Meet Your Match

RENEE ARONIS

DEDICATION

To my husband, Scott, who believes in me. He is truly
my helpmeet and he's also my favorite. And to my mother,
who read and sang to me when I was a child.

CONTENTS

Chapter One

E rin March was in trouble. She couldn't catch her breath, and that could only mean one horrible thing. *Please, God, not again! Please don't let me die this time!* she prayed as she fought the panic rising inside her. "Honey, I have to—" she began. She needed to use the bathroom, so she stood, but once the coughing started having to pee didn't matter anymore. She felt her husband, Todd, catch her as she collapsed to her knees. He made eye contact and held her while she gripped his shirt as more and more of her breath was expelled with each cough. Her body shook as her muscles fought, unsuccessfully, to bring fresh air back in.

"I'm here, honey. You'll be okay in a few seconds. It'll be over soon, try to relax," she heard him say, the same way he'd done each time he'd been forced to help her through an episode over the last sixteen years they'd been together.

She felt the sweat of her body's struggle run down her face and start dripping off her shoulder-length, salt-and-pepper hair. At last, the blackness came with its little white dots, and she was oblivious to pain and time. Consciousness

1

came back when she finally gasped, drawing in that first, painful, shuddering breath that happened after every episode of her disease, the Fertilis Defect.

"Forty-eight seconds this time, honey, two seconds longer than your record," Todd said softly, as he helped her back onto the sofa. He dabbed her forehead and patted her wet hair with the kitchen towel he'd had over his shoulder, then he covered her with a blanket.

"Thank you, honey. You are so good to me. I love you," she said and fell asleep immediately.

Chapter Two

DOCTOR DAYS

Erin didn't want to think about supper as she sat on the hard plastic chair in the exam room three weeks later. 'Doctor days' were difficult enough without that to worry about. *I'll ask Todd to bring something home tonight,* she thought, eliminating one stressor from her day.

She hated going to the doctor. It was always the same thing: *"I'm sorry, Mrs. March, there's nothing we can do for you. You're a product of your parents' selfishness, and now you've gotta pay the price."* They didn't say those exact words, but that was the truth of it.

Another episode was fast approaching, which meant that sometime within the next week or so, she'd be on her knees again, gasping for breath and thinking she might die. The worst part was knowing it would happen and feeling it creep ever closer with no way to stop it.

Until that point in her life, she'd been able to stay positive. However, the escalating exhaustion and lack of hope meant depression was an enemy she was rapidly losing ground to. Her life was becoming a never-ending struggle to survive.

The drug, Fertilis, had been a miracle pill. It almost guaranteed a pregnancy for the couples who employed it, as Erin's parents had. They didn't know until much later, though, that it created a mosaicism of birth defects in only the female children conceived because of it.

The disease took many forms, with each Fertilis-born woman having health complications unique to her. The only symptom known to affect them all was infertility, just like their parents. Fertilis was banned fifteen years later after it was linked to the birth defect, but it was too late by then.

Like every girl born as a result of the drug, Erin had been living with the Fertilis Defect symptoms since she'd become a woman and had gotten her first period. It didn't sound that bad on paper, but her symptoms were severe and getting worse as she aged. At nearly forty, it was debilitating, and she feared for her life.

She didn't care what had gone wrong with the drug or why it targeted girls exclusively. She figured it was because the mother was the one who took the turquoise caplet, so they were the gender punished. The only thing that mattered to her was finding a way to stop the symptoms, whether that meant the cure or an effective treatment. As long as it was affordable and didn't cause other negative side effects, she was desperate for it.

Doctor Nanavala entered the exam room wearing a perfectly starched shirt and beautiful tie, as usual. He was tall, with large, dark eyes and warm, brown skin. She guessed he was somewhere around fifty-five, the few strands of grey mingling with his thick black hair being the only indication of his age.

He was kind, sympathetic, and had a great sense of humor; she was grateful he was her doctor. He smiled at her lightheartedly, though he usually looked as tired and careworn as she always felt, so she hoped he had good news for her. "Looks like you're having a good day today," she said, hoping to get him talking.

"And you are having an observant one," he said with his soft Indian accent, dodging her indirect query. "How have you been feeling?"

She was sick of that question, mainly because there seemed to be no hope of ever being able to answer it differently. "Horrible, as always."

"Any changes? New symptoms? Anything out of the ordinary?"

They went through the same dance during every visit, so that Erin thought it might be easier to do it through an email or text message. When he was finished with his questions about if, when, duration, and pain scales, she spoke up. "Come on, Doctor; there's something up. I've never seen you so excited. You're no good at hiding it, you know?"

A genuine smile lit up his face. "I cannot give you details today, but you are correct. A new treatment has been approved, and it seems to be the miracle we have been waiting for."

Erin was stunned and prayed she wasn't dreaming. "But why can't you tell me now?"

"You will need to make an appointment for you and your husband to meet with me at my office in the hospital. I will tell you everything you need to know then."

It would take more than that to appease her. "Can't you give me a hint? Is it a pill, blood transfusions, surgery to remove an unnecessary organ? What?" She was sitting on the edge of her chair, grasping the seat-front with white knuckles. "Please," she added softly, as desperation kicked in.

"I am sorry—"

"I think you should tell me now. I can make up my own mind and—"

"I need for you both to be there, Erin. It involves a decision that the two of you must agree on. Trust me, you will understand after you hear what it is," he interrupted. "Plus, I simply do not have the time now. I have rooms full of patients. I will be able to give you all the time you need at your appointment, alright?"

"I guess I don't have a choice," she said petulantly. "I'm sorry, I just don't want to have another episode, you know?"

"I know, but you will understand—"

"… after you hear what it is," she finished with him.

"You will also need to go to the lab. This treatment requires additional testing and blood work, so we will get that out of the way now."

Erin knew Todd wouldn't stop her from having any treatment if she could find relief. Was it possible to be free from the hell she'd been in since turning twelve years and eighteen days old? If so, she couldn't think of anything to make them pause.

When the nurse came in, Erin asked to be seen as soon as possible. She got an appointment two days later, then headed to the lab. This was routine. She knew all the techs by name and always asked how their families were doing. She'd given vial upon vial of her blood for new tests or theories, each one promising to be the breakthrough remedy. The results of her donations were never shared with her, however.

When the blood draw was finished, she hurried to her car, shivering in the cold April winds of Wisconsin. When she got home, she crawled into bed, physically and mentally exhausted. She woke to find Todd leaning over to kiss her on the forehead and sat up, feeling only slightly better. "Hi, honey. Before I forget, we have an appointment with Dr. Nanavala on Wednesday afternoon," she said, wanting to be excited but also afraid to get her hopes up. "He wants to tell us about a new treatment and needs us both to be there. And before you say it's up to me, I already tried that. He was adamant you come along so we both have the information firsthand." Todd was changing out of his work clothes and sat on the bed next to her, wearing only his old, white cotton briefs. As he looked at her, she could tell he was gauging what to say.

"Another experimental treatment? Another drug that makes you sleep all day and cry all night? I don't know, honey, what did he tell you?"

"He told me it, 'seems to be the miracle we've been waiting for,'" she said, trying to sound like him. "He wouldn't say anything else. I seriously considered begging, but I was already exhausted and didn't have the energy. The sooner he tells us, the better, though. I feel an episode lurking in the shadows. Who knows, maybe I can get ahold of whatever it is before it happens."

"Let's hope so," he said as he took her hand in his. "I want you to feel better."

"I know, me too! What would I do without you? Wait, don't answer; I don't want to know!"

He smiled and kissed her cheek, but she turned her head to kiss him on the mouth. She touched him on his cotton briefs and smiled at how her touch made him react. After he laid her down, he took off his underwear, ready for her as she moved further up onto the mattress.

They made love in the missionary position, which had become their old standby. Gone were the days of trying new positions and making love in exciting ways and places. They were most comfortable on their bed, so that's where they did it. After nearly fifteen years of marriage, it wasn't overly passionate; it was comfortable. No worries about how she looked or what to do; she just laid beneath him and hoped it lasted a good long time.

Sex for them was Todd-focused, which she'd gotten used to. They used to try to make sure she was also satisfied, but it didn't work. Trying to bring her to an orgasm was frustrating for both of them. It never happened unless she used her vibrator, which was a turn off for Todd. He did tell her that he didn't mind if she used it afterward or during the day when he wasn't home. Sometimes she did. Sometimes she had to.

Todd finished with a small grunt, pulled out, and gave her a light kiss. "Thank you," he said and went straight to the bathroom to clean up.

Erin lay on her back with her eyes closed, wishing she could climax, even occasionally, like he got to do every time they made love. *Do other women have this problem or is it another symptom of the Fertilis Defect?* she wondered once again.

Chapter Three

LET'S MOVE

"Let's move to England or Scotland; I'm not choosy," Erin exclaimed the next afternoon as she sat on the sofa next to Todd. He didn't seem surprised to hear it. She'd said similar things many times before, although it had been a while, as she'd all but given up on the idea. "We can sell everything we own and move. It'll be an adventure! It doesn't get as cold, and everything I love is there."

"Everything you love, huh?" Todd said, teasing her, and raised an eyebrow.

"Well, if you moved with me, *then* everything I love would be there." She knew it was a losing battle. Todd would never move, but she had to keep trying.

They'd taken a vacation to the UK a few years earlier, staying in Dorset and Edinburgh. At the time, she had vowed to find a way to emigrate, but Todd wouldn't leave everything he knew to go off into the unknown. Relocating was too uncertain for him. He'd been born and would probably die in the frozen tundra that was Wisconsin.

That afternoon, Erin tried to eliminate as much stress as possible by resting. It wasn't easy, with the anticipation of her doctor's appointment the next day, and she woke a few hours later with the familiar tightness in her chest anyway. Todd had gone out to the garage to putter, and she was sitting, curled up on the couch, in a flux between dreaming and daydreaming.

She could see her old English, stone farmhouse, dressed up in a gown of purple wisteria trained up the walls. The high hedges around the garden took the island's gales with hardly more than a shiver. Up ahead was the hand-laid cobblestone courtyard that connected the barns and outbuildings with the house. Finally, she saw her favorite feature, the low dry-stone wall splashed with white and green lichen, as well as fragrant white jasmine, climbing over it.

She put on her old, ugly, well-worn barn wellies before heading outside to feed the animals. As she walked past it, the slate tiles on the roof of the old forge made random cracking sounds as the sun came up and warmed them. It made her think of popcorn kernels hitting the lid of a metal pot as they exploded.

She threw scratch out for the chickens and checked the coop for large brown, blue, and green eggs. After caring for their little menagerie, she went back to the house to warm up with a cup of strong builder's tea, taking a tea bag out of her beautiful, vintage, green tin. She set out a package of digestive biscuits but chose to bake scones to eat with jam and clotted cream instead.

After cleaning up, she decided to take a walk using her clean, comfortable wellies to wander the public trails. She could hear wood pigeons and gulls crying and also far-off dogs barking. The bright morning sun felt comforting on her face and neck, and she welcomed the breeze that tugged her hair out of the messy twist she'd put it in.

As she walked, Erin looked forward to their time after supper when she and Todd would 'run down the pub' for a pint of cider. They'd have a chinwag with the owner and a few of their mates before walking back up the street past the ancient church with its boxy bell tower. Maybe they'd take the shortcut home over the fields they leased to a local farmer, then trek through the thick wall of trees that bordered their property. When they got home, they might sit in front of the coal fire to watch a few British programs, such as *Doctor Who, Graham Norton, and Future Explorations*, which was her favorite, though it was only on reruns.

Future Explorations was a show about a time-traveling man, originally named John Thomas of Fife, though over time, his name changed to John Thomas Fife. He was thrown into the role by his predecessor, Joe Whitehall. Joe had stumbled up to the kilted man's feet in 1693 Scotland, telling him that he'd come from the end of the twentieth century. He handed John Thomas a time travel device, which would allow him to explore the future, while Joe, we find out later, could only explore the past.

Joe repeated the same advice he'd been given by the man who'd handed it to him, "Do good and help people," he said and then inconveniently died, thus beginning John Thomas's adventures. The series only lasted three seasons and had become a cult favorite. Erin loved the show and thought that David Elliott, who played John Thomas Fife, was the most attractive man in existence.

She looked up at the actor's face, so near to hers, and felt light-headed. The tingling of her body consumed her, and she wanted him. It was a warm night, full of unfamiliar noises and smells. He smiled at her and leaned in, his breath warm and sweet-smelling, like fruit, getting nearer and nearer her waiting lips.

Erin was startled awake by the slam of the kitchen door as Todd came in from the garage. "Is there anything you need at the store?" he asked loudly, bringing the grocery list into the living room with him and sitting next to her on the sofa.

"Uh," she said, trying to wake up. "I think we need milk, and, oh, I was having an amazing dream about *my* house in England, the one I always dream about."

"Oh, sorry I woke you then," he said with a hint of annoyance.

Was that contempt? she thought. "That's—okay, but it reminded me that I need more tea. I'm down to two bags."

"Anything else?"

She shook her head, knowing there would be something she was forgetting, but she'd just add it to a new list later. "I don't know, honey, get what's on the list. I'll go back sometime soon and get anything we missed. Thanks for doing the shopping. I really appreciate it."

Todd stood and bent down to kiss her. He turned to leave, and she could've sworn she heard him say, "*My* house in England, huh? Whatever." He left, slamming the door on his way out.

Erin sighed and laid down on the couch, closing her eyes. She wanted to get back into her dream, so she thought about her greatest desire. She'd always wanted British children running around the garden, calling her 'Mummy.' Children who dipped their toast soldiers into their soft-boiled eggs sitting neatly on their little egg stands at breakfast. She imagined a herd of kids running around, screaming, and laughing. Of all her UK dreams, that's the one she wanted most. It was also the one least likely to happen since she couldn't have children.

They'd looked into adoption but couldn't afford it, plus there were so many problems with the system, too many horror stories. She didn't think she could endure the heartache involved with the process. Not only that, what were their chances of being approved given her disease, anyway? It was a dream that wouldn't come true and she had come to grips with it. Still, sometimes she would wake from dreams in which she had children so real, she thought she'd be able to remember their names if she tried.

Sitting on a bench, looking at the sea and a sandy beach, she handed out fish and chips to her brood of children. They were all ages; teens, preteens, even a baby in the pram next to her. The smell of the salty air and feel of the delicious summer breeze enveloped her. Brazen seagulls edged closer and closer, trying to snatch a bite of their meal, but the middle children chased them away. A young girl came up to her, excited to tell her something.

"Mummy! Look what C— (she couldn't hear the name) found!" Just as she was about to be shown what was so exciting, the bang of the kitchen door ripped her out of her dream. She could've cried. *What was it? What did 'C—' have?* She bit her lip, trying to stay calm and not yell at Todd. No matter how many times she asked him not to slam the door, it never stuck in his mind. Sometimes she wondered if he did it on purpose, as payback for having to be her caregiver and husband.

She figured she might as well help put things away, so she sat up. Her head felt foggy, and she was still tired. *Maybe if I could sleep for longer than ten minutes without being startled awake by that damn door, I'd feel more rested,* she thought as she walked into the kitchen. The bags were on the island, so she started putting the groceries away.

"They were out of Yorkshire Gold, so I got that," Todd said, seeing the box in her hand and the confused look on her face. "I didn't know. It said English breakfast, so I thought it would be okay."

"No, this stuff isn't good. It tastes more like the bag than the tea. I'll exchange it another day," she said and put the milk in the fridge. Her energy level was so low. She needed to find some help.

Chapter Four

CRAP AT POKER

loody hell! David Elliott thought on the way home from the game. *What am I gonna tell Susannah?* He hadn't planned on going to the poker game in the first place. He was pressured into it by his mate, Martin, who had a way of talking him into going along with his schemes. His cunning, opportunistic tactics were always cooked up, so it seemed, with the sole purpose to cause him trouble. It was Martin's greatest talent, except for poker; apparently, he was brilliant at poker. *I'm crap at poker, and Martin knows it; why'd I allow him tae get me into this? Could he have cheated?* he thought bitterly. Doesn't matter; what's done is done.

He laid his head back on the headrest of the nondescript black Uber he'd hired to deliver him safely to his London home after too much liquor. His head was pounding from strong drink and cigar smoke, and he only had a vague concept of what he was in for. He knew the Fertilis Defect was out there, he knew it was a big deal, and he knew, thankfully, that it didn't affect men. He'd also heard rumors about there

16

being some controversy about the treatments but hadn't paid attention to it.

He'd also heard something about a voluntary registry but had no clue what it involved and hadn't wanted to know. *Voluntary registry, he thought. Et's voluntary now, but things like that seem to become compulsory eventually.* It was compulsory for him now, thanks to Martin. "Bollocks!" he said aloud and brought his fist down hard onto the leather seat next to him.

"Oi, mate! Mind th' leather, a'right?" the driver said, looking at him through the rear-view mirror

"Sorry." He knew he'd been tricked into wagering his commitment to the upcoming event. Martin had known and most likely planned for him to be just drunk enough to fall for it. Now he was going to have to dig in and learn what the Registry involved. *What'll I be agreeing to, and am I willin' tae do et? he wondered.* "Ahh, ex-cusse me, do yeh know annathin' about the Fertilisss De-fect Reg-istry?" he asked, still besotted enough to talk to the driver. His speech was slurred, and he forgot to use the posh received pronunciation accent he usually used.

The driver looked up. "My sister-in-law's got it," he replied.

David leaned forward, sobering up a bit. "Really? Have they found a cure then?"

"Naw, no cure, mate, jus' what they're callin' 'treatments,' like." The driver humphed and continued, "A filthy excuse ta me if you know what I'm sayin'?"

David had no idea what he was 'sayin',' but he nodded as though he did. "Right."

The driver pulled up to the address he'd been given. "Here ya are, mate. It's none uh my business, but why're you so bovered about the Registry? You know someone who's got the Fertilis Defect, then?"

"No. I overheard a mate talking about it tonight and was curious. Goodnight," he said and got out. "Cheers," said the driver and pulled away.

David stood, swaying ever so slightly. He watched the car fade away and turn down a side street before he walked, or perhaps stumbled would be more accurate, to his front door. He fumbled in his trouser pockets for his keys. *There's no bloody light out here. How am I meant tae*— The light came on, causing him to shield his eyes.

The door was opened by an excruciatingly slender, beautiful woman with an angry face. "Get in here quickly, before anyone gets sight of you!" Though she was six inches shorter than him, Susannah Elliott seemed to tower over her husband at that moment. "Oh, David," she said, with disgust, "look at the state of you."

He allowed her to lead him to the chair in the foyer so he could take off his shoes. He wasn't all that pissed up, but he didn't want to tell her about his predicament. *Let's have one more peaceful night, shall we, before upturnin' everathing,* he thought ruefully.

Susannah managed to help him up the stairs and into their bedroom. She helped him off with his clothes and then into their bed. He liked it when she took care of him and let her get on with it, even though he was fully capable of doing it himself. She leaned over to pull the duvet over him, and he reached up, putting his hand on her tiny waist. He lifted his head to kiss her, but she turned away.

"You smell like a pub; I'm not going to kiss you!" she said, but she was very nearly smiling. At least as close to a smile as she'd given him in a very long while, so he hoped he had a chance to get what he wanted.

"Come here," he said as he pulled her down on top of him. "You look lovely in yer nightdress." He rolled them both over so that he was on top of her and began kissing her neck. She tried to push him away, but that made him all the more eager.

"David, stop! Get off of me!"

"Ach, but et's been so long, my lovely. Couldn't yeh jest—"

"No, I couldn't 'jest,' now get off!" she said again, so he rolled back over and put his arm over his eyes in frustration. "And don't think of trying anything later, either; I'm not in the mood."

"Aye, as usual," he whispered as she went to her side of the bed and got under the covers.

Chapter Five

WHAT IS IT THIS TIME

Morning came, and with it, a dull, throbbing headache. David dreaded the day ahead of him and hoped to avoid the task of telling his wife he would have to sign up for the Registry. *Maybe she'll have gone out,* he thought hopefully then heard her voice coming up the stairs.

"Yes, Kitty, I want the linens pressed this time. I do believe I've mentioned it every washday since we took you on," Susannah said, rolling her eyes as she entered the room. Her hair was strawberry blond, and her eyes were blue, though, when she was angry, they took on a color more akin to the sea as the tide is coming in, dark and churning.

He didn't want to see them like that, but he figured he'd rip the plaster off in one fell swoop. "Sweetheart," he said sweetly, which was a mistake. Her eyes lit on him, and he nearly ducked for the imaginary darts they seemed to throw in his direction.

"What did you do last night, David?" she said, as though she'd read his mind.

She always did that to him, knowing as soon as he opened his gob when he was in trouble. "Martin." That was all he needed to say for her to sit hard on top of the duvet.

"What did he get you into this time, *dear*?" She said 'dear' with an exasperated condescension he didn't like but was all too familiar with.

"He's tricked me into hosting one of his charity events."

"Is that all? What for?" she said before he could go on with his explanation.

"The Fertilis Defect."

She stood and crossed her arms, facing him as an angry parent or headmaster might do with a naughty child. "The Fertilis—are you serious? Well, you will ring him and tell him you're not interested and be done with it—at once! The Fertilis Defect. Honestly!"

He was surprised at her reaction. He thought it might be strong and that she'd be annoyed, but she was livid. "I can't, and you know it," he said, trying to stand his ground. "He knows I'm a man of my word. I don't understand why you're so upset, love, it's only a charity. I'll have to sign up with the Registry, but—"

"Sign up with the Registry?" she roared, cutting him off. "There's more to it than that! Are you aware of what the Registry is for, David?"

"No, but—" he began.

She held up her hand as she crossed the bedroom and stood at the small desk where they kept their much-neglected tablet. She switched it on and began typing something. "You hide your head in the sand, David, ignoring everything unless it pertains directly to you. Had you been paying any attention, at all, you would have seen it all over the news and would never have been so stupid!" She rolled her eyes and handed the illuminated tablet to him. "Read this; maybe then you'll understand."

David hesitated, afraid he was in way over his head. The page read:

THE FERTILIS DEFECT

REGISTRY AND TREATMENT INFORMATION

This website is to be used solely for information concerning the voluntary Registry for the Fertilis Defect (TFD), its symptoms, and its treatment. We are not in any way associated with the Registry … .

Yeah, yeah, he thought.

HISTORY

TFD has been conclusively linked to the use of the drug, Fertilis … Fertilis was approved in Europe and then in the United States three years later. It was prescribed by physicians for sixteen years until the first cases of the Defect were linked with the drug … .

Okay, got it.

SYMPTOMS

Symptoms are varied and can include any number of deficiencies and mutations of organs and tissue ... .

Aye. It sounds horrible!

TREATMENT

There is no cure for TFD. The only known treatment is for a man and a woman with TFD, who have been matched through the Registry, to perform coitus on a prescribed schedule ... .

WHAT! Woah! Not likely!

Furthermore, the collection and administration of semen without coitus has not been in any way effective towards treating TFD ... .

Are they serious?

REGISTRATION

Registration is free and requires a man to be seen by a qualified physician at a licensed location. (See links below to find a location near you). The man will be expected to submit samples of blood and semen … .

I'm no' doing et. Martin is insane if he thinks I will!

TO REGISTER

To register, the man must supply a copy of his birth certificate, National Insurance Numbercard, (or equivalent identification), and must be willing to sign a waiver, allowing him to be matched with, and potentially share personal information with a woman diagnosed with TFD and/or her physician …

This is mental! Who would do this?

COMPENSATION

As an incentive, those who register may choose to be paid, or donate their "treatment time" in return for accommodations being provided by the TFD Registry Trust … .

Paid! Is that not prostitution?

IN CONCLUSION

We at T.F.D.T.E.A. (The Fertilis Defect Treatment Education Advocates) strongly

support the Registry and encourage every
able-bodied man to register … .

I'm able-bodied, but I'll no' be registerin'!

David reached the end of the webpage and looked up at
his wife who'd been studying his face as he read. He was rarely
at a loss for words, but he had nothing.

"Now, do you grasp why you must tell Martin that you
will NOT register or do his charity event? Of course, you may
offer a substantial donation or whatever you wish to promise
him, but you simply cannot register, David! I don't understand how Martin could do this to us?"

"I'll go 'round to his flat today. I'm sure he only meant
to give us a rise." At that moment, his phone rang, and the
screen read 'Martin Green.' David lifted the phone to show
who was calling. "See there, he's rung to ask if we've looked it
up." He answered, and sounding as amused as he could under
the circumstances, said, "What on earth were you thinking?"
They both heard Martin's laughter ringing through the
phone, but neither of them was laughing with him.

Susannah stood. *Fix this!* she mouthed and left the room.

"Ah, so you've done your homework, have you?" Martin
said.

David heard him take a drag on his cigarette. He knew
Martin was jealous of him and his life, but this was too much,
and he meant to let him have it for his scheme. "I don't know
how someone who considers himself my friend could stoop to
this level of … trickery! Do you find pleasure in seeing me

suffer?" He could still hear Martin laughing under his breath. "You do realize I won't be doing any such thing, don't you?" he said defiantly. "I'm willing to host the event, but you cannot force me to sign up to have sex with a stranger!" He'd expected Martin to give in, saying, "Of course not, mate. I was just having a laugh," but he didn't. The line was silent. "Martin?"

"Shall I tag along when you go, then?" he asked, and David heard him take another pull on his fag.

"I'm not going to do it!"

"David," Martin said with unexpected seriousness, "You are aware that there were quite a few witnesses at the game last night?"

David was confounded. "Yes, well, I was also quite drunk," he stammered.

"Oh, yes, you were. So much so that you added to the pledge."

"I've no idea what you're talking about. You know I can't register; there's no way. Susannah would never allow me to do it even if— Ye're off yer head if yeh think I'm goin' to ruin my marriage because of a loss in poker!" he said with his voice raised and his native accent coming to the surface

"I did consider that," Martin said, sounding cool and confident, "That is why, if you'll recall, I had you sign a pledge, saying that should you lose, you wouldn't break your word. Everyone witnessed it."

"I wouldn't sign anything like that!" David said, though he couldn't actually remember whether he had or hadn't.

Again, there was silence on the line, except for the crackle of a lit cigarette being inhaled.

"Ah, but you did, mate, and as I said, you are the one who insisted that I add the bit about signing up for the Registry. You've a Superman complex, mate, always needing to go that extra mile so everyone will pat you on the back. Well, you're gonna have that in spades now, my friend. Oh, and don't get any ideas about hiring a solicitor, or the document may find its way to the *Daily Mirror* come Monday morning."

David had had enough. "Are yeh trying tae threaten me?" he said. He could hear Martin laughing.

"You've until Sunday night to change your mind, mate. After that, there's going to be a lot of talk on the street. Cheers!" Martin rang off, leaving David sitting on his bed with his mouth hanging open.

He looked at his reflection in the dark glass of his mobile. "I can't believe it! Did that really happen?" he said out loud. "What's he thinking?" *More importantly, what in the bloody hell was I thinkin'?* He stood and made his way to the water closet. *This is gonna be a bloody nightmare if I dinnae give in, but there's no way Susannah would even consider it. Is he trying' tae split us up?* he thought, miserably. The thought had occurred to David more than once since Martin had always admired Susannah. *Perhaps he's thinking that if we aren't together anamore, he'll have a shot with her?* He knew he was caught in a trap. It was a trap, no two ways about it, but why? *Jealousy is one thing, Martin's been jealous for years, but why strike now?*

27

Martin took a long drag on his cigarette, taking pleasure in making his friend squirm. He'd only gotten involved with the charity after learning about the Fertilis Defect and what the treatments were all about. He knew he had to get David involved, and when you can influence a celebrity, people will listen to what you've got to say.

It's about time someone took you down a peg, he thought. *Things have always been easy for you. You have everything; a beautiful home in the poshest of London neighborhoods, a glamorous career with an income to boggle the mind, and the most beautiful woman I've ever seen. Why shouldn't you be made to suffer now and then?* He smiled and began thinking of more ways to torture him.

Chapter Six

NO CHOICE

"He said what?" Susannah shouted. David had just stepped out of the shower and was toweling off when she entered the bathroom. He told her what Martin had said about the pledge and the threat looming over their heads. "Wait, you've done what?" Her eyes were now like two little hurricanes heading straight for him.

"I don't remember signing anything." There were a lot of things he didn't remember about the night before, but he wasn't going to mention that. "He said everyone saw me sign it, so what shall I do, then?"

"He's going to do this to us, isn't he?"

"Yes, I think he will, though I don't understand why."

"We need to suss out a plan," she said quite suddenly, determination in her voice. Her eyes had also downgraded from hurricane to tropical storm.

"A plan? A plan for what?" he asked, wary of the change; it could mean she was accepting the situation or that things were about to get much worse. He didn't want to think about how much worse it could get.

"We're stuck, and he knows it," she said with an icy, matter of fact tone. "We can either resist and have it become common knowledge, or we quietly submit."

"Woah, wait, submit?" David stammered, not believing his ears. "Are you saying—"

"Yes, David. You've gotten yourself into this mess, and we are not able to get out of it, at least not as far as I can see, so you're going to have to pay the price." She glared at him, her petite body shaking from top to bottom.

"But I don't want to—" he began to say, but she ignored him.

"If you don't, your name will be smeared all over the country for evading a high-profile charity event. The articles, interviews, and headlines, no, David, you will not put our family through that. I'll not allow you to ruin your career and our status because of this. You know that is what will happen if you refuse."

"Do I?" he replied, thinking she was overreacting.

"Yes, you do, and you also know that the scrutiny will eventually bully you into registering anyway, although by then, the whole world will know you've done it. At present, there's still an option to remain discreet. You will have to host the event and join the Registry, so you'd better hope and pray that there isn't a match," she said and turned on her heels, removing herself from the bathroom. Water vapor swallowed her slight figure as she walked away.

He knew 'I'm sorry' wasn't going to be enough and that he'd be on his own for a while, including separate beds and quiet meals. It didn't matter much; they didn't have anything in common and rarely had interesting conversations anyway. As for the bed situation, the night before was the first time in months he gotten that close to having sex with her. No, things wouldn't be much different, except for the hostility in the air, and he'd have to walk on eggshells until it all cleared up.

David dressed and walked soberly downstairs. The toast and marmalade on the small, round breakfast table did not look appetizing. *'... you'd better hope there isn't a match.'* His wife's words rang in his ears. *Ach, dear Lord, this is bad,* he thought as he took a triangle of toast from the rack and spread the preserves onto it. He took a bite, and Francie, their kitchen help, set a pot of steaming hot tea next to Susannah, who was sitting, passively scrolling on her mobile phone. "You're sure there's no way out? You can't think of anything?" he asked her. He knew the answer but couldn't believe it.

"No, and as I said, it can be done quietly or turn into negative tabloid news. Which would you prefer?" she said, not looking at him.

He stared at his toast, the remnants of his hangover making his head throb. "I'd prefer it went away, but since it won't, I choose quiet, I suppose." His heart was pounding, and the contents of his stomach rising. He poured his tea, picked it up, and threw the rest of his toast in the bin, heading to the sunroom to sit and think.

His wife's sudden acceptance was throwing him off more than a little bit. He knew she valued fame quite a lot, and to lose public opinion at their level of society, for her, would be something to avoid at all costs. *Does she care about what it means I'll have to do?* A wave of nausea threatened to overwhelm him; even his tea tasted bitter in his mouth. *Surely people would go easy on me, seein' what's involved, wouldn't they?* He tried to imagine Monday morning's papers emblazoned with his name and face:

David Elliott seen agreeing to host charity— Backs out at last second!

Or:

Can David Elliott be trusted? Proof positive in ink says he can't!

He imagined the telephone ringing non-stop; reporters camping out on his doorstep, and his children teased and harassed at school. *Susannah is right,* he thought. *People dinnae care about the truth, just the headline.* He took his mobile phone out of his pocket and rang Martin's number.

Martin answered with an over-animated, "Yeesss?"

"You win. I don't want to hear anything more about it. I'll register today," David said and rang off before Martin could reply. He downed his cuppa and reluctantly went back into the kitchen.

"I'll go now," he said to Susannah, who was still sitting at the table absorbed in her phone, her half grapefruit untouched in front of her. "I've rung Martin, and he knows." She nodded her head as though he'd told her he was going to the shop for a bag of crisps.

"You'll need your birth certificate and National Insurance Numbercard from the safe," she said without emotion.

"I love you, and I'm sorry," he said, as he walked out of the kitchen and down the hallway to his office.

"Uh-huh," he heard her say as he left the room. The tension was going to last a long, lonesome time.

He opened the thick, wooden door of his office and walked in. He loved that room; it smelled like old books, furniture polish, and leather. The walls were lined with bookshelves holding hundreds of books and film scripts, as well as the remnants of his children's school years. They were growing up so fast, and all he had to show for it were piles of artwork and unidentifiable objects made from clay or things like cork and toothpicks.

Susannah wasn't sentimental and would've chucked it all into the bin had he not secreted them away in there. He had artifacts he'd collected over the years. Mementos from his time on *Future Explorations* as well as items he'd been allowed to keep after several of the films and programs he'd acted in. More precious to him were the things he'd collected as a child. There were fossils, shells, and bits of flotsam and jetsam he'd found on the beach whilst on holiday at his grandmother's house in Dorset long ago.

He approached the safe, camouflaged in a corner, made to look like a large, wide plant stand. It was adorned with a humongous spider plant, which added to the effect. After punching a string of numbers into the keypad, he opened the door, seeing the old flat wooden box which held his great grandfather's service medals. They were one of his prized possessions.

There was the drawer that held his great grandmother's wedding ring as well as his own father's. He'd been given his father's ring when he died, and arthritis had forced his mother to remove his great grandmother's ring, which she'd used as her own. Susannah turned her nose up at it when he showed it to her, so there it sat. He had hoped to have a marriage to stand the test of time, as his parents' had done, and held on stubbornly, though he was beginning to have some doubts.

Finding what he needed, he closed the safe and made his way to his large maple desk to find an envelope. The room beckoned for him to stay, but he knew he must do the deed right away, or he'd lose his nerve. Leaving the safety and privacy of his office, he walked through the house and out the front door into the comfortless light of day.

Closing the tall, heavy entry door behind him, he descended the five steps, which landed on a short walk and a wrought-iron gated wall that opened onto the pavement. *Dammit!* he thought as he closed the gate. *I dinnae ken where I'm goin' and I'll no' go back inside.*

Feeling utterly miserable, he took his mobile from his trousers again and typed 'Fertilis Defect Registry near me.' Several locations came up, one of them only five blocks away. *I can't be seen walkin' into one of those places. This is going to be much more difficult than I imagined.* He considered turning back, but he couldn't face Susannah again.

He remembered his motorbike, hardly ever used anymore, as Susannah thought it was undignified. *She didn't mind when we were first married, and we'd ride into the countryside,* he thought as he walked around the terraced houses to the tenant car park. Thankfully, his helmet was stored in a hard case attached to the bike, and the key was in his wallet. *Et's perfect, no one will recognize me,* he thought and then wondered if he needed an appointment. He touched the call icon on his mobile and waited, hoping he'd be told they were packed to the rafters and have an excuse to put it off.

Chapter Seven

REGISTRY

"National Fertilis Defect Registry. This is Sean; how may I be of service?" a man with a light Irish accent answered.

David swallowed hard. "Ah, hello. I'm wondering if you're busy at the moment?" He was sweating, though the morning air still had a chill to it.

"Oh, we aren't busy a'tall. Are you looking to book an appointment then?" Sean asked.

David's heart was pounding so hard he imagined Sean could feel it through the other end of the line. "Er-uh, would it be possible to pop 'round in oh, say, ten minutes? I'd rather not have my name placed in an appointment book if you don't mind?"

"Of course. Do you know where we're located then?" Sean responded cheerfully.

"Yes, I do. I … uh … I hate to ask this, but is there a back entrance I might be allowed to use? I don't want anyone to see me."

"Everyone asks that," he said, unphased by the question. "Our entrance is located down an alley, so it shouldn't be a problem."

"Well, then, I'll be there soon."

"Alright, see you then," Sean said and rang off.

David would've ridden past the nondescript, age-darkened, stock brick building, had he not connected the Bluetooth between his mobile and helmet. A cheerful woman's voice said, "You have reached your destination." He drove into the small car park behind one of the buildings, keeping his helmet on as he walked down the narrow alley toward the black metal entry door.

He removed his helmet and after checking his reflection in its visor, smoothed his hair and entered the musty, dimly lit hallway. A few steps down and to his right was a door with a plaque on the wall which read, **National Fertilis Defect Registry Clinic - Department of Health and Social Care**, along with the royal coat of arms. *Well, this looks official enough,* he thought, then opened the door and walked in.

To his right was a large desk with two chairs and two telephones, where a young man was seated. He was on the phone and put his finger up in a motion that said, 'One moment.' "It's no trouble a'tall," he said into the handset. David recognized Sean's voice and waited, thankful the waiting room was empty, and hoped Sean would hurry up.

"Of course. Our entrance is located down an alley, so I'm sure it won't be a problem. Yes, you as well."

Sean hung up the phone and smiled at David, assuming he was the man he'd spoken with a few minutes earlier. The look said, 'See, we get that question all the time,' then his eyes widened when he realized it was David Elliott standing before him. "So, you'd like to register, then?" Sean asked brightly.

"Yes, please," David said and was handed a clipboard with a stack of paperwork and a ballpoint pen. He knew someone could enter at any moment and recognize him, so he leaned in. "Do you, perhaps, have a more private waiting area?"

Sean stood and motioned for David to come through the door separating the waiting room from the examination rooms. "Follow me, please," he said and led David down a long hallway. The doors were open, revealing examination rooms as well as more comfortable-looking rooms, each containing a settee and magazine rack. He didn't need to be told what *those* rooms were intended for and hoped he wouldn't need to 'use' one of them.

Sean stopped in front of an exam room and motioned for David to enter it. "Someone will be with you shortly, Mr. Elliott. Open the door when you've completed the paperwork. Do you have proper identification with you, then?"

He reached into his coat pocket, produced the papers, and Sean took them, saying he'd be right back. David put the clipboard on the examination table and took off his coat, hanging it on the back of the door. He set his helmet on the floor, picked up the clipboard, and sat in the hard plastic chair provided.

After the first page, he was already overwhelmed. As well as wanting the basics, such as his birth name and address, they wanted a list of all medications, surgeries, or medical procedures he'd ever had. Then, he was asked to swear, in writing, that he hadn't been convicted or involved in any sexual harassment lawsuits. It took quite a while, but eventually, he finished, signing his name at the bottom of the notice of privacy disclaimer, and opened the door.

When Sean returned, he handed the envelope back to him and was about to leave when David stopped him. "This is a lot of information, isn't it?" he asked and stood to return the envelope to his coat pocket. "I mean, my entire medical history?"

"I understand, Mr. Elliott, but we wouldn't ask for any information that wasn't vital to the health and wellbeing of yourself and the person you'll be matched with."

"Right, of course; that's reasonable," he said with renewed dread. "Here it is, then." He handed him the clipboard and pen, his hand trembling.

"A'right, I'll give this to the doctor," Sean said and left the room.

After a rather long wait, there was a knock on the door, and a middle-aged man, wearing a white shirt and red tie stepped into the room. "It's nice to meet you, Mr. Elliott," he said as David shook his outstretched hand. He pulled out the stool that was under a small countertop with a computer screen, keyboard, and mouse on it and sat scanning David's paperwork. "My name is Doctor Moore, and I'll be performing your examination."

"Please, call me David."

"Alright, David, please tell me why you've decided to join the Registry?"

David didn't quite know how to answer. He knew if he gave the real reason, they might not allow him to register, but it might also cause them to probe into who'd pressured him. He didn't want them to search Martin out; that would end badly. "I've agreed to host a charity event for the Fertilis Defect, and … I'd feel like a hypocrite if I didn't do my part."

The doctor frowned at him. "That's a nice thought, though you do realize it isn't compulsory to do so?"

"Yes, I do, but I want to set a good example for … other men to follow suit," he lied.

"I don't mean to be indelicate," Dr. Moore said, obviously trying to be tactful, "but is your wife aware—I mean, does she know what's involved, and has she agreed to your signing up?"

David straightened up in his chair. "I wouldn't be here otherwise, now, I'd like to get on with my day, so can we please keep things moving along Doctor?" he said, trying to be patient.

"Yes, of course. Just making sure things are squared away at home. Wouldn't want any surprises disturbing the nest, would we?" The exam began with all the usual measurements, height, weight, blood pressure, and heart rate. "Now, take off your shirt, and sit at the end of the examination table, please." When he was seated, the doctor put a cone on the end of the otoscope and looked in his ears, nose, and mouth then took out a tongue depressor and asked him to say 'aah.'

"Very good," Dr. Moore said when he was finished with the examination. "You may step down and put your shirt back on. You seem to be in tip-top shape. We need to be sure you are healthy enough to be sexually active. Don't want to send anyone out to administer treatments who might have a heart attack in the middle of it." The doctor smiled at his own humor.

Such candor was not putting David at ease. He faked a smile and finished buttoning his shirt. *It must be nearly over. What more could they subject me to, after all?* "So, what's next, Doctor; do you draw blood now?" he asked.

Dr. Moore was entering information into the computer. The mouse was saying, 'click, click, click, drag, click' as he ticked boxes on the screen. Finally, he looked up. "Yes, we'll draw blood, but first I'm going to need a semen sample from you," he said.

David broke out in a cold sweat and must have looked a bit green around the gills. "After that, it's a quick blood draw, and you're done," the doctor reassured him. "I have a few more questions for you, though, and it's vital that you answer truthfully. Have you ever had unprotected, promiscuous sex, unprotected sex with a prostitute, or unprotected, homosexual intercourse?"

He knew they were routine questions, but it didn't make them any less embarrassing. "No, Doctor, none of them, protected or unprotected." He was handed a sheet of paper that had the same questions printed out and was asked to sign at the bottom, vowing he was telling the truth for the safety and health of all persons involved.

There was a box above the signature line that read, 'I have done one or all of the things listed above and choose to be excluded from the Registry privately and confidentially.' He was tempted to check the little box making him ineligible. The problem was, he was too honest. Not only that, if anyone got hold of it, it could become a huge mess.

Dr. Moore added the signed sheet to David's file and led him to one of the other rooms he'd seen on his way in. They both entered the room, and the doctor closed the door behind them for privacy. "Take as long as you need; there are magazines and DVDs on the shelf if you're in need of them and use a sealed specimen cup located on the table next to the settee. Please place the sample inside here." He pointed to a small cupboard next to the door. It had doors that opened on both sides of the wall, presumably, so the person supplying the sample and the one removing it could remain anonymous.

David was quite sure it would be Sean doing the pick-up, which didn't help one bit. "Ah, okay."

"Do you need anything before I go?" the doctor asked, "A bottle of water, perhaps?"

"No, thank you."

"Very well, when you're finished, please open the door, and Sean will lead you to the lab for your blood draw. After that, you may leave; we'll contact you once we have found your match. Furthermore, if you've any questions before then, don't hesitate to ring us," Dr. Moore said and left the room, closing the door behind him.

Once we have found your match. he thought miserably. *Are they so confident, then?* The thought made him feel sick, so he swallowed hard, trying to get the lump out of his throat. *Best get on with it,* he thought. The shelf against the wall held all manner of filth and debauchery, which he didn't fancy, but he took a step closer, anyway. *What're my choices, then?*

He read the titles: *Cum On, Big Daddy,* read one of the DVDs. No, thank you! he thought. *Rise Up and Stand Tall,* read another one. Then there was the classic, *Stay Calm and Thrust Hard.* He decided to peruse the magazines instead. There were *Playboys,* with skinny, buxom women gracing the covers, a *Maxim* or two, and a few hardcore options, as well.

Not caring, he picked one up and opened it to a random page. It had all the usual nudity and graphic sexual poses. He wasn't into any of it, so he unfastened his trousers and sat on the sofa. He thought about his wife, though in his mind's eye, she was soft and plump. She was lying in the bath, her nipples floating just above the water; *Yeah,* he thought, *that's gonna work.*

When he was finished, he opened the little door in the wall, placed the plastic cup on the shelf, and closed it. Before the door was fully closed, he heard the door on the other side of the wall open and shut. *Ma Losh!* he thought with a shudder, *were they waitin' outside the room?* He made sure to put the magazine back in the rack exactly where he'd gotten it from. He didn't need anyone going home and telling their partner, "David Elliott was in today. He likes to read *Fat Bottomed Girls.*"

He opened the door, and Sean appeared. They both walked to the lab, where a nurse was preparing the necessary things to draw blood. "Hello," David said to the young man and sat on a small chair.

"Hel-lo, uh, my name is Tom. I'll be performing your blood draw today. Please spell your surname for me."

"E-l-l-i-o-t-t."

"Now your date of birth, please?"

"Eighth of April," he said. Tom went about taking the blood sample, all the while peering furtively at him, then looking away. David watched as the blood flowed dark red into the vial, wishing it would go faster so he could leave.

When two vials were filled, Nurse Tom extracted the needle from his arm. Then, he asked David to put pressure on the folded cotton gauze he'd placed over the puncture wound. Next, he placed a label with David's name and vital information on the vials so they wouldn't get mixed up with another bloke's blood. Finally, he opened a fresh plaster and placed it over the gauze.

"Well, Mr. Elliott, we're all done. Do you know your way back?"

"Yes, I think I can manage."

"It was nice to … uh … meet you—" Nurse Tom said and then added shyly, "My wife and I are huge admirers of yours. We enjoy your work, but, uh … don't worry, I won't tell her you were here today, of course!" he stammered. "I mean, I had to take this opportunity—I'm just chuffed to bits that someone like *you* is doing his part," he said, "It makes me respect you all the more."

David was used to people complimenting him, but he felt like such a hypocrite. "Thank you, uh … it's the … least I can do," he said and quickly walked away with his jacket and helmet in hand, looking for the exit. He found Sean sitting behind the desk where he'd entered, nearly an hour and a half earlier.

Sean stood and handed David a folder with every pamphlet and article they had in it. "Everything seems to be in order then. We'll be in touch; have an enjoyable day," he said and, quite unnecessarily, pointed to the door.

"Thanks," David said and walked out into the short hallway. When he cleared the final door, he put his helmet back on and took a deep breath, thankful to be finished with that chore.

Relieved to be rid of the place, he wanted to go home where he could relax and forget about what he'd been through. Sadly, he realized that home might be the last place he could unwind; Susannah was there, and he'd have to face her. He was glad he'd taken his motorbike. *Perhaps I should take a nice little drive,* he thought, wanting to escape all reminders of Martin, the Fertilis Defect, and worst of all, the 'match' that the doctor was so sure would be waiting for him once all his results were processed.

Taking his time winding his way through traffic, he had a mind to keep riding past his home and past the angry woman who was waiting for him inside of it. He parked the bike, and as he shut the engine off, he heard his father's voice say, "Puttin' things off never made them easier." It was so clear, David turned around, sure he'd be standing behind him,

45

though he knew that was impossible. His father, mentor, and more recently, his friend, had died peacefully in his sleep ten years earlier.

"Oh, Da," he whispered, "I wish you could give me some advice. There's no one I can turn to about this mess." He waited a moment, hoping by some miracle, his dad would come around the corner and ask him to go for a walk to 'sort things out.' No one appeared, so David took his helmet off, ran his fingers through his hair, and resigned himself to go inside.

Chapter Eight

NEVER AGAIN

When David returned from the Registry, he didn't hear anyone in the house and was ready to heave a sigh of relief when he heard the crash of something break in the kitchen. He rushed toward the noise and found his wife standing on a chair with broken glass scattered around her bare feet.

"Don't move!" he said and rushed over to her. He easily lifted her up off the chair and set her down on the other side of the kitchen that she'd designed to within an inch of its bare, cement entombed life. There wasn't a shabby or pretty thing in sight. Everyone who saw it left saying either it was too sparse and modern or that they wished their kitchen were half as marvelous as Susannah Elliott's. "What happened?" He carefully brushed the broken glass off the chair into the bin, then finding the broom, he began to sweep up the broken crystal vase.

"I was trying to reach the vase you got me for our last anniversary. I lost my balance, and it slipped out of my hand."

He thought she seemed upset about it, so he laid the broom against the counter, and crossing the polished concrete floor, he swept her up into his arms. He wanted to hold her like that forever, but she wasn't having any of it. "Let me down!" she hissed and struggled, so he let her down gently, which was challenging with the way she was fighting him.

"Susannah, dear—" he began as he tried to get her to hold still enough for a hug, but she pushed him away.

"Don't *Susannah dear* me!" Her voice was icy and hostile. "You cannot just waltz back home and imagine things are going to be alright! It's not going to be alright for a long time."

"Susannah," he said, trying to remain calm, "I never once thought—"

"You're right, David. You never do think when it involves Martin." He opened his mouth, trying to think of a reply, but she rolled on. "You allow him to cause us trouble, and I'm the one left to clean it up. Well, this time, I can't. Do you know—can you even imagine how I might be feeling, David? Do you care at all about what this means for us?" He bit his lip and let her get it all out. "I've been *utterly* faithful to you from the moment we met, and let me tell you, *dear*, I've had many opportunities to be with other men," she boasted, "Just last week—"

"I'd rather not hear about last week," he said, knowing how men looked at her and how they talked about her as well. "I know I'm the luckiest man on earth to have you as my wife. I swear, I didn't know anything about this last night." She gave him a look that made him think she didn't believe him, which made him angry. "So, is that et? Do yeh think I've been out lookin' for an excuse tae have an affair? I never have, Su-sannah, and you know et."

"Do I?" she said under her breath.

David was dumbstruck and took a step back, hearing the crunch of broken glass. He couldn't believe what she'd said. He'd gone out of his way since they'd met, to tell her how she was the only woman for him. He only had eyes for her at events and had never once entertained the slightest notion of another woman's advances. "Really?" he said quietly.

She looked slightly ashamed of what she'd said, but the look was fleeting and replaced with more fury than before. "I have given you four beautiful children—" she continued, but he couldn't take any more of her barrage.

"Are yeh no' hearin' me? I've no desire tae be with any woman but you! I'd love nothin' more than tae have them ring me sayin' there's no' a match and that I've been disquali-fied. The idea of havin' tae do this gives me no pleasure a'tall. I wish you could understand that!" *Why can't she see how much agony I'm in over et?* "How do yeh think *I* feel?" he said and instantly regretted it.

Her eyes bulged out at this new morsel of fodder he'd thrown at her. She was a rabid pit bull and wasn't going to give up the flesh she'd sunk her teeth into. "How *you* feel, you … Scottish prig?" she screamed. "How *you* feel? You'll not get any sympathy from me! You won't be getting *anything* from me until—until I am good and ready, which won't be for a long time. And using that disgusting accent on me isn't help-ing you one bit!"

He knew she hated his native Scottish accent, so he rarely used it, but when he lost control of his emotions, it just came out. "I thought perhaps you'd feel that way, so I'll move into the guest bedroom tonight. I wish you knew how sorry I am," he said and went back to the broom he'd abandoned.

"Don't bother," she spat at him, "I'll have Kitty do it, now, leave." She sat on a dining chair, facing away from him, and drummed her fingers on the breakfast table.

She's right, yeh are an eejit, he said to himself as he left the kitchen with a heavy heart and walked up the stairs to their bedroom. He gathered his toiletries and the clothing he needed, draping it all over his arm or stuffing it into his holdall. Angrily, he snatched up his pillow, wishing he could travel back in time and choose to not go with Martin. *Never again,* he vowed to himself as he carried his things to the guest room, *never again.*

On Monday, David got a call from his agent, Becky, telling him there was an offer for a small role in an American television series. It would mean an extended weekend away from London, with a few days of shooting in New Orleans. Usually, he made sure to read the script and talk it over with Susannah, but he needed an escape, so he agreed on the spot. "I'll do it."

"What did you say?" Becky replied.

"I'll do it."

"You don't want to read the script?" she said suspiciously. "Is everything alright with you?"

"Yes," he lied, "I need to get away, and this will be good. I've a lot on my mind right now, Becks, and I need a way to escape my head."

"Well, if you're sure, I'll let them know in New Orleans. This isn't at all like you, David. Are you sure everything is alright?" She sounded concerned.

"Of course it is, Becky. What could possibly be wrong with my perfect life?" *If she only knew,* he thought. "Alright, I confess ...." He began and told her about the Registry and what that involved.

"You did what? Why don't you ever talk to me, David? Well, now you'll have to follow through, and I'll need to send a nondisclosure agreement," she said, sounding put out.

It occurred to him then that taking the job in America would be beneficial in other ways, as well. For instance, he wouldn't be available if the Registry called him. *Et's perfect; brilliant, even!*

Chapter Nine

THE BOTTOM LINE

Erin and Todd sat in front of a large desk with a plaque that read, 'Surya Nanavala, M.D.' They'd only been in the office for a few minutes when Dr. Nan entered the room carrying two beige folders. "How are you feeling today, Erin?" he asked as he walked around the desk and sat in his leather chair.

"Honestly, I've felt better. Right now, I'm feeling impatient and can't wait to hear about the new treatment. This has been the longest few days of my life," she said, not wanting to sound rude but wanting him to get to the point.

He leaned forward and opened the top folder. Inside was a set of papers and pamphlets, held together by a binder clip. He handed it to Erin. "I find I am at a loss for words. It sounds foolish to suggest the things I am about to say to you."

"Come on Doctor, it can't be that bad, or it wouldn't be approved as a treatment, right?" Todd said.

"No one needs to be sacrificed in a ritual cleansing, do they?" Erin added.

The doctor smiled and shook his head. "No, nothing like that."

"Okay," Erin said as suspicion rose up inside her, "Then what's the cost, and what are the side effects? Is it an experimental drug that will make my symptoms—maybe five percent better, but makes my—toes fall off? Yeah, and surprise, it only lasts two years! Then, lucky me, it all comes back—all except my toes, that is?"

Dr. Nan couldn't help but laugh. "No," he said, trying to regain his composure. "There are no negative physical side effects, and it is not a drug. It is a completely natural, bimonthly treatment."

"Please, Doctor, spit it out," Erin said, "I have to try it; I don't care what it is!"

"I will try to explain it in lay terms, though the pamphlets will give more details. All I ask is that you hear me out and listen to all I have to say before you get … upset." The couple frowned and nodded, so he pressed on. "There are voluntary registries all over the world where men sign up at specialized clinics. We are one of the last countries to get involved; that is why you have most likely never heard of them," he said tentatively. "The men have a thorough checkup and must give samples of their blood and … semen."

At the word semen, Erin's eyes grew wide, but she said nothing. "The goal is to match each man with a woman who has the disease. "When a man and woman are matched, they must both agree to … er, have intercourse with each other at least once every two weeks, to begin with. The men are tested thoroughly for every kind of sexually transmitted disease, so it is completely safe. Then, as symptoms improve, there may be fewer treatments necessary. However, both people must begin with the mentality of being in it for the long haul."

Todd stood; his face was red, and his fists clenched. It looked like he was either going to start yelling or storm out of the room. Erin was staring wide-eyed, her mouth hanging open. "You're … kidding, right?" she managed to whisper. "So, there might be a … guy out there who—"

"Who could free Erin from her torment?" Todd finished for her and then sat hard on his chair. He'd been angry at first, but then it occurred to him that she could die, and it would be his fault if he forbade her or made her feel like he wasn't on her side. If there was even a chance it might help her, he knew he had to be selfless, suck it up, and encourage her to at least try it.

"Are you serious? You're joking! You're not thinking about having me do this, are you?"

Todd looked at the doctor and then at Erin, tears gathering in his eyes. "Honey, you've been suffering for so long, and we are desperate, right?" He looked helplessly at the doctor. "Are you saying there's a chance Erin could live symptom-free if she has sex with some guy twice a month?"

"That is precisely what I am saying," he said.

Erin looked at them both as her face turned bright red. "But can't it be done another way? Injections, or, I don't know, a turkey baster, or something? Does it have to be actual intercourse?"

"All of those things have been tried. The semen of your match is a cocktail of proteins, hormones, and enzymes that work together to stop the symptoms of the disease. Some of them are quite fragile and cannot be overly manipulated, or they break down and become ineffective, so insemination does not work. It has been difficult to analyze, as it is—it appears to be DNA specific. We are still trying to isolate the function of each—

"Suffice it to say that it may take some time before we have a drug. This is for many reasons, including the fact that drugs need to be clinically tested and FDA approved, so even when we succeed, it won't be on the market anytime soon. It seems the only way to get a positive reaction, at this time, is through the physical act of sexual intercourse with the person you have been matched with. This method is for those with the greatest need, those who may be willing to take drastic measures to survive."

Erin was in great need, but was it too drastic for her? "I don't know—Wait, how was this treatment discovered? I mean, people with the Fertilis Defect are having sex with their partners every day; how did anyone figure it out?"

"Good question. It began when a woman came to her doctor reporting rapidly diminishing symptoms, a new boyfriend being the only change to her routine. Similar stories were soon being documented, so testing and clinical trials began and found that if a matched couple had sex at regular intervals, the woman would go into remission. However, if the treatments decreased, or stopped, so did the remission."

"But why is it only one match per person? That's like a one in a million chance of finding the right one!" Erin exclaimed.

"We do not know how many matches a woman may have at this time, as the Registry is still in its infancy. As more men sign up, we may find there are more, but for now, it seems as though it is specific to only one."

"But what if that one—"

"How long are we talking about here? Six months, a year, for … life?" Todd asked over her.

"You must have the mindset that it will be for life, I am afraid." Dr. Nanavala held up the second folder, "This file contains the name of your match. I can—"

"Woah, wait one goddamn minute!" Erin interjected, "You've already found … my match?" She didn't know what to think, but her first impulse was to light the folder on fire and throw it out the window. There was a real person in there.

What kind of man would do that?

But if he can help me?

No, NO! It's disgusting and insulting, and it's not an option, she thought wildly.

"This man will most likely allow you to live your life episode free, Erin." Dr. Nan said.

She sat mute and furious, looking between the two men. She was angry that he'd even suggest such a thing and that Todd seemed okay with it.

Dr. Nan leaned forward in his chair. "You need to discuss this thoroughly. It is a weighty decision, one with the possibility to change your lives, for better or worse. You are in shock right now and should not rush to decide. No one is going to try to force you into anything, and no one is getting a kickback or incentive for suggesting it. I am only trying to help you. Now, we need to go over all the details and have you come back when—"

"What's there to discuss?" Erin said and stood. "I'm not cheating on my husband! This is the most ridiculous thing I've ever heard!" She slammed her open palm down on the desk. Todd was right; they were desperate, but how could she have sex with a stranger? It sounded like something straight out of *The Handmaid's Tale* or an elaborate joke. *It can't be real*, she thought to herself, *it can't be*.

Todd stood and put his hand on her shoulder. "We have to get her to agree to this," he said through clenched teeth. "What other choice do we have?" He looked at his wife, "Let's go home and talk about it."

She nodded, too exhausted and furious to argue.

Dr. Nanavala stood, walked over to Todd, and handed the first folder to him. "Read the literature. Take your time and think about the advantages and disadvantages."

Todd nodded, thanked him, and they left.

Chapter Ten

THERE'S NO WAY

Todd and Erin rode home in silence. The words spoken in the doctor's office tumbled around in their minds like a bitter alphabet soup. Each of them sat in their mind's own private torture chamber, mulling over what they'd heard and trying to come to grips with the fact that there was hope, but not a realistic version of it. Erin thought about all the guys she'd dated before meeting Todd. They'd all cheated on her, and she didn't want him to feel the pain she'd felt so many times. *I'd hate myself for doing it.*

The sun was setting and blinded them as Todd pulled into their driveway after the appointment that day. The garage door rose in slow motion, and the clunk of the gear shifter sounded like a shotgun being cocked as he put his car into park and turned off the engine. He walked around and opened the door for his wife, who didn't seem to be aware they were home.

"Oh!" she said, as he held out his hand to help her out, "I'm sorry, I was lost in thought." She took his hand, feeling like she'd aged fifty years in a matter of an hour. "I need a nap."

"It's a beautiful evening for April; let's take a short walk," he suggested.

Erin longed for the forgetfulness of sleep, but she saw something in his face that made her agree. They used to walk around the block often, holding hands and talking about their day, though, now that her symptoms were getting worse and more frequent, she just didn't have the stamina anymore. Sometimes she feared she was mentally giving up and that, maybe, if there was a bit of hope, she'd have a little more energy.

Todd held her hand as they walked to the end of the driveway, where they paused, looked at each other, and smiled. They used to have playful arguments when they reached that spot about which way to turn. It had become a game between them.

"You choose," she said softly, so they turned left, away from the sinking sun.

"I honestly think—" he began, but Erin stopped him.

"No! I don't want to talk about it now. Let's just walk and talk about nothing important, please."

He nodded and sighed as they continued walking. The sun felt warm on their backs, and red-winged blackbirds sat on the telephone wires above them without a care in the world. Erin looked at her husband; he was average in height, weight, looks, and in just about every way a person could be. His hair had once been a dull dishwater-blond but was now mostly white. He sometimes grew a mustache and had touted a full goatee when they were first married.

He wasn't handsome, but she didn't care. She wasn't much to look at herself, being just over two hundred pounds, with ordinary brown eyes and dark-brown hair that was quickly turning grey. She loved him; he was more than her husband; he was her friend. She couldn't fathom allowing another man to touch her, let alone enter her bed. *How can anyone who's married do it?* she wondered, but her last episode had been so bad, the worst one so far. The thought of finding relief was surprisingly tempting, and she was ashamed of herself for even thinking about it.

But could it work? Could it possibly—

"No!" she said, not meaning to speak out loud and put her hand over her mouth. When she turned to him, he looked at the ground. "This is too much! I can't take it! Even if I could somehow imagine it, I could never actually do it; it would kill you!" she cried out. She stood in front of him, taking both of his hands in hers, and he looked up at her, "Do you honestly think you could live, knowing I was in a room, having sex with another man?"

Todd lowered his head again. His voice cracked when he finally gathered enough control to reply. "I don't know." He couldn't look at her, or he'd break down. "Will it hurt? Of course, but it hurts me to see you live like this, and with it getting so much worse? I don't know, Erin …" His voice trailed off, and he looked over her shoulder, moving her so he could continue walking. He wanted to get home, out of the view of their neighbors.

They got back to the house and started supper. Neither of them was hungry, but it gave them something else to concentrate on. Erin set the table absentmindedly, knowing Todd wouldn't let her use him as an excuse to pass on the wretched thing.

She was trying to come up with something, anything to justify not doing it in a way that would appease him. He'd go to hell and back (which was, most likely, what it would do to him) to help her. Eventually, he'd wear her down into considering it, so she decided to save the war. There was no point to it, not with Todd.

Todd knew it would be the hardest thing he'd ever be required to do, but in his mind, he was required to do whatever it took to help his wife. She'd put up with his issues over the years, after all, forgiving him, again and again; he owed her. It was the only thing promising them any hope, so if he had to teach himself to go numb while she slept with another man, then so be it. He didn't know how, but there was no question in his mind he'd find a way or die trying.

"I'll call the clinic tomorrow and ask if I can see the file of the man," he heard Erin say from across the room.

He was shocked. His wife was a stubborn woman, not one to give up on an important fight. He came and stood across the table from her. "I'm listening," he said, with a skeptical look at her.

"I know you aren't going to let this go, so I'm not going to fight with you." She stared at the silverware she was laying out. "Look, you know I don't want to do it, and I know you'll do whatever is in your power to convince me. We've been married a long time," she said and looked up at him, trying to smile.

He walked around the table and held her tightly. "It breaks my heart when I can't do anything to help you during an episode. I feel so powerless," he said, not able to explain what he felt. Here was something, albeit something impossibly difficult that he could 'allow' her to do, but he couldn't say it that way to her. There was no 'allowing' Erin to do anything, she either did it, or she didn't, and she had to do it.

That night, Todd made love to Erin in a way he hadn't in a long time. He touched her a bit more, thrust harder, and made her feel more than she was used to. *If he could just keep that up for a little while longer—then maybe*—she thought. "Yes! Just like that! Keep doing that!" she gasped. It was feeling so good, but her excitement took him over the edge. Todd reached his orgasm, grunting like he always did, and frustrated, Erin lay on her back as she always did.

"I'm sorry, honey," he said and kissed her. "I love you. I wish I could please you more. I know it's not fair."

It's not his fault it's mine, she thought, still annoyed that he didn't try harder, although she knew it probably wouldn't help, anyway. As he headed to the bathroom, her insides ached for more. "It's okay, honey. I love you too," she said and rolled over.

Chapter Eleven

MEET YOUR MATCH

"I'm not saying I'm gonna do it, just that I'll look into it. If he's gross, I won't do it, and you won't change my mind, got it?" Erin blurted out first thing after the alarm went off the next morning. Neither of them had slept well, tossing and turning.

It was a rude awakening for Todd, being reminded of everything so bluntly, but he was relieved she was still willing to consider it. "Okay, honey. Thank you," he said, and a shiver went down his spine, remembering it was sex with another man they were talking about. "Just promise me one thing."

"Okay, what?"

"Don't … tell me anything about him. I don't want to know. I can imagine he's … I don't know … but if he turns out to be … well, either way, I won't be able to handle it."

"Okay, I promise," she said quietly.

Todd left for work after kissing her goodbye. The thought of calling the doctor made Erin feel sick, but she picked up her phone anyway. I need to talk to Lily! she thought. Lily Graves was her closest friend, and the only person she trusted with all her secrets. They'd met when they were school bus drivers and stayed friends after Erin had to quit because of her health. Lily would be working but had a short break between her two morning routes, and Erin hoped she'd be able to respond to a message.

Erin: *Big news. Call me between routes! PLEASE!*

She sat on the bed, biting her nails. A few minutes later, she was startled when her phone rang.

"What is it, Erin? I only have ten minutes," Lily said.

"There's a new treatment, but I'll have to have sex with another man. Something to do with a semen cocktail that somehow works to neutralize my symptoms; I don't know, but it's a real thing, Lily. Todd wants me to do it, but I don't know if I can!" Erin said, not allowing her friend to respond.

"Sex! Like real sex with a stranger? Erin! That's crazy!"

"I know! My doctor said that there's a match for me. I don't know how they do it, but there's a file, and I'm scared, Lil!"

"Of course you are! But … do you really want to do it, Erin? Are you sure?"

"No, I'm not, but the disease is getting worse. I'm afraid that if I don't do something soon, I'll die from it and it won't be far from now. That's why Todd wants me to do it, but Lily!"

"You're too young to die! I don't want to think about that! Who is this guy? What's he like? Can you meet him first?" Lily asked.

"I'm going to call Dr. Nan and ask to see his file, but I don't know. What if I do it and Todd leaves me? What if he can't handle it?"

"God, Erin! I don't know."

"Should I do it? Should I see the file and … do the treatments?" Erin asked her friend.

"Treatments? More than one?"

"Oh, yeah, I'd have to do it every two weeks at first, then who knows after that." Erin felt rushed, and wished she had more time to discuss her options.

"Wow, Erin! But if you don't do it, you'll die? I guess you don't have a choice unless you're ready for that," Lily said, making the decision clear.

"I'm not ready to die, Lily. I guess I'll have to do it. I'll call the doctor now. Thanks for listening to me! I love you!"

"I love you too. Damn, I've gotta go now. I'm sorry, bye."

"Bye," Erin said quietly. She found the card with Dr. Nan's direct number in the folder he'd given them. Her hand was shaking as she touched the smooth glass of her cellphone and nearly hung up when he answered.

"Doctor Surya Nanavala."

His light Indian accent was usually comforting to her, but not then. She'd expected to leave a message, so she was flustered. "Oh! Hi. I didn't think you'd answer. It's Erin March."

"Hello, Erin," he said. "I'm surprised to be hearing from you so soon. How can I help you?"

"Doctor?" Erin breathed; her heart was pounding, and she was afraid she'd start bawling, though she rarely cried. She cleared her throat. "Can-I-see-the-file-of-the-man-you-said-could-help-me? I'm-not-saying-I'm-gonna-agree-to-this-stupid-thing-but-Todd's-convinced-me-to—But-if-he's-gross-or-or-then-I-won't." All the words ran together. She had to audibly inhale when she finished and was shaking from head to foot. There was silence on the other end of the line. "Dr. Nan?" she said timidly, terrified they'd gotten disconnected, and she might have to repeat herself. "Are you … there?"

"Yes, I am here. So, you and Todd have discussed it?"

Erin was annoyed; she didn't want to rehash what she and her husband had said. She wanted to see who the guy was and get it over with. "Yes, but I don't want to talk about it. Can I see the file, or not?" she snapped and then realized how rude she'd been. "I'm sorry. I know you're trying to help me, and I shouldn't talk to you that way." She heard him take a deep breath. It occurred to her then that the information might be confidential, at least until everything was set in stone. "I mean," she stammered, "If I can't, then—"

"As far as I am aware, with HIPAA laws and such, I am not allowed to tell you any detailed information about him. The process is still new to me, Erin. I am not sure what the proper procedure is. I need to make a decision, so please give me a moment."

Surya Nanavala was a man of rules, but this was unfamiliar territory. Should he give sensitive, personal information to someone on the fence? If she told people who it was, he could get into a lot of trouble. Maybe there was another path. He couldn't give her details, but perhaps he could provide her with something. "Okay, Erin, are you there?" he asked, having made an executive decision based on the information he had at the time.

"Yes," she whispered.

"I cannot show you the whole file, but I will give you his description and some information about him if it will help you? Can you and Todd stop by today at 11:30? I will allow access to an amended file. You may view it while I go to lunch, on the condition that it does not leave my office and you tell no one."

"I'll be alone today. Todd's at work, and he specifically told me he doesn't want to know anything about him. I can't blame him, can you?"

"No, I guess I cannot."

"Okay, I'll be there."

Three hours later, Erin was led into the doctor's office. She had to remind herself to breathe, as she'd found herself holding her breath several times after entering the building. Dr. Nan wasn't in the room yet, and she could see the folder sitting on his desk. She was simultaneously repulsed and drawn to it, equally. Her eyes were fixed on it as she sat facing the desk, as though she thought the man might pop out and attack her. She laughed out loud as she imagined a young Antonio Banderas appearing and kissing her hand with a flourish while bowing low.

The door opened, and Dr. Nanavala stepped in. "What is so amusing?" he asked.

"Oh, man! You startled me!" she said. "My imagination was getting the better of me, that's all." She was blushing deeply, feeling it tingling in her cheeks.

Dr. Nan walked around his desk and sat in his chair. He put his hand on top of the folder and looked earnestly at her. "Remember, this file cannot leave my office, and though much of the information is redacted, you must treat it with the strictest confidentiality." He slid the pale tan file folder across the polished desktop until it was in front of her, and she put her hand on it. The doctor stood, took his jacket off the coat rack, and opened the door. "Good luck," he said and closed the door behind him.

Erin felt like she was snooping in a secret military file and would be sentenced to life in Guantanamo Bay, being waterboarded if she were caught. Breathe, she reminded herself again and turned the folder right-way-round. She nearly opened it twice but slammed her hand down onto it, as if the contents might escape and hurt her. *You're being ridiculous!* she told herself and then managed it. The first page was legal and privacy law blabber, so she skipped it. She took a breath and flipped the page, wishing for a glass of wine, or maybe something more potent, to calm her nerves. Not able to sit still, she stood, lifted the page, and read:

Name: ████████████

Yeah, that's helpful.

DOB: April ███ 19██

Well, we were born in the same century, at least.

Height: 6'2"

That's friggin' tall! Todd's only 5'9!

Occupation: Employed: ████████

Being employed is a good thing.

Marital Status: Married.

Why would a married man sign up for this? Odd!

Residence: ████████ England, UK

Ooh! Goody—wait, shut up!

Addendum A:

Appointments are conditional, based on all arrangements being kept strictly confidential. Also, no ████████ shall be made aware of his involvement with the patient. If the agreement is breached, this, as well as all further appointments, shall be terminated.

Addendum B:

████████████ is willing to travel for treatments unless ████████ . In that case, he is prepared to have the patient flown to his location, with all accommodations arranged and supplied, so as not to burden the patient with the added cost of travel.

Erin reread the sheet several times, wishing for more information. She even tried holding the pages up to the light, but not only had they been blacked out, @ signs had been typed over everything, which was thorough but annoying. She wanted more. "I don't think I can," she said out loud and then felt her chest constricting. The coughing began, and she was unable to inhale, though her muscles fought to do so. She clutched at her throat, praying internally, *Please, please help me breathe! I'll do anything, just help me!*

She found herself lying on the floor of the doctor's office, gasping and sore from head to foot, but she could move, so it must not have been a bad episode. Her last conscious thought came back to her as she tried to get up, *I'll do anything, just help me!* and she knew she'd have to do it.

Dr. Nanavala re-entered the room as she was nearly back onto the chair. "Dear Lord, are you alright? What can I do?" he asked and hurried to help her the rest of the way up.

"You can set up my first treatment," she said, looking him in the eyes. She was furious with her body, her parents, Fertilis, the disease, and herself for giving in. She balled up her fists and closed her eyes. *What will Todd say? What will he do? How am I going to get myself to do this?* Her mind was racing, and it wasn't until Dr. Nanavala placed his hand on her back that she remembered where she was. "I need to go. Thank you, Dr. Nan."

"But Erin, you should not drive yet. I can put you into a room so you can rest—" he was saying, but Erin was determined.

"No, I need to get home. I'm fine. It's not far to drive." She grabbed her purse and took one more glance at the folder lying innocently on the desk. *I hope this is the right thing to do.* Erin managed to drive herself home. Dr. Nan had been right, she should've rested first, but she knew she'd want to sleep for a long time and didn't want to do it at the hospital. She parked in the driveway and sat, staring at the breezeway door. It took so much energy to unbuckle her seatbelt and get out; then came the arduous task of getting all the way into the house and into bed. She took the journey one step at a time and slowly managed to get to her room. The comforter and top sheet were heavy as she lifted them enough to crawl in and was asleep as soon as she lay down. Later, Todd would find her purse and jacket on the floor of the kitchen. One shoe lay in the hallway, the other just inside the door of their bedroom.

Chapter Twelve

THWARTED PLAN OF ESCAPE

Becky called David on Tuesday wanting to know what he was willing to offer his match, should they find one. He told her he would ask his assistant, Tina, to manage it. However, when Tina started ringing him daily, he gave her carte blanche to decide what might make the woman's experience easier; his only requirement was to be generous.

On Friday, his mobile rang, and he answered with his usual, "This is David," which he regretted as soon as he heard the voice on the other end of the line.

"Hello, is this Mr. David Elliott, then?" Sean's lilting Irish accent asked.

David wanted to tell him he'd rung the wrong number and hang up, but it was too late. "Hello, Sean, what is it?" he said, which he realized sounded a bit rude. He had a feeling Sean wasn't calling to chew the fat. His heart was in his throat, and his mouth became horribly dry.

"I have good news for you."

"Good news?" David managed to say without betraying the fact he thought he'd pass out at any second.

"Yes. We've found your match."

David had been walking toward his office, and at that, his knees buckled. He had to steady himself on one of the carved side tables to keep from dropping into a heap on the floor. His arms and legs had become jelly, so he sat on the hall chair, not yet ready to hear that his fate was sealed. "You have?" he squeaked and cleared his throat. "You have?"

"Yes, and we must arrange your treatment schedule as soon as possible. What is your availability, then?"

David sighed, thankful he'd taken Becky's offer. It meant he wouldn't need to lie. "Oh, Sean, I'm terribly sorry, but I've taken a job in America," he said, trying to sound disappointed.

"Well, that's ideal," Sean exclaimed.

"Ideal?" David limbs became an even softer jelly, without form.

"Yes. Your match lives in America." Sean sounded as though he were elated.

David was glad he hadn't eaten anything for some time as it would've come back up at that point. "In America, you say?" He leaned forward and put his head between his knees, hoping he wouldn't pass out, or worse, vomit right there on the polished hardwood floors.

"Are you alright?" Sean asked cautiously.

"Continue," was all David could manage.

"She lives in Wisconsin. I've no idea where that is, but I've been told it's near the middle of the country."

"Uh-huh."

"When will you be in America, and for how long?"

"In three weeks," he heard himself say. He wanted to grab the words and reel them back into his betraying gob. *Dammit! Why are yeh doing this to yourself, yeh stupid numptie!* David gathered his strength and said, as evenly as he could, "Sean, I'm going to have you ring my assistant. She is aware of the situation and is trustworthy; she'll be able to help you with scheduling, a'right?"

"Of course, Mr. Elliott. We'll get this sorted, don't you worry."

David gave Sean Tina's telephone number and rang off. He pulled himself together enough to stand, glad no one had seen him in that state. Taking himself upstairs to his temporary bedroom, he closed the door and locked it. As he lay on the bed, he didn't know if he wanted to cry or vomit. He hadn't cried in a long time, not, he supposed, since his father had died. He'd been upset since then, but this was so big, so overwhelming. All he wanted to do was weep, and he was going to be sick, making it to the toilet just in time. *Oh God, I can't do et! I've no' slept with anaone but Susannah!*

Chapter Thirteen

SECOND THOUGHTS

E rin was alone in a large crowd. He was coming toward her. She was thrilled, nervous, and confused. *What's John Thomas Fife doing here, and why is he smiling at me?* She woke just as he was about to take her hand.

"Wake up, honey. I think you'd better use the bathroom," Todd said, touching her shoulder and shaking her gently; then he was back. "Erin—you've been asleep for probably twenty hours. Supper is nearly done; please try to get up. I'll be back in a few minutes." He bent down, kissed her cheek, and walked out of the bedroom.

Did he say twenty hours? That can't be right, she thought, annoyed that she'd lost a whole day. Her stomach made a horrible noise, confirming it had been at least that long since she'd eaten. He cooked? Wow! "Why didn't you wake me before now?" she asked, hoping he'd hear her from the kitchen.

"I tried. I helped you to the bathroom twice, don't you remember?"

"No, I don't. Thank you." She sat on the edge of the bed, willing herself to get to the bathroom, but it was difficult to get up. Their landline started ringing, and she could hear Todd say that she wasn't able to come to the phone, but he'd take a message. He thanked the person, said goodbye, and then walked into their room.

Seeing she hadn't moved, he helped her to stand and then walked with her to the bathroom. "That was Dr. Nan's office. They said they've been trying to reach you all day and had to schedule your first treatment, or your match's calendar would be full. What happened, Erin? What's all this about setting up treatment dates already?" Todd was trying hard to hide that he felt wounded, but she could tell.

"I had an episode, alone in the doctor's office today, uh, I mean yesterday. The last thing I remember was praying, 'I'll do anything, just please help.' I have to do it, Todd, I don't want to, but I can't go through it again. What was the whole message? Did they tell you the dates?" She knew her anxiousness made her sound too eager. She saw the hurt in his eyes, but she was starting to get impatient.

"They didn't tell me the dates. They asked me to have you call them back," he said brusquely, as he helped her from the bathroom to the living room sofa, where they'd be eating, then he turned to leave.

"Wait! You were the one who told Dr. Nan I had to do it, now you're getting upset? I don't understand."

"I don't know, it feels different now. I need time to adjust." He took a deep breath and walked away.

Erin wanted to stop him, but what could she say? Nothing that would make things any easier. She managed to stand, walking slowly into the kitchen, and saw Todd looking out the window by the sink. She came up behind him and wrapped her arms around his waist. "I'm sorry, honey," she whispered. "I want this to be over with so we can get on with our lives."

He helped her to one of the dining chairs and looked at her, so weak and tired. "I know, I'm just shocked you made the decision so quickly and without letting me know." He handed her the message and cordless phone.

Why does it have to involve sex? It isn't fair! she thought. She called the clinic, telling the receptionist she was returning a call from Dr. Nanavala's nurse and was put on hold.

"This is Nurse Kelly,"

"Hello, this is Erin March. I'm returning your call."

"Yes, Mrs. March, I have good news! We were able to set-up your first treatment; it's on May sixteenth."

"That soon?" she said, starting to panic. *Three weeks? Oh my God, no!*

"Yep, your match has a temporary job in the U.S., so he'll be able to meet with you here. We couldn't get ahold of you, so I set it up" The woman had a childlike voice that was entirely too bubbly for the occasion. Erin wanted to ask the happy little kitten what she was thinking, scheduling it so soon! "I hope that's okay. I didn't want you to have to wait too long, you know?"

Erin sighed. "I … appreciate that," she lied, "Thanks."

"No problem, I'm glad I could help! You'll need to fly to New Orleans, but the hotel room will be taken care of, so you won't need to worry about that. You'll get an email with the details in a few days."

"New Orleans? I thought 'here' meant—here. Wow! I didn't think about having to travel."

"Also, you should set up a few more appointments, but you can do that later. You'll be meeting every two weeks for three months, then your case will be reevaluated."

"Okay," she managed to say, "I'll write it on my calendar. Is that all?" She was proud of herself for keeping her cool when all she wanted to do was throttle the little nurse do-gooder.

"That's it, good luck," she said.

When Erin hung up, her head was pounding, and her mind was reeling. *Three weeks! Can it get any worse?* Everything was far too real. She needed to wrap her head around what she had to do and didn't even want to think about her out-of-shape body. It wasn't a date or beauty pageant, but she was still embarrassed and wanted to go back to bed and avoid the reality of the mess she was in.

When Todd returned from setting up the TV trays, she told him what the nurse said. He was visibly upset with his jaw clenched and his fists balled up so tightly his knuckles were white. She knew he wanted to hit something and was glad he wasn't a violent man. He was pacing, wild-eyed. "Three weeks? That's, what, the middle of May?" he said, sounding panicked.

"May sixteenth. I should get an email with the itinerary in a few days. Are you sure you don't want to know anything about him or—"

Todd swiveled, doing an about-face to look at her, fear and jealousy contorting his expression. "No!" he said between clenched teeth. He took a breath, tried to relax his jaw, and continued in a more even tone, "I don't want to know anything! Nothing, do you hear me? If you tell me anything, I'll want to kill him, or … myself."

'Myself' was spoken in a whisper, and it startled her. "I don't know how to help you. If you can't find a way to deal with this, you need to tell me, so I can cancel it." She wanted him to tell her to call and tell them it was a mistake, but she knew he wouldn't.

"Erin," he said as though he was already tired of repeating himself, "I'm not going to change my mind, so please stop asking me. I'll find a way just don't badger me about it." After a few minutes, he stopped pacing, released his fists, and took a cleansing, relaxing breath.

This was a side of Todd she'd never seen. The treatments hadn't even started, and it seemed like their relationship was on sandy ground. Their marriage had been as solid as a rock. She once thought that nothing could tear them apart. Now she was beginning to worry. "I love you, honey," she said quietly.

Todd knelt in front of her. He was calm, though his face was still red. "I know. I'm sorry I barked at you," he said and laid his head on her lap. "I feel so useless. Why can't I give you the relief you need? I'm just angry that it has to be some-one else."

"I wish it were you too. I don't know how to prepare my-self, and I'm scared. Please stay on my side and be there for me."

"You know I will," he said.

Chapter Fourteen

FED UP

Becky sent David the preliminary script. The part wasn't big, but his lines were quite wordy, so he went about learning them as he prepared for his trip. Two weeks later, as David was packing, Susannah came into the room and sat on the bed. She had been as distant as he'd ever known her to be and walked away if he tried to speak to her.

Martin had wisely kept his distance, as well, and didn't try to contact him after the Fertilis Defect charity event. He had fulfilled that aspect of his promise, and the charity had been overwhelmed with donations. Of course, he was chuffed about that.

"When do you leave?" his wife asked flatly.

"Four days."

"Do you need anything for the trip? I can tell Kitty to have everything you need washed and set out for you before you go."

He knew she didn't care whether he needed anything or not, nor, for that matter, if his plane went down in flames. It was just an excuse to get information, that's all. "I don't need anything, and if I do, I'll buy it there," he said, with the same blunt manner she was giving him, but then changed his mind.

You should tell her about your match, don't you think?

"Listen, whilst I'm there, I'll be—"

"I don't care what you do whilst you're there, David. How long did you say you'd be gone?" she asked with a complete lack of feeling.

"I hope to return by Monday, though the room is booked until Tuesday, so—"

"Fine," she said and walked out of the room before he finished speaking.

The night before he was meant to leave for New Orleans, he put some American dollars in his wallet and set out his passport. A few quid and a credit card were also tucked away in his holdall for the way home. He tried to concentrate on the role he was meant to play and not the 'treatment' he was meant to perform, but it was difficult.

Tina had already set up the accommodations and all travel arrangements for him and Mrs Erin March, which was the woman's name in the email he'd received from the Registry. He knew that the Fertilis Defect Registry Trust wouldn't be able to put her up in a comfortable room, so he would. Susannah had set a standard of comfort he'd grown accustomed to, and he wasn't about to stay at a luxury hotel while the sick woman was stuck in a dive on the outskirts of town.

He had also asked Tina to provide her with a driver to pick her up at the airport. It was the least he could do, or that's how he saw it since she couldn't be any more comfortable about the situation than he was. People were always giving things to him, so he thought of it as giving back, and if he were honest, it made him feel good to be able to make things easier for her.

It seemed ridiculous to him to have two separate rooms when a suite offered plenty of privacy and the ability to get to know one another before they were forced to … consummate the treatment. *Is that the proper word?* he thought. He hoped his plan would be acceptable to her. Having stayed at the cottages once before, he knew them to be an establishment of distinction. It all hinged on whether she'd be agreeable to sharing a suite with a stranger or not.

That night he found himself daydreaming about their first meeting and whether or not she'd been warned who he was beforehand, genuinely hoping she had. *Is et compulsory tae disclose that information? Et must be, he reasoned. Et would be cruel not to.* There was the issue of privacy laws, but he'd been given her name, surely, she'd be granted the same courtesy. *Ach, will she even know who I am? Perhaps she's never heard of me.*

Through his sources, Martin learned that David had accepted a role in an American crime drama being produced by an online streaming service and that he'd be filming in New

Orleans. *I'm sure I can cause him trouble whilst he's there,* he thought, feeling desperate to make something happen.

He heard his mother's voice in his memory. *"You're just as good as David, Martin. He was born with a silver spoon in his mouth, and you weren't, but that doesn't mean you can't force it out of his mouth every now and then. The only difference between you is that you've got to make things happen for yourself! Use whatever means necessary to make your way, no matter what it takes, love."*

He'd never been so ruthless before, but when Graham Norton had asked David about the role of a lifetime, and he hadn't denied it, that was the final straw. *I'm tired of reading about his success, and I'm going to do something about it,* he thought. *Perhaps force-feeding him a tin of humble pie will have Susannah turning to me once she sees his weakness.* As soon as he knew the date, he called a mate who worked as a private investigator to see if he could refer him to someone in New Orleans.

"I've got just the bloke. He's been known to break the rules, so if that's not what you're after, tell me now."

"He sounds perfect. I don't know where David is staying, but last time it was at the Audubon Cottages. All I know for certain is he'll be arriving on the fifteenth."

"Right-o, I'll ring him to see if he's available on that date."

"Thanks, mate, cheers," he said, feeling the adrenaline kick in. Now for the fun part. He was acquainted with a pretty, young actress who just happened to be cast as David's co-star. He was sure a few extra dollars could persuade her to come on to him. Martin knew his plan would be tricky, as he presumed Susannah would be upset at him, but he'd be able to turn it around. *I'll chance a visit to see if she needs anything. Perhaps I'll have a few photos to show her as well.*

David woke early the next morning and set his holdall on the bed. At the last minute, he packed a black suit. *Yeh never know,* he reasoned. In went his toiletries, then his favorite book, battered, beaten, well-worn, and read often. It went with him everywhere in case he needed something to do.

It would soon be time to leave, so he decided to try speaking to Susannah one more time. She was usually up quite early, and he found her in their bedroom, sitting in her favorite reading chair. Her book was lying on her leg, and her eyes were closed. He stood in the doorway, not daring to enter his own room for fear of the consequences. "Susannah?" he said, waiting for her to snap at him or glare and leave the room.

"Mmmhh?" she replied.

That's positive; maybe I'll be able to at least kiss her once before I go. "I'm off to America in an hour. I thought … perhaps … we could spend that time together?" She opened one eye and then the other. *This could go either way.* He hoped enough time had passed that she could tolerate his existence for that long.

"I've a migraine, David. I was about to head back to bed, and don't you DARE get any ideas about asking to join me there! Your charm won't win out for you this time."

"I wasn't going to suggest that. I only wanted to spend some time with you before I leave, with perhaps … a kiss goodbye?"

"You may kiss me, I suppose."

Aye, the bloody princess deigns to offer me a kiss. He was annoyed at her attitude but decided to take the opportunity. Walking through their bedroom, he felt like a child who was told by Nanny that he was allowed to give Mummy a kiss goodnight. As he bent over her, expecting a peck on the lips, she turned her head so that he kissed her cheek instead. "See you in a few days then," he said, trying not to sound desperate or angry, which of course he was, both.

"Hmm, a few days—" she muttered.

David was fuming by then, so he turned heel and walked resolutely out of the room; back to where he'd been exiled for the last few weeks. Picking up his mobile and holdall from the bed, he walked down the hall, downstairs to the foyer, and left the house. He didn't know what he'd do for the remainder of his time in London, but he had to remove himself from that house before he went mad.

Stepping into the shop down the road, he chose a *GQ* magazine and a Mars bar, then he paid the turbaned Sikh man at the counter and left. A car was meant to pick him up at six, but he wasn't about to sit there for an hour, so he called to have one come right away. As he sat on a nearby bench, his head in his magazine to hide his face, he stewed.

Why's she bein' this way? Aye, she's a right to be angry, but what does she think behavin' this way will accomplish? Why can't we move on and deal with et? I'm tired of the 'Make David Feel as Though He's an Uninvited and Unwelcome Guest in His Own Bloody Home *game'. I'll no' stand for et much longer.* He was the one providing the house and lifestyle she was enjoying, and he'd not let her drive him out.

About twenty-five minutes later, a sleek black car pulled up, and the driver got out to open the boot. David told him not to bother, so the man nodded and opened the rear door for him instead. He slid inside the dark, quiet sedan. "Take me to Heathrow, please, terminal three," he said before he realized he'd already told the dispatch person where he'd wanted to go.

"Right," the driver said, cheerily, as he pulled away from the pavement.

It was morning rush hour on a weekday, so it took a while, but they eventually pulled up to the terminal. After thanking his driver, David walked into the airport and found the check-in kiosks of the airline he was flying with. He took out his passport and placed it into the machine's reader, but it wouldn't scan. An attendant with a name badge that read Trina S. came over to help, so he handed it to her. She tried again, and that time it worked. "Alright, Mister Elliott, we have a round-trip, first-class flight to Louis Armstrong, New Orleans, stopping at Chicago O'Hare?" she confirmed with a deep Texan accent that caught him off guard.

He very nearly quipped, 'Yes ma'am' in an accent to match hers but thought better of it. "Correct," he said, instead.

"Do you have any baggage ta check?"

"No, I'll keep my holdall with me."

"That's fine." They waited for his boarding passes to print. "You have a safe flight now, Mister Elliott," she said and smiled as she handed the long slips of paper to him.

"Thanks," he said and walked away, seeking the VIP lounge, where he'd be able to rest and read his magazine without being bothered.

Chapter Fifteen

PREPARATION FOR THE UNKNOWN

Erin had to visit the hospital once more to sign the confidentiality agreement. Dr. Nanavala seemed to be under quite a lot of stress. He was distracted, and his desk was piled with stacks of manila folders. "Wow, Doctor, what's up?" she asked.

"I have my hands full with new matches and am a bit disorganized lately. Now, I know there is something that I am forgetting." He closed his eyes, seeming to be going through a mental checklist, then he shook his head. "No, I believe we have covered everything. Do you have any questions?"

"I guess not," she lied. She wanted to beg him to tell her more information about her match, but he'd already told her that he couldn't, and she didn't want to stress him out any more than he already was. She figured she'd find out eventually. "So, that's it then?"

"That is it. I will see you when you return."

Erin drove home contemplating her new reality. She was glad they were meeting on neutral ground, far away from home. At first, she thought she'd have to bring him there and dreaded inviting a stranger into her home, having to play hostess and whore at the same time. It wasn't whoring, of course, but it damn well felt that way.

She presumed Todd was also relieved that it wouldn't happen on his bed, though he'd started flinching if there was any mention of the disease or its treatment, so she didn't bring it up. It probably didn't help that she was going to a beautiful, romantic city without him. She started packing her things a week ahead of time, keeping the small suitcase under the bed. He didn't need to be reminded of what it represented every time he saw it.

She'd be away from home for three nights and wasn't sure what to bring. *New Orleans in spring. What does that mean for clothing options?* In Wisconsin, she knew what to expect, generally cold unless it decided to get hot. There was no predicting the weather there in spring. New Orleans, on the other hand, would be much warmer.

She stuck with lighter things, including her favorite summer dress and the only bra she had that looked good under it. It had matching panties and just happened to be really pretty. She made sure Todd didn't know, even though they weren't for the benefit of the mystery man at all. What if she wanted to see a show, or whatever people in New Orleans did in dresses?

She managed to pack her clothing but couldn't decide what she'd sleep in. Her preference was wearing nothing, but she packed a purely practical, middle-aged-looking night-gown, just in case. As for what to wear for the 'treatment,' she was stumped. *What does one pack for something like that? Surely not lingerie or fancy underwear, she thought. Holy Moses! I won't be expected to get fully naked, will I?* The thought made her feel sick.

Excitement and nausea took turns beating her up, so she was packed and ready two days before the trip. All she'd need were her toiletries. She usually didn't wear makeup, but if she went out one night, she'd want it. Not optional were her hair styling products and ever-faithful straightening iron to tame her naturally wavy and often frizzy hair. Most important of all was sunscreen. The last thing she needed was to get sunburned and be miserable the whole time she was there.

Maybe Mr. Mystery man can help you apply it, said the naughty voice inside her head.

Woah! Where'd that come from? Damn, Erin, pull yourself together! You can't be thinking like that!

The night before she left, Todd surprised her with a small gold locket. Her initials were surrounded with filigree swirls on the front, and his were etched on the smooth, un-decorated back. Inside, it read, 'All my love, forever.'

"So you don't forget me," he joked.

"No chance!" she countered.

They made love that night in the usual way. It was nice, yet bittersweet. She felt like she had to remind them both that she'd be back soon. "It's just a few short days. I'll be back before you know it."

"I know, but I'm afraid things will be different when you get home."

She didn't blame him for thinking that way. To tell the truth, she had the same nagging fear as they fell asleep, wrapped up in each other's arms.

In the morning, Todd got ready for work, looking miserable. "I know it's dumb, but please remember I'm here waiting for you to return and that I love you."

"I'll miss you, honey. I'll call you every day if you want me to," she offered.

He looked at her sadly, "I don't think I do. It'll make what you're there for too real. Maybe it's better to let the days blend together, like when you're with your girlfriends. Only call to let me know that you got there safely, the room number, or if anything changes in your plans, okay?" he said, as though he'd given it a lot of thought.

"Really?" She couldn't hide her confusion. "I thought you'd want to hear my voice."

"I know it's confusing to you, but I think it'll help me … cope."

"Okay, if that's what you really want."

"It is. Now, I have to go, or I'll be late. You have a taxi coming to take you to the airport, right?"

"Yeah, I'm all set. Have a good day at work, honey," she said, knowing it would be impossible.

He kissed her goodbye, smiling as best he could, and walked out the door.

She watched him get into his car and back out of the driveway. He turned right and was out of sight in a few moments. The strongest desire came over her to run after him, yelling, 'Wait! I've changed my mind! It's all a mistake!' Instead, she gathered her toiletries into their black bag and put it into her suitcase, then she sat on the bed, wanting to cry. She couldn't, so she made sure she had everything she'd need; money, cell phone, charger, and carried them to the front door.

She used the online check-in for her flight. Then, after setting her purse on the suitcase, she paced the floor, wringing her hands while she waited for the taxi to arrive. *Why is time so fickle?* she thought. It couldn't seem to make up its mind whether to speed by or to drag on miserably. Whatever you wanted it to do, it was sure to do the opposite! She washed the coffee cup Todd had left in the sink and put it on the drying rack, then she paced a bit more, finally deciding to dry the mug and put it away. She was closing the cupboard door when she heard the car horn.

It was as if she were watching herself as she walked to the taxi and got into the back seat. The driver was an older man with sandy blond hair and kind, blue eyes. He confirmed they were headed to Austin Straubel airport and, they were off. After backing out of the driveway, they went the same direction Todd had gone on his way to work an hour earlier.

"Business, or pleasure?" the driver said, making small talk.

"Uh, neither."

94

"Don't matter to me," he said with a smile, "It's just something I always ask."

"I'm not in the mood for chit chat, sorry," she said, not wanting to be rude but not wanting to talk either.

"Fine by me. I like quiet just as much as I like talking." He smiled at her in the rear-view mirror, and she smiled back, liking him more every minute.

She lay her head back on the headrest and tried to think of something pleasant. She thought of dressing up and going to an amazing jazz club or show. The problem was that her imagination had her standing next to a tall, unknown man. She wasn't planning to go anywhere with the mystery man, so why was her brain including him?

It was a short ride to the airport, and they soon pulled up to the terminal. He stopped in the taxi lane and got out to open the door for her, which was unexpected and sweet. Erin thanked him and gave him a small tip.

"Have a nice trip, Mrs. March. I'll probably be here when you get back. Just look out for me, and I'll be happy to help," he said as he got back into his taxi and drove away.

Chapter Sixteen

UNPREDICTABLE

An airport was an unpredictable place for David. Sometimes he could walk through one, and no one noticed. At other times it was as if he was a powerful magnet, drawing everyone's eyes towards him. That day, thankfully, he was left alone. No one ran up to him demanding a selfie, and it was demanding. They pretended to ask, 'Can I have a selfie,' but their cameras were always right there, ready to snap their photo. He also had to have a natural smile and be friendly, no matter what he was dealing with in his life.

It was a violation at times, but he didn't have a choice; he must play along or find out later that he'd offended a hotshot internet mega personality. His name would then be smeared all over the internet without a chance to defend himself. It was part of his job description, he understood that, but some days were much tougher than others. It would've been difficult that day.

He made it through security to the executive lounge and was thankful for the soft, comfortable seats. A waiter asked if he'd like a drink, so he requested a Guinness if it was available. The young man returned three minutes later with a pint of liquid heaven on earth. It was just what he needed to help him relax and wait the three hours until his flight was called. The dark, velvet draft went down far too well, and when he ordered another, he vowed to drink it more slowly. The man returned with his second pint, and he immediately broke his vow.

This isn't gonna make anathin' better, yeh ken, his inner practical side tried to warn him. His inner coward, on the other hand, didn't care and drank it down. He wanted to forget everything for a while.

What's the harm in tryin' tae get through this with a bit of liquid assistance? he asked the nagging voice, which was gradually getting more and more muffled as the creamy, black stout worked its magic.

"Jus' one more, please," he said when the waiter came back. This time he didn't notice how many minutes it took, and he didn't get through the whole pint. He woke to someone *repeatedly* saying his name.

"Mr. Elliott!" said a member of the ground staff, who looked to be no more than twelve. She had a blond ponytail, braces on her teeth, and was trying to bring him back into his harsh reality.

"Hmmm?" *Wha' d'yeh want?* he thought to himself.

"Mr. Elliott, wake up. You are being called for an earlier flight."

"Wha'?" He was having trouble focusing. He saw his blurry pint, half-drunk, on the table next to him and fought the urge to down it, hoping no one would notice. *Wait, ach, aye, the pigtail, I mean girl.* "Did you say … an earlier flight?" *Did I ask tae be bumped to an earlier flight? I can't remember.*

The girl-child was quite anxious. She alternated, looking at her tiny wristwatch and over her shoulder at the departures screen hanging on the hazy wall. He could tell by her face and voice that it wasn't the first time she'd had to deal with someone of notoriety sleeping drunkenly in one of those chairs. *Ach, I see; that's why I was bumped. Passed out, second-rate actors aren't appealing to their V.I.P. clientele.* "A'right, aye, a'right," he said in that disconnected stupor one finds oneself in when disturbed in the middle of a deep, blissful, alcohol-induced sleep.

"*Please* follow me, sir." She was already out of the lounge doors by the time he managed to get up off his chair. He looked down at its soft leather curves and wanted nothing more than to sit and drift off again, but then she was back and sounded more urgent than before. "**Mr. Elliott**, we must leave *now* if you want to make this flight."

"Aye, I'm comin'!" *Ma bag—and ma mobile. Dammit! Wake up, you git!*

"Please hurry, sir."

This is hurryin'! They sprinted through the crowded terminal halls and into the empty departures lounge. He was then, indelicately, pushed through the gate and onto the airplane. The flight attendant led him to his seat, and he was told to buckle up as they were meant to taxi to the runway at once. Everyone seemed put out at having to wait for the 'big shot' actor.

Ah-righht, et's no' my bloody fault they called me tae this flight. I was happily out cold, oblivious tae your damnable time-line. Lay off, would yeh? his inner dialog spewed, while on the outside, he was calm and well mannered. He might've been tempted, in his state of intoxication, to say something about it, but the pilot was speaking, and he just wanted to go back to sleep.

He awoke sometime later to use the toilet and then ate a meal. When they landed in Chicago, he notified the car service in New Orleans that he'd be arriving earlier than planned. Having slept for most of the first flight, he finally managed to read most of the *GQ* he'd purchased in London. He noticed that he did feel a bit lighter (minus the splitting headache) than he had before leaving. After all, he was about to begin a new job, and, well, to be blunt, doing something different. It certainly wasn't anything he'd ever planned to do in his life, but by God, he would do his best to make it as comfortable for the woman as he could. He didn't know how, but he could be charming, right?

Chapter Seventeen

DAVID ARRIVES IN NOLA

David arrived in New Orleans and found his driver via a sign reading '*Elliott.*' The uniformed woman drove him to the French Quarter, one of his favorite places on earth. The city was beautiful, music spilled out from somewhere, day and night, and then there was the food; there was nothing like food in New Orleans! Jambalaya, crawfish, and then a trip to the Cafe du Monde for a bag of beignets and a cafe au lait. His mouth was practically dripping by the time they pulled up to the Audubon Cottages.

As he stepped out of the car, a lady saw him and asked for a selfie. *You used tae keep count. Now yeh smile like a trained monkey and exchange pleasantries until they're satisfied,* he thought as he thanked her for her kind words. One of the resident butlers was near the courtyard door, and after a warm welcome, he showed him to cottage number two, his home for the next week. *Perhaps I'll stay on a bit longer as I'm not wanted at home,* he thought.

The cottage was homelike and comfortable; he needed comfort if a 'treatment' was going to happen successfully.

He'd had enough of posh hotels where he was afraid to sit on the fine furniture. *Yeh mean as yer home has become?* he mused.

Having no idea what her standard of living might be, he hoped his guest would be comfortable as well. To him, it was the perfect blend of privacy and shared living space. Though, if she were anything like Susannah, it would be the absolute bottom of what she'd consider acceptable, *'for a person of my stature,'* which was her point of view, not his.

After wandering through the cottage, he chose the bedroom with the smaller bathroom. All he needed was a clean bed, toilet, and shower to sustain him. He set his holdall on the bed and put everything away. Susannah had broken him of the habit of living out of his suitcase long ago. Gone were the days of clothing strewn about the room as though a hurricane had ripped through it. He thought about calling his wife to let her know he'd arrived safely but remembered her coldness and decided against it.

Stop thinkin' about Susannah! he thought severely. She's no' here, and ye're glad of et, correct? Well then, leave her in London and get on with et where yeh are. Instead, he took a quick shower and afterward looked in the mirror for quite a long time. *David, you're lookin' old, mate! Ye're no' what yeh used to be!* "Humph," he replied out loud to his own critical analysis.

The early evening warmth outside was proving to be a great lure; he had one night alone and was determined to make good use of it. He got dressed, trying to look casual and blend in; he wasn't in the mood for selfies and autographs. After looking through a tourist pamphlet, he decided to take a walk, needing fresh air and interesting things to see. Gathering his wallet, sunglasses, and room key, he opened the cottage door and was met with a beautiful, sunny afternoon.

Leaving his sanctuary, he walked out of his private courtyard. He took his time as he walked down the brick path, flanked on either side by smooth, thin, tree trunks, potted ferns and foliage, and the outer walls of cottages one and two. The green door was soon open, and he was on Rue Dauphine, zig-zagging his way through the French Quarter to the Cafe du Monde.

His first mission included a bag of beignets and a cafe au lait, so he stepped underneath the green awning that read 'Original French Market Coffee Stand.' He dodged small, round tables and green, vinyl-covered chairs where people's wayward legs stuck out, ready to trip him up at any second. He had one aim, and a pair of strappy sandals would not keep him from it.

At the takeaway window, he placed his order, the smell of fried pastry and coffee lulling him into a sense of peace he'd not felt in quite some time. The cook made his order, throwing small squares of dough into the fryer. David watched them bubble and crackle as the man ladled the hot oil over it all, bathing them so that they puffed up, light as air.

His coffee and pastries were handed to him, and finding an open table in the corner, he sat, anticipating the plume of icing sugar awaiting his first bite. He opened the white paper bag to allow them to cool and sipped his coffee as he listened to the lone trumpeter standing on the pavement nearby. The older man was playing 'Oh Susanna,' which had him thinking about her again, so he stood, grabbed his pastries and coffee cup, and walked over to him. "Hello. I'm sorry to interrupt you, but would you mind playing something else? Your song has me feeling homesick."

"Homesick?" he said, a little confused, "You don't sound like you from Loo-siana," he said with a thick accent.

"Yes, well, my wife's name is Susannah, you see. She's in London, and she's not happy with me at the moment."

"Hoo! I understand that, yeah! Now, I have just the thing to cheer you up." He opened the spit valve on his horn and blew a few puffs of air through it, causing several drops of water to splash onto the pavement, then he played something sweet and beautiful that David didn't recognize.

He was spellbound, standing under the bright, big sky, with all the sights, sounds, and smells around him. It was probably jet lag setting in, but he could've cried for joy. He put ten dollars in the trumpet case at the man's feet and went back to his table.

His beignets were no longer scalding, so he reopened the bag, which crinkled happily as he unrolled the top. The aroma of oil and yeast rising from the crispy delights was intoxicating as he reached into the sugary bag of goodness, like Tom Thumb. However, instead of a plum, he pulled out one of God's greatest gifts to man.

Remembering too late to make sure he wasn't breathing in when he took his first bite, he inhaled a head-full of icing sugar. He coughed and sputtered, laughing out loud whilst tears ran down his powdered face. After catching his breath, he finished his treat without any further ado and threw the bag into the bin at the corner of the covered alfresco dining area.

Noticing a busboy, bedecked in his white paper hat, black bow tie, and white apron, clearing dishes from the tables, David handed him his cup and thanked him for the most wonderful evening. Either the boy had a good sense of humor, or people said similar things to him often enough that he didn't miss a beat. "Happy to have been of service," he said and continued wiping the sugar-dusted tabletops.

Behind the cafe, he sat next to the bronze statue of a young woman sitting on the edge of a small fountain and sighed. It wasn't much fun wandering around a beautiful, foreign city alone. Thinking about his family, he knew Susannah wouldn't have joined him, but he imagined it would be a grand adventure to explore it with his children, sharing the sights and smells of the French Quarter.

Feeling a bit depressed, he stood and headed to the French Market. His children might not be with him, but he could get them each a gift to say he was thinking about them. There wasn't much room in his holdall, so he found a few small things and decided to return to the suite and work on his lines.

David would've loved to take his leisure and explore the beautiful French Quarter that night, but he needed to adjust to the new time zone. Also, he had to be on set the next day with no traces of jet lag, so he knew he'd better get to bed early. Feeling tired, he walked through Jackson Square, past the banana trees, until the pristine front of St. Louis Cathedral loomed over him. He stopped and gazed at the crisp white church, its black-capped spires sitting atop the building like witches' hats in the setting sun.

Taking his time, he strolled down Pirates Alley. *There's somethin' romantic about that name,* he thought, imagining men with large, plumed hats, long waistcoats, silk sashes, and tall, buckled boots. There wasn't anything special about the small road; he fancied it on name alone, though his favorite book was *Captain Blood,* by Rafael Sabatini, so that might've been a factor.

He turned left onto Rue Royale; the iconic, wrought iron balconied buildings, painted peach and pink, and bedecked with hanging ferns and multi-colored flags smiled down on him as he walked past. Trying not to make eye contact with people, he continued slowly, looking into gift shops and admiring the architecture.

Rounding the corner onto Toulouse Street, he was nearly bowled over by a group of young adults. As they apologized, he knew by their accents that they were from the north of England. They recognized him and asked for a group photo, as well as several autographs, which he didn't mind giving, except it was drawing attention from the other tourists passing by.

David continued winding his way through the narrow streets, but now his stomach was rumbling, so he used his mobile to search for places to eat. Finding a restaurant near the cottage, he stopped and got a catfish po-boy to go.

Hank Roberts, P.I. got the call to observe David Elliott at the perfect time. He'd just completed a boring case involving insurance fraud and needed something interesting for his next job. Someone wanted the actor surveilled with photos, so he got a paid trip to New Orleans. There were worse things to do on an extended weekend.

He waited at the Audubon Cottages until a luxury sedan pulled up, and a man who looked like David Elliott got out of it. A lady asked him for a selfie, then he spoke with someone who worked at the place. "I believe I'm in cottage two," the man had said, plain as day. How much easier could the job get?

Hank would wait for him to leave so he could go inside to plant a few cameras. Was it legal or ethical? No. He did it for his own entertainment. He had the equipment; why not use it? He watched David leave the cottage on foot at five o'clock. *Perfect! I can at least get one or two devices inside before he comes back,* he thought. He reached into the back seat of his nondescript black electric car and grabbed his black duffle bag.

It was still light outside, but if he was quiet and confident, people would usually assume he was allowed to be there. He opened the green door and walked down the shaded path to number two. As he was about to open the private patio door, he heard a man's voice. "Hey there! Now, what you doin'?"

It was the employee he'd seen earlier, so Hank thought quickly. "Mr. Elliott is expecting me."

The butler looked at his duffel bag and shook his head. "Mr. Elliott ain't here," he said, reaching up to hold the door shut.

"I'll come back later, then," Hank said calmly and walked back out to the street. It didn't do any good to get angry or make a scene. He'd try again another time, and maybe he'd get lucky. *Hell, if all else fails, I always have the drone,* he thought.

When David entered the cottage, he saw his bedroom directly to the right of the front door. Although it was tempting to skip supper and go to sleep, he had work to do and wanted to go to bed at the local time, anyway. He sat on the comfortable, welcoming sofa in the living room and ate his supper, then spent the evening going over his copy of the script, which was boring by himself.

The production company had chosen him, at least partially, for his Scottish accent, so he didn't need a dialect coach, which was good. There was enough on his mind already; having to remember how to pronounce his lines would've been difficult. He studied the script for a few hours, and when the words began to blur, he got up, stretched, grabbed a Coke from the mini-fridge, then went back to it.

He must have dozed off, as he woke an hour later, his neck stiff and his right arm completely numb, having fallen asleep as well. *What time is it?* he thought as he shook his arm gently, waiting for the blood to flow back into it. He turned on the telly and found something interesting, though apparently, it wasn't all that interesting, as he woke up an hour and a half later with an even stiffer neck and a sore throat from snoring.

Knowing when to admit defeat, he stood and went to his room. He undressed and folded or hung up his clothes, then he crawled under the covers, kicking the thin duvet off the end of the bed, thankful for the comfortable mattress.

Chapter Eighteen

A JOB TO DO

David woke before his alarm. *Thank God! I hate that thing!* He didn't want to get out of bed; the sheets were deliciously smooth and had the faint smell of lavender. Reluctantly, he got up, showered, shaved, and got dressed. It was still early, so he chanced going out to the 'Garden House,' a small building in the courtyard where they served breakfast.

There was one older couple there when he entered. They smiled, said good morning, then went about their business, not recognizing him, so he chose what he wanted. The po-boy from the day before still had him feeling full, so he went easy. He filled a ceramic cup with dark, fragrant chicory coffee and walked back to the cottage, sitting out on the private patio to eat.

They would be filming his part in *Definite Action*, a TV series made for an internet streaming channel that day and the next. It was also the day his guest arrived, as both the Registry and his assistant had reminded him in an email with the woman's name and arrival time. The thought made his stomach do flips, and his breakfast lost its appeal.

How does one prepare for this? Should I do anathin'? I'll call the butler and ask tae have somethin' waitin' for her. Aye, I'll leave a note as well, he thought. Those things were easy enough, but what about the rest of it? *Don't go gettin' yer knickers in a bunch again.* He was ruining his appetite, so he decided to put it out of his mind.

He ate as much as he could and binned the rest. Then, he called the butler to ask for a basket of snacks and a bottle of wine for his guest. He found a sheet of stationery with *Audubon Cottages* engraved as the letterhead and wrote:

Please make yourself at home. I have taken the liberty of installing myself in the first room to the right and will most likely return between 3:00 and 7:00. If you require anything, please ring the butler, and he will be happy to help you.
—David

"That'll have tae do," he said aloud and placed the note on the small round dining table, where she would hopefully see it. Gathering his things, he made sure to close the door to his bedroom, then he left the cottage, leaving it unlocked for her. He wished the butterflies in his stomach would have stayed behind as he headed out to the street.

He could've walked to the film site, but a hired car was waiting in front of the building, the driver leaning patiently against the rear passenger side door. "Good morning," David said, as the gray-haired man, dressed in a clean, crisp uniform opened the car door for him. "Mornin', suh. My name is Benjamin LeFeite, but mostly people just calls me Ben."

"Nice to meet you, Ben," David said. The windows of the plain, black sedan were tinted for privacy, and the air-conditioning was already on to cut the humidity, for which he was grateful. It was a comfortable car; the tan leather seats were soft, making him sorry they were only traveling a few blocks. *Later you could tell him tae keep drivin' past the cottage and the woman waitin' in et,* he thought. He had forgotten her name, so he read the email from Tina again and sighed.

Ben walked around the car and got in. "You comfortable, suh? If you too warm or too cold, they controls back there for you. If you have any problem, you just ask ole' Ben here, a'right?"

"I'm fine, thank you," he said, enjoying his accent. He suddenly wondered whether Tina had remembered to have a car waiting for—He had to look at the email once more. *Mrs. Erin March—don't forget et again and stop worryin'! Tina knows what she's doin'.*

In a few minutes, they were turning into a cordoned-off area dedicated to filming crew and actors. A young man with security moved the orange safety cones, allowing the car to enter the restricted zone. Ben got out to open his door, and David stepped out into what appeared to be utter chaos. "Thank you, Ben."

"My pleasure, suh," he said as he closed the door. Then he walked back around the car and drove away.

David was used to the tumult of a film set and knew what to do. He spoke with the young security man, asking where to find the second Assistant Director. The man checked his name off the list on his clipboard and pointed to a long trailer about thirty meters away. "Over there, suh," he said, and David set off in that direction.

He made his way through base camp, past the portable loos, AKA the honey wagon, then the catering truck, and the 'talent' trailers. Since he was only slightly above a walk-on and already had accommodations, he passed them by. The hair and make-up trailers were in sight, so he continued to his destination.

After speaking with the second AD, he located the call sheet finding the times he'd be needed on set. The day's schedule was relatively sparse. He'd be doing most of the work the next day, although he knew he'd still be knackered after a long day of shooting. Standing around waiting, blocking, and monotonous retakes were surprisingly exhausting.

Chapter Nineteen

ERIN ARRIVES IN NOLA—
—THIS CAN'T BE RIGHT

E rin entered the sliding glass doors of the terminal, taking a deep breath. Austin Straubel airport wasn't large or new. She walked inside, heading to the stairs in the center of the building. The gift shop was to her right, with its display of green and gold Packers apparel and bright yellow cheeseheads. To her left, there was a cheese shop. *Leave it to Wisconsin to have a cheese shop at the airport,* she thought, as she took the escalator to the next floor.

After sailing through security, she waited for the plane. Then, after a two-hour layover in Minnesota, she finally made it to Louis Armstrong airport. Her stomach was in knots, which tightened at the realization that she didn't know where she was supposed to go. She wasn't paying much attention as she entered the arrivals gate, where she stopped to look for her paperwork and nearly missed the man with a sign that read *March.* Surprised to see her surname, she asked the uniformed driver, who he was waiting for, reasonably sure it wasn't her.

He looked at the back of his sign. "Now, that would be Mrs. Erin March," he said with a delicious accent that made her smile.

"Really? Well, that would be me. I wasn't expecting to have anyone waiting for me."

"Well, then, I'm glad to be of service. If you're Mrs. March, then follow me, please. I'll make a pass by your hotel." He led her to a sleek black Lexus and offered to take her suitcase, but she said she'd keep it, so he opened the door to let her in.

She found herself in an immaculately clean, luxury vehicle, with soft leather seats that were so comfortable she nearly fell right to sleep. As he wound his way through the streets heading away from the airport, she read through her itinerary. There wasn't much to read, and the sights on the freeway really weren't different from any other city, so she dozed. Eventually, they pulled up to a green wooden door with a brass plaque on the wall next to it that read *Audubon Cottages*.

"Thank you," she said to the driver when he got out and opened the door. She wasn't sure if she was supposed to tip him, so she held out a dollar and apologized for not having any more to give him.

"Aww, ma'am. Now that's *real* kind of you, but there's no need, ya hear? Everything has been taken care of for you. Now you have yourself a *fine* day," he said and touched the brim of his hat as if he were tipping it. Then, he got back into the Lexus and drove away.

Erin slung her purse over her shoulder, pulled up the handle on her suitcase, and entered the door. The scenery changed from nondescript buildings to a shaded brick walkway lined with tall, pale trees, which lead to the courtyard pool and more green wooden doors. Her itinerary said she was in cottage number two, and finding a door with a number two on it, she lifted the latch. She found herself in a private patio surrounded by tall, red brick walls, where she was greeted by a fountain carved into the shape of some sort of beast, obscured by a thick layer of ivy.

Her printout said that her key would be on the table inside, so she timidly tried the handle, and the French doors opened. Feeling overstimulated, she stepped inside. All she wanted to do was lay down and rest, free from stress and away from people. Her stomach did a somersault as she remembered the mystery man she'd be meeting sometime that day.

She walked into a beautiful living room furnished with antiques and comfortable places to sit. *This isn't so bad,* she thought as she shut the door. There was a closed door to her right, and her heart skipped a beat. *Dear God, please don't let him be in that room right now!* She didn't hear anything, and no one came out, so she timidly walked through the long, narrow room toward the small dining table that had a basket on it.

She saw an open room to her right that looked like a bedroom. *Wait, if this is the bedroom, then what's behind the closed door? The bathroom—or maybe it connects to an adjoining room?* The open door did lead to the bedroom, so she walked in and laid her suitcase on the bed. She turned around and saw a bathroom, making her even more curious about the door near the entrance.

The bathroom had a walk-in shower and a whirlpool tub. The horrible thought of being in it with the mystery man made her turn around and walk out. She went back to the kitchenette and was about to head for the living room, intent on opening the door when she noticed a note on the table. It was next to the basket, written in a man's rather neat hand-writing.

Please make yourself at home. I have taken the liberty of installing myself in the first room to the right and will most likely return between 3:00 and 7:00. If you require anything, please ring the butler, and he will be happy to help you.
—David

His name is David—Okay, relax, Erin—Wait! She was confused. What did he mean by he'll 'return,' and he's 'installed himself'—*That sounds like—Oh no! What is this?* She stormed through the cottage to the closed door and tried the handle. It opened freely, so she peeked inside. It was another bedroom. The closet door was ajar, and she could see clothes hanging in it. This must be a mistake! She closed the door and walked back to the small table, trying not to panic.

She thought of Todd and decided to call him. Opening the cellophane wrapped around the basket, she grabbed an apple and found a bottle of water in the mini-fridge. She walked into her room, closed the door, and fumbled in her purse to get to her phone. Her hands were shaking, but she was *not* going to sound upset on the phone. She sat on the antique chair next to the bed and called Todd's cellphone.

The time on her cell was 4:07; plenty of time to get home from work, so she thought he'd answer, but his voicemail kicked in. "You've reached Todd March. Please leave a message... Beeeeeeep."

"Hello, honey, I made it here safe and sound. The parts of the city I was driven through are so beautiful! I wish you were here with me!" *Well, that was insensitive,* she thought. "I'm at the Audubon Cottages in cottage number two." She looked at the phone on the bedside table and read off the phone number. "I'll be home in a few days. I love you, and I miss you already. Bye!" She ended the call and sighed.

In her panic, she unpacked, putting all her clothes into the top dresser drawer. A few minutes later, she changed her mind and put everything away neatly into the drawers or closet, like she imagined most people did. Usually, she lived out of her suitcase when staying in a hotel. Then, she brought her toiletries bag into the bathroom, and everything was set out neatly on the shelf above the sink. She looked in the mirror, wondering who the old lady was. Her hair was quite grey, and the lines on her face seemed to have multiplied since the last time she looked. *I'm too young to look like this!* Feeling old and frumpy, she decided to put on a little makeup, first impressions, after all.

She had just finished putting on her lip gloss when she heard the door open. *Good night nurse!* After washing the smudges of eyeliner off her hands, she slowly walked out of the bathroom. Taking a deep breath, she paused, then bravely opened the bedroom door. She thought she'd have a heart attack when she saw who was standing by the dining table with a bottle of water in his hand.

Chapter Twenty

END OF THE DAY

The day was finally over. David was pleased with how well he'd gotten on with the cast and crew but was glad to be headed back so he could relax. He then remembered who would be there and sighed. *So much for relaxing.* Ben took him back to the cottage, and David thanked the man as he opened his door.

"See yah t'morrow," Ben said and left him there, alone.

David inhaled and bravely walked through the main entrance. The closer he got to number two, however, the more he paced himself. His stomach dropped as he thought about the woman waiting for him. *Relax, you meet people every day, dinnae panic!* He opened the door and timidly stepped inside, taking off his sunglasses. He heard a tap running and waited to see what would happen next. When no one appeared, he walked through the living room and set his key, mobile, and sunglasses on the small table in the kitchenette.

Something had been removed from the basket, and he was relieved. *Good, I'm glad she wasn't afraid tae do that.* His mouth was cotton wool, so he went to the mini-fridge and bent over, extracting a cold bottle of water. Her bedroom door was closed to his right, but as he straightened up, it opened, and the woman stood in the doorway. She was about his age, with dark, greying hair. Those were the first things he noticed before he saw the recognition of who he was on her face. He watched her expression change from trepidation and fear to utter astonishment, and his heart sank as he realized that no one *had* told her whom she was meeting.

She stood completely still, staring at him for a long time. He was about to say something when her mouth opened, then she took a step back and staggered, as though she might fall. He rushed over to steady her, praying she wouldn't faint, but he was too late. She had tripped on the edge of the area rug and landed on her rear end. "Damn!" he heard her say under her breath as he stepped into the room and crouched down beside her. *What is that scent?* he thought and took her hand, feeling an instant connection. Something akin to electricity passed between them, which made him slightly aroused. She cautioned a glance at him, and he smiled, gazing into her large, hazelnut brown, or better yet, afternoon-tea-colored eyes.

"Are you alright?" he asked as he helped her up and led her to one of the ornately carved dining chairs that he pulled out for her. *That smell! Is it her perfume or shampoo? Et's verra nice.* Whatever it was, he wanted to smell more of it, burying his face in her hair, or was it her neck? It smelled … familiar, like something from his earliest memories, and it was intoxicating. He pulled out another chair and set it near hers, then handed her his unopened bottle of water.

She took it with a shaking hand, then her mouth opened again, but nothing happened. After a moment, she peered at him and looked away quickly. "Good night nurse!" she said, "But you're—"

"David Elliott; pleased to meet you," he said. He smiled, holding out his hand in greeting, and she shook it tentatively. The energy from earlier was there again. She must have felt it as well because she looked at her hand and pulled it away.

"I'm … Erin, uh, pleased … to meet you, too?" It came out as a question. As if she wasn't quite sure whether she actually was pleased to meet him or not. They made eye contact for a split second before she looked down at her knees and picked at a thread on her capris. "I didn't know … I mean, dammit!" she said and looked up again, smiling nervously. "I'm making a horrible first impression, aren't I?"

Her cheeks were red, but her smile was utterly disarming, and he instantly liked her. He thought she had a comfortable way about her and felt some of his awkwardness and embarrassment over what they were meant to do, begin to dissipate. "I was going to try fainting as well, but you beat me to it," he teased.

She set the wet bottle on the table. The condensation ran down the sides, pooling up at the base. "For the record," she said, in a blatant attempt to keep a bit of her dignity, "I didn't faint, I … tripped. Well, that doesn't make it much better, does it?" Her pink cheeks flushed a bit darker, "But I wasn't going to faint." She smiled a bit more boldly, that time.

Oh, we're gonna get along right well, he thought, then shrugged, melodramatically. "If you say so, but I'm not con-

121

vinced." Humor won the day, and the ice was cracked, if not broken. They both laughed, and she was finally able to look at him for slightly longer than a second. "I'm sorry for the shock," he said. "I had hoped someone would warn you." She looked back down at her legs and shrugged. "Never mind," he continued, "too late now, hmm? I do hope it's a pleasant surprise, at least?"

"Well, yes," she said, and then reacting to something internal, her eyes darted away, and her smile vanished. She looked down again. David watched as her earlobes became bright red, matching the rest of her face. "To be honest, yes, and no." Stealing a glance at him, she bit her lower lip. She must have seen his puzzled expression because she looked uneasy and continued haltingly, slipping her wedding band on and off her knuckle. "Well ... I mean you're—" She dropped her voice, so it was difficult to hear her say, "amazing, but that means, well ... things are going to be even more embarrassing, I guess." Closing her eyes, she smiled ruefully and knit her brows together. She put one elbow on the table and rested her forehead in the palm of her hand, then she looked up at him and frowned, continuing to bite her bottom lip.

He didn't know what to say next, but she spoke for him. "This is so awkward." She was now twisting the wedding ring on her finger, looking worried and shy. "I can't believe this whole thing. I'm married and—"

"Yes, I know just what you mean," David interjected. "I've been in a right state these last few weeks, but there's no rush. We've time to get to know each other. We'll just have to find a way to get through it, right?" He tried to sound reassuring, though he didn't have a clue how they'd manage it. He laid his hand on hers, not sure why he did it, and a surge of energy made his heart start beating faster.

Woah! Steady yerself, lad!

They sat for a while, lost in their own thoughts. He didn't move his hand, it was comforting to have that small connection, and she didn't seem to mind. "Why don't we go for a walk?" he suggested. "I reckon it'll be easier to get to know one another if we're not worried about where to put our hands or where to look. What do you think?"

"That's an excellent idea," she said and looked at him. She opened her mouth but then closed it again.

"What is it? Tell me, whatever it is."

"It's stupid, but what should I call you? You've always been 'Davidelliott,' one word in my mind. I think I'd feel weird calling you by your first name alone. Damn! I feel weird being in the same room as you, alone," she said and laughed, rolling her eyes.

"Don't feel weird. You're welcome to call me anything you'd like. Wait, I take that back, call me David, please." That made her smile, and he consciously determined to keep doing that, making her smile. They both stood and replaced their chairs under the table.

"I'll get my purse," she said and walked into her bedroom.

"Let's make out as though we haven't seen each other in a long time and are catching up," he said, without thinking it through, and then realized how it may have sounded. "I don't mean for us to make out ... ah, what I mean is ... let's act as if

123

we're mates, um … you know what I'm trying to say, don't you? Does that sound ridiculous to you?" he asked, feeling quite flustered. *Ridiculous? Childish and daft is more accurate. Well done you, putting your foot in your mouth!*

"Not ridiculous at all," she said as she came back into the room, smiling and holding her handbag. "I think it's a good idea. It's easier to get past something difficult by pretending to be someone you're not, isn't it?" She looked up at his smile, "Oh yeah, I forgot who I was talking to. I guess you would know what I mean, wouldn't you? Is there somewhere you want to go?"

There's that smile again, he thought. "I say we walk out the door and not think overly much about the 'where' part. What do you think?"

"Sounds nice. You lead the way."

Chapter Twenty-One

CLOSE ENCOUNTERS

E rin had a lightheaded, slightly nauseous feeling come over her. *David Elliott, of all people,* she thought. He was really nice, and he looked and smelled really, really nice too. *Okay, don't get ahead of yourself.* She had to stop that train of thought right then and there. She'd liked him as an actor for so long, and to have him standing there in the flesh was nearly more than she could stand! *He held your hand, Erin! And did I imagine the electricity I felt?*

David led the way through the living room; Erin followed, noticing the decor. She should've been looking front and center, but *he* was there, and it was difficult to look at him, even if it was only his back. *Holy Moses, how am I gonna get through this? At least he's not a smelly, ball-scratching, ass-crack-showing creep!* She had just moved her gaze to one of the large portraits of what looked like French nobility on the wall and wasn't paying attention to what was happening in front of her.

He stopped unexpectedly and spun around. "I've forgotten my—"

Erin nearly ran into him but somehow stopped with her hand up just in time. Her palm landed flat against his stomach. She could feel the warmth of his skin through his pin-striped dress shirt, as well as the rise and fall of his breathing. There they were, almost face to face since he was much taller.

Both were utterly surprised, and as their eyes met, Erin's heart leapt into her throat. She caught her breath and looked away, shifting her gaze to her hand, not knowing what to do. *Holy Moses! This can't be real! Am I dreaming? Is this another dream? If it is, Erin March, you'd better live it as though it's real!* She was stunned, frozen in place while everything around her seemed to move in slow motion. It took a moment to recover before she slowly moved her hand away. "Forgotten what?"

"My key ... and ... things," he finished quietly.

They stood like statues for a long awkward moment. David could smell her fragrance again and liked the feel of her hand on his stomach. Finally, she turned to the side to let him pass. Something had happened between them; his heart was fluttering, and his breath was still playing catch up. *Ma Losh, what was that?* he thought, as the air seemed electrically charged up.

He stepped past her, weak all over, fighting the desire to kiss her. *What's wrong with yeh?* he scolded himself, *You've only just met, and ye're already wantin' tae snog her? Control yerself!* He tried to conjure up a memory of Susannah to bring him back to earth but could think of nothing.

Erin's insides were wibbly-wobbly; she was out of breath, and goosebumps spread up her arms and neck. *Holy Moses! Maybe this won't be so difficult after all,* she thought, standing there with her eyes closed.

Shut up, Erin! Do you hear yourself? This isn't a date! You have Todd, and he loves you! Cool your jets, lady! Her mind gave her a mental slap in the face.

She waited while David crossed the room, grabbed his things from the table, and made his way back toward her, smiling self-consciously, as he got close to her again. "Wow," she whispered as he stepped past her and held the door open.

"Mmmh," he said and closed his eyes as she passed him, stepping outside. Her scent had him spellbound, seducing him already; he felt like he was going mad and couldn't get that moment out of his head. *This isn't like you!* he chided himself, wanting, aching to grab the lovely stranger by the arm and pull her up to him for a long, passionate kiss. Instead, he followed her as they walked, single file, to the sidewalk on Rue Dauphine.

It was a beautiful afternoon, mild with a light breeze. They could hear frogs, crickets, and hundreds of other insects making a lovely symphony of sound all around them. As they wandered the French Quarter, they didn't keep track of where they were; if one of them saw something interesting, they'd go in that direction. Occasionally, they got close enough to brush up against each other; when that happened, they both had to catch their breath. After a few hours, they were almost used to each other's company, and as long as they didn't touch, they were comfortable together. The exception was when someone recognized David, then Erin felt ugly compared to his beauty.

Hearing live music coming from a nearby nightclub, they decided to go inside. The jazz club was filled with a delicious mix of people with every skin shade known to man, gay, straight, and everything in between. They sat at the bar, and Erin found herself flirting with the demigod sitting next to her. It seemed like he was flirting back, but she knew he was just being kind. It had to be an act to make her feel more comfortable. She figured he must be dreading the thought of performing a treatment on her and was trying to make the best of it.

It was supper time, and they were both hungry, so when a small table near the door opened up, they moved to it and looked at the menu. The bar only served appetizers, but they managed to have a lovely, albeit light, meal. The building was quite crowded, and with the band, it was hard to hear anything unless you were speaking directly into the ear of the person next to you. Needless to say, there wasn't much conversation.

After they ate, David excused himself to use the toilet. Erin watched him walk away to the farthest end of the building and disappear. She thought back to the moment he'd nearly run her over at the cottage. How she'd desperately wanted him to kiss her: to bend down, take her into his arms and kiss her, like something from a silly romance movie. Who was she kidding? The complete awkwardness of the encounter proved that kissing her was the last thing on his mind.

Oh, Erin, you're an idiot! You need to snap out of the fantasy world you're creating in your mind! It's not going to be like that with him, and you're going to be disappointed, not to mention, you're being a terrible wife!

Chapter Twenty-Two

CHAMPAGNE

Erin sat back in her chair and sighed. The atmosphere of the club wasn't anything she would've enjoyed at home. In Green Bay, its equivalent would be a sports bar near Lambeau Field during a Packers home game. Crowds and noise were not her thing, but that night, she was having the time of her life. *Must be the good company,* she thought and then felt something brush against her shoulder.

"*Ma chérie!* He sure like you, yeah!" a woman's slightly husky voice said in her ear.

Erin was startled and looked at the person who was talking. She nearly gasped, as next to her stood the most beautiful drag queen she'd ever seen. Her flawless, deep-brown skin was like silk. It contrasted with her bright blue eyes making them appear to shimmer, like wading pools filled with a million lapis lazuli and sapphire gemstones. Around her neck lay a massive diamond and sapphire necklace that made her eyes all the more mesmerizing. As she moved, the gems danced with the flames of the candles on each table.

She was dressed in a sequined, skin-tight evening gown the color of spun gold and wore painfully high stilettos with gold-plated backs on the heels. Her hair was a magnificent mass of curls, styled perfectly for her oval face, and her makeup was impeccable. She appeared to have just walked off an elegant vintage movie set.

"I'm sorry, but who are you talking about; who likes me?" Erin asked, confused, and in awe of the goddess standing next to her.

The grande dame eyed her as she gracefully stole around the table, positioning David's chair so they'd be sitting next to each other. She sat elegantly, crossing her delicate ankles, and leaned in so she could be heard in the noisy cafe. "Dat man, *che bébé*, dat man you actin' timid with. You are plainly *les amoureux*, no?" she said, in a Creole accent, with a little extra French flair added for effect.

"*Les amoureux?* Oh! You think I'm in love with him?" Saying it out loud made her blush. "We aren't a couple if that's what you mean? I mean … this isn't a date. We've just met, actually." She was flustered; how did the diva see through her like that?

"Now *bébé*, you want dat man, I could see it from across the room. You don't need a history to be in love, *oui*?"

"I guess not," Erin said, imagining everyone in the club was whispering about the two unlikely lovebirds by the door.

"Now, he like you too, *ma chérie*; no doubt about it!" She nudged Erin's arm and smiled, showing perfect little pearls for teeth.

"Nope," Erin countered, "Not a chance; didn't you see him? He's … well, he'd never be interested in someone like me! There's no way." Erin was a realist and wouldn't allow herself to be deluded into a fantasy world where the handsome prince falls in love with the toad; real life didn't work that way.

"Do you not see it? He is under your spell, honey." She looked at Erin again, "*Oh mon Dieu!* You can't see it, can you?" She leaned in even closer and dropped some of her flamboyance. "Now, I may be dressed as a beauty queen right now, but underneath it all, I'm still a man, and I know when another man is attracted to a woman, I sure do! You don't see it, but when he thinks you not lookin', he's lookin' at you, no mistake!"

Erin looked askance at the beautiful storyteller. "Now you're telling lies, well, unless he's looking at me in disgust?" Erin said this with a smile; she knew she wasn't completely ugly. There were a few things she didn't hate about herself, but she was far too overweight for David Elliott to consider attractive. She'd seen his wife, who was the complete opposite of her.

"You are wrong, *ma chéri*. You know what I'm gonna did for you? I'm gonna prove it. Mistah will return shortly, no?" she said.

"I hope so!" Erin said, enjoying the quirks of the drag queen's accent and praying David hadn't decided to escape out the back of the building.

"*Oui*, he will, and when he do, you watch him; if he come out lookin' for a distraction, then maybe you right, and you win. Now, I am of the mind he gonna come back lookin' only to be right cheer; where I am sat right now."

Erin shook her head and smiled. "Okay."

The bet was on. They saw him emerge from the depths of the club, surrounded by people. It was a long, narrow building, and he was having a difficult time moving through the swelling crowds. "You watching now?"

"I'm watching," *How could I NOT watch? He's beautiful,* Erin thought and felt her cheeks get warm. "By the way, I have to tell you, I've never seen anyone as beautiful as you! How do you do it?" she asked the mysterious match-making stranger with trepidation. "I'm truly awestruck!" As her blush deepened, she was envious of the Creole queen's dark skin.

"*Merci, ma petite*; it takes many years of practice. Now, you take this callin' card; I'll wager a makeover, seein' I'm gonna win our bet. I want you to call me before you leave New Orleans, ya hear? I'm gonna did you up so dat man won't know he been hit, but once I am done with you, he will be on the floor, beggin' for mercy!" She magically produced a card from somewhere on her body and held it out.

Erin laughed at the mental image and took the delicate card out of her perfectly manicured, gold-polished fingers. "Okay, thanks."

"Now, most people call me Champ."

"Champ?" Erin jerked her head away from the matte black cardstock, which was quilted with little champagne glasses, and embossed with a dazzling sapphire 'C' surrounded by gold filigree.

"*Oui*. Champ, short for Champagne, *bébé*," she said, then laughed and winked.

Erin smiled at her and looked back down at the card; it read,

Champagne Lagniappe
"CHAMP"
(504)-555-2222

The little piece of artwork was exquisite. Erin didn't know that someone could buy anything so fabulous! She held it like it might break or dissolve in her hands. As though her Muggle touch was enough to break the magic holding it together. She put the card in her handbag, hoping it wouldn't get crushed or dented in there.

They watched David try to make his way back to the table; he'd seen Champagne sitting in his seat and was obviously curious. His eyes fastened upon Erin, and they saw him smile, only looking away to navigate through the crowd. He was halfway to the table when he stopped, closed his eyes imperceptibly, and reluctantly turned.

The ladies looked at each other, both sure they'd won the bet. They couldn't hear what was being said, but Erin guessed it soon enough. David was smiling his winning smile and shaking people's hands. She saw his mouth say 'thank you' more than once, as well. He allowed several people to take selfies and took a pen someone handed to him from out of the crowd, and wrote something on a woman's chest, above her heart (or breast, if you weren't feeling romantic). Then he was finally able to excuse himself.

"What is this now?" Champ asked, looking at Erin. "What have you not told Champagne?" She'd obviously not recognized David or wasn't aware of who he was, for she looked genuinely shocked.

"Oh, I thought you knew, he's David Elliott; haven't you heard of him? He's a British actor."

"*Mon Dieu! Oui*, I have heard his name, but I had never seen his face before. Now, you have no choice! I will require you to call my number, *ma chérie*! I will teach you how to be fabulous for him!"

Erin was flattered by the attention of the heavenly creature, but she had to end the charade. "Thank you so much for your kind, generous offer, Champagne, but I have a confession. We, me and him, are both married to other people. We're not lovers." *In the traditional sense,* she thought uncomfortably.

"No matter. If it is meant to be, and somethin' tells me it is, well, you cannot stop it," Champ said and waggled her finger at Erin. "Child, you already know this. You have a chemistry, yes? Now, don't try to deny it, *che bébé*."

People were still pointing at David and taking pictures; some discreetly, like the man sitting at the bar, and others, not so much, like the woman who'd been lifted into the air, so she could get a good shot. He finally made it back to the front of the cafe, and Champagne rose gracefully, standing at least three inches taller than him.

She held out her hand. "*Enchanté, monsieur*, it is a lovely night to be in New Orleans, no?"

David took her hand and kissed it lightly. Photos were still being taken all over the room, and it was becoming a spectacle. "*Enchanté, madame*," he said and smiled at Erin, so she stood to introduce them.

"David, this is Champagne; Champagne, this is David—" She didn't know if she should say his last name or not, was there an etiquette to it? She didn't want to sound like she was name dropping. She floundered for only a second before he helped her.

"David Elliott," he said, smiling as he noticed the blush on Erin's face. "I see you've been thick as thieves, planning my destruction, I presume?"

"*Quoi?* No, not destruction, *beau cher*. I saw a beautiful woman sitting all alone and wished to keep her company. Do you blame me, *monsieur?*"

"No, I don't blame you one bit," he said.

It was now David's turn to blush. He recovered quite well, but Erin saw it and knew by the twinkle in Champ's eyes that she had too. He seemed sincere, but Erin's first thought was that his blush meant he'd been lying, agreeing so she wouldn't feel bad. She could sense he was uncomfortable and attributed it to Champagne's flamboyance. *Though, I'm sure acting like he's interested in me could have something to do with it, too.*

"Well, I do believe it is time to leave this cafe, *mes amis*," Champagne said abruptly. "I must go where the people need me." She stepped forward and kissed David on each cheek.

More camera flashes, more spectacle. "*Au revoir, Monsieur* Elliott.*" She slipped elegantly around the table to stand before Erin and took hold of her hands, "I do look forward to hearing from you soon—I believe I have forgotten your name!"

Erin realized she'd never actually told her. "Erin March."

"*Mon Dieu*, such a beautiful name! *Au revoir*, Erin," she said, and then she was gone. She seemed to float away in a cloud of gold and diamonds, leaving Erin, at least, speechless.

They sat in the relative calm after the storm of Champagne. David would've liked to leave the place as well. Too many people recognized him, and too many pictures were being taken of him with women. He didn't imagine there were any paparazzi in the crowd; how could anyone know he'd be there? Still, the wrong photo, sold to the right website, and there would be trouble. His thoughts were interrupted by Erin.

"Isn't she wonderful?" she asked, looking dreamily into the crowd.

"Yes, I reckon she is, but she's not my type. Don't get me wrong, I'm sure she's a lovely person, but to me, she's too much," he said candidly. "I think I'd soon tire of so much bravado."

Erin looked at him, seeming to consider what he'd said. "I suppose you're right, but what I wouldn't give to look even a little bit like her," she said. She looked in the direction

Champagne had gone and sighed; it was a tiny sigh, but it said a lot.

David wasn't sure what he should say. He wanted to correct her, saying she was lovely exactly how she was and that he genuinely preferred her honest simplicity to the other woman's grandeur, but didn't know how to word it. He racked his brain, trying to think of something to say, but in his hesitation, Erin finished off her drink and smiled at him sheepishly.

"And we know your type, don't we?" she said with a smile, knowing she'd never come close to comparing with Susannah Elliott, feeling even less attractive in the wake of the Creole queen, and wishing she had another drink so she might drown out her insecurity.

"Well, I wouldn't—" he began, but there was another camera flash, so he leaned in close to her ear. "Let's go. I'm a bit tired of the noise and attention."

"I agree," she said, relieved to have something other than her self-loathing to consider.

Chapter Twenty-Three

RUE BOURBON

D avid and Erin left the club and walked a few blocks until they found themselves on Bourbon Street. Music came from everywhere, strangely dressed people danced around, having a fine 'ole time, and drunk people tried to stay upright by leaning against buildings as they staggered to the next bar. They saw someone crouched in a doorway and hoped he was only resting, not defecating, but they couldn't be sure. As they headed further down the street, they came to a place selling hurricane cocktails the size of an elephant and decided to share since neither of them would be able to drink a whole one and remain standing.

Erin waited outside while David went in to get it. She could hear whoops and shouts from different corners of the street and hoped they had nothing to do with David Elliott's presence in the vicinity. People were bumping into her, so she found sanctuary against a red building across the street, a gas lamp post in front of it illuminating the area. There was a bench next to her, but a couple was sitting there just then. She wasn't impressed with Bourbon Street; it had the pungent stench of spilled booze, vomit, and she didn't want to know what the other odors were made up of. She was saved from contemplating that topic by David's lovely English accent, with just a hint of delicious Scottishness.

"Erin? Where are you?" With a quick wave, he spotted her and had to catch his breath. The gas light above her head haloed her lovely face, and her smile lit it up even more brilliantly. "There you are," he said and lifted the cup to show he'd fulfilled his errand successfully.

She had to catch her breath as she saw him coming toward her. There was more handsomeness in him than in every man she'd ever laid eyes on put together. He stepped up to her and handed her the plastic cup that was at least a foot tall *and as big around as one of my upper arms,* she noticed sadly.

She took a small sip to gauge whether she'd want more. "Oh, it's good!" she said, feeling the ice-cold liquid flow all the way to her belly. The bright pink concoction was like a slushie and didn't taste like alcohol.

He took a sip and smiled. "Not bad," he said. "Tart."

"Hey, it's not polite to call people names," she said and laughed.

"And fruity," he said, narrowing his eyes at her.

Erin was having a wonderful time, and though they were getting used to each other, she still felt nervous, like she was on a first date. She took a long draw from the straw that his lips had just touched and instantly got a brain freeze. Handing the cup to him, she sat on the now vacant bench, holding her head in her hands.

"Cold headache?" He crouched down in front of her, putting his hand on her knee to steady himself, then he set the cup on the pavement. *She's so bonny!* he thought as he waited for her to be able to speak again.

"Mmm-hmmm," she managed. "Good night nurse that hurts! That was almost as bad as one of my episodes!" she said and smiled to show she wasn't serious. As their eyes met, she felt the energy that had made her insides do the somersault they'd done in the cottage. His hand was on her knee, and she willed herself not to think about that. *It's to keep his balance,* she had to remind herself.

David had felt it as well and forced himself to look away. He was fully aware of the placement of his hand and was trying not to focus on it while also not wanting to move it. He put one knee on the pavement and cringed as he looked down to see how utterly filthy it was. Bourbon Street was most definitely not the place for him.

He stood and took Erin's hand to help her up, not wanting to let go, but he had to. She put her hand on his bicep and turned to him, standing on her tiptoes, wanting to say something, so he leaned in, putting his hand on the small of her back so she could speak into his ear. She was so close. Her hand felt warm on his arm. He knew all he'd have to do was move his hand down a few inches—

David! What the fuck are you thinkin'? he scolded himself.

"I'm not crazy about the smell and filth of this place," she said, echoing his thoughts. "Let's find somewhere a little bit less crowded to walk, okay?"

"Aye, that's just what I was thinking."

Erin saw a camera flash and then noticed a few people standing nearby with their heads bent together, watching them. People were now staring openly at them, pointing fingers and phones their way, having recognized David. She had never experienced that kind of attention before and could *feel* the stares. Every whisper was amplified as though they were in the center of Lambeau Field and all the energy was focused on them. "I ... don't think ... I like this," she said, feeling her heart skip a panicked beat. Imagining the crowd was pressing in and surrounding them, she started backing up without realizing she was doing it.

"Alright, it's a'right, don't panic," he said, taking her gently by the arms and making eye contact with her. "Just pretend they're not there. Et's something I have to deal with." He started looking for somewhere to go, away from the crowds, and noticed a commotion nearby as a group of women stumbled out of a bar at the same time.

He could tell they were looking for trouble and hoped that none of them knew who he was. "I think we should leave right now," he said, casually leaning closer to Erin's ear. He motioned with his head to the group of ladies who were obviously in the middle of a bachelorette party and were clearly too drunk to be discreet.

One of the ladies pointed at him and said something to the bride-to-be who wore a small tulle puff on her head, meant to signify a bridal veil. They made a beeline toward David and started pawing at him, speaking to him with their faces far too close. He was trying to be nice, but they were getting way too friendly. One of them reached around and grabbed his ass, saying something completely incoherent, while another one was taking pictures of it all on her phone.

"Alright, ladies," he was saying, trying to get them to settle down, but the bride-to-be, undeterred, walked right up to him and put her cheek against his chest, posing for a photo.

"You're hot," she said, although it sounded like 'Yerr hut.'

Before he could make a sound, she unexpectedly grabbed his crotch just hard enough that, being caught off guard, he groaned and staggered backward, dropping to his knees. He managed to put one arm out, hand splayed, to stop her from advancing her attack any further.

Erin watched the whole thing unfold, feeling overwhelmed and helpless. She'd been shoved out of the way, but when she saw what the bride-to-be had done, she got angry. She managed to get between David and the group of wasted women and had to raise her voice to be heard over their rude comments. "How dare you do such a horrible thing?" she shouted.

The future bride was laughing and falling over her friends. "Whhat do ya-hoo ca-hare, Pahorky?" she slurred, which made her girlfriends roar with laughter. She smelled like she'd vomited at least once that night, and it appeared as though she might do it again at any moment.

Her friends began crowding around her, but Erin didn't care; they'd been out of line, and she was going to say something. "What do I care?" Her face was hot, and she knew she was going to lose it. "If you were sober," she said, "which I doubt happens often," she added under her breath, "and a

143

drunken idiot grabbed your tits, you'd be furious. You'd tell the police you were sexually assaulted, wouldn't you?" The woman looked at her friends and started laughing, but Erin wasn't giving up. "Wouldn't you?" she said much louder and right in her face.

The drunk woman rolled her eyes and shrugged. "Maybe," she said only slightly more soberly than she'd been speaking before. She casually looked down at David, who was mostly upright again. "Ssorry," she continued, halfheartedly, as he tried to get ahold of Erin's arm.

"Just go away!" Erin said.

The woman mocked her, saying "Jusst-go-aawayy," but she rounded up her brood, whooping and gyrating as they moved on.

One of the bridesmaids turned back and yelled out, "You're the sexiest man alive!" She lifted her top, flashing David, and a few unsuspecting guys, as she made her way toward the next club, having already forgotten the damage they'd done.

Chapter Twenty-Four

FIRSTS

David was in full retreat as he took Erin by the hand and dragged her away from the noise and stench of Bourbon Street. He pulled her down a side street, then they rounded another corner and found themselves in the entrance to a hotel parking garage, which was quiet and secluded. He leaned against the wall of a building, knowing full well it made him look drunk, but that was irrelevant. There were more pressing matters to deal with. He waited a few minutes, first, to catch his breath, and second, to make sure no one had followed them. When he didn't see any evidence of being watched, he straightened himself up the best he could with the slight ache in his groin. "Erin," he said, as he stood in front of her, putting one hand on each of her arms.

She was about to defend herself, making it clear why she had the right to stand up for him, when he brought his head down and brushed his lips against hers, feather light. Her whole body tingled as he did it again, this time kissing her gently. He parted his lips and began touching his tongue to her mouth, asking her to yield to it. When she did, a powerful wave of energy seemed to join them as they kept time in an unchoreographed flow of movement. He let go of her arms and placed his hands on her face and neck.

His hands were smooth and cool; they felt good on her angry, burning face. The stench of Bourbon Street was gone, and in the still quietness of their newfound hideaway, she melted. She hadn't been kissed like that in a *very* long time, and she wasn't about to push him away. Her breath was staggered, and she was shaking terribly, but she stood on her tiptoes, letting her hands drop to her sides. He was kissing her urgently, as though he honestly wanted to. As if she were someone he'd been eyeing all night.

Ridiculously, she thought about the hurricane they'd left near the bench on Bourbon Street but didn't miss it. It all seemed like a dream, not real life. *Am I really here with him, and is he really kissing me? I mean, I didn't ask him to do it; he did it himself.*

Coming back to himself, David realized she didn't respond as he had hoped she would. "I'm sorry," he said and backed away from her, staring into her upturned, glowing face. She hadn't lifted her hands or touched him at all, which he took to mean she wasn't happy about his advances.

"You are?" She placed her hand against the building to steady herself, trying to keep her balance.

"Well … I mean," he stammered, "actually, no, I'm not." He leaned against the wall again and closed his eyes. "That is … I mean … I've wanted to do that since the moment I nearly ran you down in my haste to retrieve my key in the cottage, but I didn't think it was appropriate, as we'd just met, and—"

She put her finger to his lips to make him stop talking. "You did?"

"Aye, I truly did."

"Really? I'm so glad you followed through."

"You are?"

"Oh yes!" She closed her eyes, breathing deeply. "Mmm, that was lovely!" It felt to her as though she were hovering an inch above the ground. She wanted to hold on to the moment and not let it go too quickly. People were talking and laughing on the busier streets, oblivious to their presence, and she wanted to remain there, hidden all night.

"Aye, it was," he said as he stood in front of her once more and lowered his head. He kissed her again, placing his hands on her waist. Her lips were warm on his, and he could taste the tiniest hint of the hurricane on her tongue. There was no one in sight, and he wanted to snog her all night long.

She reached her hands up over his shoulders and ran her fingers through his clean, soft hair as they leaned against the building. He wrapped his arms around her, and she could feel his excitement as his kiss became more urgent. *Please, take me now, don't stop!* Her thoughts were wild, and it wasn't like her. She was usually level-headed, perhaps a bit emotional at times, but this was far beyond that! Her thoughts were flying, and her body was quivering. *One treatment? Only one? But what if one treatment, every-other-weekend, isn't enough?* She needed to break away from him, to get herself under control, but how could she?

Erin! She gave herself another mental slap in the face. *Calm down! It's only a kiss!*

It feels like much more than a kiss!

The thought suddenly occurred to her that maybe this was something he did. *What if he's a playboy accustomed to using his wealth and celebrity status to get what he wants from women? Taking less-than-attractive women out to show them a good time, and then—bedding them.*

Oh my God, Erin! How could you even think that! Now you're being paranoid.

David abruptly stopped kissing her and backed away again. He had seen a flash in his peripheral vision, but when he looked in the direction it had come from, there was nothing there.

"What is it?" she asked, a little afraid he'd read her mind.

"We need to get out of here," he said. *And I need tae be more careful. The last thing I need is ma face gracin' the front page of a dozen tabloids with an unknown woman in ma arms,* he thought, baffled at how he could be so reckless.

What's gotten into yeh! You're never this excitable. Take a step back and think about what you're doin'. You're snogging a married woman in a dark alley, the reasonable side of his brain said.

But I like snoggin' her, the rest of him responded.

He smiled down at Erin. Her back was against the rough bricks of the building, and her eyes were closed. She was still breathing deeply and looked slightly drunk. He took her by the hand, and they continued walking, eventually ending up at the Cafe du Monde, where they shared beignets and strong, delicious coffee.

"Holy Moses! This is good!" Erin said after her first bite of a beignet. He had warned her about not breathing in, but she forgot, so her face was peppered with powdered sugar. She coughed and sputtered while they both laughed. He took a napkin and gently wiped the white powder off her face, wishing he could touch her cheeks, caress her neck, and kiss those sugary lips again.

Later, the vacant French Market building was dark and deserted as they meandered through it. Erin leaned her back against one of the iron support poles to rest. He watched as she stood with her eyes closed, her hands behind her back, leaning on the painted metal. Her chest moved slowly, up, and down as she breathed in the warm, fragrant breeze blowing through the building. He wanted to approach her, to touch her, but he hesitated, not wanting to take his eyes off her. She opened her eyes, smiled at him, and he could resist no longer. In two steps, he was standing in front of her, holding her tightly and kissing her soft, welcoming lips.

Her hands slid up his chest as they made their way slowly to his shoulders and then ended up tickling the tiny hairs on the back of his neck. He knew they needed to stop, but self-control was becoming more difficult every second they were together. He almost took hold of her ass at one point, wanting to pull her against his erection. Instead, he stopped abruptly and backed away from her. She looked confused and so lovely in the dim light coming from the streetlamps. "I ... we need tae stop. It's too dangerous ... out here ... like this." He was breathing heavily and desperately wanted to get back to the cottage. Using a whole lot of willpower and keeping a wary eye out to make sure no one had seen them, he took her hand, hoping the feeling of being watched was all in his mind.

That evening was turning out to be the most romantic one Erin had ever had. Maybe it was because they hardly knew each other, or perhaps it was that both were so far from their other lives that made it so electrically charged. She couldn't tell the reason, but it *was* electricity. Lightning passed from one to the other, making the anticipation of what lay ahead of them, in their shared cottage, with nobody watching, intoxicating. They sat on a bench, holding hands, and looked out on the Mississippi River rolling past them, thankful for the darkness of night. The lights on the opposite shore painted the river in a wash of rippling watercolors. Stars looked down on them and winked, and they forgot about time.

"How far do you live from here?" David asked.

Erin was glad for the respite, not wanting him to see how tired she was or that she was just starting to have trouble breathing again. "I live in Green Bay, Wisconsin. It's about 1100 miles away, give-or-take, pretty much straight north from here, as the crow flies. What part of Scotland are you from?"

"I'm from Edinburgh—Duddingston, to be exact."

"I think I've been there, amazingly enough. Todd and I went to the Sheep's Heid a few years back. We walked around there a bit too; it was beautiful. I remember a lake and a garden having to do with a doctor—"

"Dr. Neil's Garden; I used to go there when I was young. My children still do. It's lovely, isn't et?"

"Yes, it is." *What a small world,* she thought. "I have to know; how on earth did you end up choosing to register?"

He told her, sparingly, about agreeing to do a charity event and that registering, to his mind, was part of it. He didn't tell her how he'd been snared in a trap by his oldest mate or the mess it made with Susannah. "Tell me about the Fertilis Defect, if you feel comfortable telling me, that is," he asked, wanting to change the subject.

"Oh, well, it's different for everyone who has it. For me, it 'temporarily blocks the production of the surfactant that keeps the insides of normal people's lungs from sticking together,'" she said with air quotes. "That's the only technical stuff I can remember. Basically, for the duration of what's called an episode, I can't pull any air into my lungs because they're stuck together, something like what can happen when a latex balloon is deflated. The walls won't separate until the episode runs its course, so all I can do is wait and pray it's over quickly."

"Ma Losh! How long does et last?" he asked.

"When it started, it was only a second or two; hardly enough to notice, but the older I get, the longer it lasts. An easy episode might last twenty seconds, but sometimes it's pretty bad. My last bad one was forty-eight seconds. I can hold my breath for that long, but an episode is different. It starts with a cough that expels any air already in my lungs. Then my muscles, accustomed to normal breathing, try to continue their habit. When they can't, they keep trying harder, creating painful spasms until I pass out from lack of oxygen and exhaustion."

"That's … terrible." He was genuinely shocked, knowing there was no way for him to fathom what it was like. "And it happens without warning?"

"I usually get 'lead up' symptoms, like shortness of breath, warning me I'm due for another episode, but there's no way of knowing exactly when it'll happen. It might be the same day, or a week later."

"Wow, Erin, it sounds utterly traumatizing."

"Yeah, it's scary. I'm always afraid it won't end, and I'll die, but so far I've made it through, knock on wood," she said and hit her knuckles on her head since the bench they were sitting on was metal.

"Do they know why it happened? What the drug did to cause it?"

"I couldn't even begin to tell you the scientific reasons. I've been told, but there's a lot of medical jargon that I can't remember. Actually, I'm not sure anyone really knows, for sure."

"I'm glad I'll be able to help you," he whispered.

"Me too."

They were much more sedate as they began their walk back to the cottage. The electricity was still there, though it was tempered with a bit of reality, mixed with nerves and a touch of guilt. Occasionally, David would steal the courage to hold her hand, and sometimes Erin would lay her head on his arm. They were happy to be walking together, even if they weren't saying anything. However, the closer they got to the cottage, the more the anticipation and electricity started to build again until it was almost palpable. The simple act of taking the key out of his pocket and slipping it into the lock was somewhat erotic, bringing them one step closer to where they were headed. David opened the door, and as they both stepped quietly into the dark living area, he bent down and kissed her.

Chapter Twenty-Five

LIGHTS OUT

David was torn; *Should we be doin' this already? Is et too soon?* he thought as he took a step back and looked down into Erin's large, tea-brown eyes in the unlit shadowy room. She put her forehead on his chest, breathing heavily, with her hands on his waist. He laid his hands her shoulders, knowing there was no turning back once the decision was made—wanting and fearing it, together. "Do you … want to—" he breathed, hoping she'd say yes. She looked up at him and nodded, so he took her hand and led her to his bedroom.

This is going to happen! I can't believe it, right here, tonight! she thought.

It had been over fifteen years since either of them had experienced a new lover. It was awkward and frightening, yet, it also had the familiarity and comfort that comes with age and experience. They both shared desire and guilt as they began to undress. Erin timidly untucked his shirt and had just finished unbuttoning it when the landline phone rang. They both jumped, looking at it and then at each other.

"Who would be ringing this late?" David said, more than slightly annoyed. "I think we should let them ring back later."

"Yes, later," she agreed and touched his bare chest, running her fingers over his dark chest hair.

Her touch sent shivers through his whole body, and he wanted to pull her up against him, but *ring—ring,* the telephone yelled. He turned on the bedside lamp, trying to find the volume or a mute button on the blasted thing.

Rinnngg—rinnngg—rinnngg.

Erin was about to give in and answer it when whomever it was, finally gave up. They looked at each other again, feeling guilty.

"Which one of us would've answered?" he asked as an afterthought. "It could have been your husband or my wife." The look on Erin's face said it all. It was better to let ringing phones ring in that circumstance. They sat on the edge of the bed, the memory of the shrill ringing still fresh in their memories until David stood and smiled at her. "Where was I?" He pulled her up to standing again and began unbuttoning her blouse. Slowly, he unfastened each little round disk, enjoying the anticipation it created.

Erin unbuckled his belt and then unbuttoned his slacks, hands trembling. She pulled the tiny zipper tab down, hardly able to breathe as his trousers fell. His belt buckle made a loud thud when it hit the hardwood floor beneath him. She longed to touch him, to pull down his underwear, and finally see the erection she'd felt against her earlier that night, but she hesitated. He continued with her top, moving a bit faster. Her intoxicating smell had him ready for her, and he longed to feel her soft hand on his cock. The last button was released, and the thought of seeing her filled his mind. Without warning, she pulled away and looked down at the floor, holding her blouse shut with a clenched fist.

"Wait!" she gasped, shaking.

"What's wrong?" he asked, desperate to touch her.

"Please, I don't want you to … see me. I'm so … well, I don't want you to see me," she whispered.

He wanted to see her, feel her, the whole experience. "Not see yeh? But—"

"My body isn't—"

"I don't care about that. I'm attracted tae you, not the size of your clothes." He lifted her chin with his first finger.

"You are?"

"Aye. I don't care if you don't have the body of a super-model, Erin, honestly." *I actually prefer yeh this size,* he thought. She nodded but still held her shirt closed in front of her. "But," he added, seeing she was genuinely uncomfortable and not playing the 'I'm so fat' card even the thinnest of women played, "if you'll feel more comfortable with the lights off, it's a'right with me."

"Thank you," she whispered.

He reached over and clicked off the lamp. Once their eyes adjusted, the glow of the streetlights through the closed shutters and the tiny LEDs on the electronics in the room gave off enough light so they could make out where they were. Everything was shadowy and vague as David kissed her mouth.

She allowed him to open her blouse, and it fell off her shoulders. One of her bra-covered breasts was then in his hand, and she gasped sharply in anticipation as he reached around her back, attempting to unfasten her bra. One by one, the hooks slipped free of the eyes, and she heard that little voice again.

Oh yeah, he's a pro! He's done this a time or two, hasn't he?

"Wait!" she said, pushing him away again, "Wait, stop."

"What is it? Did I pinch you?" he asked, stunned and breathless.

"No, you didn't hurt me." She sat on the edge of the bed with her head down again. "I'm sorry, but it occurred to me that—" *What are you doing?* her internal voice questioned.

"Maybe ... maybe you do this with women—" *Shut up!*

"... get them to fall head over heels for you, and—" *Don't say it!*

"... bring them to a hotel room and—" *Erin! What in the hell are you doing?*

"... Oh, God! I don't want to believe that, and ... and I know I shouldn't even care. It's none of my business what you do with ... anyone." *That's right! You're ruining everything!*

"... I know it's not supposed to be like that with ... us, only please, I beg you ... please say you don't?" *Yeah, and what if he does? Is he going to tell you? You're an idiot!*

One tear ran down her cheek. The room was dark, but David could see glints of light reflecting off it as it trickled down her face and fell off her chin. "Oh, Erin," he said and sat next to her. He felt a tenderness that surprised him, seeing she'd come close to accusing him of seducing lonely women so

157

he could have his way with them. "I've never done anathing like this before in my life. I've never been unfaithful to my wife until, well, now, I reckon." He closed his eyes and took a deep breath, confused and mystified about his feelings for her. It was meant to be a simple 'treatment,' but it had already become much more than that.

"You should know it's never been like this with her, my wife, I mean. We've never had any kind of spark or connection. I married her because, well, she was a beautiful supermodel, and for some reason, she was interested in me. I was flattered, and then everyone told me how lucky I was, so I made my decision based on that." He didn't know how much to tell her, but it was flowing, so he carried on. "I've never felt the way I'm feeling right now with anyone, not even other actresses. I haven't been with anyone since I met Susannah; that's the truth."

"Oh," she said quietly, "I'm sorry. I didn't mean to accuse you. The horrible thought of you having a scattering of women all over the world, with me about to become the next notch on your bedpost, so to speak, just filled my mind. I truly am sorry," she said and a few more tears escaped her pretty eyes. He wiped them away and stood to finish undressing while she did the same. They lay on their backs in his bed, staring at what they could make out of the high ceiling. "I'm so sorry. I feel like a big, fat idiot."

David rolled over to face her, placing his hand on hers, which she'd placed strategically over her stomach. "Don't worry, Erin, and please don't say that about yourself. I've a confession to make—it's something I've never told anyone." *What are you doing?*

"… And I can't believe I'm tellin' you now, except—" *Shut your gob!*

"… I think you need to hear it, so please, hear me out." There was already a damper put on the events of the evening, so he figured he would tell her the truth about himself.

"Holy Moses! Are you gay?" she asked and sat up, feeling humiliated that she'd allowed herself to fall for a gay man.

"What? No, I'm not gay! Are you gay, after the way we kissed in the alley?" he said, laughing, and stroked her cheek with his thumb. "I'm married to the most beautiful woman in London, or so I've been told by many people."

"She is beautiful."

"Aye, but—" *Steady!*

"… I'm … not attracted to her. I thought I was. I mean, she's a woman, and *I am* attracted to women, but she's so verra thin and has no … no meat on her. Even after four children, she's all skin and bones." *You don't have to do this!*

"… I live in a world, well, I reckon we all do, where it's assumed you'll be happy if you have money and a 'perfect-looking' woman at your side. Well, that's no' who I am. I married Susannah because she was what everaone told me was the best, and at the time, I bought into it." *DON'T! You'll regret it!*

"… But … I'm not, in all honesty, attracted to thin women. There, I've said it. I'm not, and never have been, actually." *She's not going to believe yeh, yeh ken? She's gonna think et's a line tae get what you want from her. She'll tell someone, and ye'll be a laughingstock in the tabloids!*

Erin was shocked; she hadn't expected him to say anything like that. "Really?"

"Really. At home, we use 'fit' to describe a skinny woman, but Susannah isn't fit. She won't eat, and when she does, she can't keep et down for longer than twenty minutes. I've tried to get help for her, but she'll not hear of it. Thousand-pound-per-plate meals at charity benefits, down the toilet, wasted." *Why are you talkin' about her? Shut up!*

Erin listened, feeling sorry for Susannah. She thought it must be hard to be the wife of a famous person, and she could see how it might easily give a woman an eating disorder.

She was frowning, so he continued trying to convince her. "Ma mate Martin, well, I thought he was my mate—" *She doesn't care about this!*

"… He's been jealous of me 'acquiring' such a beauty as her, but she's not a nice person. She only cares about money and status, not about having fun or being spontaneous." *Stop talkin' about your wife!*

"… Listen; I'm not telling you this for any other reason than to let you know, you need tae know—I'm attracted to you, every part of you. You've been drivin' me mad all night with yer curves." He ran his hand up her torso and caressed one of her breasts, now braless, making her catch her breath, then he looked at her as best he could in the darkness. "You're the only person I've ever told that to, and that I've ever thought about doin' this with since I met Susannah and … and you are the only one I intend to do it with after this."

Did you just say that? Do yeh mean et?

He kissed her, and the electricity was back. *I mean et.*

"I'm sorry I've ruined everything," she said softly.

He rolled on top of her, kissing and touching her body. "You've no' ruined anathing," he whispered. The feel of their bodies together was too much to resist. "May I?" he asked.

"Yes, please!" she panted.

He lifted her leg with his arm and kissed her thigh. He could hear her breathing heavily and wished he could see her body as he entered her. She felt so good; soft and supple, not boney and fragile. He grabbed the flesh of her leg as he eased himself into her, and her body yielded to him. When she placed her hands on his arms, he felt goosebumps pop up at her touch. He knew he wasn't going to last long, which had never been an issue for him before. Each tiny move was bringing him closer, and it was taking all his effort to keep going.

Things were building up in Erin's body, too. Every move was intense, and she felt like she was either going to melt or explode, over and over. She had never felt anything like it. *Holy Moses,* she thought again as her body released in a powerful orgasm and she felt the pulsing waves overtake her. She then heard him moan and felt the echo of his release inside of her.

David didn't want to move. Sex had never been that charged up for him. He'd never been as turned on, or at least it had never been like that before. It was as if he had lived his entire sexual life with a sort of sensory deprivation and was only now coming out of it, exploring a new world.

Good night nurse! Did that actually happen? she thought. It was so powerful and different. *Do other people have this experience every time they have sex,* she wondered? She had never actually had an orgasm during intercourse before, ever. Rarely during foreplay or with her vibrator, but not like that. It felt so natural, so freeing, and incredibly powerful. Her body had responded to him without her having to try, concentrate, or will herself to feel more than the basic movement of sex.

He moved as though he was going to get up, and she was filled with a kind of dread. "Please don't move yet!" *I need it to last a little while longer. I might never have anything like this happen again.* At that thought, the tears started; she couldn't stop them. No delicate trickle, running down her face that time, and to her utter horror, her body was shaking with uncontrollable sobs. She internally pleaded, begged, and willed them to stop, but she was powerless. Her whole body's senses were overwhelmed, and that was the way it had chosen to deal with it.

David raised himself up. "What's wrong?" he asked, "Are yeh in pain?" *Or are yeh disappointed?* he thought, which, at the moment, was his greatest fear.

"Please, let me up now," she whispered between sobs. She was mortified, and as soon as she was unpinned, she practically leapt off the bed and hid in the bathroom, sobbing and gasping for breath.

Fuck! Fuck! Fuck! Why? Why are you acting like a baby now? Why can't you be cool and hold it together?

She turned on the light and accidentally caught a look at her face in the mirror. She cried even harder then, seeing how

162

ugly she looked with her face all red and splotchy. She wanted to break the horrible thing for ruining her imagined loveliness; for showing her the harsh reality of what she really looked like.

"Erin?" came his delicious Scottish accent at the door. "Are yeh a'right? Did I do something wrong? I know I didn't last verra long—I'm sorry for that."

He sounded so worried and alarmed that she turned out the light and slowly opened the door. "No, it's nothing like that at all. It's just, I've never had it—sex, I mean, feel so good … I mean, I've never been able to … uh, I mean—"

He took her by the hand and pulled her to him. Then he reached over to the box of tissues on the nightstand and handed it to her so she could try to stem the flow of tears. "That was the best sex of my life," she said quietly and full of emotion, feeling another sob rise up inside of her. "I don't want to cry. I honestly never cry!"

David kissed her face, pressing his lips to her forehead, her cheeks, the tip of her nose, her leaking eyes, and finally, her mouth, then he held her to him and stroked her hair. "I'm glad," he said. "I was afraid, well—I understand, let it out. If it felt anathing close tae how it did for me, you are allowed tae cry." They crawled back into the bed, and she nestled up against him, tiny ebbing sobs shaking her body every few seconds. After a while, the sobs stopped, and all was calm. "What were you afraid of?" she asked.

David stared at the ceiling. He inhaled her beautiful, feminine scent and marveled at what had happened between them. *Why is it like this with her?* he thought. *Why have I never felt this with Susannah?* "Ach, I thought maybe yeh were … I

163

don't know, disappointed. I didn't last verra long, and ... I was worried that maybe you wanted or ... needed more," he said, blushing so deep Erin could feel the heat radiating off his neck.

"I don't think I could be more satisfied. It was perfect. Thank you so much!"

"Aye. Perfect."

Chapter Twenty-Six

NOW WHAT

Erin could hear David's breathing change and didn't want to wake him, but she needed to use the bathroom, so she waited as long as she could. She smiled as she washed her hands. She'd had good sex before, but what had just happened blew it all out of the water. She imagined an Acme bomb, sporting the classic sparkler-like lit fuse cast into a pond, the explosion raining flotsam and jetsam everywhere.

Now what? she thought, her smile fading. *How do I go home after this?* She heard him walking around the room, so she opened the door. The bedside lamp was on again, making her feel self-conscious and exposed. Timidly, she walked across the polished wooden floorboards and saw her clothing laid out neatly at the end of the bed. David looked at her and smiled. It was the same smile that had driven her crazy on *Future Explorations* and other things she'd seen him in. It had shown through photos on IMDb, Instagram, or Facebook, when one of his fan profiles posted one, greeting her when scrolling on her wall.

She saw his beautiful, flawless features and marveled that she was standing naked in front of him. How was it possible that he was smiling at her with those irresistible, large brown eyes or that he'd given her the best sex of her whole life? She felt like a peasant, or more accurately, a villein having been with her King. Her heart sank as she realized she was only a villein, lower than a peasant, and she would soon have to leave the King's presence. She'd have to return to her ordinary life, knowing what was possible, and knowing she couldn't have it permanently.

"You look so sad," he said, after walking over and kissing her.

He was still naked, and the feel of his warm, welcoming skin against hers made her feel tingly again. She wanted him to hold her, touch her, and smile at her, just the way he was, every day for the rest of her life. It struck her again, like another slap across the face, how she couldn't 'keep' him. It had been magnificent, but her treatment was done. Consequently, she'd have to wait until her next appointment to have another one. *Well, at least you've got that to look forward to,* she thought, trying to cheer herself up.

"What happens now?" she said as she backed out of his arms and gathered her things, preparing to take them back to her room. Her blouse made a handy screen to hide all her lumps and rolls, as well. "I mean, how do I go back to my life now? And how do I wait another two weeks until my next treatment?"

"Ah, I see." He frowned, sounding a bit heavy-hearted, and allowed her to gather her things. "I hadn't thought of it as being the treatment just now, but—"

"You didn't?" she said, her heart feeling much lighter.

"Well, no. I wanted to make love to yeh, Erin, not execute a medical procedure that I was obligated to perform."

She couldn't help but smile, relief washing over her. "I'm so glad. I was dreading having to wait."

There you go again, talking out your ass. What makes you think he'll want to do it again? her critical side thought. Her face burned, so she tried to busy herself to hide her embarrassment.

He said so, didn't he? She thought back to what he'd said. *He said he'd wanted to have sex with me. Presumably, that would mean we might do it again, doesn't it?* Her mind was at war within her, so she decided to change the subject. "I still don't know how to return to my—"

"Aye, neither do I," he interrupted, "Though my wife and I don't get on very well anamore. She doesn't enjoy my company. For instance, she would have refused to go out on the town without a plan as we did tonight." He stood in front of her and took one of her hands in his. "By the way, she would *never* have stood up to those sodden women, either. What you did was pure brilliant, Erin." He kissed the top of her hand and smoothed it away with his thumb, then he looked into her eyes, "I wanted to thank you for et."

She hadn't thought about it at the time, she'd just acted. She smiled up at him and shrugged, her cheeks coloring a bit more from the memory of it. "You're welcome. I couldn't help it. They were so horrible! I know fame has its price, of course, but that was too much! I mean, I've been to a few rowdy bachelorette parties but would never have even thought of doing that. Not to anyone, but especially not a celebrity!" She grinned, shocked at her realization. "Wow, that was fast."

"What's that?"

"I don't think of you as a celebrity anymore; you're simply David now. I thought it would take a lot longer to get past it."

"Glad tae hear et. I'm a normal guy who doesn't have anathing more worked out about life than anaone else."

"How do you define 'normal?'" she teased.

"Truthfully, I wouldn't know, as I've never met anaone who actually *is*," he said as he touched her cheek and then ran his thumb over her earlobe.

"I thought you were angry when you pulled me away from them."

He sat on the bed in front of her and pulled the clothing out of her firm grip. Then he pulled her up close to him and lay his cheek against her chest. "No, not angry, the opposite, actually. I truly don't know what I'll do when these few short days are over. I reckon I'll have to look forward to the next fortnight when I can be with you again." He looked up at her, resting his chin on the top of her belly, and smiled his heavenly smile.

See, I'm not so stupid after all, she said to her critical side. *He does want to do it again!* "This is crazy on a level too high to climb, you know?" She smiled back at him and ran her fingers through his dark chestnut, ever-so-slightly graying hair.

"We don't even know each other!" She laughed, a wicked smile playing on her face. "I might have the advantage, though, now that I think about it."

"Oh really? How's that?"

"You had my name before I had yours, but, well, I have looked you up before on IMDb." Giggling, she tousled his hair, and he tried to tickle her, but she rolled out of his grasp. He stood and tackled her, pinning her onto the bed by her wrists, but she didn't struggle. *Who'd want to get away from him?* He could pin her down for eternity. That was where she wanted to be, and she was loving every second of his company.

"Bide yeh here t'night, Erin," he said, so tenderly and so Scottishly, she couldn't refuse.

"Okay, but I snore like a lumberjack!" she said, looking up at the most beautiful human she'd ever laid eyes on. He released her, and they both crawled under the covers, which were far too much for the warm night. They kicked off the blanket, and she nestled her head on his shoulder between his arm and chest and laid her hand on his sternum. Again, she felt the rise and fall of his breathing. "This is nice. I'm glad we have a few days together. And to think, I was scared out of my mind we wouldn't get along." She looked up at him; he was smiling, his face pointed at the ceiling with his eyes closed. She could see his long, thick eyelashes and the crow's feet at the corners of his eyes.

"Aye, et's verra nice. I wish I didn't have tae work tomorrow. I'd been glad for the excuse to get away, as I had no idea what we'd do together, but now, well—" He nudged her gently with his elbow.

"Oh, I see, now you're thinking of two treatments for the price of one?" she said as he reached over to turn off the bedside lamp.

"Sounds like a win-win to me," he said.

She could tell he was nodding off, so she stopped talking and snuggled in beside him. She could smell his cologne and something else, probably his soap. It smelled staggeringly good and made her feel calm and comfortable. Within minutes, they were both sound asleep.

Chapter Twenty-Seven

TOO REAL

Erin needed to use the bathroom, so she got up and headed toward the minuscule amount of light coming from that direction. While washing her hands, she saw the words 'NIGHT LIGHT' on a sticker above one of the light switches. She flipped it on, and a dim light shown above the toilet. "Huh, that would've been handy a few minutes ago," she whispered and opened the door.

She made her way back to bed and crawled in, pulling the sheet up. She rolled over and got a close-up view of David, sleeping peacefully, looking like a middle-aged Adonis. *Fuck!* she thought, fighting the urge to jump back out of bed; he was so impossibly beautiful. She imagined if he woke up and saw her with her hair messy and smelled her foul breath, he'd bolt, considering he'd fulfilled his part of what the whole weekend was about.

She felt even more starstruck than when she'd first seen him in the doorway. At least then he was animated, and she could see the expression on his face. Seeing him like that was far worse; he was just too real! Her body trembled uncontrollably. She was seriously considering getting up again and at least brushing her teeth, or maybe even going to her own room, when he opened his eyes, which made her jump.

"What's the matter?" he asked, propping himself up on his elbow.

She knew she had a deer-in-the-headlights expression on her face, but she couldn't help it. She wanted to run away. "I ... I'm sorry," she said, not knowing what else to say.

He furrowed his brow. "Sorry? Whatever for?" He could see the look of terror on her face and realized what was wrong. She had the sheet pulled up to her chin and looked panic-stricken. It was the same look as when she'd seen him for the first time, only intensified, and his heart dropped.

"I'm sorry, it's just ... you're here, and you're ... real, and I just forgot, and I'm sorry." She closed her eyes, trying to remain calm.

"Et's still me, Erin, the same person I was last night; I haven't changed. Look at me, please."

She felt his hand on her burning cheek and opened her eyes. He was smiling at her but looked sad. "I know, and I'm sorry for freaking out, but I got back into bed, and ... there you were. It was just so overwhelming, and I panicked." He placed his hand on the back of her neck and pulled her in for a kiss, but she shook her head. "Mmm-mm!" She covered her mouth with her hand as her eyes grew wide.

"I don't care," he said and pulled her hand away. He laid her down on her back and kissed her. His hand held the side of her face, and his forearm lay between her breasts, over the covers. She was suddenly hot and tugged on the blankets, so he took hold of the sheet and pulled it down for her, revealing her bare body. She lay naked, longing for him to touch her.

Propping himself up on his elbow again, he looked at her in the light that was no more than the glow of a single candle. He ran his finger along her sternum, then brought it toward him, over her breast, stopping at her nipple. The skin pulled together, lifting the center up, tall and firm as he watched. The smallest hint of light touched and highlighted her skin, making the highest points of her body glow. *Ma Losh! She's perfect,* he thought. "Ach, Erin, you're lovely. Look at that; et's so bonnie!"

"You really think so?" she asked as he leaned down and touched his tongue to the top of her nipple.

"Aye! You're beautiful." He took her raised nipple into his mouth, suckling it gently until she was moaning and arching her back. He cupped her other breast with his hand and then moved it slowly down her ribcage to her waist. Her skin was soft and giving as he brought his hand up over her belly-button, making his way down into her pubic hair. His fingers ran through it as they continued moving down, down, until he was cupping her in his hand.

He watched her face as he gently pressed his middle finger down, feeling her soft, warm, wetness envelop him as it entered her. Her face went through a cycle of shock, thrill, impatience, and then she knit her brows in concentration as he pushed his finger in a bit further. She was panting, with one knee raised. Her hips flexed, and she made little noises, letting him know she was enjoying his touch.

"Oh," she whispered, and her eyebrows shot up as he pulled his finger out and ran it across her clitoris, making her inhale sharply and then let her breath out in halting, staggered puffs. "Oh yes!" Suddenly, her body began to climax; he could feel the pulsing, rhythmic spasms and needed to be inside her. He removed his hand and got on top of her, pushing himself into her, feeling her surround him completely. He thrust hard, making her cry out, and watched as her breasts moved in time to each stroke, then he buried his face into her neck as he reached his orgasm.

They lay that way for a long time, breathing heavily. Neither of them wanted to let go of the intense feelings or each other. After a few minutes, he felt her breathing change into soft sobs, and he kissed her neck, taking her hand in his. Their lovemaking had been so remarkable and overwhelming, he could understand her inability to control her emotions. He rolled to his side and held her, allowing her to let it all out, not far from tears himself. "Thank you, Erin. I never imagined anathing like this was possible, except in films," he said and laughed lightly.

"Agreed," she whispered. As the sobs began to wane, her breathing slowed with only the occasional shutter dotting its steady rhythm as she fell asleep.

Chapter Twenty-Eight

MORNING

The alarm coming from David's mobile phone pierced the air. Erin was now facing the wall and woke up confused and disoriented to the theme song from *Future Explorations* exploding into the room at a volume to wake the dead.

"Shut up!" he barked as he fumbled with the phone, trying to shut the alarm off. After a few seconds, he groaned, got up, and headed toward the bathroom, having to walk around the bed to get there.

She watched his naked body in the gentle glow that the bathroom nightlight was giving off, as well as the soft morning light sneaking into the room through the wide wooden slats of the blinds on the windows. *He truly is magnificent,* she thought. Not muscular or toned, he was simply lean and slender. Some women might call his body type skinny, but Erin thought he was perfect.

He turned on the bathroom light, and as if just remembering that he had a roommate, stuck his head out of the room. "Good mornin', hen, did you sleep well?" he asked, bestowing upon her his impossibly beautiful smile.

"I did until all the ghosts in the French Quarter were awakened by your alarm. I liked the song, though, real catchy." She raised an eyebrow at him, and he rolled his eyes.

"Narcissistic, I know, but it's the only thing that'll wake me up lately. I'd have lowered the volume if I'd thought of it."

He stepped toward her as she lay watching him. Breathing became much more difficult, and her body tingled as he reached the side of the bed, bending over to give her a kiss. "So, what time do you have to be on the set?" she asked with a wily grin as she ran her fingers down his arm.

He kissed her on the forehead and backed away. "Ach, no! I'm not gonna be lured back into bed with you, yeh cunning temptress! I have to be ready in an hour, and I'm not skipping my shower; that's final."

The room was still quite dark as the shutters on the windows were closed, so Erin got up and stood in front of him, naked body to naked body. His chest hair felt soft, and his skin warm against her breasts and stomach. He wrapped his arms around her, clasping them below her ribcage. She stood on her toes and buried her face into his neck, breathing in his scent. "I think you smell amazing just the way you are but have it your way. I'll go take my own shower, or even better, a nice long bath in the whirlpool tub!"

Needing to stand even higher on her tiptoes to reach his lips, she kissed him, putting her arms around his neck. He pressed himself against her, and by his physical reaction, she could tell his resolve was waning. "I'll be here when you get back." She rotated them both around so she could get past him, then looking down to admire his erection, she reached her hand down to gently caress it. He let out a moan at her touch. "Oh, David, that's so nice!" she said as she backed away.

"Yeh she-devil! I'll be ready for you when I return, so be forewarned," he said, falling onto the bed with a groan.

"I'll be ready for you always," she said and leaned over from the opposite side of the bed to kiss his forehead. As she walked out of the room, she heard him groan again and smiled to herself. That was a side of herself she didn't know she had. In the past, she was the one trying to talk the guy into a quickie, not teasing and making him desire her even more. Her unspoken motto in that kind of situation was, 'a good erection is a terrible thing to waste,' but here she was, calm and cool, allowing anticipation to work its magic.

The shower started, and she heard him call out to her. "In case you're interested, it's cold water, thanks to you!"

Erin laughed as she walked to her bedroom and sat on the taupe, upholstered chair next to her bed. This absolutely can't be happening, she thought as she leaned back, savoring the memories from the night before. *Can you believe **The** Da-vid Elliott is on the other side of this wall—in the shower—a cold shower, because of you?*

Hearing the water running, she placed her hand on the wall, shaking her head in disbelief. She walked to the dresser at the end of the bed and sighed, wishing she'd packed more clothes. As she decided what to wear, she wondered what she would do alone all day. *I brought my swimsuit. I could spend time in the pool and then bask in the sun; maybe I'll get a tan.*

I'll probably burn and then spend the next few precious days in pain. Sunbathing was out. *There's always clothes shopping,* she thought.

She heard the shower water shut off then the sink faucet run. *Brushing his teeth, I bet.* She pictured him standing at the sink, naked, then she imagined him getting dressed. As she finished laying out her clothes, she heard footsteps and that same old fear of being seen washed over her. She quickly grabbed the hotel robe and held it up in front of her to hide her body as David stepped up to her door. He gave a little knock and smiled at her, making her melt all over again. He wore jeans and a dress shirt with a light suit jacket and looked like a million bucks.

Crossing the room, he stood in front of her, smelling like everything manly; pine, musk, and something heavenly that reminded her of burning leaves. She teetered a little, and her knees trembled as she inhaled deeply. *He smells like two million bucks!* "You smell delicious," she said as she drew in another deep breath. "Good. Night. Nurse! How much would it cost for me to hire you to stand here and let me smell you all day?"

"More than you can afford, I assure you," he said, feigning importance, and wrapped his arms around her, "I am almost an A-list actor, after all!"

"You're A-list to me," she said, making him smile.

"So, tell me, what *will* you do *without* me *all* day?" he said, dramatically.

"Well, I was getting ready for a shower of my own, but mine won't be cold!" She shot him a naughty look. "After that, I have no clue. Any suggestions?"

"You could come to the set and watch me work my craft? I can have security add your name to the admittance list if you'd like?"

He was trying to sound nonchalant, but she could tell he wanted her to say yes. "I'd never be ready in time to go with you!"

"It's not far; you could walk there when you're ready."

"But won't I be a distraction to you while you work?"

"Erin, from this point forward, you will be a constant distraction to me. Having you there won't make a difference."

His breath smelled like fresh mint, and she knew hers did not, so when he leaned down to kiss her, she turned her head. "I haven't had a chance to brush my teeth! My breath is disgusting!" She put her hand over her mouth.

Undeterred, he gently moved it away. "I don't care," he said, and French kissed her passionately. Then he looked into her eyes while smoothing her hair back with his hand, clearly not wanting to leave. "I have to go; my driver is waiting for me. Will I see you later then?"

He looked so hopeful. "Okay. I'll need directions, though."

"I'll write them down for you." He was as excited as a kid and hurried out of the room. He returned a few moments later with a crude map, drawn on the back of the note he'd left her the day before. "There you are, it's easy to find, but if you get lost, ask someone to point you to the film set. I imagine most people around here know where it is." He looked at his platinum and diamond watch and exclaimed, "Damn! I *have* to go!"

Erin threw on the robe and tied the belt as she followed him through the living room. As they got to the door, he abruptly turned to face her, and they crashed together. That time, he didn't hesitate and kissed her deeply, lifting the robe above her legs. He placed his hands on her bare hips and pulled her up against him.

She wanted to grope him, to touch the growing excitement she could feel against her, but that would only delay him longer. "Holy Moses, go already, or I'll melt into a puddle of goo right here, and the cleaning staff will have to mop me up!" she said, panting. Her body was aching for him, but she had to push him away. "I'll see you later, now go!"

He laughed and turned toward the door. She watched him turn around again to pick up some papers he'd left on the armchair next to the couch. Finally, he opened the door and was gone.

She was weak in the knees and soaring as she walked to her bathroom, that is, until she caught her reflection in the mirror. She grimaced and turned away, *What on earth could he possibly see in me,* she thought. Her body was bumpy where she should've been flat and was, at least in her own eyes, unattractive.

She had been married to Todd long enough that he didn't seem to notice. In fact, they hardly looked at each other's bodies anymore, not that it was a bad thing; it was nice to not be self-conscious. Todd was comfortable and safe; she knew him, inside and out, and could predict what he would say and do. *Todd! This would kill him,* she thought. *He's already afraid of this exact thing happening. He doesn't deserve this!* She suddenly felt horribly guilty.

Erin, you're acting like a foolish little girl. Yes, this is amazing now, but what are the odds it could ever go any further than weekend excursions and stolen moments? Even if it could, you're both married, so rein it in!

She turned back and looked at her reflection in the mirror again, torn between loving Todd and desiring David. She placed the bathmat on the black tiled floor and turned on the shower. Much of the bathroom was tiled in black marble with white veins, while the walls were painted a lovely sage green and had Pieter Casteel flower basket prints hanging on them. The hot water felt good washing over her, and some of her guilt washed away with it. Feeling like a young woman, in love for the first time, she didn't want it to end and started humming a song the band had played in the club the night before. It was an old standard, "The Way You Look Tonight," which was one of her favorites, so she sang it out.

After her shower, she realized she'd left her bra in David's room, so she wrapped the robe around her again and walked to his side of the cottage. The scent of his aftershave and cologne lingered in the air, so she walked into his bathroom, sniffing it like a bloodhound. *Maybe I'll camp out in here all day,* she thought, intoxicated by the smell of him. As she was about to leave the bathroom to search for her bra, she saw a small photo with a clear vinyl cover on the black marble toiletries shelf above the sink.

She picked it up and saw that it was the first of many in an accordion picture holder, the kind men usually keep in their wallets. The first one was of his four children; three handsome boys and a beautiful girl. They looked like the people on the throwaway paper inside purchased frames.

She flipped to the next one, which was of the eldest boy. He was strikingly handsome, looking so much like his father, except he had deep blue eyes while David's were brown. She carefully slid the photo out of the vinyl, only enough to read the back. It read, 'Peter, age 15.'

The next sleeve showed a younger boy with wavy hair a little lighter than David's, and brown eyes. The back read, 'Charlie, age 10.' The third photo was of a freckle-faced boy who looked like mischief. He had a big, beautiful smile and a perfect dimple on each cheek. His hair was dark, and his eyes were hazel. The back read, 'Daniel, age 10.' *They must be fraternal twins,* she thought.

Next was his daughter, she was beautiful, like her mother, with strawberry-blond waves and deep blue eyes. The back read, 'Rosie, age 8.' Erin looked at each face, wondering what their personalities were like. She presumed, because of the nature of his job, David didn't get to see them often. *I wonder, do they treat their parents with respect, or are they spoiled brats?*

She turned to the next picture, which was of the three boys dressed in soccer uniforms. Peter was holding the ball, and they were all smiling happily. Next was one of Rosie in a ballet leotard, tutu, tights, slippers, and a top bun. She was posed *en pointe* with her arms over her head, and it looked painful.

The last two were family shots, probably something they put into their Christmas cards. The first was quite old; Rosie was an infant, and the three boys were very young. Everyone was smiling, wearing matching pink dress shirts and blue jeans. David was so youthful, and his smile was the same one he'd flashed at her an hour earlier. He was sitting next to his wife, Susannah, who was stunning. She had three small children and had recently given birth to the fourth, but her body was perfect.

The last picture was much more recent, probably from the previous autumn. They were all dressed in white; the girls wore lacy linen dresses, the boys wore tan, linen pants and clean, white linen shirts. The boys were tall and fit, and their sister looked like a miniature adult with makeup and perfectly styled hair. Their mother looked exactly the same as she had years earlier, and David looked like the man she knew then, though his smile wasn't quite as natural in that one.

She thought that was the last one, but then she noticed another picture tucked behind it. For some reason, she hesitated, having a sense of misgiving warning her not to look. As usual, though, she threw caution to the wind and wasn't able to catch it as it flew away, up in the air, out of reach. Slowly, she tugged at the top edge of the paper, revealing a photograph that was so stunning, it made her gasp.

It was a black and white wedding photo, a close-up of the bride and groom. It was a candid shot taken after a formal pose when they were laughing and acting naturally. Susannah was looking down and had a happy, unguarded smile. David was looking at Susannah with adulation as though he couldn't believe he was with her. It resembled how she felt when they were together. They looked like a fairy tale couple, the prince and princess in a Disney movie where they all lived happily ever after.

Erin gently pushed the beautiful image back into place, then she folded everything neatly into the compact album it had been before she picked it up. As she placed it back on the shelf, her heart was conflicted. It wanted to be free to take the road that leads to falling in love, but she couldn't compete. Eventually, the newness of their passion would fade and—

And what? she thought, *And she would've loved in vain? Are you kidding me? Stop being so melodramatic! Have fun and be yourself. Who cares if you fall in love or if all you do is fuck like bunnies every two weeks? God, Erin! He said he likes you. He said he doesn't care about your weight. He said you were driving him crazy with your curves! You need to get over your idea of perfect, dammit! You have a once in a lifetime opportunity to be with the man of your dreams! Don't get all emo and make him regret you. He's not yours, you're not his, so live your life accepting his passion for you and give it back to him in return!*

Her thoughts had never been so empowering before, and she felt revitalized, at least for the moment.

Chapter Twenty-Nine

SOMETHING'S DIFFERENT

At the film site, David changed his clothes in the wardrobe trailer. He sat in hair and makeup, no different than the day before, but he had changed. He felt as light as air and like there was a hurricane inside of him that didn't resemble the drink they'd shared the night before in any way. The thought of it made him happy. He must have been smiling because the lady doing his makeup looked up at his reflection in the lighted mirror.

"You seem much happier today. Looks like you're in love," she said and smiled, returning to her task of applying his foundation.

Bloody hell, ye're gonna have tae be less obvious, yeh dolt! "I've had a good breakfast," he lied. Just then, having not actually eaten anything, his stomach gave a horribly loud grumble, as if to catch him in his fable. He smiled sheepishly and was glad she was done so he could leave. The woman smiled at him and winked, actually winked. *Do people do that anymore?*

He walked to the set to read the call sheet, knowing he'd never get though the day if he didn't pull himself together.

Thank God it was Friday, and he'd have the next two days off unless they needed him for something. There was always the possibility of being called back. *Let's hope that doesn't happen.*

What? That's no' like you! Yeh love yer job, now, suck et up and think of somethin' sobering!

Sobering, what was sobering? The thought of returning to London to a wife who wouldn't talk to him, children who hardly knew him, and a bedroom all to himself. Yes, that was a sobering thought, indeed. *I wonder when Erin will get here,* he caught himself thinking before the last thought had fully left his mind. "Christ!" he said out loud when one of his co-stars came up behind him and startled him. He was younger than David and much broader around the shoulders; he couldn't remember the man's name.

"Whoa, looks like you have a bad case of indigestion!" the guy quipped, "What's the matter?"

David suddenly regretted inviting Erin to the set. *I have tae find a reason other than infatuation* (he made a mental eye roll at that thought) *tae be behavin' so differently than yesterday.* "Ah, yes ... well, I must've eaten some ... shrimp that had gone off last night," he said.

"Gone off?" the actor said, looking confused. "Oh, you mean went bad?"

"Ah, yeah, went bad." David imagined a cocktail shrimp with a thin black mustache, a bowler hat, and a Tommy gun. The toothpick it would've been speared with was sticking jauntily out of its imaginary mouth. He smiled at his concocted villain. "Don't worry, I'll be a'right."

"The honey wagon's right over there," he pointed in the direction of the portable toilets, "if you think you might need it," he said with a wink.

Winking, is that an American thing? "Ah, yes, thanks," he said, as the man walked away, shaking his head and chuckling. David wanted to get to work, but his first scene was an hour away, so he headed to the craft table. He picked up an enormous muffin; blueberry, he guessed, by the purple spots all over it. He pinched off part of the top and put it into his mouth, causing his stomach to give him a loud *thank you!*

A cup of tea was what he really wanted, but the American idea of tea was quite different from anything he was able to drink. He wasn't a snob until it came to tea, so he poured a cup of coffee and looked for a place to sit. *I should've taken a spoon tae eat this thing with,* he thought, after sitting alone at a table.

He was about to get up when one of his female co-stars walked over with a piece of toast and a fork. She handed him the fork and sat beside him. Young and pretty, with skin the color of a cafe au lait, light brown eyes, and long, dark, curly hair, she was sitting entirely too close for comfort. "Thanks. I was about to get up and get one," he said, hoping she'd move along. The smile she had on her face was far too bright, and he was beginning to feel hot under the collar.

"Oh, it's no problem, sugah," she said with a soft southern drawl. She finished her toast and began licking the crumbs off her fingers sensually. "I saw you sittin' here and decided I'd help you out."

David had just taken another bite of his muffin, using the fork that time, so he had an excuse not to speak. "Mmm-hm," he hummed in response. She suddenly leaned in too close, putting one of her hands on his thigh. Her other hand was cool on the back of his neck, and he froze as she spoke low into his ear.

"I thought you might wanna go over our scene before we have to be on set."

It was then he remembered who her character was. She was the prostitute his character hires for the night; the one who finds him murdered in the morning. He raised his eyebrows. "Uh, no, thank you. I'm sure it will go fine," he said, trying not to look too disgusted. After all, he'd have to work with her later and was already dreading it.

Why did you invite Erin here today, yeh naff wanker?

She started playing with his hair and was not-so-subtly moving her other hand up the inside of his thigh. "Well then, would you like to meet me after our scene tonight? I have a room at the—"

David sputtered, muffin crumbs flying from his mouth. He stood too quickly, which upset the table. His coffee spilled, and the cup and muffin fell onto the dirt below. He coughed, having inhaled a few crumbs, then he saw her. Erin was standing five meters away, watching the girl try to entice him. When they made eye contact, she frowned and turned away. The girl grabbed his hand, "Oh fuck! He's choking! Oh, David, do you need mouth to mouth?"

He pulled his hand away and hurried toward Erin. "Wait!" he said a bit too loudly and caught up with her. "I'm glad you're here. Listen, I'm no' interested in her. She was coming on tae me. I didn't invite her in any way." He was desperate for her to believe him, though he didn't know why.

Why should I care what she thinks, he reasoned to himself, *we're no' together,* but he did care, very much. *Why should she care, for that matter?* he thought, and then remembered her tears from the night before, and what she'd said: 'Maybe you do this kind of thing with women—' Her look of confusion was nearly more than he could stand, but it wasn't the time or place for that conversation.

"Are you sure you want me to stay?" she asked softly, not making eye contact.

"Yes, I'm sure. Come sit with me. Would you like something to eat or drink? The craft table is only—"

"No, I'm fine," she interrupted. The last thing she needed was to be seen eating. Back at the table, he picked up the muffin, fork, and empty paper coffee cup. He threw them into the nearby bin. *At least the girl is gone, thank goodness,* he thought, but then his heart fell. *Dear Lord! I have a sex scene with her today.*

You just had tae invite her, didn't yeh? Fuck!

"Ah, I don't have a trailer, or I'd take you there. I'm sorry you saw that."

"I guess I don't blame her. I mean, you're … well, I would want to do the same." Her voice was low, and he knew she was upset. She shook her head and took a deep breath. "So, this is a film site, then?"

"Aye, I'm meant to begin shooting in thirty minutes. We should make our way to the set, I reckon," he said nervously.

People were watching them, and he didn't like it. They walked into a building that looked like a temporary garage with an interior room built inside it.

"David … this is a bedroom," she said and slowed her pace. "You're doing a bedroom scene?"

"I wasn't thinking when I asked yeh to come here, but aye, et's a sex scene with the actress you saw earlier. I'm terribly sorry, Erin. You don't have tae stay, although it's not a'tall sexy when et's being filmed," he said, trying to put her mind at ease.

Just then, the young actress walked in wearing a thick robe. As soon as she stepped into the building, though, she took it off, revealing a red, see-through, lingerie robe and sheer panties. The robe was untied and open, showing off her perfect, flawless, *braless* body. Erin turned around. "Okay, I shouldn't have come. I didn't need to see that. I have to go now," she said, but then heard a voice behind her.

"Aren't you gonna introduce me to your *friend,* David?" the woman said, her voice full of saccharin and spite.

Erin straightened her back and turned around. She looked at David, and he could see the panic in her eyes. "Kessa, stop. You're making a fool of yourself. If you're trying to turn my head by parading around like that, it's not working, so go away," he said and turned his back on her, leading Erin away. "I'm sorry, Erin. I understand why you need to go, and I feel horrible. Please trust that this isn't going to be pleasant for me, no matter what yeh might be thinkin' right now."

"Right, but you'll be … and— Right. Okay. I'm gonna go now. I'll see you later."

David could hear her breathing heavily; he presumed she was panicking and felt sick inside. "This was a mistake. I will never be able to deal with this," he heard her say under her breath as she walked away.

He was gutted.

Chapter Thirty

GET YOURSELF TOGETHER

Erin hadn't expected what she'd just witnessed and felt sick. She managed to get off-site and turned down a few streets before hovering over a trash can, not sure if she'd throw up or not. It was obvious David wasn't enjoying the woman's attention at the table; he'd jumped up and tipped it over before he'd seen her standing there. What made her sick was the thought of him touching and kissing her perfect body, then coming back to the cottage and seeing her far-from-perfect one. She was also full-on jealous; she couldn't help it. It was too much for her, and she wondered how his wife could take it?

You're gonna have to get used to that kind of thing. He's David Elliott, for goodness sake! Women are going to want to be close to him. What matters is, for some storybook reason, he likes you.

But he chose to do a role where he would be pretending to have sex with a younger woman, knowing full well that there would be kissing and touching involved. At that thought, she very nearly did heave into the trash can.

He said it wasn't going to be pleasant for him, but why would he accept a role like that unless—

Erin! Shut up! It's none of your business what he does, especially since he chose to do it before he met you! You're being an idiot, so snap out of it! You've gotta let this go! You've known him for less than twenty-four hours!

She decided to take the rest of the day to go shopping. Anything to get her mind off the things he might be doing, what he was going to do, and what he'd probably already done with that woman. She hadn't brought a lot of cash, but she had her debit card, so when she saw a woman who looked like a local, she asked her if there were any resale shops nearby. The woman told her about one only a few blocks away, so Erin walked in the direction she pointed.

The store was clean, organized, and well-stocked. Between the owner and herself, they miraculously managed to assemble a few outfits in her size. The one she liked best was a grey-and-white-striped, knit dress, with flowers splashed here and there all over it. It also, amazingly, matched the pretty bra and undies she'd brought with her. As she walked back to the cottage, she was nervous and excited, wishing she were good at hair and makeup. It then occurred to her that she knew someone who was, so she carefully took out Champagne's delicate black calling card from her purse and typed the number into her phone. A deep, male voice answered, which startled her.

"Hello," he said.

"Ah, hello. This is Erin March."

"*Oui! Ma chérie!*" came the voice she recognized as Champagne's from the night before. "I am so glad you've called me! Now, what can I did for you?"

She smiled at Champ's theatrics. "Well, I need a tiny makeover if you're not too busy, that is. I mean, I know it's last minute, but ..." she trailed off, not wanting to impose.

"I will make time for you, *che bébé!* You want to come here right now?"

Erin was relieved she was so accommodating. "That would be great! I'm not sure what time, uh, I'll be ... picked up tonight," she fumbled, not wanting to come out and say she was staying with David. She wasn't sure when he would be done, so she wanted to be prepared for a night out before he got back.

"*Mais*, now do not worry, *mon amie*, you come here to me. We gonna did you up!" Champ said and gave her the address.

Erin typed it into her phone and headed in that direction. "Okay, I'll be there soon," she said, forgetting about lunch in her excitement. It didn't take her long to find Champ's tiny apartment and was buzzed in as soon as she touched the button. As she climbed a tall staircase, she heard Champagne tell her to come on in and be comfortable.

The apartment was something Erin could never have imagined. It was a perfect mix of masculine and feminine. The walls were painted in rich chocolate mocha, taupe, and deep scarlet red, which gave the space intimacy, and seemed to embrace rather than smother. There were bronze statues of out-stretched nude women and tribal artwork, showing nearly naked ebony people dancing or in the midst of a ritual or ceremony.

A perfume hung in the air that made her think of fresh-baked cookies, a campfire with sweet-smelling smoke, and—Erin sniffed the air, trying to place it, gardenia. The place was sensual and erotic. She was enchanted. "Your apartment is amazing! I love every inch!" she said as she scanned the small room, finding surprising things everywhere she looked.

"*Merci beaucoup*," Champ said and walked into the room wearing a cherry red kimono with an embroidered gold dragon wrapped around it and a purple silk turban that would've looked ridiculous on anyone else. She came over and kissed Erin on both cheeks. "Now, what we gonna did with you, then?" She walked around her in heels and stockings that had a seam up the back, eyeing her up, as a sculptor might do to a piece of clay.

"I don't know what we'll be doing tonight, but I want to look nice," Erin said.

"You will be with *Monsieur* Elliott?" she asked, and Erin blushed.

She told Champ about the beauty she had seen all over David and what she had experienced earlier. "I just want to look a little better than I usually do and learn to do some magic myself." Champ led Erin into her boudoir, which was crammed full of the most beautiful gowns, wigs, shoes, and jewelry. It was a scene from a stage show dressing room. "Oh, Champ! This is every girl's dream! I feel like I've left earth and climbed up into heaven! Can I just stay here forever?"

Champagne smiled, showing those beautiful, perfect teeth. "*Ma petite*, you are welcome here anytime! Come sit on that chair right here. Now, what you gonna wear?"

Erin showed her the dress she'd found at the thrift shop. It was so far below the grandeur and quality of any of the dresses surrounding her that she felt ashamed.

"Now, you go behind that screen and try this on for Champagne."

Erin did as she was told, feeling frumpy and plain as she walked back around the silk-paneled screen.

"That fit you well, *chérie*. If we had the time, I'd put you in somethin' of mine, but that would take trussin', no mistake." She saw Erin's face fall a bit and continued, "Now, don't you worry, girl, it takes me a hell of a lot of trussin' myself!"

They spent the next few hours fixing her hair, and Champ taught her a few tricks for her eyes, lips, and cheekbones. A little contouring and a spritz of hairspray, and they were done. Champagne pulled a stunning red gown off her full-length mirror and stood behind Erin, towering over her, smiling broadly.

Erin gasped; was it really her standing there in the reflection? "Champagne!" She didn't have any words to say how grateful she was. She looked beautiful, not overdone or theatrical, but pretty. Her good parts proudly welcomed the eye, and her not-so-good parts were carefully shaded and hidden, overlooked under the glow of the rest. "I'd cry if it wouldn't ruin my makeup!" She turned around and hugged her new friend, her face landing only slightly above her breasts, or at least the bra making them look like breasts.

"Would you please take a photo of me, and then maybe a selfie of us both?"

"Of course, *chéri*! You are a masterpiece, *mon ami*!"

They took a few selfies first, then Champ took a few of only Erin. They looked so amazing she decided to share them on Facebook but made them private until she got home. She didn't want Todd to see them and think Champagne was her match! It was getting late, and Erin needed to get back to the cottage. "You've been a lifesaver!" she said, wishing she could say more to show her gratitude. "Will you friend me on Facebook, so we can keep in touch?"

"*Oui*, but you cannot laugh at my real name," she said, looking serious.

"I won't; I promise!" Erin said.

Champagne raised her eyebrow at her. "My name is Marvin Brunet," she said and waited for Erin to laugh, but she didn't. "That's not a funny name. Champagne is much more … effervescent, but Marvin is a good, old-fashioned name. I like old names."

"Oh, *mon ami*, you are a dear; *merci beaucoup*! Now, you must be off to your *amour*."

Erin looked once more at her reflection in the full-length mirror and sighed. "Thank you again!"

"*Bonne chance*!" Champagne replied.

Erin smiled as she made her way down the stairs. She didn't have far to go to get to the cottage; she only hoped she would make it there before David.

Chapter Thirty-One

READY

When Erin got back to the cottage, she was relieved to find it empty. She hurried to her bathroom to freshen up and spray a bit of her favorite Givenchy perfume onto her cleavage, wrists, and the back of her neck. Changing into her miraculously matching panties and bra, she put the dress back on and slipped into her pumps. She remembered the bottle of wine in the basket, so she went out to the kitchenette and opened it. *I hope this is good. Maybe I should try it to make sure.* She poured a bit into one of the wine glasses provided by the cottage. *Not bad,* she thought as she drained her glass and washed it in the bar sink.

David managed to get through his scenes well enough. He was playing a Scottish businessman in the states for a conference who hires a prostitute and ends up murdered. The sex scene was miserable. *Playing the whore, he thought, not much of a leap!* During one take, the girl was all over him. She tried giving him tongue and kept running her hand up his leg, far up his leg.

"Who's the big girl you was fussin' ovah earlier, huh?" she sneered at him during a scene reset. "I'm sure your little wifey waitin' at home, would love to know how you looked at her."

What he wanted to say was 'Mind your own goddamn business, yeh fuckin' minge!' Instead, he said, "She's a friend."

"Looked like a helluva lot more than that, seein' how she left so sudden!" she said with a grin.

It was all he could do to get through the rest of his scenes with her, but he managed and was told it was most likely his last day on set. Everything had gone so well, they didn't think they'd need any pick-ups or retakes from them, so he made sure to give her a wide berth. She disgusted him, and he wanted nothing more to do with her.

At the end of the day, David got into the hired car. It was quite warm, and he appreciated the cool interior of the air-conditioned sedan. Ben took him back to the cottage without saying anything except, "Mistah Elliot," as he got in. He was glad, as his mind wasn't in a place for chit-chat, dreading the drama he anticipated when he got to the cottage.

Susannah generally didn't get upset about women being too friendly or sex scenes, but he thought about what her usual anger reaction entailed. All her things would be packed, her suitcases sitting near the door. Then, she'd not speak to him until her hired Lexus came to get her. He had no idea what to expect with Erin. When they arrived, he thanked Ben and got out of the car, not waiting for him to open the door.

"Have a fine week-end, suh," Ben said and drove away when the door was closed.

David stepped through the street entrance door. He slowly walked down the lush, shaded walkway and took a deep breath as he entered their private courtyard. He had just taken out his key when the cottage door flew open. Erin stood before him wearing a light summer dress. Her hair was pulled back, and a few stray waves haloed her face. Her makeup was done differently, and he liked it. He could smell the perfume she was wearing, which was quite different from her other scent, spicy and sweet, and so sexy he was instantly aroused. "Come in, David," she said, smiling brightly at him and greeted him with a kiss. "Are you hungry? I thought we could go somewhere nice for supper tonight."

Is this a trick tae catch me off ma guard? "Erin," he said dubiously.

"I'm sorry," she interrupted, "I'm sorry I made a scene today."

"But you didn't—"

She put her finger to his lips and continued. "Let me finish, please. I was just startled by what I saw. I've been thinking about it all day. I know she was the one who was … well, you didn't look happy about what she was doing at the table. Also, I believe what you said about sex scenes not being sexy. Not only that, I shouldn't even care, it's not like we're in a relationship or anything, right?"

She was so lovely he couldn't resist. "Is it too early to say I love you?" he said, relief washing in waves over his tired body and worn out nerves. She walked over to the dining table as he sat on the sofa.

"Just a leettle too soon," she said, but her face was beaming, and he thought she looked happy he'd said it. "Would you like a glass of wine? There was a bottle in the basket." She stepped up to the counter and upturned two wine glasses before he could answer.

"Yes, please. That actress was terrible today."

"Doesn't matter," Erin quietly interjected, not wanting to hear about it.

"It was in one of the scenes. She was horrid and wouldn't leave me be, even threatening to tell my wife how I'd looked at you. I wanted to tell you, in case … I don't know, she said something," he said miserably.

Erin stopped pouring and left the glasses on the counter. She took a deep breath to steady herself, then crossed the room to sit next to him. "Thank you for telling me. I'm not good at this kind of thing. I've been the insecure and jealous type all my adult life, and to be honest, I don't know how I'll ever be able to see you with another woman in your arms. Even if I know it's all an act, I'll want to kill her." She smiled ruefully up at him, "But, I'm not going to ruin this weekend with you. It didn't feel good to see it, but if I let jealousy have any say in things, it'll all be ruined. I'm determined to get past it, no matter what it takes."

David looked at her, thankful for what she was saying. Susannah used her jealousy or anger against him. She manipulated him and wouldn't forgive without a huge battle; he'd expected a battle. "That mean's a lot to me, Erin. To tell the truth, I wasn't sure what to expect when I walked in tonight. At the minimum, I expected the silent treatment. I'm used to that and can deal with it. What I dreaded most of all was finding you crying, or worse, saying you were leaving and didn't want to see me again. I'm glad you didn't." He hesitated, having a thought cross his mind, "Unless—"

"Unless what?"

"Unless you're only saying this because I'm 'David Elliott,'" he said, inserting air quotes.

She looked sadly at him. "First of all, not want to see you again! Are you crazy? Because of that skank? Not a chance! Second, while I admit it's crazy that *you're* my match, and meeting you has been amazing, I don't care that you're a famous actor. Honestly, it's scary when people crowd around you, but I can deal with that." *I hope,* she thought to herself. "I *do* care that you're attracted to me, for some reason I'll never understand, and I'm head over heels attracted to you, 'David Elliott' or not," she said, also using air quotes. "We have fun together, and the fact that you are, quite literally, the cure for what ails me helps a lot, too."

David smiled and took her hand. "Aye."

"I know you're an actor, and part of your job is to work with beautiful women. You'll be kissing and touching them." Her body involuntarily shuddered. "Truthfully, right now, I feel downright nauseated thinking about it, but it's your job, and you're bloody good at it! For me to be childish and freak out when it happens would be unfair." She got up and walked back to the counter to finish pouring the wine.

David followed and stopped behind her, resting his hands lightly on her waist. She picked up the delicate glasses and turned to face him. "How can I not fall for you, Erin?" he said and took the glass she held out for him. He put it back on the counter and placed his hand on her cheek, feeling that energy once again.

He needed a relationship where he could be himself and not have to act or pretend. Where he could communicate and be heard. He didn't have that with Susannah. To be with someone who could admit when they thought they'd been wrong. Someone who'd tell him what they were feeling or thinking without yelling about it or blaming and accusing? He'd never known a woman, except perhaps his mother, who was like that, and he wasn't sure how he'd ever be able to let her go.

Being jealous and even insecure was something he also understood. Only a few days earlier, when Susannah had mentioned the 'offers' she'd been given—he'd hidden it from her, but it made him want to kill every man who'd ever looked at her. He could guess what Erin was feeling when she saw the actress in that outfit, and knowing he'd be getting rather intimate with her as well wouldn't help. For him, it would've been a venomous rage, making him want to hit things. For her, he guessed, it probably felt as bad but took a different form.

He bent down and kissed her, putting everything he was feeling into it, then he reached down and put his hand on her leg, slowly inching her skirt up. Her legs were smooth and soft, and so was her bottom as he gently squeezed it under her dress. She set her glass next to his, allowing him to take her hand and lead her into her bedroom. He brought her to the bed and then went back to turn off the light.

It was all he could do to fumble with his belt, trousers, and pants. It seemed as though they wanted to stick to him, to hinder him in every way they could. He managed to kick them away and pull Erin further onto the bed. The dress she was wearing was stretchy and soft. When he lifted the skirt, he saw in the light from the kitchenette that she was wearing panties that matched her dress. *Where do women find these things,* he thought in amazement as he pulled them down and threw them onto the floor to mingle with his own. It was useless to try to take the dress off her; he wanted her so badly he didn't want to take the time, and she didn't seem to mind.

Remembering how quickly things had gone the previous night, he desperately wanted to last longer that time. Not knowing how he'd be able to slow things down, he hesitated, but when she said 'Please,' he didn't need to be begged. He got up onto the bed, lay on top of her, and entered her, holding her thigh as he kept a steady rhythm.

He tried to hold out, to think of everything non-sexy he could, but with the smell of her perfume, and the way she was reacting, it was so difficult. When she moaned, it sent him over the edge, and they were both overwhelmed, gasping for air as they reached orgasm together. He could feel her spasms and marveled at their strength, sending waves of intense pleasure through his body with each one. Susannah had never responded that way to his lovemaking. She used to make noises that sounded as though she were enjoying herself, but her body never did that for him. It was like a drug, a powerful one he knew he'd never be free from again.

"Thank you," she whispered as the last waves passed over them. The tears were there again, though without the sobs that time.

"I should say the same to you," he said and then rolled onto the mattress. They lay facing each other, holding hands. He traced the lines on her palm with his thumb, although he could hardly see them.

"I mean, for now, and for doing this for me; all of it," she said. "You didn't have to register. I know you said you did it because of the charity benefit, but you weren't forced to do that, now were you?"

One could argue, he thought.

She closed her eyes tightly, trying to find the words swimming around in her mind to express how she felt. "For you to agree to meet a complete stranger and have sex with her? You! I might have been a stalker, super-fan, or ... weirdo." She looked at him, waiting for the joke about her being a weirdo and how he liked them, but he didn't say anything.

He gently pried her fingers out of the fist she was making and kissed her palm. "Go on, you could have been a freak."

"Weirdo," she corrected, "or a freak, that works too. But you decided to follow through, and now we're here, and I've never felt like this. Oh, I can't get my words out the way I want them to sound."

"They sounded perfect to me," he said, leaning forward, so he could kiss her. "And you're welcome; I'm verra glad I did it as well.

Chapter Thirty-Two

THE PERFECT MATCH

Eventually, David and Erin got up and he searched for his clothes in the poorly lit room. "This might sound odd, and I honestly can't believe I'm saying it out loud," David began as he crouched down to pick up his shirt, then paused.

"Go on."

"Well, it seems ... between us ... similar to how it must be when two people are made for each other. I imagine when that happens, they click, and everything is right. Do you know what I mean?"

Why do yeh say these things out loud? What's come over yeh? Erin stopped groping around in the dark for her panties. She stood upright and stopped him from passing her, since he'd spotted his socks on the floor next to the bathroom door. He gave her a sheepish look, having a sudden dread envelop him, thinking she'd laugh at his ridiculous romantic notions. Instead, she kissed him tenderly.

"That's exactly what I've been thinking, but I was too afraid to say it."

He let out the breath he'd been subconsciously holding, relief washing over him. "Good." He'd learned the hard way that saying how you truly felt in front of Susannah meant certain judgment, so he didn't understand why he was revealing his every thought to Erin.

Letting go of him, she said, "I'm gonna go in there," pointing to the bathroom, "and get myself all dolled up again so you can take me out for a night on the town." She walked over and flipped on the bathroom light switch, wincing at the brightness, then returned to grab her panties, which were under the edge of the bed. She straightened up, smiled at him, and walked away, closing the bathroom door behind her.

Still reeling a bit from their excitement now fulfilled, David sat on the edge of her bed and bent down to retrieve the rest of his clothing. *Ma Losh, this feels nice!* he thought as he recalled the feel of her skin and the taste of her mouth. *I'd like tae feel like this every day.* He closed his eyes and sighed, enjoying the calmness he felt within himself. He stood and carried his clothing out into the shared living space. He noticed the wine glasses that had been left on the counter, and taking a sip, he made a sour face; it wasn't revolting but he was accustomed to much better.

Erin came out from the bathroom, having fixed her smudged makeup and tousled hair. David was no longer in the bedroom, so she stood in the doorway, entranced by the sight of him standing naked by the table. He had his clothing draped over his arm and was holding one of the wine glasses they'd abandoned.

"The wine isn't great!" he said as he lifted his glass toward her.

She was enjoying the view and couldn't take her eyes off him. She wanted to devour him, to touch every inch of his flesh, but he was talking to her, and she had to pay attention.

"Earth to Erin," he said, as he watched her eyeing him up.

"Oh, I didn't mind it, but I haven't had a lot of wine in my life, so I wouldn't know," she said smiling sheepishly, "I tried it when I opened the bottle."

David set his glass down and went to her, wrapping his arms around her shoulders. The hanging belt buckle on his trousers tapped against the middle of her back. "You mentioned going out earlier, didn't you? Let's find something to eat."

"I'm famished! I've been too double-minded all day to think about eating until now. Let me grab my purse, and we can go."

"I reckon I'll get dressed first," he said and heard her say, "*Awww*" as he walked toward his bedroom.

Making sure her cell phone was on silent, Erin put it, along with her lip gloss and face powder, into the light blue interior of her small, white satin clutch. It was her favorite purse. She'd gotten the delicate handbag as a gift from her mother-in-law when she and Todd were married. It had filled the 'something new and something blue' items in her wedding attire and went with the dress she'd packed. It matched the new dress even better, so she decided to use it that night. She walked out into the kitchenette as David stepped out of his room. He made his way toward her, resplendent in his suit coat and tie.

"All set? You look well braw," he said and held out his hand.

"All set." She took his hand, silently thanking Champagne for helping her feel pretty that night.

David took Erin to the Bombay Club for supper, which was only a short walk from the cottage. He managed to make a reservation before they left, so they were seated at once. The atmosphere made it feel like they had stepped back in time and into a 1950s-era, members-only, supper club. She half expected to see Bing Crosby or the Rat Pack sitting at one of the tables.

The walls were covered in dark wood panels, and the rooms were bespattered with rich leather upholstery in green, brown, and red. A large grandfather clock looked down on them as they were led through the bar to a table for two. Set into a cubicle with hunter green velvet curtains hiding them from view, the half circle booth gave them complete privacy. Erin had never been to a place like it before. *Is he trying to impress me? Consider me impressed.* she thought.

"I would've taken you somewhere a bit more elegant, but I knew we'd have privacy here. I hope it's a'right?" he said.

"I wouldn't know what I was doing in a fancy restaurant, so it's perfect. All I want is to be with you."

The food was excellent, and the atmosphere cozy. Half-way through the meal, David realized he'd left his mobile at the cottage but didn't think he'd miss it enough to go back. They talked and ate and laughed for an hour, not concerned about people watching them or photographs being taken.

Chapter Thirty-Three

DON'T WANDER OFF

When they left the restaurant, they were both full and satisfied. David had resolved to curtail their public displays of affection, but as they roamed the city, it became increasingly more difficult, so he tried to keep to the quieter, more secluded streets. He and Erin wandered around the French Quarter in the glow of the gas lamplights that lit their way. After a while, they stopped paying attention to the buildings and street names; they were too absorbed with each other to notice. The night was lovely, and they didn't have to be anywhere until Sunday morning.

They turned a corner and heard a vicious-sounding dog barking and someone yelling inside a house nearby. They looked up and found themselves in a shady-looking neighborhood with bars on most of the doors and windows and graffiti on some of the buildings. "We should turn around," David said, just before two young men stopped and began talking to them. There was something wrong with the situation. The men were asking them questions but were mumbling, so they couldn't understand them. When they began crowding them toward a side street, David knew they were in serious trouble. "I think we'll be going now. It was nice speaking with you." he said, trying to sound calmer than he actually was.

"I think you won't be goin' nowhere, Mr. English. No, you and your 'spensive clothes, and your nice, plump woman ain't goin' nowhere, no sir," one of the men said.

"You want money? I'll give it to you," David said, wanting to appease them and be left alone.

They were being herded—like sheep being shorn into the darkness of a narrow path between two houses on a side street. "We gonna take yo money, but that ain't all we want." The man laughed and looked from his companion to Erin, eyeing her up and down.

One man opened a small, dark red door, and the other one pushed them into the enclosed gap that reeked of stale bread and animal feces. As soon as the door was closed, someone tall came up from behind them and put a large hand across Erin's mouth. He grabbed her around the waist with one long, strong arm, lifting her off the ground as she struggled. She let out muffled screams and thrashed around like a worm on a hook.

"NO! Wait! Please!" David yelled, feeling utterly helpless and scared beyond anything he had ever felt in his life. He tried to get to her, but one of the first two men grabbed him and wrapped a strong arm around David's waist. He could feel something cold and hard at his throat and knew it was a knife. He was incapable of doing anything and didn't dare move for fear the man would slit his throat and then really hurt Erin.

"Please, take my money, take what you want, just dinnae hurt her."

"Take those 'spensive shoes," the one holding Erin said to the remaining thug.

"Never mind that now. I got somthin' else I'm gonna do first!" said the man who seemed to be the leader.

The man holding David turned to look at his accomplice. "Now, hold on! We ain't got time for that shit!" he said, while the leader was looking at Erin and adjusting himself in his jeans.

"NO!" David tried to scream, fighting to get free, but he felt the blade sink into his flesh. "No!" he said again, but this time he didn't struggle.

The leader pawed at Erin, wrapping his large hands over her breasts. Then he buried his face in her cleavage and took a deep breath. "Ooh boy, she sure do smell purty. I want me some uh this nice, white pussy," he said and put his hand up her dress.

Erin fought wildly, trying to scream as tears ran down her face. She looked directly at David, though he could do nothing but watch, hating himself for not protecting her and for leading her into that neighborhood in the first place. The man took hold of her panties and ripped them off her with force.

Oh, dear Lord, God, David prayed silently, *please help us!*

The leader tried to put his hand between her legs, but she twisted and kicked, trying to get away, so the man put his face right up to hers. "You want your man to die right here in this place?" he hissed. "Then you just keep on a thrashin', bitch.

You gonna stop, right?" Erin nodded, tears still rolling down her face. "Good! Now I needs me some of this! Whoo, boy!"

She could smell his breath; garlic and stale tobacco. The stubble on his chin rubbed against her face as he began to grind against her leg. She wanted to fight, to try to get away, but she didn't want them to hurt David.

"Hold her tight!" the leader hissed to the man holding her.

"I ain't your slave!" the man said. "We ain't got time for this! Now tighten your belt! We gotta go! Jus' grab the man's wallet an whatever you want. I want outta here, I feel like they po-lice 'round, and I ain't goin' back to juvie! You with me?" he said to the man holding David.

"Yeah, I ain't doin' this with you no more!" The one holding David said to the man threatening to rape Erin.

"Aww fuck!" the leader said and stepped away from her, grabbing her purse, which had fallen on the ground. He wrenched David's shoes off his feet, then took his wallet and watch and put them into the shoes. "I'm outta here!" he said and ran off down the alley, out of sight.

"That goddamn, fuckin' prick!" The one holding David said. "Leavin' us here to be got by the po-lice!"

"What we gonna do now?" said the one holding Erin.

"I say we find a way out of here, and right now!" The one holding David said, and the other one nodded in agreement. "Now you, Mistah English, you gonna be cool, right?" he said, "Ima let you go now, but you bettah not run or yell out or do nothin' stupid, a'right?"

David nodded his understanding.

"Your woman gonna do the same, right?" He looked over at Erin, and she nodded. "Ima count three, and you bettah stay right here, you understand?" They both nodded. "A'right, one- two- three." They both let go and ran through the red door, off into the night.

Erin and David both fell to the ground, panting as they found each other and held one another tightly. Erin was shaking and gasping for air, having trouble catching her breath. The smell of rotting garbage surrounded them, and they could feel the grime on the grass between the old clapboard houses.

"Are you a'right? Did he hurt yeh? Oh, Erin! I'm—" David began to say, but then they heard a noise nearby. "We need to go!" He helped Erin to her feet, and they both walked out through the tall, narrow door and turned in the opposite direction the thugs had run, back to the street they were on before they'd been attacked.

Erin had her arms wrapped protectively over her stomach and was having a tough time standing upright. She kept gasping and was shivering from head to foot as if she were freezing cold, though the night was quite warm. David wanted to stop and talk to her, but he had to get them the hell out of there first. As he was trying to decide what to do, a squad car drove around the corner.

Chapter Thirty-Four

BLAME

The officer pulled up next to David and Erin. "Two-nine-one-four to headquarters; I'll be out with a male and female on Rampart and Kerlerec," they heard him say through his open window.

"Ten-four, 2914," a woman's voice replied through the radio.

"Are you okay?" The officer asked them.

"Officer!" Erin exclaimed and started crying.

"We've been attacked," David said, feeling numb and as if he were about to lose consciousness. "I need tae sit," he said to Erin and they both sat on the curb.

"Can you describe the people who attacked you?" the policeman asked.

"There were three of them; they were tall. Two were African American, and one was white. I think they were in their early to mid-twenties. The one who seemed to be the leader was the one who tried to assault me. He was wearing a red baseball cap and had pockmarks all over his face. Oh, and he had his hat on backward," Erin said. "I didn't see the one holding me, but the one holding him had his head shaved. I also don't think they were from New Orleans. They didn't have your accent; theirs sounded more typically southern."

The officer was taking notes and looked up at David. "The third man had a wide, flat nose. His hair was bleached; et was orange and untidy," David said.

The policeman lifted his radio handset and called in, "Two-nine-one-four to headquarters: subjects are victims of assault. Send another car and rescue. Suspects: two Black males, one white male, tall, early to mid-twenties—"

David and Erin sat numb and dazed as the officer called in their situation. Erin was still shivering, so David took off his jacket and wrapped it around her shoulders. She seemed surprised he was still there, even though he hadn't let go of her since they were released from the thug's grasp.

"I'm not cold," she said and looked at him like she was sleepwalking.

He took his jacket back and laid it across his lap. "You're shivering."

"Am I?"

"I've called for an ambulance, so they can see if you're all right," the officer told them. When he said that, Erin started sobbing. The man got out of the SUV and opened the back door so they could be more comfortable sitting in the vehicle.

He held out his hand to help Erin stand, then reached out to help David, who was trying with all his might not to be sick. As soon as he was up, though, David turned and vomited into the gutter, retching, and spitting, feeling like a useless git. Erin moved toward him, but he held out his hand to stop her until the tide of nausea had receded, and he could stand erect again.

The officer helped them into the squad car. "Sir, where are your shoes?" he asked.

David looked down, only then remembering they were gone. "They took them, as well as my wallet and watch. They also took her handbag," he answered.

Erin nodded and started crying all over again. "It has my phone in it. It was a wedding gift from my—" She buried her face in David's shirt and bawled.

"A'right, you're doin' good. Now, can you tell me anythin' more about the men who did this, ma'am?"

She managed to pull herself together enough to answer the question, shuttering breaths scattered throughout her speech. "I think I told you everything. There were three men in their early to mid-twenties." Through her sobs and while trying to catch her breath, she told what had happened.

"A'right, ma'am, that's real good. Now can you think of any more details about what happened here?"

"Oh! The one holding me said he didn't want to go back to juvie, so he must have been under eighteen, I guess," Erin said and then blew her nose into one of the tissues the officer had provided.

The ambulance and second squad car came up behind them, lights flashing. Three EMTs got out, walked up to the SUV, and asked Erin and David to exit the vehicle. One of them took David aside, and one spoke with Erin, asking if they were hurt or in need of medical assistance. The third one talked to the original officer and the officer from the second squad car, who was now standing with them.

David was treated with antiseptic cream and a band-aid for the slight cut on his neck. Erin was forced to relive everything as she answered in-depth questions about the assault. When that was over, they were asked if they wanted to be taken to the hospital, but they declined. They just wanted to go back to the cottage and be alone, so they signed a waiver saying they didn't want medical attention. When the officer was finished talking to the EMT, they were driven back to the cottage.

Thankfully, David still had the cottage key in his pocket, so he fished it out and managed, with trembling hands, to unlock the door. They entered, and he locked it, fastening the deadbolt behind them. He turned around, and Erin grabbed him, holding him to her as she sobbed and shook. He leaned his back against the door, still feeling useless as he held her in his arms, and they both slid to the floor.

When she could speak, Erin whispered, "Oh, David, I was so scared! I didn't know what to do. I could see you couldn't do anything, and I didn't want them to hurt you!"

"I'm so, verra sorry, Erin! How could I let that happen tae you? I couldn't help yeh! Oh, Erin, please, please forgive me!" The words caught in his throat. He was exhausted and couldn't stop the tears. *I'm useless,* he thought. *I ken et, and now she does as well!* They both cried and held each other for a long time.

Once she'd calmed down, Erin thought about what he said, that he was sorry and that he'd let it happen. *He's blam-*

ing himself! "David, I want you to know, you need to know, I don't blame you!" She looked up at him, his eyes red and puffy.

Tear stains streaked down his cheeks, and she realized he'd forgotten to wash the foundation off his face from his day of filming. She smiled and rubbed her thumb across his wet cheek, showing him the smudge of makeup clinging to it. "Aren't we a sight?" she said, trying to lighten the mood if only a little.

He tried to smile and kissed her thumb. "I feel as though I ought to have done somethin', and I didn't. If I'd struggled more and broken away—"

"Then you'd be dead, and so might I. You did the right thing," she said and lifted her head to kiss him. He turned away, but she turned his head back with her hand and gently kissed his mouth. "Please, David, I understand that as a man, you have a deep desire to protect and keep the people you care about safe. I know you're going to blame yourself, and nothing I say is going to sway those dark thoughts but listen to me!"

She got up on her knees, facing him, and looked him straight in the eyes. "I don't blame you. And if that's not enough, if you still feel guilty, even though I don't think it's your fault in any way, I want you to hear this. I forgive whatever you think you did. I forgive you, and I think ... I'm beginning to ... I mean, I might be starting to have feelings, the kind that might turn into love for you ... eventually."

You idiot! What are you saying to this amazing man! You are going to ruin everything!

She hadn't expected to say that. He'd said it when he came back that day, but he'd been kidding around. It wasn't something she'd allowed herself to imagine, even, but there it was, and she couldn't take it back. He opened his mouth, but she put her finger up to his lips and closed her eyes. Taking a deep breath to clear her mind, she decided to keep going. "We have two more days here, right? So please, I beg you, don't let those assholes steal our joy in each other's company. Don't let them ruin this time we have together!"

He tried but couldn't smile. Instead, he frowned. "I ken you're right, of course, but I'm no' sure how tae shut up the voice tellin' me I'm a failure," he said, still feeling ashamed and angry at himself.

"I don't know how either, but you can listen to my voice instead, can't you?" she asked, seeing his sad, tormented face.

"Aye, I can try."

"Good, now, please help me off the floor; my knees aren't what they used to be."

He managed to smile that time and helped her up, then they walked into his bedroom. Erin turned to look at him; he could tell she wanted to say something but was hesitating. "What is et?" he asked, worried she'd found something to be upset at him for.

"When we were talking just now, and at other times, I've noticed that your, well, your accent gets much thicker. It sounds more Scottish." She smiled and blushed.

He couldn't imagine why she was blushing. "Well, I reckon that's because I'm Scottish. I'll not do it if—" he said, glad for the change of subject.

"I know you're Scottish, silly. That's not what I meant. I'm saying I like it," she said, rolling her eyes at him.

"You do?"

"I do."

"Susannah doesn't like it, so I've tried tae neutralize it. I reckon when I'm knackered, pissed, er, I mean drunk or stressed, it comes out more," he said, relieved he wouldn't need to continue a posh accent with her.

"Well, I really, truly, like it. It makes me feel happy."

"Aye? Then ah'll take et oot a wee bit more often for yeh," he said in an overly thick accent, making her giggle. He hugged her and kissed the top of her head.

"I'd like that." She wrapped her arms around him and placed her head on his chest, listening to his heartbeat, thankful they were safe once more. "Do you mind if I take a quick shower in here?" she asked after a few moments.

"Aye, I think I'd prefer that as well. I'd like you to stay near me." He wanted to add 'Can I watch?' but mentally chided himself for thinking that way so soon.

"You can watch if you want," she said quietly, seeming to read his dirty mind, and he smiled a real genuine smile.

"Maybe I'll join yeh."

Chapter Thirty-Five

REALITY BITES

Todd had a rough time on the day Erin left. He even broke down and called her room, but the phone rang for a long time, so he hung up, presuming she was asleep. The next day was worse, so after work on Friday, he decided to call the number of a helpline in the folder Doctor Nanavala had given them. He hoped to talk to someone who could help him remain calm and get past his fears.

The man he'd been connected to told him about a meeting in the area for men in his situation starting in a few hours and that he'd be welcome to join them. Todd figured it wouldn't hurt, so he drove to the Quality Inn and Suites in downtown Green Bay. In the lobby, he saw a sign taped to the wall with an arrow that read, *Dealing with F.D. Treatments* in bold type.

He made his way down the hall to the meeting room. The carpet was a dizzying floral pattern in brown and green, and the walls were painted an ugly peach color, which, because of the fluorescent lighting, made him think of vomit. He sat in a green vinyl upholstered conference-room chair. It had been set up with several more of its companions in a circle, like what you might see in an Alcoholics Anonymous meeting. Half a dozen men came in and greeted one another, each finding a seat.

He shook hands with the man who sat to his left. "I'm Todd," he said. How long have you been coming to these?"

"Jim. This is my second meeting. I think it'll help, but it's still rough."

"This is my first one," Todd said, "My wife left for her first treatment yesterday, and thinking about it is driving me insane. I was told about this group and thought I'd sit in."

The group leader stood and asked everyone to give their names and briefly tell their stories. The treatment plans were still new in that part of the world, so most of the men's wives or girlfriends hadn't been doing it for long. The exception being a man who'd recently moved to the area from France, where they'd been using the treatments for about eight months.

His wife had been matched six months before. The man's name was Jean, and he was in a horrible state. Todd could tell he'd been crying recently by his puffy, red eyes. Jean told them how he and his wife of twelve years had been happy and in love and were about to adopt a child. His wife had been matched when they were halfway through the adoption process.

"She assured me it would be fine, and she'd be 'ome soon, promising things would be back to normal in no-time. But my Nadine never came 'ome," he said with his thick French accent, tears rolling down his face. "She called me weeping after the second day with him, the one whom she had been matched with. She told me he was her soul-mate and said she was sorry, but she was not coming 'ome. She has filed for a divorce and is now living with *him* in Avignon."

This did absolutely nothing to help Todd; in fact, it only made things worse for him. He imagined Erin speaking to lawyers behind his back and telling the new man his faults and that she'd never actually loved him in the first place. He would've left the meeting, but it was his turn to say his name.

"Ah, I'm Todd. My wife has been gone for about a day and a half now, on her first treatment weekend, and she won't be back till Sunday. I was up all night, pacing the floor, and today I made countless mistakes at work from being overtired and distracted. I don't know how to do this. I thought I could, but now, I'm not sure."

All the men nodded and said some form of 'Uh-huh!' "I thought this might help me, but after hearing Jean's story, I'm even more worried. Has anyone had a good experience with this? Have any of your wives come home, and everything's worked out okay, you know what I mean?" The men looked at each other and shrugged. It was plain to see they didn't want to worry him more, but none of them could ease his fears.

Most of them stared at the floor, except for one man, sitting three chairs away from him. "You know, man, I can't say things are the same. To be honest, it's really different in some ways, but it's not all bad. I know part of the difference is in how I see her now. Being with another man changes the way you look at your woman. When she first came back, things were awkward, and she was shy with me, but it's getting better. She still says she loves me and hasn't said anything about leaving."

"Yeah, but when's her next treatment? My wife is on her third, and for us, it's getting worse, not better," the man sitting across from him said.

"We made a game of it; it adds a little spice, you know? I didn't know it beforehand, but it turns out I'm into that kind of thing. Maybe I'm just more open-minded than other guys?" This came from a balding man with a large beer belly. He was wearing a Brett Favre Packer jersey, and after his confession, both his face and the top of his head were bright red.

"Okay, who can tell me one way to deal positively with your fears—" the group leader began, but Todd was only half listening; he didn't want things to be different and definitely not worse. He just wanted everything to stay the same or maybe even get better, though he had a feeling it probably wasn't going to be that way for him.

After the meeting, Todd was invited to join some of the men for a drink at the bar across the street, but he declined. He needed to call Erin and hear her voice telling him it would be okay. A few of the men gave him their phone numbers to call in case he needed to talk, so he thanked them and left as soon as he could without being rude.

When he got to his car, he called Erin's cell phone. It rang forever and then went to voicemail. He imagined all sorts of reasons why she wouldn't answer her phone, and none of them were good, so he drove home as fast as he could. He called the phone number she'd left in her voicemail message, but it also rang endlessly with no answer.

Irrationally, he thought he could talk to her before she'd had the treatment and hoped she would decide to come home before she did. It was ridiculous, and he couldn't expect her to do it, but it was his only thought at that moment. He tried both numbers once more and gave up. *I'll try again in the morning,* he thought and poured himself a large glass of whisky, downing it in only a few gulps. He was going to get to sleep, even if he had to drink himself there.

He woke up with a horrible headache and couldn't remember how many glasses of whisky he'd drunk before stumbling to bed, not bothering to take his clothes off. Her cell phone still got no answer. *Stay calm! Maybe her battery died, or she turned it off, or it was on silent all night.* "Yeah, that's right, she puts it on 'do not disturb' after 8:30!" he said out loud and then tried the room number again, thinking that he'd been an idiot, worrying for nothing. *Just be calm,* he reminded himself again, but he about pissed himself when a man named David, with a British-sounding accent, answered the phone in her room.

Chapter Thirty-Six

PANIC

In the morning, Erin and David woke to the landline phone on his bedside table ringing. Without thinking, he picked up the receiver. "This is David."

"Dear God! Uh, is … is Erin there?" an American man said, sounding distressed.

"Ah, yes," David stammered. Erin rolled over and looked at him. He put his finger up to his lips to keep her from saying anything. "One moment, I'll get her." He got out of bed, put the receiver on his pillow, and motioned for Erin to follow him out of the room. They walked in silence all the way to her bedroom, where he whispered, "I think et's your husband."

"Oh!" she said and instantly turned scarlet as a wave of guilt and shame washed over her. "Oh, shit!"

"Erin?" David called out loudly, hoping it sounded like he was calling her to come to the phone.

"Yes?" she replied at the same volume, feeling like a betrayer and a horrible wife, which she already knew she was.

"The telephone is for you," he said aloud and kissed her on top of her head.

"Okay, thank you." She picked up the handset in her room and said, "Hello?"

"Erin?" It was Todd, and he sounded miserable. "Erin, why … why did he answer your room phone? Did he stay the night? Did you sleep with—Oh, dear God!" he said, his voice shaking.

"We have a suite with separate rooms. I didn't know about it until I got here. I should've mentioned it in my message. I'm sorry. There's a phone next to each of our beds; he must have answered it out of habit."

Todd calmed down enough to continue. "I know I said I wouldn't call you, and I didn't want to hear from you while you were gone, but … well, I can't wait that long. I'm afraid you won't come back to me." He'd planned on staying calm, but now that he finally had her on the line, he was too worked up.

He knew he sounded terrible, but at that point, he couldn't control his emotions. "I called your room Thursday night, but you didn't answer, then I tried your cell phone last night and this morning, but still no answer. Are—are you avoiding my calls, Erin?" He was unhinged, not letting her answer as he spewed out all his fears and jealousy.

She listened patiently, waiting for an opportunity to speak. "Todd—"

"... unless you've decided you don't want to come back—" he was saying.

"Todd, honey, calm down. Take a deep breath."

David stood near the table for a moment before he went back to his room. He'd overheard some of her husband's agony and felt a wave of guilt wash over him. Her poor husband was in a right state, worrying himself to death. Even from across the room, he could hear the torment in his voice. He went back to his bedroom and replaced the receiver, but not before hearing Todd say, "... and he had to answer the fucking phone, didn't he? Oh, God, Erin! I thought ... I thought I could take it."

"*Dear God! Ah, is ... is Erin there?*" David could still hear her husband's voice haunting his memory. *The man's been torturing himself because of what I was meant tae do to his wife once, as a medical treatment. Now, look at us, acting as if we're kids, no' thinkin' about the people who love us at home.* He could hear Erin's voice in the other room trying to console her grieving husband.

"I'm sorry you couldn't get me on my cell phone, but ... well, it got stolen last night." There was a pause, and then, "Yes, I'm fine. They took it and ran away. Yes, we were together when it happened. We were walking back after supper." She lowered her voice, but he could still hear her. "No, he couldn't do anything. Yes, they got away, but—" She stopped talking and after a while said, "Yes, I'm still here. No, he's not in the room with me. No, I don't think he can hear me."

David didn't want to listen anymore. He didn't want to hear her loving words or the tenderness in her voice and could feel jealousy welling up inside him.

Todd has the right tae her affection, far more than you do, he reminded himself.

He had to get some fresh air, so he put on his robe and walked to the kitchenette to get a bottle of water. Looking briefly into Erin's room, he could see her sitting on the bed with the phone nestled in her lap. The receiver was at her ear, and tears ran down her face. He turned away and walked back to the French doors. After unlocking them, he stepped out into the warm, beautiful morning. He sat on the wrought-iron furniture, listening to the gargoyle head fountain bubble and spit. *What's happenin' here? It's as if I'm livin' in a film,* he thought and opened the bottle of water, throwing the cap on-to the table.

A fine mess ye've found yourself in, David Elliott, he imag-ined his father saying and shook his head to clear it. When David was upset as a boy, his dad would take him for a walk to 'sort things out.' That's what his father used to call it. He closed his eyes, missing him so much. When he opened them, Erin was standing in the doorway, wearing the hotel robe. Her eyes were red, and she looked utterly worn out.

"What have I done?" she said and put her hands up to her face.

"I heard some of what he said. I can't imagine—"

"He's giving himself massive panic attacks. He told me that he imagines us here, being all romantic and falling in love," she said. David opened his arms, and she sat on his lap, crying. "I'm a horrible wife! How can I do this to him? The thing is, when I'm with you, I forget about everything else."

"I'm sorry," he said quietly into her hair. "What should we do now? Should we cut this off; call et quits, as it were, with only one treatment per visit from now on? I'm no' sure I can do that at this point, could you?"

"I know I can't! That's why I'm a horrible wife. I'm gonna have to go home to my husband and act like nothing is wrong; like things were before I left. If I don't, he might ask me not to continue the treatments."

"Would he really? I mean, I know we have somethin' special, but I *am* actually treating your symptoms as well, aren't I?"

"Of course you are, but I told him before I left that if he couldn't stand it, I'd stop; to hell with the symptoms."

"I dinnae ken. I could hear his suffering on the line. He's in pure agony, Erin."

She laid her head against his robed chest, nodding in agreement, then she looked up at him again, her eyes wide. "He's going to want to make love to me when I get home; he said so on the phone. I mean, how will I be able to do that? Oh, David!"

He knew she was right, and if he ever wanted to be with her again, she'd have to do just that. The thought made his insides burn. "I reckon you could pretend et's me, couldn't yeh? You could close yer eyes and imagine I'm the one makin' love tae you," he said softly, although he knew it was wrong and still felt sick to his stomach at the thought.

Two days and yeh feel this strongly? Maybe yeh ought tae back off? he thought.

"That's what I've been doing my whole life, David, pretending. Pretending to enjoy sex with him. Pretending not to care that he's the only one being satisfied and that he … well, never mind. I'm tired of pretending. I guess I'll have to do it, but it's all a big lie, and I don't want to do that. This is such a mess, and I don't know what to do."

She had her nose pressed against his neck. He could feel her breath on his skin coming out in little puffs as she exhaled. Her hair was tickling his earlobe, and he could smell whatever it was that drove him mad. Opening her white, waffle-patterned robe, he cupped one of her breasts in his hand, wanting her desperately.

He moved his hand to her backside and squeezed her rear end, pulling her closer. She lay back, and he caressed her erect nipple. He wanted her to imagine him, and only him, touching her. The need was so strong that he sat her up and pushed her off his lap, which startled her. He stood, opened his robe, and spun her around to face the table in front of them.

"Here?" she said breathlessly.

"Aye, here." He gently pushed her forward, so she bent over the wrought-iron tabletop. Lifting her robe, he flung it over her back, then stood behind her and entered her, right there, outside. He knew someone could walk out onto one of the second-story balconies or simply walk into their private patio and see them, but he didn't care.

He was done thinking about Todd, or Susannah, or anyone but Erin, the woman he'd been waiting for all his life, though he hadn't known it until then. The one who made him feel like no other woman had ever done before, physically and emotionally. He grabbed her hips and plunged himself deep inside of her, knocking his bottle of water over. The cold water ran through the open-work tabletop, splashing over their legs and feet.

Erin loved the dangerousness of what he was doing, out in the open, without the safety of closed doors. She felt the cool metal against her chest and the vibration of the table legs scraping slowly across the bricks on the courtyard floor. Air-conditioners hummed, birds sang, and people talked near the pool outside their secluded hideaway. She tried to be quiet, but an occasional moan escaped her, nonetheless.

He thrust deeply, one more time, and she let out a powerful, low moan, sending him and her both over the top. Wanting to feel her every spasm, he held on as she clutched at nothing on the table. A few moments later, she laid her cheek down and went limp. He kissed the outline of her spine, which he could see stretching all the way from her tailbone to the base of her skull.

"I have to move now," she said.

He gently reached underneath her and cupped her breasts, pulling her up so she stood with her back against his chest. "I don't want to let you go!" he said as he kissed her neck.

"I don't want you to either, but my legs are falling asleep."

"Oh, sorry," he said and released his hold on her.

She smiled as she turned to face him, her legs pins and needles. "S'ok. Thank you, that was wonderful," she said and kissed him before she took a few timid, tingling steps toward the door, and they both went back inside. She walked to her bathroom, and he went into his.

Looking in the mirror, David saw the age on his face. Lines that hadn't been there a few years ago were now quite conspicuous. *I dinnae feel old when I'm with her. I feel as though I'm seventeen again, and I can't keep ma hands or ma cock off her! How am I gonna go without her for a whole fortnight?* He put his hands on the rim of the sink basin and bowed his head. *I can't think about et, or I'll go mad, what with her bein' held by him.*

He's her husband, mate. Yeh have tae accept that. She said herself she's never had fulfilling sex, except with you; relax already. Yer gonna have tae snap out of this—or do yeh genuinely believe she'll leave him and then be expected tae move a quarterway 'round the world for you? It's highly doubtful, yeh ken, no matter how unfulfilled she is with him. You heard the way she spoke tae him. Anaway, why would she leave Todd when she can have yeh each fortnight without the commitment? He was at war with himself as he got dressed and then waited for her on the sofa.

Erin stood at her bathroom sink, breathing heavily.

What are you doing? You just got off the phone with Todd, and now what? What's your plan here? Are you gonna leave him? Do you really think David Elliott is gonna divorce his perfect wife and choose to be with you? Don't take Todd's love for granted, she thought as she got ready for the day.

She was conflicted and torn beyond anything she'd ever felt before. Not knowing what to do, she told her mind to shut up and decided, selfishly, to put Todd to the back of her memory again.

Chapter Thirty-Seven

MAGIC SUN REPELLANT

When Erin emerged from her room, she was dressed in capris, sandals, and a striped sailor blouse. "Yeh look lovely!" David said, and she made a silly little curtsey before walking to the couch.

"So, what should we do today?" she asked, all thoughts of Todd having, once again, flown right out of her mind. As she fell asleep the night before, she decided not to dwell on the attack. Yeah, the guy had touched her breasts over her dress, but he didn't rape her, and she was determined to be thankful for that. Plus, continuing to be upset would ruin the short amount of time they had together, and she wanted to make the most of it. "I heard about a bar that spins like a carousel, or maybe we could see a show?" She sat next to him, holding a bottle of sunscreen in her hand. As they talked, she started applying it to her legs, arms, and face.

"I've heard of et, it's in the Hotel Monteleone, on Royal," he said as he wiped a streak of the white lotion off her earlobe.

"Oh no!" she said, looking heavy-hearted. "It's Saturday; the city is going to be busy with tourists. Would it be wise for you to be strolling around town with a woman who isn't your wife? I mean, people will recognize you, I'm sure."

David stood, held up his finger, and walked to his room. He came out a few moments later brandishing a baseball cap and a pair of dark sunglasses. "Hah-ha!" he said, "Ma foolproof disguise!" He placed the hat on his head and put the sunglasses on. "You can't tell et's me, can yeh?"

"Does that actually work?"

He took his disguise off and sat next to her. "Truthfully, not as much as I'd like, but as long as we dinnae make too much of a show, I reckon we'll be okay."

"I suppose we *should* be more careful anyway. We don't want your wife reading a tabloid headline about her husband being seen kissing and fondling another woman, now do we?" she said and smiled wickedly.

"Fondling, eh? I'll show you fondling! Come here yeh minx!" He took her arm and tried to pull her toward him on the couch, but she let out a little squeak and pulled away.

"No, no, no, no! I'm not going to waste this beautiful day, not after bathing myself in sunscreen! Now, come here, and I'll put some on you, too. You don't want that delicate Scottish skin frying to a crisp when you might have filming to do on Monday. Continuity, after all."

"Very well then, m'lady, I shall allow you to anoint me with your magic sun repellant," he said with the most delectable Laurence Olivier style accent.

"That was yummy!" she said and spread the thick, white SPF 50+ lotion on his body. It was nice running her hands and fingers along his skin. *I need to find an excuse to do more of this,* she thought. She finished up and carefully closed the cap on the bottle, but now her hands felt gross. "I'm gonna wash my hands, and then we need to go! It's getting late!" She walked to her bathroom sink and washed the sunscreen off the best she could, then checked the mirror to make sure everything was in order.

When she returned, David was asleep on the couch with his head back and his mouth open. *Are you kidding me?* she thought and then remembered the morning they'd had. First, Todd calling, and of course, the hot sex on the patio furniture, he was bound to be tired. *I guess I can let him take a short nap before we go out. The idea! You, allowing him to do anything! You're crazy!*

An hour later, he woke with her head on his lap as she lay next to him. She was reading his book, which he'd set on his bedside table the evening he arrived. He made a little snort, and she giggled. "Lovely," she said, smiling up at him. "This book is interesting! I can't wait to find out what happens between Peter Blood and Arabella Bishop."

"Oh, Erin, I'm sorry! Why didn't you wake me?" He sat up and stretched.

"Well, I tried, but you started choking me, saying, 'Kill the commie bastards,' and referred to me as 'Charlie,' so—" She laughed out loud at her own joke. "We had a full morning. I decided to let you sleep so you'd be bright-eyed, bushy-tailed, and ready to go."

239

"Well, thank yeh, hen," he said, "I didn't realize I was so tired. How long did I sleep?"

"About an hour."

"Well, I'm famished! Let's find somewhere tae eat."

"Good idea." They stood and headed toward the door.

"Bullocks!" he said and stopped. "Ma wallet."

"Oh yeah."

The night before came crashing back down over her; he could see it on her face. "Never mind, love." He walked into his room, and she followed.

She watched him take his holdall out of the closet and set it on the bed. Reaching inside, he unzipped a small pocket and took out a credit card and some British pound notes clipped together neatly in a monogrammed silver money clip.

"I had these prepared for the trip home. I'm sure we'll be able tae have et exchanged; now, let's go, lassie. I wish ye'd stop delayin' us!" he said with a laugh. She smiled, but there was still a shadow clouding her face, so he went to her and kissed the top of her head, "Let's go, love, so we can put et out of our minds, a'right?"

"Alright," she said.

Chapter Thirty-Eight

CHARTRES HOUSE

David and Erin wandered around the city looking for a place to eat. On Rue Chartres, David stopped to look in the windows of a jewelry store. He saw something on display and wanted to buy it for Erin as a keepsake and token of his affection. *How will I manage et without her seein' me?*

Across the street, Erin saw a hanging sign in front of a salmon-colored building that read, *Chartres House Cafe.* "This looks nice, doesn't it?"

He turned and looked at her, not what she'd pointed to. "Beautiful," he said tenderly and gazed down at her, making her blush.

"Not me, silly, the restaurant across the street."

"Right," he said with a grin. They crossed the street and entered the building. It was cozy, and the food smelled delicious. "You *are* beautiful, though, Erin March," he said as they walked in, followed by a man who sat at the bar and ordered a rum and coke. David was about to remove his hat and glasses when she nudged him.

"I think that man knows who you are, David; he's staring at you," Erin said, feeling uncomfortable.

David stole a glance at him and shrugged. "Dinnae worry love, just ignore him."

Soon the host came and led them through the restaurant. The man was old; his face had so many wrinkles, Erin thought it looked like a topographical map of jagged mountains. They walked under a large brick archway and were seated in a room toward the back. He handed them each a menu and asked if they wanted anything to drink. Erin asked for water with lemon. She hadn't been drinking enough water and could feel her skin was nearly as dry as paper. David asked for a pint of Guinness.

"A bit early in the day for a pint, don't you think?" she teased.

"It's never too early or too late for a pint." He smiled at her and looked down at his menu.

Their waiter arrived with two glasses of water and Erin's lemon wedge. He looked to be in his early twenties, with sandy, blond hair and blue eyes. "Hello. Welcome to the Chartres House Cafe, my name is Jack, and I will be your server today. Have y'all had a chance to look over the menu, and are you prepared to order?" he said, smiling pleasantly at them.

"Yes, I believe so," David said, and Erin nodded.

"For you, miss?" he said, making Erin laugh.

"Miss? You're looking for a nice tip, aren't you?" she said. He smiled at her and shrugged. The boy's smile was indeed charming. "Well, it might work." She smiled back at him and ordered her food. He then turned to David, resuming a more serious demeanor.

"And for you, sir?" he said. David ordered, then the young man took their menus and walked away. David smiled as he watched Erin. She was squeezing the wedge of lemon into her glass, which was beading up with condensation.

"What?" she asked when she noticed his gaze on her.

"Nothing. You and the waiter were flirting."

"I wasn't flirting. I was being nice; there's a difference." She took a sip of her drink and smiled back at him.

"Right. Well, he was flirting with you."

"I can't help it if I'm so appealing that men can't resist the urge to get my attention. It's a curse," she teased.

"It worked on me."

"Well, there's no accounting for taste."

Jack returned with David's pint and went back to the kitchen. When he brought out their food, it was steaming and smelled heavenly. "Oh, this looks amazing! Thank you, Jack!" Erin said as he placed her meal in front of her.

"You're welcome. Now, is there anything else I can do for y'all?"

"No, everything is perfect," David said, smiling at Erin.

Jack saw the way he was looking at her and grinned. "If you need anything, please get my attention. *Bon appétit!*" he said and walked away.

The food was delicious, and as they ate, they talked about their lives. When Erin excused herself to use the toilet, David stood, put on his disguise, and asked the host to hold their table, saying he'd return shortly. He was out the door before the old man could say anything. The man at the bar watched as David ran across the street into the jewelry shop.

"Mistah!" the host cried out, then he saw Jack and beckoned him to come over.

"What is it?" Jack asked. "Dat man—dat one at table nineteen, yeah?"

"Yeah, what about him?" he asked, trying to be patient.

"*Mais*, he done gone out across the street, ovah there, and walk right into the silversmith place. What are you making of that, now?"

The young waiter looked at the shop and shrugged. "Maybe he wanna buy his girl somethin' purty without her knowin' about it?"

"Oh! I think maybe you right. Look now, here she come; go distract her."

Erin found the table empty when she returned. She looked around to see if David was nearby and was about to ask the host when Jack appeared.

"Your companion has gone to the men's room. If you'll please take your seat, I'll show you the dessert tray," he said, thinking fast. He rushed off to the kitchen to retrieve the tray of desserts before she could protest. He returned a moment later with a selection for her to choose from.

"But I don't know if David will want anything," she said, then spied a ramekin of crème brûlée, and paused. "I love crème brûlée! I guess David can order something for himself when he gets back, right?" She smiled and looked at Jack, who nodded enthusiastically at her.

"Of course," he said, wanting to keep her attention away from the open doors. He noticed her wedding band and asked, "What brings y'all to New Orleans, then? A second honeymoon, perhaps?" He saw her flinch and frown.

Ah, well, it's a bit … uh—" she faltered. We're not on our second or even first honeymoon. We're good friends and are spending the day together. Have you seen him?" Before Jack could respond, David walked around the table and sat in his seat again, slipping his hat and glasses onto the chair next to him. "Are you alright? I was getting worried. You were gone for quite a while."

The waiter smiled and winked at David, showing him the dessert tray. "*Mademoiselle* was considering the crème brûlée; would you care for anything, sir?"

"No, I'm quite finished, but please bring '*mademoiselle*' whatever she would like." Jack went to the kitchen, and David smiled at Erin. "I'm fine, I assure you. I was stopped on my way out of the water closet. I'm sorry I took so long," he fibbed, and she looked at him a bit closer.

"David, you're sweating! Are you sure you feel okay? We can go back to the cottage if you feel sick!"

"I'm no' sick. I'm just a bit warm from the spice in my food."

Erin seemed appeased by that explanation and leaned in towards him. "The waiter asked if we were on our honeymoon! Do we have signs on our backs saying 'lovers?'"

David looked at her hand. Her gold wedding ring flashed with a reflection of light from an unknown source. "I'm thinkin' he noticed your ring and presumed."

245

Erin looked at her left hand and placed it on her lap. "Oh, yeah. I forgot about that." Jack returned with her dessert and set it in front of her. "Oh, I do love crème brûlée!" she said again, but with much more passion that time. She lifted the dessert spoon and gently tapped the top of her dessert. The crystalline layer of caramelized sugar cracked and made the most beautiful noise.

David thought she looked like a schoolgirl, fully engulfed in an amazing discovery. He watched her, amused, as with each spoonful, she closed her eyes and said something like, 'so good!' or 'this is heaven!'

It was nearly gone before she thought about sharing. She stopped suddenly and looked up at him. "Oops, I'm so sorry! Would you like some?" she asked, embarrassed at her rudeness, but he only laughed.

"No. I'm enjoying watching you devour it, the same way I want to devour you," he said wickedly.

"David! You are a naughty boy!" She laughed, feeling her face flush and her insides tingle again as she ate the last few bites. Jack came to take her plate away and asked if it was good.

"Good? No. I don't believe it was good," David said with a smile, "I think perhaps my friend here has had an out of body experience! We may need to get medical assistance." He laughed as Erin threw her napkin at him.

"It was perfect, Jack, thank you," she said.

"It was my pleasure," Jack said and then brought the bill to the table a few moments later.

David paid, leaving a substantial tip, both for good service and for stalling Erin while he made his stealthy purchase across the street. They walked through the now empty bar as they left the restaurant to continue their adventure.

Chapter Thirty-Nine

TEASE

"I love this music," Erin remarked to David as they walked through the tourist shops playing Cajun or Zydeco music. They tried on hats and played with adorable stuffed crawfish in one of the stores. David bought them both matching alligator tooth keyrings as a joke, saying they could keep them in their pocket to remind them of their weekend. Erin was delighted. She was sentimental and having the reminder would mean a lot when they weren't together, if only to prove it had actually happened. They were completely comfortable together, enjoying a lot of the same things, and had a similar sense of humor.

David's disguise worked fairly well, and for the most part, they were left alone. When someone did recognize him, he spoke with them, allowing selfies and autographs. Erin loved how kind he was to the people who approached him. He made it seem like he didn't mind people interrupting him, whereas she would've been aggravated long before he seemed to be. "What do you say we order take out and stay in tonight?" she suggested as they made their way through Jackson Square since her feet hurt after walking all day.

David wanted to grab her by the waist and pull her out of sight behind a banana tree. To press himself against her and ask, 'What else would you like to *do* whilst we're in?' but he wouldn't allow any more public displays of affection. Instead, he found a bench in the shade and sat on it. "That sounds nice. My feet are hot from the pavement, and et's early in the year. I can't imagine what et's like here in August." He put his ankle on his knee, then laid his arms out along the top of the seatback, as though he were only resting.

Erin sat next to him, but not too close, trying her best to act like she wasn't turned on by everything he did and said. His thumb was ever so lightly touching her shoulder, and it sent shivers through her. She closed her eyes, enjoying it. Will this ever stop? she thought. Would there come a time when he'd touch her, on purpose or accidentally, that she wouldn't shudder or feel her insides go squishy? Eventually, it probably would, but she knew it would take a long time, and she didn't want to think that far ahead.

She wanted to reciprocate his tiny show of affection, but she could come up with nothing, so she sat back and enjoyed the sense that they were being dangerous in public. *Is this how the Victorians felt at every minor touch from the person they desired? What glorious torture!* Oh, what she wouldn't give to straddle him on the bench and kiss him until their lips were chapped and people formed a line to take pictures with the 'kissing couple' statue.

David touched her shoulder to wake her from her day-dream. "What's goin' on in that head of yers? You were smil-in' like the Cheshire Cat just now."

"Oh, nothing. I was just thinking of things I'd like to do to you on this bench." Not waiting for a reply, she stood and began walking in a general cottage-ward direction.

David stood and followed her. When he caught up, he leaned in close to her ear. "You're makin' me pure radge, woman; absolutely barkin', ravin' radge!" he said quietly, but with a great deal of intensity.

She figured 'radge' was a Scottish way of saying crazy, or maybe horny. It didn't matter; it seemed like something she wanted him to be. Standing on her tiptoes, she put her hand up as though she were telling him a secret and nibbled on his earlobe. "Too bad there isn't a private place we could go. Somewhere we might conversate more about these things."

His legs were wrung out. They'd been washed in the agi-tating tub and were then squeezed through the rollers. How would he be able to walk back to the cottage without working legs? "When we get back Ms. March, I'm going to take you over my knee."

"You think you will!" she interrupted, and skipped in front of him, then she turned, walking quickly backward. "You'll have to catch me first." She let out a tiny squeak as she sprinted ahead, knowing he wouldn't come after her since it would cause people to notice him, but she could do whatever she wanted. She stayed at least ten feet ahead of him as they wound through the busy streets filled with people.

She managed to keep her distance except once, while they were on a deserted stretch of a small side street, and he caught up to her. His unexpected touch on her shoulder made her yelp. He grabbed her by the arm and pressed her up against a building next to a dumpster. As he pawed at her, kissing her savagely, she rubbed the front of his jeans.

They both moaned as she felt him, hard and ready for her through the denim fabric. He wanted to take her right there—he'd show her for teasing him, but a minute later, they heard voices nearby. They reluctantly collected themselves, and she grinned, darting ahead of him again.

They got back to the cottage and made it into the safety and privacy of their oasis. David took off his belt and acted as though he was going to take her over his knee as he'd threatened earlier. Erin shrieked like a little girl and miraculously made it to her room, closing the door before he got to her, so he knocked politely.

"I'll be out in a moment, darling," she said sweetly.

"Et had better be one verra quick moment, or I'll be accused of trashin' the place when I kick down the door." He paced in front of her room, dying to go inside.

Erin freshened up as quickly as she could, then tore through the dresser drawers, looking for her pretty undies. That's when she remembered they were lying on the ground between two old houses. Her heart sank, but she did have a pair of plain, black underwear. He was drumming his fingers on the door, so she put on her pretty bra and the black undies. She added a tiny spritz of her perfume and lay on the bed. "You may enter my chambers now," she said regally.

David opened the door slowly and saw her lying on her side with her head propped up on her hand. He wanted to ravish her without hesitation, but he figured that's what she wanted him to do. He also realized it was the first time she'd left the lights on, and he wanted to look at her. He prowled around the bed like a panther, eyeing up its prey. He stalked to one side of the bed and took off his shirt. When she reached out to him, he retreated to take off his trousers, which made her moan. Each time she tried to touch him, he managed to escape until he was naked.

She could stand it no longer and got up on her hands and knees, crawling to the end of the bed. *Look at him! Look at that hard-on because of me!* she thought, amazed at being able to do that to him. She gently took hold of it, wanting to taste his skin, so licking her lips, she took his cock into her mouth.

That was something Susannah wouldn't do, and after only a few moments, he had to stop her. If she made another move, he knew he wouldn't be able to stop himself. *Why is everathin' so sensitive? Everathin' she does brings me so close, so quickly!* He unfastened her bra, and pulled it off her, then she lay down, and he got onto the bed, hovering over her on his hands and knees. He had to let himself settle down before he would allow her to touch him again. He kissed her soft, pale neck, leaving small red hickeys all over it.

She arched her back as he kissed her breasts, making his way down her body, working his way to her navel. *Oh, please don't stop there!* she thought as he reached her belly button. *Keep going, a little further.* He kissed her all the way to her panties, and then stopped, seeing the bruises on her legs, a remnant of the thug's assault on her. "Ach, Erin," he whispered and gently kissed the bluish-purple splotches on the front of her thighs.

"Don't!" she said defensively, not wanting him to notice and not wanting to remember it, either. "Please, just keep going, okay?"

"A'right," he said and began to pull her underwear down slowly, inch by inch. She writhed beneath him, trying to get him to go faster, but he took his time. When he finally got them past her feet, he buried his face between her legs as though he were famished. She moaned and panted as he enjoyed her thoroughly, wanting to please her so badly.

Holy Moses! I can't believe he's doing that! "Don't stop! Please keep doing that!" she said breathlessly since Todd always stopped long before she was ready. David seemed happy to oblige. With each rotation of his tongue, she let out short breaths and gasps. "No, don't go faster—like that, yes." Soon, her body was pulsating like it did when they made love. "I need you; please make love to me now!"

He did as she asked and felt her waves of climax envelope him. It didn't take long for him to join her, their breath sounding like bellows stoking a smoldering fire. Neither of them wanted to move for fear it might break the spell.

"You make me feel so good," she said as everything settled down. "Wouldn't it be wonderful if we could do this every day?"

Et would be perfect, he thought. He longed for that so badly himself. To come home to her smile and to feel her touch every day. To laugh and not worry about image, money, and especially ridicule. That was what he wanted most in life, but he knew he couldn't make it happen, and his frustration was getting the better of him. "Oh, God, I wish we were free, Erin!" he said suddenly and got up.

She was surprised by his intensity. He was clearly struggling with something internal as she watched him cross the room and then return to her, only to go back and retrace his steps. Experience told her that sometimes it was better to remain quiet and let a man sort things out in his head before asking for an explanation, so she waited patiently, figuring it was his turn to have a meltdown after sex.

A sudden and unwelcome ball of emotions had formed inside of him. It came charging up to the surface, and he didn't know what to do with it. *If we were both free et would be easy, we could live happily ever after, but et's so complicated.* He wanted to tell her that he really did think he was falling in love with her, but it would be wrong. It was far too soon for him to say such things, even if he did feel it. Plus, how could he say that with no real hope of having her long-term love in return? *Even if she loves me, as well, I can't expect her tae leave her husband for me, can I?*

He finally had what he truly wanted within reach, but he couldn't have her. He'd give up everything he had for her, but she wasn't available. Saying that he wished she were free just then wasn't fair to her; she still loved her husband. He realized with a heavy heart that he and Susannah weren't in love, never actually had been, and the recurring epiphany of his failed marriage made him angry. He'd bought into the lie that looks and status meant something, and now he felt trapped.

Frustrated and upset, he wanted to punch something, but there wasn't anything to hit. He also didn't want to frighten Erin. He ached to claim her as his own—to know they were they, and that was that. He knew she had feelings for him, not the actor, 'David Elliott.' It didn't matter though, none of it mattered. Looking at her waiting patiently for him, he couldn't bear it any longer and walked away, wanting to scream.

Breathing hard, infuriated, and fuming, he stormed to his room, not understanding why he couldn't contain his feelings. He wasn't the kind of guy who became an emotional wreck. Instead, he took things in stride, calm and steady, like his father, the example of strength, who never allowed things to affect him, at least not on the outside.

He leaned over his bed, both hands on the mattress, and pounded it several times with his fists, feeling hot, stinging tears forming in his eyes. *Fuck! I dinnae want her tae see me like this,* he thought and hurried into the bathroom, turning on the shower. *Please, dinnae let her come after me—not yet.*

The water was freezing cold, but he didn't care. He stepped in and leaned his forehead on his arm against the wall, allowing the tears to come. They were tears that had been years in the making, a time bomb, waiting for the trigger to set it off. Each silent meal, each condescending comment Susannah threw at him or said about him to their friends, not caring whether he could hear her or not. All of her arrogance, pretentiousness, and contempt for anyone lower than herself. She didn't love or respect him. There was no honor in their marriage. He wanted out, but what was the point?

Here was a woman who made him laugh, who showed even the most common person respect and courtesy. Erin never scoffed at him when he was interested in what someone was saying, even people whom Susannah would think of as not worth his attention. She was kind and civil, witty, and spontaneous. He'd finally met her, **the one**. *What am I gonna do now?*

Chapter Forty

WEAK IN THE KNEES

Erin stayed on the bed after David left the room, wishing she could help him. When she was younger, she would have thought she needed to fix or discuss whatever it was, following him, nagging, and pestering until he either talked to her or, more likely, got angry and stormed out. She knew he wasn't upset by anything she'd said or done, it was something he needed to do to get his emotions under control, so she decided to wait for him. She heard the shower start and pictured him, only a thin wall away from her. She wanted so badly to comfort him, to go in and hold him, but knew she shouldn't. Instead, she placed her hand on the wall, hoping for a telepathic connection.

She decided to take her own shower, not understanding why she was so calm. She'd done nothing but cry the first three times they'd made love, now he was a mess, and she was feeling strong. *One of us should remain sane when the other one's lost it*, she thought as she stepped under the water. Memories of the sex they'd just had were still vivid in her mind, the feelings so tangible, they made her heart beat faster.

She hummed one of her favorite songs until she remembered all the words. Since David wasn't there, she started singing "Whenever You Come Around" by Vince Gill. It was a song about having a crush so bad you couldn't breathe; your knees got weak; you couldn't talk, and your world flips when they smile. When she was finished singing, she laughed. "Not bad, Erin," she said out loud to herself.

"Not bad a'tall," she heard from the other side of the shower curtain and froze; she hadn't been singing to be heard.

"I didn't know you were in here," she breathed, feeling mortified and self-conscious.

"I didn't hear et all, but that song was nearly word-for-word ma own thoughts. Did yeh come up with et yourself?" he asked.

"Don't I wish!" she laughed. "It was a country music song in the 1990s. I've always loved it, and it popped into my head so, I sang it."

"Et was beautiful. Would yeh sing et again for me, please?" he asked.

She heard something in his voice, either longing or sadness, so she made herself suck-up her embarrassment for him. Water vapor filled the room, and she was turning into a prune, but she'd be damned if she came out or opened the curtain. She turned off the water and sang the song again.

Though there wasn't much demand for her voice anymore, she knew she could sing. She had a love/hate relationship with performing, and it was difficult for her. The only way she could do it was to imagine he wasn't there. So, leaning on the wall, she closed her eyes and let go, then she waited with bated breath for his reaction.

He sat silently through the whole thing, and when he opened the curtain, his eyes were red, but he was smiling. He stepped into the wet shower, boxers notwithstanding. "You're gonna get soaked!" She laughed as he pulled her up to him.

"That was stunning, both the song and the one singing et."

Why can't I seem to stop blushing, she thought, as she felt her cheeks bloom pink. She laid her cheek on his chest and shrugged. "Thanks, it's one of the few things I can do well."

"I can think of others," he said under his breath, making her smile.

"I used to sing in church and wanted to be a famous singer when I was younger, but now I'm glad it didn't work out that way. I wouldn't want to be watched and judged by people when I do something they don't like. I'm not that kind of person."

"I'm glad ye're not," he said. He kissed her for a long time and then held her. "I'm sorry about earlier."

"It's okay, I understand. Do you feel better now?" she asked, running her pruney fingers through his hair.

"After hearing yeh sing—and the words tae that song, I feel like I'm fallin' in love with you," he said, softly.

Erin held him tightly around his waist, her wet, chilly head, against his dry chest. She could hear his heart beating and smell his soap. "I don't want this to end," she said.

"Neither do I."

Chapter Forty-One

REALITY CHECK

Later that night, David and Erin walked to a sandwich shop. Several autographs and one selfie later, they brought their meals back to the cottage. "How can you stand it?" Erin asked, thinking back on all the selfies posed for and each hand he'd shaken as they sat on the sofa. "I've never valued my anonymity as much as I do now. It never ends, does it?"

"Do yeh mean what happened tonight or on Bourbon Street?" David asked.

"Well, all of it, I guess. Being watched and followed."

"Ach, et's not so bad."

Erin gave him a look that said, 'Are you kidding me?'

He smiled at her and shrugged. "No, really, I dinnae think I'd be able tae do this at all in England. There are places I can go where I'm left alone, but there have been times when I've had tae bring a security guard with me tae keep from being mauled," he said, and she looked horrified. "Dinnae be frightened. People don't want tae hurt me, they only want tae get close, and some people will do anathing tae do so. Et's no'

260

so frequent now, but when *Future Explorations* was on, et could get pretty bad. A woman once climbed into a tree, and when I passed under et, she hung down from one of the branches; scared the livin' bejesus out of me!"

"I bet it did, but it makes me feel uncomfortable. I'm not sure why, but it makes me feel like, oh, what's his name? Icarus? Yeah, that's it, and I'm getting too close to the sun," she said, making him smile.

"Aye, but there are benefits—cars, houses, clothes, money ... things." He frowned. The truth was those weren't good enough perks. None of those things made him happy anymore. It was nice not to be poor, yes, but fame was still more than he'd bargained for at times. The attention was something he was used to, though he remembered quite well how frightening it could be to someone new to it. He then noticed that she was looking at him in a way he didn't understand.

"What does it profit a man to gain the whole world and lose his own soul?" she said softly and then smoothed a stray hair from above his ear.

"Mark 8:36." He took her hand in his and kissed her fingertips. "I attended a Faith school until fifth year." *And ma da' used tae quote et to me every time I came tae visit after I met Susannah. Where'd this woman come from?* he thought. He was used to people in his life wanting more and feeling as though he had to do more to make more to give them more. Here was a woman not wanting anything from him.

"I hope you know those things don't impress me. What impresses me is kindness, love, thoughtfulness, understanding, and—"

And doesn't Todd give you that? she heard her conscience say.

"Oh, God! I'm such a hypocrite!" she said and stood. It was her turn to pace and ball up her fists while David sat watching. "Here I am telling you all the things I value in a person, and I'm nothing like that myself! I have a husband at home who's given me all the things I've listed, and I'm down here doing what?" She was finding it hard to breathe suddenly. "Making believe that I could have your life? Pretending that what you have and who you are is what I truly want, instead of the stability of what I already have." As soon as the words left her mouth, she wanted to take them back.

"What I have and who I am?" he said, wounded, as though she'd slapped him in the face.

"I—I didn't mean it like that," she said, trying to figure out a way to explain herself.

David felt stung. *"… what you have and who you are …"* he heard again in his mind.

"I only meant … I mean … I'm not someone who was made for the rich and famous lifestyle, that's all. I didn't mean who you are as a person. I meant the fame your name has acquired." She sat on the floor in front of the couch, hugging one leg, and laid her head on her kneecap, trying to figure out what she wanted to say.

"What are we doing, David? I hate myself for forgetting Todd, but when I'm with you, you're everything. I don't want to think about anyone or be with anyone but you. My mind, my heart, my very soul, is being torn to shreds and beaten black and blue. One minute, I'm in the clouds, being with you, this incredible, wonderful man, but then I'm drowning at the bottom of the ocean, knowing I'm essentially killing my husband and yet not willing to give you up," she said miserably. "I'm so selfish."

David had been quite upset by what she'd said, but as he listened, he knew she was right. The only difference was that he was fully willing to let Susannah go, whereas she wouldn't be able to do that with Todd. "Erin?" he said after a long time.

"Yes?" she said, leaning her head against his knee.

"Maybe we need tae look at things a bit differently," he said. She looked up, waiting for him to continue. "We're behavin' as though we won't see each other again after Sunday, but we will, won't we? I mean, aye, ye'll have tae go home to Todd, and I'll have tae go back to London, but it's not the end of us, is et?"

"No, but—"

"Why does et have tae be black or white—yers or mine? We have the opportunity tae have, I reckon you could say, the best of both worlds, right? Who says yeh have tae love me exclusively?"

What are yeh sayin'? That's no' how you feel! Where are yeh going with this? Haud yer wheesht, yeh eejit!

His mind was trying to get his mouth to shut up, but it didn't work. He just *had* to come up with *something* or he was going to fall apart.

"What are you saying?"

"Well, I've not stopped tae think about it, but et seems to me ye're just gonna have tae learn to be in love with two men." The room was silent.

Erin didn't know when he was going to add the punch line. "I—"

"Wait, hear me out." He stood and began pacing, then he stopped and knelt in front of her, taking her hands in his. *Don't push her!* "Tell me first—" he said, looking anxious and afraid.

She could feel his hands shaking. "David, calm down," she said as she saw his face grow red.

He waved his hand, dismissing the thought of calming down, and continued. "Do yeh … I mean, on Friday night, yeh said … yeh might be fallin' in love with me."

Her face burned, remembering her foolish confession. "David, I—" she began, but he waved his hand again.

"A'right, fine, but do yeh … want tae love me? Do yeh think et would be nice tae fall in love with me?" he asked, praying she'd say yes.

Erin held her breath; she could hear a heavy truck on the street outside and thought she could even smell its exhaust. There was a piece of lint on the shoulder of his shirt, and she wanted to pick it off. She wasn't sure where he was headed, but it was getting very real. "Yes, of course, I do. What are you—" she began, and he leaned in, putting his hand on her cheek.

He could smell her scent and felt the tiny soft hairs on her face. "I want, with all ma heart, tae fall in love with yeh, Erin," he said, his chin quivering slightly. "I selfishly want you tae love me as well, but I can't ask yeh tae do that." He kissed her lightly and stood, pacing again. "You love yer husband, and yeh should. I can't ask yeh tae stop just because yeh also love—want tae love me.

"I can't have yeh for my own now, and maybe not ever, but yeh don't have tae choose, do you? You love him for the reasons yeh do, and yeh love—want tae love me as well, right? Is et impossible they should overlap; happen at the same time? Why should one of us be the one yeh want and the other cast aside?"

"Cast aside? What do you mean, I never said—"

"Making believe that I could have your life? Pretending that what you have and who you are is what I truly want," he quoted.

"Oh, yeah, but I didn't mean ... I mean ... this is going so fast. I didn't expect to feel so much for my match, you know? We're going to have to figure things out as we go, David."

"Aye," he said, feeling wretched. He sat on the floor next to her and laid his head on her shoulder. "Erin?" She looked at him. "Do yeh think if Todd knew how we feel about each other, he'd truly stop yeh from havin' treatments?" He took her hand, absent-mindedly rubbing her fingernails.

You dinnae want tae know the answer. Why are yeh askin' her this? he thought.

"I don't know," was all she could come up with. The thought of telling Todd made her stomach drop. She didn't think she could do it. No, Todd wasn't the kind of man who could share her long-term, possibly not even short-term. Emotionless sex as a treatment was one thing, but if he knew she had feelings for her match, it would be bad. "David, why don't we slow down a tiny bit?"

What are you saying? Shut up! Don't tell him that, are you crazy? her mind was screaming at her.

"I mean, we've known each other for what, two and a half days, and I leave for home tomorrow. Oh, shit, I leave tomorrow," she said and wanted to cry. It was all gone; their time was up. *No wonder he's freaking out!*

"What I'm trying to say is you don't know the real me. I have lots of flaws and annoying habits. I whine a lot!" She smiled at him, trying to get him to relax. "Anyway, to quote my favorite Scottish time-traveler, 'We cannae guess the future, all we can doo is work at makin' et the best we can with what we've been given,' right? It suddenly dawned on her that he was afraid; of what, she wasn't sure. "What are you afraid of?" she asked bluntly.

He raised his head, ready to deny any fear at all, then, realizing she'd caught him out, he decided to lay it on the line. "Of losin' you. Of losin' what we have here, now. I'm afraid ye'll go home to the man who's nursed yeh through this horrible disease for—"

"Over fifteen years. Since before we were married."

"That long? Oh, God. That ye'll remember how much yeh love him and … forget about … me," he said and hung his head.

"Forget about—"

"Yeh dinnae understand, Erin. I don't have this at home. I can't be me; there's no love or even friendship. More than wantin' tae fall in love with you, I want this friendship tae last, to grow. I'm sure yeh think that because of 'what I have and who I am,' I must have more friends than I could ever want, but that's no' true. Your friendship, how we get on, et's, well, et means everathin'.

"I'm terrified that when we meet again for yer next treatment, you'll be all business, and et won't be as it has been any longer. Or—perhaps they'll find a way tae administer the treatments without me bein' involved with yeh a'tall. What if yeh go home and Todd says yeh can't have treatments from me anamore? Erin, ma insides are bein' torn out by an invisible hand, and I dinnae ken how tae stop et," he said, clutching his stomach.

She had no idea he felt so strongly; she knew he had feelings for her, but she didn't realize all of that was going on inside his head. How was it possible for him to feel so much for her already? Taking his hand away from his stomach, she held it with both hands, looking him in the eyes. "No matter what happens, David Elliott, I will *never, **ever*** forget about you. You're what I think about when I go to bed and when I wake up. You're my daydreams when I'm awake and my sweet dreams while I'm asleep.

"Your friendship and affection mean everything to me too, and I'm not going to throw it away. *I'm afraid* I won't be able to hide my passionate obsession with you when I get home, and Todd will be hurt. I'm also terrified you'll look back and be embarrassed about being with someone … like me and regret it. None of us know the future of medicine, but

I can't imagine Todd would deny my treatments. He's not that kind of man, at least I don't think he is.

"He's been there, holding me while I cough and then can't pull a breath back in, the muscles in my chest clenching, trying with all their might to breathe. He's been there to revive me after I've passed out from not having any air for nearly a minute. And he's nursed me when I've been too weak after an episode to feed myself or get up to use the toilet. He's a good man who loves me, and he's not going to tell me that I'm just going to have to live with it from now on," she said, hoping she was right.

"I didn't realize yer symptoms were so bad," he whispered.

"As I told you before, they weren't when I was younger, but it got worse from there. I've been treated for asthma and COPD. I've used inhalers and had to sit in oxygen tents for hours and even days while my parents paced the floors and bit their fingernails, wondering what was wrong with me and not knowing what to do."

"They didn't ken et was the fertility drugs?"

"Not right away. I was one of the first Fertilis babies born in my state, and no one put the pieces together until I was fifteen. I think there were rumors in Europe, but the drug company didn't want to give up their cash cow, you know?"

"Yer parents must've been beside themselves when they were told. I can't imagine the guilt!"

"Yeah, it was bad. My mom cried pretty much twenty-four hours a day for weeks. My dad shut himself in his basement workshop every night after work, sitting on his stool, staring at nothing. I was angry for a long time. I mean, they wanted a baby so badly they were willing to take a stupid drug, not considering the cost of it. When I found out I couldn't have children of my own due to it, I brooded and moped because of their selfishness. Gradually I got over it and realized they only wanted what they couldn't have, and the price was high. They didn't know it would happen. If they had, they wouldn't have done it, and I wouldn't have been born, and we wouldn't be here right now."

"I'm sorry," he said and kissed her hand. "I've been so selfish. Ye're right, this is goin' so fast. Three days is fairly soon tae talk about lovin' each other isn't et?" He gave her a weak smile and sighed. "You should know, I've never spoken tae anyone this way before, not even my therapist."

"You have a therapist?" she asked, trying not to laugh or tease.

"Hmm, I've not been happy for some time, and I thought et would help tae talk to someone. I most certainly was *not* gonna tell Susannah or Martin. I'm no' one tae tell people what I'm feelin' or my thoughts. I dinnae ken how, but you bring et all out of me, makin' me trust yeh. I've never trusted, well, anaone as I do you."

"I'm glad you do. It means a lot to me, truly." Her rear end was getting numb sitting on the floor, so she stood and helped him get to his feet. He followed her as she went to the mini-fridge and poured them each a glass of Coke, then she turned and handed one of them to him. "I don't remember my departure time for tomorrow," she said glumly. "I'd better check. My paperwork is in my suitcase, so I might as well pack while I'm in there."

She took a drink, set the glass down, and walked into her bedroom, sighing as she took her suitcase out of the closet and set it on the crumpled-up bed linens. "One-twenty-eight pm departure." She read the printed sheet out loud and heard David make a groaning noise, perfectly echoing the one in her head. She opened the dresser drawers, stuffing her things into her suitcase, not caring about what it looked like. All she left out were a shirt, socks, and her last pair of clean underwear for the trip home.

Chapter Forty-Two

PRESUMPTION

A re you hungry?" David asked from the kitchenette.

"How about a pizza?" Erin proposed.

"Pizza? In New Orleans? I reckon that'll do. Any preferences?"

"No, whatever you like." She made her way to the living room and sat on the sofa while David called in their order. "Wanna watch a movie or something?" she suggested, thinking how nice it would be to cuddle on the couch together.

"A'right," he said and sat next to her. He picked up the remote, found the channel guide, and scrolled through it so quickly, she was starting to feel sick.

"Slow down, or I'll be running to the toilet to vomit!" she said.

"Et's all yours," he said and handed her the remote.

"Hmmm, I didn't think I could like you any more than I already did."

"Do yeh mind if I check my mobile whilst yeh search? I've not looked at et in quite a while, and I should tell Tina tae cancel my credit cards."

"Fine by me; is there anything you're in the mood to watch?"

"No, I'll let yeh choose."

He left the room and she scrolled through the channel guide, stopping at BBC America. The station was running a marathon of The Graham Norton Show reruns. She loved the show and selected it without bothering to read the descriptions.

The episode nearly finished, Graham was speaking to someone in the Red Chair. The man, who was wearing an ugly white cable-knit sweater, was recounting how he'd farted at his best mate's wedding, just as he was handed the microphone to give a toast. Everyone at the head table had been thoroughly disgusted, and he had photos to prove it. They showed a photograph of the wedding party's hilarious faces. Everyone on the couch laughed, and Graham let the guy walk. The show ended with the thumping bass of Graham's theme music.

Erin decided to run to the bathroom before the next show came on, so she missed the British announcer, with her RP accent reveal the list of guests on the next episode. The doorbell rang and David stepped out of his room just as Erin came back and took hold of the remote again. He paid the delivery person and then set the pizza on the coffee table. "I love Graham Norton, don't you?" she asked as he sat next to her and picked up a slice.

"So, I come to America, and am forced tae watch British programs?" he lamented.

"Well, only if it's *Graham Norton, Doctor Who, Sherlock*, or—"

"A'right, I get the idea; who's on this one?" They watched as Graham began his opening dialogue.

"No idea. I ran to the bathroom and missed the line-up," she said truthfully, then David's face appeared on the enormous screen Graham used in his teaser.

"*Houlihan's Flat?* More like Houlihan's Hunk!" Graham said.

Erin froze, and David nearly leapt off the couch. "Holy Moses!" she exclaimed.

"Ach! You knew et; yeh had to!" He looked at Erin suspiciously and tried to get the remote away from her.

"I did not! I told you, I was in the bathroom, now stop being a baby," she said, laughing. "I sang the song again for you in the shower even though it embarrassed the crap out of me. I think you should suck it up and let me see this."

"Help ma boab! A'right, but I'm warnin' yeh, it won't be any good. I'm crap on chat shows."

"Help ma what?"

David shrugged, waving his hand to dismiss it, and sat, pretending to sulk.

Graham introduced his first guest. "You know him from *Underground* and *Viking Express*, Thomas Boyd McMillan!" He greeted the young, red-headed actor and assisted him in finding a place to sit on the long red couch.

"My next guest played two queens in middle age! Olivia Colman!"

"Oh, I love her!" Erin said.

"Aye, she's fantastic! We did a film together. That's why we're on at the same time."

"Oh, that's right! I can't wait to see it! You know Olivia Colman! That's so awesome!" she said, and David smiled.

"My next guest is known for his plucky know-how and scant attire in *Future Explorations*; please welcome David Elliott!"

Had Erin been watching alone a week earlier, she would've whooped and fallen back on her couch. But, since she was actually with the man, she bit her lip, leaned closer to him, and held his hand. He walked onto the stage, wearing a casual suit and tie. His hair was immaculate, and his smile, bewitching.

"This is exciting! You look so handsome!"

"Susannah hates that suit; she thinks it's tired and shabby."

"She's blind!" Erin said passionately, which made him smile and kiss the top of her head. "Is that couch as uncomfortable as it looks?"

"Worse!"

She noticed David had been called last, which, at least on that show, usually denoted he was the most prominent of those on the couch. She giggled when Graham showed pictures of all the guests in their early teens. David's photo showed he was already on his way to becoming the attractive man he'd turned out to be. *Not all that different from his eldest son, Peter, wasn't it?* she thought, trying to remember the name on the back of the photo she'd seen in the small album.

Olivia Colman was brilliant and funny as usual, and Thomas Boyd McMillan was hilarious. His quick humor and slight inebriation kept everyone on their toes and laughing. At one point, Graham suggested David had been chosen for the shortlist to play 007, James Bond. "Is it true?" he asked bluntly, in the flirtatious way Graham was known for.

Erin snapped her head to the side and stared at him, open-mouthed.

David pointed to the screen. "I cannot confirm or deny any of your information," was what came out of his mouth as he sat looking smug, but his smile seemed quite telling.

Turning her head, Erin stared at him once more. "David! Are you? Oh, you'd be fabulous as James Bond, except," she said and lowered her head a bit, looking back at the television screen.

"Except?" He put his hand on her hair and could smell her lovely scent again.

"Except a lot of things. First, you'd be gone for a long time shooting for a movie like that, wouldn't you?"

"Well, yes, but—"

"And second, well, if you get recognized now, you'll need a full-time bodyguard after a role like that!"

And there won't be any room for you in his life either. Not to mention the nearly naked, perfect, sexy women in it, she thought, starting to feel miserable.

Graham was talking to Thomas Boyd McMillan about his upcoming role, and Erin was feeling less than attractive again. She started to worry about treatments if he was off on publicity tours and interviews. *But how could he pass up such an opportunity? Erin, stay calm, this is huge, and you can't ruin it for him. You have to suck it up.*

David could sense the mechanisms moving in her head. The dial was turning, and the tumblers were falling into place, unlocking something in her mind. He reached over and grabbed the remote, hitting mute on the musical guest, who looked to be twelve and wearing practically nothing.

"I can't fathom what's going on in that fascinatingly complex head of yours, but I didn't say I was on a list or that I'd take et if I were. Frankly, I hadn't heard anathin' about et, and as of the last time I spoke with her, neither had my agent, so dinnae get excited, love. I reckon Graham was trying tae cause a stir, that's all."

Erin nodded, feeling torn about the whole thing as Graham was wrapping up with the red chair. The first to sit was a woman dressed like a slutty version of one of David's sidekicks from *Future Explorations*. Graham offered to let David control the lever, which made the chair tip backward, and he did it without hesitation.

"No' my kind of thing," he told her.

The next person was a man with a kilt and tam-o'-shanter, but Erin wasn't interested anymore. She was tired and wanted to crawl under the soft, sweet-smelling sheets of David's bed and spoon with him until they fell asleep. She yawned so hard her eyes watered, which caused a chain reaction.

He stood and took Erin's hands to help her up, saying in his best Victorian Queen's English, "To bed with us, I say."

She smiled, loving his charming sense of humor. "But I'm not tired, nurse!" she objected playfully.

"Now, listen here! There's a bed in that room over there, with our names on it, see, and we're gonna use it, no ifs, ands, or buts!" he said in a James Cagney-esque, 1930s gangster voice that cracked her up.

They leaned on each other as they walked the short distance through his door and got undressed. There was no flinging clothes around in the throes of passion that time, just taking their clothes off and getting into bed. David snuggled up behind Erin and held her, crossing his arm over her chest as she leaned into his embrace and sighed a nice comfortable sigh. The next day would be busy, but just then, they could relax and enjoy each other's touch. He kissed her shoulder, and she held his hand until they both fell asleep.

Chapter Forty-Three

UNEXPECTED TURN OF EVENTS

David and Erin woke in the morning to the bedside phone ringing again. He answered, fumbling, and nearly dropping the handset. "Bollocks," he swore as he recovered it. "This is—David," he said into the receiver. He heard breathing and then a sigh.

"I'm sorry to wake you up, but I need to speak to Erin again."

David recognized the voice as Todd's, albeit much calmer than the last time he rang. "Certainly, I'll get her." Once again, they made the pretense of him going to find her, but this time she took the phone around the corner by the couch, and he went back into his room.

It was early; the living room was dark, and she could still hear the faintest sound of the nighttime insects outside. "Todd? What is it? Is something wrong? You know I'm coming home to—"

"Have you seen the news, honey?" Todd cut her off.

"No, I just woke up. What is it?"

"There was a shooting at the airport about twenty minutes ago. I was afraid you might be there. I couldn't remember what time your flight left and—"

"Oh, no! At this airport?" she said stupidly.

Of course it's at this airport, you idiot! Why else would he be calling you this early, to tell you there was a shooting at JFK or Amsterdam?

David heard the concern in her voice and came out to see what was wrong. "What is et?" he asked her as he walked, naked, to the kitchenette and went about brewing coffee for them in the small pot provided in the suite.

"There was a shooting at the airport about twenty minutes ago," she replied.

"Is he in your room, Erin?" Todd was saying into the phone.

"No, Todd, I'm on the couch. Hold on a minute," she said while she searched for the remote; she found it and turned on the TV.

The BBC America newscasters were already covering the story with live footage. A ticker ran at the bottom of the screen, relaying the story as well as the latest information. It read, "All flights from Louis Armstrong New Orleans airport have been canceled, and there is no further information as to when they will resume. Please stay tuned to BBC America for all the latest news …"

"Ma Losh!" David said, stunned.

"Erin?" came Todd's voice from the telephone handset.

"Oh, Todd, I'm sorry, we just turned on the news and—"

"Erin, listen, can I speak to David?"

Her heart jumped up into her throat. "What? Did you just ask to—"

"Honey, please, while I still have the resolve."

David looked up at her, hearing her confused tone, and mouthed, 'What?'

Erin looked at the headset and then up at David with her eyebrows raised. "He wants to speak to *you*," she said, not believing what she was saying.

David reached out and took the receiver from her. He looked like he was dreading it as much as Todd must have been. "Ah, this is ... David," he said with trepidation. He didn't know what was going to happen next, a lightning bolt, perhaps?

"Um, I need to ask you to do something for me," Todd said, tentatively.

"All right, what can I do?" *What on earth could I do for him?* He watched Erin, also naked, get up and prepare two cups of coffee, bringing them back to the sofa with her.

"Would you be willing to allow Erin to stay with you, only until things are better organized at the airport and until other arrangements can be made? Do you have a room for her for that long? If not, I can cover—"

David breathed a long, quiet sigh of relief. "Ah, Todd," he interrupted, "That won't be necessary. The suite is booked for a few more days. The cost is already covered, so don't worry about that." He then remembered that Todd wasn't aware of who he was, except his name was David.

"Oh, thank you, that's a load off my mind. I was so worried about her," he said casually and then seemed to remember who he was speaking with. An awkward silence fell between the two men.

"Ah, was there anything else, then?" David finally asked. *Please say no.* He wanted to get off the phone with the man. Todd March wasn't someone he wanted to be overly friendly with.

"No, that's all. Thank you again."

"My pleasure," David replied out of habit and then regretted it.

Fuck! Sure, et's my pleasure tae be fuckin' yer wife for a few more days whilst you sit at home and worry.

He handed the phone back to Erin and went to get himself dressed. He was feeling slightly light-headed and wanted to get Todd's pleasant, concerned voice out of his ears.

"Todd!" Erin exclaimed into the phone, "It's only a saying … No, I'm sure he didn't mean it that way at all … Well, it's not as though he was going to kick me out … Yes, I'm glad you did … Yes, it's fine … No, he's a good man … Yes … Yes … I'll stay here until we can work something out … I'll call you if I get any news, okay? I love you too, bye." She put the handset down and sighed.

The television was on mute, but the ticker read, "All forms of transportation into and out of the airport are now restricted … this includes private vehicles, shuttles, busses, and car hires until further notice." Erin stood; she felt her chest tighten, and it was hard to breathe. It would've scared her a month ago, but she was getting treatments. *Surely, I won't have an episode now.* She walked back into the bedroom where David was pulling on his jeans, her emotions all over

281

the place. She was glad she hadn't been at the airport, worried about Todd, happy to be safe with David, and thrilled to be able to have more time with him. She tried not to think about how she'd get home or why her chest felt tight. "I'll be in my room getting dressed," she said, holding her fist over her sternum and taking deep breaths.

David was facing away from the door and didn't see her walk in. He turned to her, but she wasn't there. "Wait," he said as she walked away. She stopped, seeming impatient. He stood next to her, wondering what he should say. There was something wrong, but he thought maybe he didn't want to know what it was.

She was lookin' forward tae goin' home, yeh dolt! She misses her husband, he thought miserably, as he looked down at her guarded face.

"Are yeh a'right?"

She looked up at him, not knowing how to express her potpourri of emotions. "I'm fine, just stressed," she said. The sun was now coming up, turning the natural light in the living room from grey shadows to whispery beams shining through the louvers on the window shutters. All the morning birds were awake and making their voices heard. She could see the concern on his face, so she relaxed and laid her head on his chest.

"We could've been there, David! What if it had happened later today?" She shuddered, thankful he was there, and she could hold him. "I read on the ticker that all forms of transportation into and out of the airport have been restricted. How are we going to get home?"

"I'm no' going to worry about et right now, and neither should you. We're safe, and together, that's all that matters." They heard his mobile phone begin to ring from his bedroom. "That'll be ma agent, makin' sure I'm a'right. I should take it."

Erin nodded and followed as he walked into his room to answer the call. "This is David … Yes, I know, I'm fine … No, I wasn't there … Ah yes … I'm not sure how I'll be getting back, but I'll think of something … Yes, alright, you too." He set his phone back on the nightstand and saw Erin standing at the door.

"Now what?" she asked as she stepped into the room and sat on the edge of the bed. She was torn. Her chest still felt tight, so she wanted to be at home in case she did have an episode, but she also wanted to stay there with David for as long as possible.

"Hmm, let me think. I'm sure we could find somethin' tae occupy us," he said with a mischievous grin. He stood in front of her, eyeing her up like a starving person would a filet mignon.

"You think so?" She smiled and felt that tingle of electricity once more between them. Since she was already naked, she didn't have much to do to be ready to make love to him.

He'd only gotten into his jeans before she'd interrupted him, so he took them off and stood naked in front of her. Pushing her gently back onto the bed, he cupped her breast in his hand and took it into his mouth. He loved the feel of the soft skin around the hardness of her nipples. She arched her back as he moved his way up to her neck, kissing her as he went, but then he stopped.

"What is it?" she asked and looked at him quizzically.

He smiled at her, having seen the damage he'd done to her fair skin when they'd made love the day before. A dozen or so red marks peppered her neck and chest. "Et's nothin'. I gave you a hickey yesterday. I'll show yeh later." He hoped that would be enough to appease her curiosity for the moment.

His chest hair felt like a carpet, soft and warm on her skin, and he smelled delicious. He nibbled on her earlobe, his breath hot and urgent on her neck. She raised her knee, putting her foot into his waiting hand, giving her the leverage to lift herself higher onto the bed. He pressed himself against her, and she inhaled as she heard him let out a moan. He surprised her by retreating and taking a knee.

Starting at the inside of her calves, he began moving upward, kissing and nuzzling, kissing and nuzzling, until he reached the place he wanted to be, between her legs. "Oh," she cried out, evidently wanting him to be there, as well. He took his time, not in a hurry. Her breathing was deep and gasping as he touched her with his tongue, manipulating her folds. Then, he entered her with his fingers and pulled himself up so that they were face to face. He kissed her while she writhed with pleasure. She moaned as his fingers thrust into her deeply, and soon he no longer wanted it to be his fingers inside of her. He extracted them and lay on top of her, entering her once again.

She gasped and let out a strange cough. Her eyes widened with fear. She tried to sit up, but he was pinning her down with his body, so he moved off her as she clutched at her throat.

Chapter Forty-Four

EPISODE TWO

*O*h, God! NO! Not here, not now! Please, help me! Erin's mind was reeling. She wished she'd warned David or told him what to do in case it happened while they were together, but she'd been foolish and tried to ignore it.

"What's wrong?" David breathed.

She couldn't talk as she continued coughing and got up onto her knees, holding him for dear life.

"Oh, God, Erin, what should I do?" Her face was turning red as her body exhaled in hoarse coughs but didn't pull any air back in to replace it. He realized it must have already been fifteen or twenty seconds since she'd drawn a breath, and he was terrified. *What should I do? What did she say last night?* He racked his brain, trying to remember what she'd said Todd had done for her.

"... He's been there, holding me while I cough and then can't pull a breath back in; the muscles in my chest clenching, trying with all their might to breathe ..." He was already doing

that. "Oh God," he said as he felt her chest heaving and her muscles working to try to bring the air back in. *What else?*

"*… He's been there to revive me after I've passed out from not having any air for nearly a minute …*" It had already been nearly a minute, and she was growing weak. He could feel it as she lay against him, and her grip on him loosened, gradually.

"*… And he's nursed me when I've been too weak after an episode to feed myself or get up to use the toilet …*"

"Please breathe, Erin, please! Please, God, dinnae let her die!" he prayed. "Erin, please stay with me!" Suddenly she collapsed like a flag that had abruptly lost its wind. "Erin! Yeh said he revived yeh; how'd he do that?" He put his head on her chest and listened for breathing. Nothing. Her face had been dark red when she passed out, and because she still wasn't getting any oxygen, it was starting to appear purplish-blue. Trying not to panic, he repeatedly said her name, watching her muscles quake as they continued to spasm.

The only thing he could think to do was mouth-to-mouth resuscitation and put his ear on her chest to listen for her heartbeat and to hear if there was any air movement. Unfortunately, his heart was pounding so loudly in his ears that he couldn't tell if hers was beating or not.

Finally, he saw her pulse on her neck, and relief washed over him. With his hand holding her forehead, he gently lifted her neck to open the airway and took a shaky breath. He pinched her nose shut, making sure his mouth was sealed over hers, and gently breathed out, hoping her chest would expand as air filled her lungs. At first, nothing happened, but when he tried again, her chest expanded. He had to move away quickly as she gasped and coughed, finally able to breathe again. He sat against the headboard to collect himself and then went back to her. She was conscious and drenched with sweat.

"I'm sorry, Todd, did I wet myself again?" she said anxiously.

"No, it's—"

"Please help me to bed," she said.

He helped move her to the dry side of the mattress and kissed her forehead, tasting her salty perspiration. She hadn't wet herself, but one side of the bed was soaked with the sweat of her exertion.

"Oh, honey, thank you! You're so good to me," she said sweetly.

"Erin, I'm not—"

"I love you so much. You're my favorite." She smiled at him blindly and fell asleep.

David's heart was racing; she'd looked right at him but didn't know him. He paced the room, still feeling as though he should be doing something. He'd just had a tiny glimpse into her and her husband's life together. *This is what they deal with every, what—month? But how?* The gravity of providing treatments for her hit him hard, right in the center of his chest. It made him stagger backward and then sit on the floor against the wall. For him, it had been making love, having fun, and feeling like a young man again, but for her and Todd, it was lifesaving.

Chapter Forty-Five

THANK TODD

David wasn't sure what to do; he thought Todd would want to know, but Erin's phone had been stolen. Wait, he thought, and stood, walking through the cottage to her bedroom. He upended the purse she'd been using since the attack onto the dresser, hoping to find an address book or something with their phone number on it.

Nothing.

"Fuckin' think!" he said out loud. *Where do they live? Wisconsin, but where in Wisconsin? Dammit! Oh wait, she said et. "I live in Green Bay, Wisconsin …" I'll try the telephone directory.* He went back to his room for his mobile and watched her sleeping, so peaceful and calm after the hurricane that had ripped through her body. Fifteen minutes earlier, she'd been enjoying his attention, and now she lay resting, exhausted after something not meant to happen anymore.

He searched 'Todd and Erin March in Green Bay, Wisconsin.' There was no listing, so he broadened it to 'March'. There were over two hundred Marches, and most of them had unlisted numbers, but as he scrolled, he saw it, 'T & E March 1324 Whistler's Way, GB.' The last thing he wanted to do was call Erin's husband. He held his mobile in his hand as he paced the floor at the end of the bed. There wasn't anything else he could do; he had to call. If something had happened to him, he'd want Erin to call Susannah, wouldn't he? *Not that she'd care overly much.*

Oh, shut it, yeh bampot, just call him!

He realized he didn't have any clothes on, and couldn't call the man whilst naked, so he started to get dressed. He had just managed to get his underwear on when Erin made a noise in her sleep, so he rushed to her side. She was only dreaming, so he touched the link to call their number. As it connected, he heard it ring; not the short double taps like they had at home, these were long and drawn out. On the fourth ring, he heard someone pick up.

"Hello?" the familiar male voice said.

"Ah, hello. This is—"

"Oh, God, what happened? Is Erin okay?" Todd asked.

David supposed he would know that the only reason he'd call their house would be if something serious had happened. "She's a'right now, I think. She's had an episode, and as far as I can tell from what she'd told me, et was a bad one," he said, reverting back to his Scottish accent with the stress. He could hear Todd breathing and the television playing in the background. It sounded like an old sitcom with canned laughter.

"What happened?" Todd asked, now able to relax.

"One minute she was fine, and the next, she began tae cough …" David told him all the pertinent things about the episode while Todd listened and sighed.

"There's nothing you can do now except take care of her. Give her water and food and help her get to the bathroom if she has the strength to stand. How long did it last this time?"

"I wasn't lookin' at the clock, but et seemed an eternity. I'm sure et was nearly a minute before she passed out and a long time again until she came to. Then, when she started talkin' … she thought … I was you, even though she was lookin' right at me. She kept apologizing and said … she loves you and that you're her favorite."

"Thank you for telling me that."

"But I dinnae understand; aren't these treatments supposed tae keep her from goin' through this?"

Todd let out a groan that only a mortified husband could make at hearing details of his wife's affair. *That means they've already … done it,* **and** *he* *said treatments, plural,* Todd thought, having one of his worst nightmares reveal itself like an arrow in his heart, *Thunk*; one in his guts, *Oomph*; and finally, *Gasp*, one in his mind. That one hit the hardest and sunk in the deepest.

"Oh, fuck! I'm so sorry! That didn't come out verra well. I just meant, why is she still havin' attacks?"

"I don't know," was all Todd could say. He wanted to vomit and kill the man, to reach his hand right through the handset and strangle him to death. "I'll call her doctor and see what he says. Then I'll give him the number Erin gave me to call if he needs to talk to you."

"Aye, that would—"

"I—I can't talk to you anymore. I have to go," Todd said and hung up the phone.

David's heart sank.

Why'd yeh have to say et that way?

Chapter Forty-Six

HOUSEKEEPING

David knew housekeeping would be coming eventually, and the bed linens would need to be changed, so he went out to the kitchenette and brought a glass of water to Erin. He hoped she'd be able to get to her room with his help, so he woke her by smoothing her hair and kissing her forehead. "Erin, I've some water for yeh. Can you sit up for me?"

She frowned and grimaced. "I'll try." She attempted to roll herself up but didn't have the strength. "I can't, honey, I'm sorry," she said and laid her head back down on the pillow.

"I need tae move yeh to your room, love; can we do that together?" he asked, knowing he wouldn't be able to carry her all the way across the cottage by himself.

"What? Move me to my room? I don't understand. Please, honey, let me sleep."

He was trying not to be upset about her thinking he was Todd, but it was difficult. She was too weak to help him move her, so he would have to wait for the cleaning help. He hoped they might have an idea about what to do, though he realized she was naked and didn't want anyone seeing her that way.

In her room, he saw her small black suitcase lying on the bed, ready for her to go to the airport. Feeling like he was trespassing, he unzipped it. When he saw the state of the clothes she'd thrown into it, he laughed softly. *How's that for organization?* Rummaging through her clothing, he found her nightdress, then the pile of things she'd laid out to wear that day caught his eye. He grabbed the underwear, *that'll have tae do, for now,* he thought and hoped it would be a woman housekeeper.

When he returned to his room, he lifted the top sheet off her and slipped her feet through the leg holes in her underwear. It was remarkable how childlike she was. It reminded him of the few times his children had to be carried up to their rooms after falling asleep in the car. They would sit up, half-awake and confused, asking where they were. He would shush them gently and help them on with their nightclothes; he'd enjoyed being a parent then.

He managed to get her nightdress on her only moments before housekeeping knocked on the door and then entered the cottage. He went out to the living room and saw that it was a middle-aged woman. She hadn't expected him to be there, so she was startled when he walked out of his bedroom. "Hi—hello. I have a situation here and was hoping to get your help," he said.

She took a step back and glanced at his legs, only faltering for a moment, then she looked up at his face. "You need help with what, sir?" she asked, looking at his legs once more.

She looked up again at once, and he frowned at her. "Well," he said, and she did it again. *What's wrong with her?* he thought. "What are yeh lookin' at?"

"I'm sorry, sir, but—" She looked again and pointed that time.

He looked down and realized that in all his efforts to get Erin clothed, he'd forgotten about himself. After he'd thrown on his underwear, he'd gotten distracted, so that's all he was wearing. "Shit! Sorry," he said and turned, walking back into the bedroom. He put on his jeans and came back out, explaining that Erin had a medical condition. "I need yer help moving her to the other bed, so you'll be able to change the linens."

The woman followed him into the bedroom cautiously. She looked at Erin and then at him, obviously wondering what he was doing with her. "She's not dead, right?" she asked, timidly.

"What? No, I mean yes, she's not dead. She's had an episode of her disease and is verra weak."

Erin heard the commotion around her and woke up. "Todd? Who are you talking to? Who's here? Please, honey, I don't want to see anyone. Tell them I'll be fine and send them away."

"I know who you are, sir, and your name ain't Todd. I think I'd better call someone."

"A'right now, you dinnae need to call anaone," he said, holding up his hands in a strange combination of 'I surrender' and jazz hands. "This woman has the Fertilis Defect, and she's here tae have a treatment. Her husband's name is Todd, she

295

thinks I'm him, and yes, he knows we're together. As I said, she's had a verra bad episode, and I need help. Do yeh think between the two of us, we can move her?" Just then, the land-line phone rang. "Bollocks— A'right, please, just do whatever you'd otherwise do, and we can figure et out later. I must take this call.

Chapter Forty-Seven

DR. NAN'S HOUSE CALL

David walked into Erin's room and answered the phone. "This is David."

"Hello, Mr. Elliott? This is Doctor Surya Nanavala. I have been treating Erin; how is she?"

"Ach, Doctor! Thank yeh for callin', she's restin' now. Honestly, I dinnae ken how she's doin'. She thinks I'm her husband and is callin' me Todd. I can understand that; the thing troubling me is I'm no' sure she can see, at least no' clearly."

"Okay, slow down. What makes you believe she cannot see clearly?"

"I was standin' beside her, speakin' with the housekeeper, and et seemed as though she couldn't see her or me. Is that normal?" David knew he sounded panicked and couldn't tame his Scottish accent, but he didn't care.

"Honestly, there is no normal, David, but I can tell you it is not *usual* for Erin. How long did the episode last?"

"I dinnae ken. Et seemed as if she wasn't breathing for at least a minute. Then, she passed out and still wasn't breathing.

I didn't ken what tae do, so I performed mouth-to-mouth on her, verra gently. On the first try, nothing happened, but on the second, she gasped and was able tae breathe again."

"Okay, please tell me exactly what happened before the episode."

David wasn't about to discuss his romantic escapades in front of the housekeeper, and he didn't know where she might be. "Can yeh hold the line for one moment?"

"Of course," Dr. Nan said.

David hit the hold button on the telephone and searched the cottage. When he walked into his room, he saw that the bed had been remade with clean, dry linens, and Erin looked as though she hadn't been touched. He kissed her on the cheek, making sure she was okay, then heard the housekeeper in his bathroom, so he stepped up to the doorway. "How'd you manage—" he began to ask, and she smiled.

"I managed. Are you finished in the other bedroom? I can clean it now if you'd like."

"No, can you do et tomorrow, please?"

"Whatever you want, sir, I'll leave extra towels. If you need anything, call the butler," she said, then gathered her things, and left.

He sat on the couch and picked up the handset. "Doctor, are yeh still there?" David asked.

"Yes, go ahead."

"First, is everathin' I tell yeh confidential? I can't have any of this leaked to the media or my wife, or, well, Todd."

"I will not tell anyone. I may need to use the data for research, but all names and situations will be kept strictly confidential," Dr. Nanavala said.

David told him what had happened, the fooling around, and everything. Then, he braced himself for the chiding he figured would come next.

"Hmm, amazing, completely astonishing!"

"Doctor?" David hadn't expected him to come back with that reaction.

"This seems to be happening with most of the matched couples," Dr. Nan said, a little too excitedly.

David thought he sounded amused and was fighting the urge to get angry. *Is this professional behavior in America?* "I'm no' sure I like yer tone. This is serious, and yer makin' it out tae be—"

"No, wait, I am sorry. I was not referring to the episode."

"Doctor, please, is she gonna be a'right?"

Dr. Nanavala sighed. "I am sorry, David, yes, she will be okay. Erin and I have been dealing with the disease for a long time, but it is new to you. I need to remember that. What she needs is rest and someone who cares to look after her. "As for not being able to see, that could be temporary. The blood vessels have been strained. She has also been deprived of oxygen for over a minute. Hopefully, once she rests, it will return. May I ask you some more questions for research purposes?"

"If it will help." David was unprepared for what would come next.

"Let me ask you, David, how long has Erin been in your company?"

"She's been here since Thursday afternoon, so roughly three days," David said.

"And how many times, er, treatments have you performed in that time?"

David didn't want to tell him but figured it was important to be truthful. "Well, every day, though we didn't get that far today. Oh, and … uh … twice yesterday, as well as the day before. I haven't been countin', Doctor." He was utterly embarrassed.

"Amazing! You had sex on the first day she was there?" the doctor said.

David took a deep breath, aggravated at the man's astonishment and feeling like he was under a microscope. "Is there a point ye're tryin' tae make?"

"Please bear with me, and then I will explain. When you first learned that you had a match, were you worried about it and what you would be required to do with her?"

"Ah, honestly, I was terrified."

"That is normal. When you met Erin, what happened? Was there chemistry, maybe even at first sight?"

"Well, yes. I fancied her at once, and aye, we were attracted teh each other within moments of meeting," David answered, smiling at the memory.

"Good. Do you now find it difficult to keep away from each other?"

"Truthfully, we can't keep our bloody hands off each other, but what's that have tae do with Erin right now?"

"Nothing, exactly, though it seems that nearly every matched couple is experiencing the same phenomenon as you and Erin. They are magnetized to each other and cannot get enough. It is truly astonishing!"

"But why is she still havin' episodes after the treatments? Are we a false match? I read about that in a pamphlet. Is et no' workin' for her?" David asked.

"I do not believe that is the case for you. Couples who are not a good match seem to be the only ones who do not have the chemistry you and Erin share. Her body needs to process the treatments, and that takes time. I know her last episode was over three weeks ago, so she was nearing her next one anyway. It is slightly early, but that can happen, especially in a stressful situation. Has she seemed out of breath at any time over the last few days?"

"Only when we're … ah—Wait, she did have several moments where she seemed winded. She didn't say anathin' about havin' symptoms, though."

"I imagine she was having lead-ups and either did not associate them with the disease or was hoping the treatments would keep her from having an episode. Has she been under any extraordinary stress, other than the obvious?"

"Aye, she has. We were mugged on Friday night."

"Oh, my! Was she hurt?"

"Erin was assaulted by one of the men, but no' physically hurt. Then Todd rang her yesterday mornin'. She had tae talk him down from a panic attack, and have yeh heard about the shooting at the airport?"

"Yes, how frightening."

"Erin was meant tae fly home today."

301

"It sounds as though she has had enough stress to last for a few years! I am not surprised it was a bad one this time."

"Aye," David said, still feeling guilty about the mugging. "Doctor, how long should she remain here before she's able tae fly? I wouldn't want her sent home too soon." He selfishly wanted him to say a good month or two, so she wouldn't have to go back home to Todd so soon.

"That depends on how quickly she recovers. In the past, it was usual for her to stay in bed for several days after a bad episode. With the treatments, she may recover faster. Hopefully, she will be much better tonight and even stronger tomorrow. Has she had any water after coming to?"

"I brought her some, but she couldn't sit up and didn't seem interested."

"Try to get her to drink fluids. Also, has she used the toilet today?"

"Ah, not that I'm aware of. She's been asleep the whole time, except for short moments of consciousness."

"You should try to get her to the bathroom if possible. It may not be romantic, but she will thank you when she does not wake up in her own waste, trust me."

David was feeling much more at ease after speaking with the doctor. "Is there anathin' else I can do for her? Oh, and should I correct her when she calls me Todd?"

"What you can do is hold her hand, or better yet, lay next to her and hold her. Human contact is good for healing of all kinds. Make sure she stays relatively hydrated and be patient. I would say she should not fly before Tuesday but let her decide. As far as not knowing who you are, you can try to correct her, but she will either be confused and ignore you or confused and frightened. Let her reload. She will remember you, I am sure of it."

"Okay, thank you. Ah, I've an unrelated question, if yeh don't mind," David said.

"Of course," Dr. Nan said.

"Why wasn't she told whom she'd be meeting? I find that grossly unfair; after all, I was given her name."

"Yes, it was unfair, and it is entirely my fault. I was distracted when she came in for the final paperwork, and I missed that bit of information. I will apologize to her when I see her."

"A'right."

"One more thing, David."

"Aye?"

"I do not wish to worry you, but you should be aware that there can be short and long-term effects from lack of oxygen. I do hope the blindness goes away, but she may have other problems, perhaps with coordination or speech. For instance, finding the right word or stuttering, which would be frustrating for her.

"Additionally, it can affect how she deals with stressful issues and events. Something that may seem minor to anyone else may appear enormous to her. Also, she may tend to overreact or be impassive. These things may not happen at all; they may come and go or have triggers that might set her off without warning into a panic or euphoria. They may be temporary or permanent, as well, so be patient and try to see things outside of the box for her. Please consider this as she wakes and you both move forward."

"Aye, I reckon that makes sense. I'll remember et, thank you."

"Do not lose heart; she needs you. Now, I must return to my practice. If you need help, call 911, or call me, my number should be in Erin's phone as an emergency contact."

"Her purse and mobile were stolen in the attack. I have ma mobile though, so I'll save the number if ye'll give et to me?"

"Of course. She is a strong woman, David, she will pull through," Dr. Nanavala said and gave him the information he needed.

Chapter Forty-Eight

SIGNIFICANT OTHERS

David walked into his bedroom and woke Erin, asking if she needed anything. She took his hand with effort and smiled, keeping her eyes closed. "No, I don't think so, honey, ask me again in a few hours," she said, sounding exhausted.

"Are you beginning to feel better?" he asked, but all she did was mumble something he couldn't understand, so he kissed her cheek and smoothed her hair with his hand.

It was nearly 11 am, and since he hadn't eaten breakfast, he was hungry. He didn't want to leave the cottage, so he called the butler, and in about thirty minutes, a meal was delivered to his door. He sat in the living room and watched the continuing news about the shooting while eating his lunch, although he didn't learn anything more. Then, he watched an episode of *Seinfeld* and the last half of *Forrest Gump*.

As he turned off the television, he heard a loud thump come from his bedroom. He launched himself to the door to find Erin sitting on the floor, back against the side of the bed, with a confused look on her face. He knelt beside her, but when she saw his face, she acted scared, as though she didn't remember him.

"Who are you? Wait—what happened?" She shook her head and frowned. "My head is pounding." She looked at him and said, "David?"

"Yes, Erin, et's me. What happened? Why are yeh on the floor?" Her eyes were wide, with the same look of amazement, mixed with bewilderment she'd had when seeing him for the first time. She was looking at a famous person, not at him. "Don't you remember me?"

"David Elliott is in my room? Holy Moses! Now I'm hallucinating. Todd? Todd!" she called out.

He was absolutely gutted. "Let me help you; do yeh need the loo?"

"The loo? Where's this coming from? I'm the Anglophile in the family, not you. Who stole my husband and replaced him with a Brit?" She laughed, allowing him to lead her to the toilet. When she was done, she let him help her back into bed.

He tried to get her as far from the edge as he could. When he was finished pushing and prodding her into a safe position, she rolled away from him. Her hair was damp and sticking to her neck, and he could see one of the hickeys, blue and purple, standing out against the paleness of her skin.

"I had a crazy dream, honey. I was in New Orleans, and it was beautiful. Oh, and the food, the food was amazing! I ate things I didn't even know existed. And I think, I think David Elliott was there. Yeah, I think he was, but it's fading now. It was an amazing dream."

To say David was devastated would've been grossly inaccurate. *Et **was** a good dream,* he thought. *At least she thinks so as well.* He sat next to her, wondering what he should do; he couldn't sit on the side of the bed all day. He figured they'd both be needing clean clothes before they left for home, so he took the bag of dirty laundry out of his closet. Then, he walked to her room, relieved to see she'd been putting hers in the provided bag, as well. It saved him having to rifle through her suitcase again.

On second thought, he knew her clothing would become a wrinkled mess if he didn't do something about it. He called the butler, and within a few minutes, he was at the door. David handed him the two plastic bags, then walked back to Erin's room and carefully laid everything she'd thrown into her suitcase onto the bed. He picked up one of her tops and held it to his face, inhaling deeply. It smelled like her detergent, which was one of the things he smelled on her whenever she got close. He folded it carefully and placed it inside the suitcase.

When he reached the end of the pile, he noticed there was a greeting card on the mattress. *It must've stuck tae somethin' when I lifted her clothes out. The envelope's gone, so I'm sure she's read et.* He picked up the pale green card which had a bouquet of lily of the valley on the front and said, 'My Love.' He opened it and read,

I WILL STOP MISSING YOU

WHEN I AM WITH YOU ONCE MORE.

Handwritten underneath was:

Handwritten underneath was:

> Please don't forget about us.
> I love you,
> Todd

David sighed and placed the card back into Erin's suitcase, tucked underneath the short pile of clothing. He closed the flap and thought about his wife. It occurred to him that maybe Susannah would like to know he was safe, so he picked up his mobile and dialed his wife's number. It rang without an answer until her voicemail kicked in.

"This is Susannah Elliott. I am unavailable currently. Please let me know how to reach you, and I will ring when I'm available." Not wanting to leave a message, he ended the call and rang their landline. He waited for one of the people Susannah had hired to clean, cook, and whatever else they did to pick up.

After quite a while, someone answered. "'Ello, Elliott residence, 'ow may I 'elp you?"

"Hello, Kitty," he began.

"Aww, 'ello, Mr. Elliott. It's good ta 'ear your voice! Ya know, I were just saying to ole Francie—" she started to say.

"Kitty," he interrupted. "I need to speak with Mrs. Elliott, please."

"Aww, right away, sir, just 'old on," she said cheerfully.

He heard her place the handset on the table and then the sound of her shoes, walking across the wooden floor. He hoped she wouldn't forget about him as she was, well, flighty.

After a few moments, he heard high heels tapping on the floor and knew it was his wife.

"Hello David, is everything alright?" Susannah said in her posh, received pronunciation accent.

He thought she sounded a bit more formal than usual. "Hello dear, I thought you'd be keen to know I wasn't in the airport shooting this morning, and I'm still alive."

"Oh, dear, was there a shooting?" she asked, sounding as though she were only pretending to care.

"Yes, there was. I thought you would've heard about it." There was silence on the line. "Anyway, I've also rung to tell you I may be coming home later than I'd planned because of … it." Thankfully, he remembered that he hadn't told her about meeting his Fertilis Defect match whilst in America. *She didn't want tae hear yer voice before yeh left, so et wasn't yer fault.*

"Will Mr. Martin be stayin' for supper, ma'am?" he heard Kitty say in the background.

There was a slight pause, and then Susannah replied harshly. "Kitty, I've told you not to ask me things like that when I am on the telephone. Now please leave me, and I will answer you when I am finished."

"Yes, ma'am, I'm sorry, ma'am, only I figger'd with it bein' Mr. Elliott, and all, it were a'right." He could hear the distress in Kitty's voice.

"Kitty, leave," Susannah hissed. "David, I am perfectly aware of your escapades with that big woman, so do not lie to me about being late due to a shooting at the airport. Now, I have company, so I will have to ring you back another time to discuss what we will do about it. Goodbye." She rang off without letting him respond or defend himself.

Chapter Forty-Nine

MARTIN'S SCHEME

E arlier that day, Martin rang the doorbell at the Elliott home, as he'd done hundreds of times before, and waited for one of the *howss-hould stahff* to answer it. The tall wooden door swung open, and their maid, whom he thought was named Kitty, greeted him. "'Ello Mr. Martin, please come in," she said pleasantly. "Mr. Elliott isn't 'ome at present, sir."

He walked into the bright and airy grand entrance. "I'm aware. I'm here to see Mrs. Elliott."

"Aww, a'right. I'll fetch 'er right away, sir," she said and scampered off.

He walked around the small room, admiring the crown moldings and wood paneling, which had been painted white. There was an envelope in his hand with proof that the man whom they all thought was incapable of doing wrong was, in fact, doing just that. *I can't wait to see her face!* he thought.

Her heels were heard clicking on the hardwood floors a few seconds before she appeared, looking more than slightly put out and tired. *Ah, yes, she'll be angry with me, won't she? I've caused more than my share of mischief here in the last month.*

"Hello, Martin. You know David is away, so what brings you here? Are you now going to torment me as well?" Susannah said without any humor in her voice. Her face looked pinched, as though she were in pain but was trying to hide it.

"Hello Susannah, dear, you are looking as lovely as ever to—"

"Stop your flattery," she interrupted. "I'm not in the mood for your games, so unless you have an important reason for intruding on my day, I'll say good evening."

Ouch! She is angry, Martin thought, but he did have an important mission. "Listen, I understand why you would be angry with me, but I have something you must see."

"Oh, please, Martin, out with it already." She had her arms crossed and was tapping her index finger on her bicep.

He knew he'd better be quick and shrewd about his next move. "I think we should go someplace more private," he said and held out the envelope.

She rolled her eyes and led him into the sunroom, then closed the door. "Now, what could be so important?" she asked impatiently.

He had the photos Hank sent him in order and pulled out the first one. It showed David kissing Champagne's hand, which he knew wouldn't bother her much.

"Is this all? You must be joking. He's kissing the hand of a drag queen; what's so important about that?" She was about to open the door, but he placed his hand on hers.

"Susannah, I think you should sit and allow me to show you the rest of these," he said with grave sadness and concern. It was a much-practiced tactic he'd used on David many times. "Do you see the woman sitting there?" He pointed to Erin, who was in the background.

"Yes, what about her?" She sat on the narrow, straight-backed sofa, and he joined her, sitting too close.

He was in heaven. Having loved Susannah for over a decade and a half, being so near to her was a thrill. The next photo he revealed was of David leaning in to say something to Erin.

"Alright, now he's sitting with a woman in a club, I still don't—"

"Please be patient; you'll understand in a moment."

She didn't want to understand; she'd been feeling unwell for weeks and had planned to lie down before supper. It also wasn't the first time Martin had come to her with pictures, trying to accuse David of having affairs. They had all turned out to be from movie sets or taken at odd angles. She knew David wouldn't cheat on her; it wasn't in his nature.

The next photo was of David with one knee on the pavement in front of Erin. She was sitting on a bench, head in her hands, and his hand was on her knee. There was an enormous plastic cup on the ground next to him which read, 'Spirits Bourbon - To Go.' Martin knew Susannah would see it. They both knew it didn't take much alcohol to get him pissed up, and there would be quite a lot in that cup.

In the next image, Erin looked angry, standing in front of a woman wearing a small, white veil in her hair. David was kneeling, holding his crotch, and appeared to be quite uncomfortable. "Who—is that woman? She seems to be defending him. Who does she think she is?"

Martin knew he had her full attention and took out the second set of photos; they were the hooks. *After these, she'll be filing for a divorce, and David will lose his precious wife.* The first was taken whilst David kissed Erin in what looked like a secluded alley. His hands were on her face, and she wasn't pushing him away.

"This does look bad, but it could be a scene from the program he's there to film. If this is one of your pranks, I'll have you taken to court for libel," she said and paused, a thought suddenly occurring to her. "Wait, from where have you gotten these photographs?"

He had her so close to the breaking point; a bit more patience and it would be done. "It's not libel, my dear. I was informed that this was a real kiss. You see, I had a bad feeling when I learned of this trip, so I called a friend to have him—followed."

"You did what? What gives you the right? How dare you!" she snapped and placed her hand on her chest.

"Trust me, darling, you'll be glad I've done so in a moment." He took out the next photo, taken in the French Market. David was leaning against Erin, kissing her, and her hands were draped around his neck. The camera must have been some distance away, as it wasn't a clear image, but it was obviously not staged.

The next showed David and Erin standing in front of a jewelry shop. He was looking down at her, and she was looking up at him, showing their affection for each other. The picture was beautiful, and Susannah wanted to rip it up.

He'd saved the last few specifically for that moment, when Susannah was finally doubting and worrying. The first was of Erin laying across David's lap on a wrought-iron patio chair, outdoors. Her head was back, and one of her breasts was exposed, as was her ass, which David had firmly in his grasp.

Susannah took the photo out of his hand and stood. Her face flushed, deep red. She stared at it and then at Martin as if she couldn't believe it was her husband. She opened her mouth, but nothing came out, so he silently handed her the last three, which were taken in succession. Erin was bent over, her torso laying on the iron tabletop. Her robe was up over her back, and her rear end was front and center. David's erection was clearly visible as he stood behind her, and there was no doubt he was having sex with her in all three images.

She recognized the face he was making when the last shot had been captured. She'd seen it many times while she stared at him on top of her, after waiting for him to finish so she could go to sleep or get back to whatever she'd been doing. *But—she's heavy! I don't understand.* she thought, *This must be a trick. Perhaps Martin has used a computer program to alter the face of another man to look like David. It could be Bran, but ... that's impossible.* "Who is that woman?" she hissed again with her jaw clenched.

I have her! The deed is done! "Her name is Erin March, she's an American, and I've no idea how they met or why they are together." Martin stood and went to her, placing his hand tentatively on her shoulder. She turned, nearly allowing him to embrace her, but in an instant, she was pushing him away.

"Oh, no, you don't," she said and then noticed Kitty outside the door, waving to get her attention. *Now what?* she thought. She calmly walked over and opened the door, ready to tell Kitty to go away.

Before she could say anything, Kitty said, "Mr. Elliott's on the phone for ya, ma'am."

"Oh, is he?" Susannah said caustically. "I think, perhaps, I'll take this call." She walked to the hall phone, picked up the handset, and graciously said, "Hello David, is everything alright?"

Martin stood near the sitting room door, eavesdropping on their conversation.

"Oh, dear, was there a shooting?"

Her voice is like ice, Martin thought gleefully. Just then, Kitty came back and interrupted her.

"Will Mr. Martin be stayin' for supper, ma'am?" The look on Susannah's face told Kitty, without words, that she was on the verge of explosion. "Kitty, I've told you not to ask me things like that when I am on the telephone, now please leave me, and I will answer you when I am finished."

"Yes, ma'am, I'm sorry, ma'am, only I figger'd with it bein' Mr. Elliott, and all, it were a'right."

"Kitty, leave," she said, not allowing David to hear her distress. "David, I am perfectly (*and photographically*) aware of your escapades with that big woman (*and I'm going to make you pay when you get back*), so do not lie to me about being late due to a shooting at the airport. Now, I have company, so

I will have to ring you back another time to discuss what we will do about it. (*You fucking prig!*) Goodbye."

She placed the receiver down, took a moment to collect herself, and walked back to the sitting room. Martin was standing there with a stupid grin on his face, as though he'd witnessed a victory. *God, I hate him!* she thought, sickened by his meddling and games. "Please leave," she said to him without emotion, still holding onto the photos. "I've things to do; you can see yourself out." She turned and walked away, leaving him without his expected pat on the back or 'well done.'

David will be sorry. He won't be able to get away with this! she thought as she made her way upstairs to her bedroom. A plan for revenge was brewing in her mind as she dialed Detective Chief Superintendent Clive Dawson on her mobile.

Chapter Fifty

THINGS TO DO

How could anyone in London know about Erin? David pondered as he turned off his mobile. He wondered who else might know and thought about calling Martin but remembered that Kitty asked if he'd be staying for supper. *Why's he in ma home when I'm no' there? What's he up tae now?* he thought. Whatever it was, he didn't feel good about it.

His body ached from the stress of the morning, so he decided to take a long, hot shower to ease his tired muscles and hopefully make time pass more quickly. He walked back to his room, feeling exhausted. Erin was still asleep; she looked so peaceful and lovely. He leaned over the bed and kissed her cheek, smelling her scent, now a mixture of something indescribable and the saline smell of sweat, but it was still pleasant.

Being alone was something he had grown accustomed to in London, but now that Erin was incapacitated, he felt like a piece was missing. He was lonely. He missed the banter and humor of his newfound friend and ached for her company. Until she was feeling better, he was going to have to find things to do. *A nap might be a good place tae start.* As he stepped under the showerhead, he imagined spooning with her, wrapping his arm around her, and smelling her scent. The mere idea of lying next to her made him excited.

After his shower, he decided to shave since he had a good amount of stubble and didn't want to be scratchy for her. Once that was done, he put on his boxers and got into bed with her. The sheets felt crisp and clean on his body, and he wanted to feel her skin on his. He longed to touch her creamy white arms, which weren't all that white anymore. Even with reapplying sunscreen every four hours or so, she was developing a deep, golden tan. Her freckles were standing out bold against the lighter shade beneath them. He'd have burned to a crisp if she hadn't insisted on putting some on his face and neck. *She would've made a fantastic mum,* he thought, with a twinge of sadness.

He nestled himself against her back, desperately needing her to remember and respond to him again. She woke a little and placed her hand atop his, which he had lying on her hip, then she rolled back against him, which made him slightly aroused. For a moment, he thought maybe she had come to her right mind and would say his name, instead of her husband's.

"Mmm, honey, not now. I'm sorry, but I'm too tired. Maybe later, okay?"

"A'right, do yeh mind if I hold yeh?" he asked softly.

"That's fine," she said and pulled his hand around her, so he was hugging her tightly. The tenderness and consideration with which she spoke to the man she thought was her husband, moved him. They clearly had a history of love and re-spect. *She'll never leave him; why would she,* he thought.

David woke sometime later to Erin twitching and saying something he didn't understand at first. "What is et, hen? Do you need somethin'?" Her limbs jerked as though she were struggling with something or someone.

"Help, David!" she cried out, which startled him. "Please! Oh, God, don't touch me! Help, I can't breathe. David!"

He figured she was dreaming of the attack. His heart was racing, and he wasn't sure what to do. Should he wake her and risk her freaking out again, or should he let the dream play out since she wasn't actually being hurt? He decided to talk to her and try calming her down. He gently pulled her shoulder to-ward him, so she was lying on her back. "Erin, et's okay, I'm here, let me help yeh. Come, take ma hand," he said tenderly, relieved when her limbs relaxed for a moment, *Hopefully, she'll dream of more pleasant things now.*

"DAVID!" she yelled and sat up. Her eyes were open, but she didn't seem to be awake.

Chapter Fifty-One

WAKEY-WAKEY

"Dav—Todd, what—" Erin said, sounding disoriented, and turned to sit at the edge of the bed.

"Erin?" David said, after getting out of bed and kneeling before her. He laid his head on her lap and held one of her hands in his. "Erin, please, please wake up."

She placed her other hand on his head, smoothing his slightly damp hair. "I need to use the bathroom," she said calmly and rose slowly.

She seemed to have a bit more strength, but he stood anyway, to support her as she walked, just to be safe. When she was finished, he helped her back to the bed, and she crawled in, seeming like a child again, then she rolled on her side, away from him.

"Todd, honey, would you please call Doctor Nan? There's something wrong with me," she said meekly, "I keep having dreams that are like real memories of things that are impossible." She started to weep, saying, "I don't think my head is right."

He remembered the glass of water he'd poured for her earlier and walked to the other side of the bed to get it. "Will yeh take some water now?" She nodded, opening her eyes, then looked at him and smiled. She sat up and let him put the glass to her lips. She was cool to the touch and no longer sweating or clammy. He looked into her eyes and smiled. She seemed to recognize him again, but he didn't know if she was still dreaming or fully awake. She took small sips of the water he presented to her, saying nothing, only looking at him like a little girl taking her medicine as she was told.

"That's all I want right now, thank you, David," she said when the glass was half-empty.

He could've flown around the room, bounding off the picture frames and then alighting on the windowsill, singing a grateful song. "Yeh ken who I am?" His voice was shaking with emotion.

"I had dreams," she said with uncertainty, closing her eyes, "I didn't know if I was awake or asleep. I thought you were part of my dreams, and I didn't want to wake up, because if I did, you'd be gone, and I'd lose you. Then, I'd wake up with Todd taking care of me, but I missed being with you in my dreams. Then, he'd change into you, and it scared me. I couldn't tell what was real and what wasn't. Tell me what happened. I can tell it was bad."

David didn't know whether to laugh or cry. She was back, in her right mind, and most importantly, she knew him again. "You did think I was Todd and spoke tae me as though I were him."

"Oh, David!"

"You were kind and grateful and loving, showing consideration and respect toward him. I could only wish for a woman tae love me as much." He walked around the bed, placing the glass on the bedside table, then he got onto the bed and sat with his back against the headboard.

She rolled on her side to face him. "I'm so sorry, David, that must have been really painful for you," she said and placed her hand on his.

"At first, et honestly didn't matter. You were breathing and conscious, but most importantly, no' dead. Yeh could've called me Father Christmas, and I wouldn't have cared. After a while et began tae sting a bit, though. Do yeh remember what was happening before the episode?"

She closed her eyes and smiled, squeezing his hand. "Uh-huh." Her breathing deepened as she remembered what he'd been doing to her.

"I'm glad." He leaned over and kissed the top of her head. "Well, I'd just started makin' love tae you when yeh coughed and continued coughing. Et was awful, Erin, and I was so frightened! Et truly seemed as though you'd die!" He told her everything that had happened. She listened in amazement and interjected, 'I'm so sorry,' many times. When he told her about calling Todd, she gasped.

"You didn't!"

"I did."

"But how did you get our number? My phone was stolen," she said.

"I remembered that yeh live in Green Bay, so I did et the old-fashioned way; I searched Google. Whistler's Way is such a pretty name for a street."

"But what did you say! And what did *he* say?" She looked quite scared and was biting her lower lip.

"I asked him what tae do, and I'm fairly certain I broke his heart," he added with regret.

"I'm afraid to ask, but how?" Her eyes were large as she squeezed his hand tightly.

"I didn't think before I spoke. I said, 'Aren't these treatments supposed to stop this from happening?' or something similar."

"I don't see what's wrong with that. It seems a fair enough question to me." *One I'd like to know myself.*

He closed his eyes and put his head back against the wall. "Ye're no' hearin' what I said. In one careless sentence, I told him first; that I had, in fact, succeeded in sleeping with his wife, and second, that et wasn't one treatment, they were treatments. He made a sound that made me want tae be sick."

Rolling onto her back, Erin lay her forearm over her eyes and didn't say anything. Her breathing was regular; he could see her ribcage rise and fall with a normal resting rhythm. "I'm sorry." It was something he'd regret for a long time. He was sure there were ways to ask the same question a bit more delicately or, better yet, kept his gob shut. "We didn't talk for much longer. He said he'd call yer doctor and give him the number here."

"You talked to Dr. Nanavala too?" *What other things could possibly have happened while I was delirious?*

"Before that, if ye'll recall, you were quite naked, and with yer exertion, the linens were soaked. I needed tae move yeh, but I didn't think et wise to try tae do et alone, in case yeh fell and hit yer head." He then told her about getting her dressed in what she was wearing.

"I wondered how I got into this ugly old thing."

He told her about the housekeeping lady and not putting anything on except his knickers.

"Thank God for them, huh?" she said.

He told her about speaking with the doctor and what he'd said about the other couples in the treatment program.

"That's crazy! What do you think it means?"

"I've no idea, but he was thrilled tae talk about et with me. He reassured me you would be okay, and the blindness would probably—"

"Blindness? What blindness?" she interrupted.

"Oh, I thought I'd mentioned et. There were times just after the episode when yer eyes were open, but yeh didn't seem tae see anathin'. For instance, when I was talkin' with the housekeeper, we were standin' right in front of yeh, and you didn't see us. Yeh asked Todd who he was talkin' to, and for him tae ask her to come back at another time."

"This sounds like a movie or something."

"Oh, there are plenty more plot twists tae come, if ye're ready?" he said, and she nodded her head. "Well, yer doctor asked me questions—things unmentionable in front of house-keepin', so—"

"Wait, he wanted to talk to you about us? You mean like, personal, intimate things?"

"Aye, he did." He told her about the one housekeeping lady managing to change the linens with her still in the bed and without help.

"No way!"

"I assure you," he said earnestly. "I told her that she could change the rest of the linens tomorrow, then I told yer Doctor Nanavala everathin'."

Erin's face and red cheeks said, plainly, that she wished he hadn't. "Everathin'?" she repeated with his accent, and he nodded. "David! You didn't! I have to see him a lot!" She'd taken her arm off her face, but now she replaced it.

"I'm sorry, hen, I had tae. I didn't ken if somethin' I'd done had been a trigger, but if et makes yeh feel better, he didn't seem one bit phased by any of et. I think he's been hearin' the same thing from others like us."

"But what did he say? Why aren't the treatments working?"

She seemed to be getting agitated, so he wanted to take a break, but she insisted that he continue. "Well, he said et will take time for yer body tae process what et needs tae become stable. He also said you were probably havin' symptoms but were no' aware they were, well, symptoms, or perhaps yeh were ignoring them, hoping that because of the treatments, et didn't mean anathing. He thought yeh were probably right on time with—"

"Okay, I understand," she interrupted, not knowing why she was feeling defensive and impatient. Closing her eyes, she took a deep breath, thinking it over, and realized she had known. "I'm sorry for snapping at you. I did suspect I was having lead-ups, and he's right; I did ignore them. I'm so sorry I didn't warn you. I should've told you what to expect and what to do. Please, forgive me?"

Erin rolled over and laid her head on his leg. She smoothed the hairs on his thigh, waiting for him to say she was right and that he was angry. Instead, he scooched himself down so that he was laying on his back beside her. She rested her head on his shoulder, between his arm and chest.

"I've learned a lot today. I couldn't understand what yeh went through, or what the treatments would mean tae you and—Todd," he added quietly. "After we met and got on so well, et was all about makin' love and the excitement of bein' with yeh, but this is far more serious than I ever imagined. I think, perhaps I should ask yer forgiveness for bein' so insensitive and selfish."

"I guess we're even then, aren't we?" She ran her fingers through his dark chest hair and asked, "Did anything else happen?"

"I think yeh had a nightmare about the attack. You were talkin' just as yeh are now, beggin' me tae help yeh. I didn't know what tae do, so I spoke teh you and tried tae calm yeh down. I told you that I was here and tae take ma hand, which seems tae have worked because here yeh are, right as rain," he said.

"Right as rain," she repeated.

Chapter Fifty-Two

NETFLIX AND CHILL

Erin was still too tired and weak to do much, so David lay with her on the bed. They ordered food and watched *Notting Hill* on one of the movie channels and couldn't help but notice the similarities in their situation. They laughed through the birthday scene, and Erin quoted to him with Julia Roberts, "The fame thing isn't really real, you know? And don't forget, I'm also just a girl, standing in front of a boy, asking him to love her." She already felt a lot better and her energy level was improving substantially, especially after their meal.

After the movie, David received a text message. "Et's my assistant, Tina. She wants tae know when to reschedule our flights." They discussed when it would be best and decided on Tuesday, as that was when he was meant to check out of the cottage, anyway. He thought it would be better to call to make the arrangements and stepped out of the room. "Hello Tina, it's David ... Yes, it's fine ... Yes, please reschedule our flights for Tuesday afternoon ... A'right, thank you!" He walked back into the bedroom and saw Erin lying on her side in the middle of the bed, looking at him.

"David?"

"Aye?" he replied as he set his mobile on the bedside table.

"Do you still want to love me after all this?"

"With all ma heart, and I think, even more than I did before," he said, looking into her eyes.

"Okay, good. David?"

"Yes, hen?" He smiled at her.

"Will you make love to me, right now, slowly and gently?" she asked, and he raised his eyebrows at her.

"But I wouldn't want to hurt yeh."

"That's why I added gently."

"I'd like that."

"Okay, good."

He lay behind her as he'd done earlier, but this time she responded to his touch, using *his* name, and didn't ask him to come back later.

She lay back and turned her head to face him. "I missed you today," she said.

The memories of that horrible day rolled like a film in his mind. "I missed yeh as well, love, and I'm so verra glad you came back tae me." They made love as they spooned, slowly, methodically. Every move mattered.

Her muscles were sore and tired, but she needed him. "I'd like to roll onto my stomach," she said, so they repositioned themselves. "I know I told you to be gentle, but I need more." He thrust deeper inside of her, making her moan long and low, it was akin to an animal noise, something primal and ancient. "Don't stop, please." Erin was oblivious to the muscles in her torso aching and burning, needing the connection, and craving the climax that only his body supplied. She rocked against him, wanting to feel him deeper and deeper. "You aren't hurting me, David, I need you."

He responded by pounding her over and over again. She moaned and accepted his thrust, desperate for the release, and there it was, as the strong waves on the ocean, washing through her. Then he shuddered as his orgasm followed hers. "Thank you," she whispered. Exhausted and feeling the strain all over her, she rolled onto her side and curled up, waiting for sleep to rejuvenate her body; her mind, calm and serene.

David got out of bed to turn out the lights in the cottage. Flipping the switch for the crystal chandelier that hung over the dining table, he remembered standing under it the first time he'd seen Erin. He laughed, thinking about how she'd fallen for him, literally. He turned off the lamp next to the couch in the living room and then checked that the French doors were securely locked. By the time he returned to the bed, she was fast asleep, looking peaceful. He listened to her breathe, soft and slow, with a little whiffle noise as she exhaled; the sound was precious to him, and he cherished it. He crawled back into bed, lulled by the inhale and exhale of untroubled dreams, and was asleep soon after his head touched the pillow.

Chapter Fifty-Three

SUSPICIOUS PERSON

I n the morning, Erin thought she'd better call Todd. He needed to know she was okay and that she'd be flying home the next day. She knew she should have called the night before, while he was home, but to her utter shame, she hadn't thought of it. David was at the garden house to get them some breakfast, so she picked up the landline and dialed their number. He'd be at work, so she'd leave a message. After a few rings, their voicemail kicked in, and she heard her own voice say, "This is Todd and Erin, please leave a message."

"Hi, it's me. I wanted you to know that I made it through again. I'm tired, but I'll be okay. I should be flying home tomorrow, but I'm not sure of the time yet, so I'll see you then. Love you, bye." She heard David come back into the cottage and called out for him to help her get to the bathroom. She was feeling much stronger but one small cough or sneeze, and she'd be on the floor, and she didn't want anything else to go wrong before they left.

He heard her say his name and crossed the stylish living room, pausing for a moment to look at the enormous portraits of what looked like French nobility in their gilt frames. They creeped him out, giving him the feeling of being watched. As he entered his bedroom, he saw Erin standing precariously, testing her limitations. It was obviously still a bit arduous for her, but her strength had improved rapidly since the day before. "Ach, hen, let me help yeh! I'm sorry I took so long; I've been imagining the portraits had eyes."

"It's alright; I just don't want to fall and have another setback. Wait, what about the portraits having eyes?"

After helping her reach the bathroom, he stepped out and remembered what Susannah had said. He felt as though they were being watched, though he didn't know to what extent. "When I spoke with Susannah yesterday, she said she knew about us. She didn't tell me how she knew or who'd told her, but I have my suspicions, and I'm afraid someone is watchin' us. The sooner we leave here, the better, though I dinnae want tae be apart from yeh," he said as he waited, facing away from the bathroom door.

"You spoke to her ... and she knew about ... me? Do you really think someone would take photos of us in here? Oh, David, I hope not!" she said while washing her hands and looked in the mirror. Her face was drawn, and she could see a dozen more wrinkles and several light purplish-green splotches that looked like tiny bruises all over her neck—*Wait!* "David? What is this on my neck?" She made it to the bathroom door, and he helped her get back into the bed.

"Ach, that's the hickey I mentioned just before yer episode. They're quite faded now." He laughed when he saw the look on her face, glad she'd changed the subject.

"Are we in high school? I swear, giving a grown woman a dozen hickeys! How am I supposed to go anywhere like this?" She tried to be serious but couldn't help laughing with him, secretly thrilled to have gotten hickeys from David Elliott, though she wasn't about to admit it to him. "Wait, when did you do this to me? The day before I was supposed to go back home? Good thing they've had time to heal, or I would have had a huge fight on my hands!"

"Ach, ye're right. I'm sorry, love. I'll never do et again, I promise," he said and made an X over his heart with his index finger.

"Don't be hasty! Never is a long time!" she shot back, hoping he'd have another chance, someday, when it didn't matter who might see it.

David laughed at her, and then his phone dinged. He picked it up and read Tina's reply. "Yer flight leaves at 3:55 pm tomorrow, so that's that, sorted. It gives us a bit more time than I thought we'd have, anaway."

She smiled at him, loving the way he said things. They heard a knock on the cottage door, and she looked at David to see if he'd been expecting anyone.

He shrugged and looked through the blinds, seeing the butler holding their cleaned laundry. He unlocked and opened the door, feeling the warm air, though it was still early in the day.

"Here's your laundry, Mistah Elliott," the butler said.

"Thank you," David said and took the clothes from him. The man jerked his head a bit to indicate he'd like to talk to him privately, so he stepped out into the beautifully warm morning, and the man spoke quietly to him.

"I thought you should know that a man was hangin' 'round here ovah the last few days. He told one of the other butlers that he knows you, and you'd been expectin' him. You weren't here when he stopped by, so he was sent away. I also saw him lookin' into your windows on our security cameras. I've notified the po-lice, so hopefully, you won't have any more problems with him."

"Thank you. I'm glad you told me. I think that may explain a few things that were puzzling me. By the way, we'll be leaving tomorrow afternoon."

"A'right, sir, I'll make a note of it," the butler said and walked away.

David reentered the cottage, closing and locking the door behind him. He was glad Erin didn't hear what he'd been told, not wanting her to worry any more than necessary. When he walked back into his bedroom; she looked at him, then at the pile of clothes he laid on the end of the bed. "I forgot to tell you I had our laundry sent out."

"Good thinking!" she said, remembering that she'd been on her last pair of underwear.

"I had to find something to do whilst you were in recovery."

"What was the butler saying to you?"

He had to lie, or at least tell a half-truth. "Ach, nothin' to worry about. I told him we'll be leavin' tomorrow afternoon."

Chapter Fifty-Four

FAMILY MATTERS

D avid brought his holdall to the bed to pack as they divvied up their laundry. Then, he took Erin's clothing to her room, placing the things not needing to be hung up into her suitcase. It was nice being helpful and accomplishing domestic tasks. At home, he was rather useless. Susannah had hired help for nearly everything that needed doing, and he mainly sat in his office, trying to look busy. He walked back to his room and finished packing up the toiletries he wouldn't need, bringing them out to his holdall.

Erin watched him put the little accordion of photos into his bag. "Tell me about your family." He looked up at her, obviously wondering what had made her ask. "I saw your photos the other day when you were filming. Your kids are beautiful, and I was wondering what they're like?"

"Ah, snooping, were yeh?" he said with a smile.

"I wasn't snooping. I'd left my bra in here, and the bathroom smelled like you." She turned pink with her confession, "I stepped in and saw it. I didn't think you'd mind. Sorry."

"I dinnae mind." He took the photos out of his bag and sat next to her on the bed. "I keep these with me since I dinnae get tae see them often. They've been sent off to a fine, verra expensive boarding school, far away, in Scotland. Susannah seems tae think et's what they need in order tae turn out the way she wants them to." *Aye, rich snobs!* he thought. "I attended the same school; I know how brutal et can be at times, and I wish they were closer tae home."

"I bet you miss them."

"Aye. When they were wee, they'd run around the house, tryin' to outrun their nanny, especially at bath time. I loved those days!" he said with a laugh and a nostalgic smile. Then he told her that the first photo had been taken during their summer break the year before. "Professionally shot, of course," he said with contempt. "Heaven forbid we go outside and take a photo of our own children." He turned the next page and told her about Peter. "He's verra smart and has a passion for—" He paused, trying to remember. "Et'll come to me."

Erin could see guilt wash over his face. "He looks so much like you! All the girls must be wild about him."

"Aye, he looks like me, but he's much more focused. He kens what he wants tae do—Plants! That's et! He's also a brilliant older brother, so good with his siblings. They look up to him quite a bit," he said. "Ach, and here's wee Charlie, I'd say he's the most like me, or how I'd like to be again. He's verra affectionate; he's the one who'll come runnin' tae find me when they arrive home on holiday." He smiled warmly at the photo, making Erin's heart melt.

"Daniel, right?" she said, as David turned the page.

"You remember their names?" He looked at her, startled and impressed.

"I looked at the backs," she said. He was still looking at her with an amazed expression. "What? I care about you, why shouldn't I care about your kids?"

"Thank you," he said softly and kissed her head. "Daniel is my troublemaker."

"I knew it! I can see it in his eyes, and I just love those freckles!"

"He's a handful, to be sure. I can usually predict when the school will be ringing to inform his shocked and appalled mother and me that he's done somethin' naughty again. I don't believe he means tae be bad; he just doesn't think things through." He sighed as he turned the page and looked at his daughter. "Ma wee Rosie, though no' so wee anamore. She's turnin' out tae be much like her mother. I've tried tae correct her when she makes nasty comments about people who are less fortunate than us, but et doesn't seem tae have any effect on her."

"Don't give up too easily," she said, "Little girls need their daddy to be an example, showing them what to expect in other men. I'm sure she hears you. Maybe what she wants is her mother's approval and says those things to please her."

"Yeh may be right. Et's no' an easy task, gaining mother's approval." He told her the next photo had been taken at their school, during football practice. "I couldn't believe how tall Peter had grown over the spring. I hadn't seen them since their Christmas holidays." He looked sad when he said it. "Ach, look at that!" he said with pride when he turned the page, revealing the ballet pose. "Apparently, she has perfect form, whatever that means. Her mother pushes her so; et makes me angry, listening to the wars and tears durin' our precious short times together."

He was about to put the album away, but Erin stopped him. "Wait, what's next?" She knew what was next, but she wanted to hear his thoughts on them.

"Yeh truly wish tae see them?"

"Yes, I do," she said and took the album from him, looking at the older of the family portraits. "You all look so perfect. How on earth did you get the boys to sit so nicely?"

"I dinnae remember, but I imagine et had somethin' tae do with their nanny; she was a fierce woman. She'd have given them a good smack had they no' obeyed the photographer."

"Harsh! They were just wee bairn!" she said, and David laughed out loud.

"Wee bairn, lassie? Ach, I didn't ken you were familiar with the term!"

"I'm familiar with a lot of things, laddie!" she said with a poor Scottish accent and laughed. "You look happy in this picture."

"I was. Ma bairn called me da', and I was allowed tae play with them," he said and swiped his thumb across the photo as if caressing it.

"I was allowed tae play with them," rolled around in Erin's mind as she turned the page.

"This year's Christmas photo," he said without emotion.

"You look like the pictures in store-bought frames." Erin looked at Susannah, utterly jealous that she had four beautiful children and David for a husband. She pushed the thought away and took a peek behind the picture, but the candid black and white wedding photo was gone.

"I binned et," he said simply. "I had et in there because et helped me imagine that there may have been love in ma marriage … once. I dinnae need et anamore."

Erin caught her breath. *He threw it away because of me?* she thought.

He kissed her hair and took the album out of her hands. "I've somethin' for yeh," he said and stood. He opened the closet door and searched the pockets of his sport coat.

"David, you don't have to buy me things," she said

Sitting on the bed in front of her, he held out a small purple box, tied with a shimmering golden bow. "I saw this in the window of the shop across the street from the Chartres House, and I had tae get et for you."

"What? So that's what took you so long? I thought you were sick!" *He got me a gift!* After untying the bow, she lifted the lid while he smiled at her expectantly, waiting for her reaction. She couldn't imagine what it could be as she lifted the cotton square and then gasped at what she saw. Inside was a charm about the size of a quarter. It was a small, silver compass that looked quite old.

"So we can find our way back tae each other," he said quietly. He lifted it out of the box by the long, delicate, silver chain it was hanging on and then placed it over her head. "I was told it was used by sailors in World War Two."

"Oh, David! It's the most beautiful, thoughtful thing I've ever been given!" Holding it in her hand, she watched as the arm spun until it found north and stayed there. She couldn't help it; her eyes sprang forth tears of joy. One of them rolled down her cheek and landed on her thumb. "Thank you," she whispered, and he took her hand to kiss it.

"I—love you, Erin," he said and held his breath. *Please say yeh do as well, but say et because yeh mean et,* he thought anxiously.

She could hardly believe what he'd just said. *Do you really love him, Erin, or is it infatuation?* she thought while she stared at the most perfect gift any man could've given her. She looked up at him. He was smiling, and she knew they were meant to be. If it meant she had to learn to love two men, then so be it. "I love you too, David, honestly, I do."

Chapter Fifty-Five

LE POTAGE

Again, the butler came to the rescue, having lunch delivered. David helped Erin to the dining table, although she was improving rapidly, faster than she'd ever done before. "I was lookin' at a map on ma mobile whilst you were sleepin' on Sunday and noticed that Nashville, Tennessee isn't all that far Green Bay, at least no' as far as New Orleans. I think we should meet there for a treatment someday, what do you think?" he asked as they ate.

"I've never been to Tennessee."

"I know et's cliche, but I've wanted a Stetson hat and cowboy boots since I can remember," he said and looked sheepishly at Erin, who smiled. He was relieved that she wasn't making fun of him. He'd said that to Susannah once, which was a mistake. She'd looked down her nose at him, saying, *"And where on EARTH would you wear something so gaudy, David?"* He stopped telling her things after that.

"You'd look fantastic in a cowboy hat! We can go out dancing while we're there! I love country dancing, and as long as you don't mind me dancing with other men—"

"Who said I couldn't dance?" he interrupted, "I've been known tae step out a time or two," he said proudly.

"Were you on *Simply Come Ballroom?*" she asked, surprised, and he laughed.

"No, ma dear, I had dance instructions with Mrs. Williams every week from the age of ten until, oh, sixteen or so. She was old school. Thick hosiery, thick makeup, and several long, plastic beaded necklaces around her thick neck."

"Sounds amazing! Did you like it?" She was excited to hear some of his life story. "I love ballroom dancing too!"

"Actually, I did, although I'd never have admitted et to ma mates! I wasn't bad either and became the teacher's pet, I reckon. I was entered into a small dance competition once. We took second place. Et was fun but a lot of work. Havin' tae dance in front of a crowd, includin' ma parents and a row of judges, was terrifying, though I think et helped give me the confidence tae become an actor. I knew if I could perform a complicated, choreographed dance, no' bein' allowed a mistake, I could stand in front of a camera, where I could usually get a retake if et wasn't any good."

"You can act, you can dance, next you'll be telling me you can sing and sew and bake; a regular Davey Homemaker!" She took his hand and squeezed it, smiling up at him. "I can't wait to dance with you!" she said and leaned over to kiss him on the cheek.

"Is there anathing you'd like tae do today?" he asked as he cleared away the remnants from their lunch.

"I can't think of anything that doesn't involve walking. I'd love to wander around one of the grand, old cemeteries, but I'm not sure how much stamina I'll have today."

"What about a ride on a streetcar or a nice, ro-man-tique carriage ride?" He said the last part with an amusing French accent, which made her laugh.

"Ooh, nice! I think I could walk to the Carousel Bar, if you'd like to have a drink, instead?"

"That sounds brilliant. How soon can yeh be ready?"

"I need a shower, then I'll have to fix my hair and find something nice to wear. I'd say an hour," she said.

The Hotel Monteleone was only five blocks from the cottage, but it was warm for May, so they took their time, making sure Erin didn't get worn out. They overheard someone exclaim that it was eighty degrees, so they were thankful for the air-conditioning when they arrived at the tall, white, wedding cake of a building. The doorman greeted them and held the door leading into the luxurious lobby.

They entered the Carousel Bar and sat at the pewter-wrapped countertop. Over their heads was an authentic 1940s carousel top, complete with at least a hundred white light bulbs. The bulbs outlined ornate gilt mirrors and colorful carved masks that embellished the outer edge of the old circus showpiece. Around the circumference of the bar stood twenty-five seats with circus animals intricately hand-painted on the back of each one. The whole thing sat atop a platform that spun slowly, making one revolution every fifteen minutes. The view changed continuously as you sat with your drink, making it unique.

On the slate-colored walls of the room there hung antiqued mirrors and stunning portraits of jazz era and *Ziegfeld Follies* icons. Each of them was ornamented beautifully with an intricate embroidery of pearls, beads, and crystals, which sparkled as the flashy bar made its slow pirouette. The large glass windows along Royal Street reflected the many lights garnishing the festive room and provided an opportunity to do some people watching. Erin was delighted.

The bartender asked what they wanted to drink and listed several of their most popular cocktails. Erin had a Fleur de Lis, and David decided on the Vieux Carré. "I'd have thought you'd get the French 007," she commented slyly, hoping he'd give something away after Graham Norton's inquiry.

"Sounds too sweet," he said, laughing. They watched people passing the windows outside and spoke with the bartender about the history of the bar and hotel, which he said was haunted.

"There are unexplained phenomena everywhere; you can't always blame it on phantoms and ghosts," Erin said skeptically.

David smiled, and the bartender shrugged. "She's got a point, but I've heard my share of chilling tales from some pretty reliable people over the years," the man said and walked away to help someone who had stepped up to the bar.

"Ach, a skeptic! I'm Scottish, so et's pretty much mandatory for me to believe in ghosts," David said and kissed her cheek without thinking about it. "Bollocks! I forgot."

"I don't blame you; I'm irresistible!" Erin said and smiled at him. After a while, she got the bartender's attention again and requested a Pimm's cup. David chose to humor her and ordered a French 007, though they ended up switching drinks.

A couple sitting at a table nearby got up to leave, but the woman stopped as they reached the doorway to the lobby. She said something to the man she was with, took a deep breath, and walked up to David, blushing and apologizing. "I'm so embarrassed, but I had to come over and tell you how much I loved you on *Future Explorations.* I'd be angry at myself forever if I didn't find the courage," she said and seemed ready to bolt.

"I'm so pleased you liked it," he said in such a lovely, sincere way that Erin could see the woman melting with every word. "Thank you for coming over. What's your name?"

"Diane," she said shyly.

"It's nice to meet you, Diane." He held out his hand as if he'd shake hers, but instead, he kissed it in an old-fashioned, continental way.

She blushed, looking at Erin as if to ask, 'Did that really happen?' Erin smiled as the woman walked away, her face beaming. She was so distracted that when her date said something to her on their way out, she had to ask him to repeat it twice. "That was sweet, David," Erin said when the couple had gone. "You've succeeded in making that woman's day. Hell, you've probably made her year!"

"People like her are easy to accommodate. She didn't ask for anathing. No demand for a selfie or tae sign my name on one of her body parts. She was lovely; if only every fan were like her!" He paused, thinking about what he'd said. "Don't get me wrong, I dinnae mind doin' the rest as well, but when it's a demand instead of a request, et gets tiring."

"I imagine so, but I haven't noticed anyone demanding selfies from you."

"Ach, they always have their mobiles at the ready, though. Makes et hard tae say no."

"But that's not how I see it. I think of it as a courtesy, so you don't have to wait while they find the app and get it set up. They want to bother you for the least amount of time possible by being ready."

"Well, I've never thought of et that way before. I reckon et makes sense," he said, seeing it in a completely different light.

They finished their drinks and David asked what else she'd like to do. "I'm not sure I'm up for any more walking," Erin said. "I think I'd rather head back and take a nap." They took their time window shopping at antique stores and art galleries as they headed down Rue Royale, soaking up the last few hours they had in the Big Easy. They turned onto Rue Bienville and passed Bourbon Street with no regrets, making it to Dauphine Street without anyone recognizing David.

They were only a few blocks away from the cottages, and Erin was glad of it. She'd enjoyed sitting at the bar, but in hindsight, drinking alcohol was probably not her best decision. They walked past the Compac General Store on the corner and finally arrived at the cottage. She was sad not to have been able to ride the streetcars or take a carriage ride with him, but she was glad to be back at their private oasis.

They entered the cottage, and she felt her legs give out. "*Le potage*!" she said as she lost her balance, and he caught her. To her utter horror, she'd quoted a line from *Future Explorations*. She sometimes used quotes from the show in her everyday life but had managed to keep from doing it around him.

"*Le potage*, huh?"

"I can't believe I let that slip in front of you! I feel ridiculous!" she said as he led her to the couch.

"Are you a'right?" he asked, looking at her face. It was pink with exertion, and her forehead was peppered with beads of sweat. He half-feared she might have another episode.

"I'm fine, dinnae *fash*—I mean, don't worry, I'll recover. I'm just out of shape and walked too far, that's all."

"Dinnae *fash*?"

"*Outlander*, sorry," she said as her blush deepened.

"Ach, I see." He smiled at her and then frowned, knitting his eyebrows together.

"I'm not going to have another episode if that's what you're afraid of," she said and smiled at him. "I can see the fear in your eyes. If I feel like I'm going to have one, I'll warn you this time, I promise, plus, they usually don't happen so close together."

"How far apart are they usually?"

"It used to be every six to eight months when I was younger, and for a long time, they were spaced about two months apart. This time it was only three and a half weeks since my last one, though it was mild. I even drove myself home from the doctor's office, where it happened. I slept for about twenty hours afterward, though. Major stress seems to speed them up."

"Your doctor mentioned somethin' about stress bein' a factor. We'll have tae take et easy until yeh leave."

"You know what I think?" she asked, grinning.

"I couldn't tell yeh; your mind is a mystery tae me," he said.

"Never mind," she said sadly. "I just don't have the energy. I thought maybe we could—"

"Ach, darling, I'd love tae, but it can wait. Why don't yeh take a wee kip, and I'll figure out some food for later, a'right?"

"Mmm-hmm. Okay," she said, already half-asleep.

He helped her stand and led her to her bedroom. With his help, she got undressed and into bed, smiling as he covered her up. After kissing her temple, he walked out to the living room, leaving the door open a crack. He thought he'd try to surprise her with something better than a po-boy. The butler assured him he'd have an extra special meal delivered to them in an hour and a half.

Chapter Fifty-Six

A MAGICAL NIGHT

Precisely one and a half hours later, there was a knock on the door. David allowed several young men wearing suits and carrying many different sized containers to enter the cottage. The men set the small dining table as though it were in a five-star restaurant. Remembering that Erin wasn't dressed, David slipped into her room to make sure she put something on before she came out. "Erin, darling," he said as he smoothed her hair with his hand. "Et's time tae get up."

"Mmmhh, okay," she said and then heard a noise in the living area that startled her. "What's that, David? Is someone here?" She grabbed his hand and held it tightly.

"Shhh, et's a'right, hen. Please get yourself dressed and come out for supper." He kissed her forehead and left the room, opening the door as little as possible.

He marveled at the transformation of the minuscule dining area. There were lit candles placed deliberately around the room, and music played softly from a small, portable CD player on the floor. Champagne was chilling in a silver bucket on the small table, and a young man standing nearby was waiting to serve them.

It was far beyond anything he'd expected, and he intended to personally thank the butler later. David excused himself and went to his room to change into something more fitting to the occasion. He put on his dark suit and tie, cufflinks, cologne, the whole shebang, only wishing he had his kilt.

Erin knew something was up. She could hear things being moved, and she could smell something mouth-watering coming from the other room, so she decided to play along. Rushing to the bathroom, she brushed her teeth and fixed her hair the best she could, then she put on some makeup and spritzed perfume on her wrists and cleavage. She got dressed in one of the outfits she'd bought at the resale shop, a black skirt and a red top. She'd been told that she especially looked good in red.

David walked back to the kitchenette and heard the water running in Erin's bathroom. He was suddenly nervous, wanting her to be as enchanted with the metamorphosis as he was. After a few minutes, the door opened, and she gasped, putting her hand over her mouth as she stepped into the room.

"Oh, David! It's beautiful! But how—?"

"Dinnae worry about how just now, love," he said, as he went to her. "Ye're stunning!" He led her to the table, pulled out a chair, and pushed it in as she sat down.

Her heart was fluttering; David looked ridiculously handsome in his suit. "Your tie, is it Monet's *Poppies*?" she asked, and he looked down at it by reflex.

"Aye, do yeh like et?"

"It's beautiful." Her eyes were as large as a Keane child painting while she scanned the room, trying to notice all the things they'd done to it. "This whole thing is extraordinary." As the waiter poured them both a flute of champagne, Erin slipped one shoe off and ran her toes along his calf. She wanted to touch him, to know it was real and not a dream she was having while lying in bed or on her couch in Green Bay.

They were served several courses, each one better than the last. For dessert, they watched the waiter use a small butane torch to melt the sugar on top of Erin's favorite, crème brûlée. She couldn't help but make delighted noises as she spooned it into her mouth. David smiled, and she giggled when she noticed him watching her.

"But it's so good! Can you believe some people have personal chefs who cook for them like this every day? Good thing I don't have that kind of lifestyle, or I'd be twice this size," she said and then saw his face fall. He smiled, but she could see she'd hit a nerve. "Oh, David, I'm sorry; I was only kidding." The waiter hurried over to pull the chair out for her as she started to stand. She went to David, waiting while he pushed his chair back, then she sat on his lap. Laying her head on his shoulder, she buried her forehead in his neck. "I love you."

He turned his head and kissed her, taking her hand in his and intertwining their fingers together. "I'm glad. I love you, as well. Do yeh think et's wrong—Ach, never mind."

"Go on, do I think what's wrong?"

"Well, tae have a personal chef, and … I mean, is that a bad thing? Is et too posh or … over the top?" He knit his brows, looking anxious.

She looked at him seriously and narrowed her eyes. "I presume that means you have one, then?"

He nodded, looking ashamed of himself. "Aye."

She raised one eyebrow and smiled. "No, I don't think so, not unless it's only to impress people. What I meant was that I can't imagine having something like that, not that it's bad."

"Ach, good, because she's the best cook in London," he said and laughed.

A few moments later, they stood, and David thanked the waiter, who was given a generous tip when they shook hands. The man said something quietly in David's ear, which had him looking around the room. He then went into Erin's bedroom, searching for something.

"What is it?" she asked when he came back out.

David nodded to the man, who took a CD out of his apron pocket and handed to him.

The wait staff was suddenly back, cleaning everything up. She could hear the "Flight of the Bumblebee" in her head as they whizzed around the room, gathering dishes and utensils, wiping everything down as they went. It was precision at its best.

"Wait," she said to the waiter as he was about to leave, "Could you do one more thing for me?" She went into David's room and brought out his phone. "Please unlock it; I'd like to get a picture of us tonight," she said and handed it to him. He placed his thumb on the fingerprint sensor and opened the camera, then she handed it to the waiter. "Would you mind?" He took the phone and snapped a few photos, some close-up and some full-length. Before looking at them, Erin thanked him, and he left. "Mr. Elliott? Could I please get a selfie with you?" she asked, playing at being shy.

"I'm a trifle busy right now, but I reckon I can take a moment for *you*," he said, using his RP accent, and then stood next to her, posing for a few shots. It was odd having someone take selfies with his phone. He couldn't wait to see them, but before he could get a look, she was gone, back to his room. "Oi!" he said, but she'd vanished.

Remembering he was on a mission, he walked back into her room and brought out the CD player/alarm clock from off her bedside table. He set it on the small countertop and plugged it in. The waiters had pushed the table out of the way so there would be room to dance, and as Erin came back in, he put the CD into the player. They heard the Five Satins croon, "In the Still of the Night."

"This song is perfect, isn't it?" Erin said as he took her into his arms and danced with her. "You're a good dancer!" she said.

"And yeh follow beautifully."

"I don't know how you did this, but it was magical. Thank you," she said as they continued dancing.

"I'd love tae take the credit, but ye'll have tae thank the butler; he arranged et. I'm just as spellbound."

"Can we bring him home with us? He's so handy."

David liked how she had said, 'home with us,' it sounded beautiful. *Maybe someday, just no' yet,* he thought, as Sting sang "Fields of Gold."

"I love this song! It's on my all-time top twenty list."

"If I see Gordon again soon, I'll tell him you said that," he said, wanting to impress her.

"Well, alright, then. You'll have to tell me that story someday."

"Aye, I will. How do yeh feel, darling?" he asked. "I dinnae want you tae overdo et."

She *was* getting tired, but she didn't want to stop. "Just a little while longer," she said, hoping she'd last through that song. The next one was "The Very Thought of You," sung by Steve Tyrell and Robbyn Kirmsse. "I have the album this is on; it's one of my favorites," she said.

David held her tightly as they listened to the lyrics and Erin sang along, then she kissed him, running her hands through the hair on the back of his head. "Okay, I think I'm done now." They walked to the couch, and Erin laid her head on David's lap, putting her feet up on the cushions.

She wished with all her heart that the night would last forever. Never, in all her life, had she imagined an evening like that. It was something that other people experienced; people in movies, not real life, ordinary ones like her. David was playing with a wave of hair that had come loose from the hasty twist she'd managed earlier in the evening and humming along softly with the music.

"David," she said, "To Make You Feel My Love" playing in the background.

"Yes?"

"I'm going to miss you more than I can say," she said and gently ran her fingernail down one of the threads in the weave of his suit pants, willing herself not to cry.

"I dinnae want tae go home. I've been livin' this weekend in a dream and … feel as though I'm returnin' to a nightmare."

"I'm still afraid things will change between us after we go back and then see each other again. It terrifies me and I don't want that to happen," she said.

Don't you dare cry, Erin March! You've done nothing but cry this whole weekend!

"God, Erin, ma insides are in knots. I'm worried ye'll go back tae Todd and resolve tae stop lovin' me, whether et's out of guilt or because he's the better man," he said and put his hand to his eyes, pinching the bridge of his nose.

Erin rolled onto her back and looked up at him. He looked like he was the one about to cry. "That won't happen. It's impossible," she said and pushed herself up to lay her head on his chest.

Monet's *Poppies* felt their first drop of rain as a single tear ran down David's cheek and fell off his chin. "Damn! I can't believe how many times I've done this since meetin' yeh! Et's been years since I've allowed maself tae cry," he said. "I feel ridiculous."

"I don't understand it either—I mean, I rarely cry anymore, at least it takes a lot to get me going, but I feel like all I've done is bawl since I got here. I'm determined not to tonight; my eye makeup would ruin your suit!" They both smiled, and Erin sat up. "I'm gonna take it off now. I've been dying to rub my eyes for over an hour." Ed Sheeran's "You Look Perfect Tonight" began to play. "I adore this song," she said.

He leaned over and took her into his arms, cradling and kissing her. She placed her hand on his face, tracing his ear with her fingers. He didn't want to let her go. It seemed like this was their goodbye, even though he knew they had most of the next day for that. Eventually, he did let her go, and she made her way to her room while he went to his. He took off his suit and hung it back up in the closet, then wrapped the lightweight garment bag around it, prepared to go into his holdall the next day. Next, he put on his boxers and went back out to the living room. He was about to resume his seat when Erin emerged from her room, completely naked, so he went to her and held her.

Just as he was about to ask her to come to bed with him, his phone started ringing. "Who'd be ringing this late? The only people who have this number are in London. Et's what, four in the mornin' there?"

Erin followed him to his room. She'd noticed there'd been a missed call when she'd asked him to unlock his phone but had forgotten about it.

"This is David," he answered as she climbed up onto the bed. "No, I didn't see that you'd called, I've been busy, and my mobile was in the other room. What could be so important?" he said and then walked out.

Erin had been reading David's book, *Captain Blood*, waiting for him to get off the phone and come to bed. She was lying on her back, naked. Her left hand was resting atop the open book, which was on the mattress next to her. Her right arm was above her head, elbow bent.

"Blimey, look at that! How bonny!" he exclaimed when he walked in and saw her lying there.

Erin opened her eyes, expecting to see an extraordinary sunset, although it was much too late for that. Or maybe an exotic bird outside the window, or an enormous full moon. What she saw was him admiring her, her breasts, in particular.

"They're like two soft, pillowy dumplings. Ach! They're magnificent!" he said and touched the one closest to him, causing her nipple to rise in response to his touch. Erin caught her breath, enjoying his attention. He was acting as if he'd never seen breasts before, though she knew it wasn't unusual for standard-delivery newspapers and magazines to feature bare-breasted women in Britain. He ran his hand down her ribcage to explore her stomach, then moved his long fingers down the sides of her hips. His hand squeezed the flesh of her creamy, pale thighs, then traveled to the soft parts between them.

"Every time you touch me, it feels like the first time," she said, breathing heavily, "and each touch makes me want you more."

He took off his boxers, picked up his book, and set it on the nightstand. Then, he rolled her onto her side and strad-dled her bottom leg in the 'pretzel' position, with her top leg wrapped around his waist. Deciding he didn't want to rush, he brushed his fingers, oh so lightly, like a feather over her skin, causing her to break out in goosebumps.

She moaned, so he continued up her leg, over her buttocks, then up her side, which caused her to squirm and giggle. He held her arm out and did the same thing. Starting at her palm, he worked his way over her forearm and all the way up to her shoulder. When he let her arm down at her side, she put it above her head, bracing herself against the headboard, unable to stay quiet as he entered her.

He watched her breasts move as he thrust, and when he repositioned himself to get more leverage, she made that low, primal noise again. He didn't know a human could make a sound like that, and it drove him over the edge. The pressure continued to build as he released inside of her, and then it was her turn. *How am I gonna make et for two weeks without this?* he thought.

"How will I live without this for two weeks?" she asked, breathing heavily. "I don't know if I can." He pulled out and laughed as he lay spooning with her. "I wasn't trying to be funny."

"I realize that, love; I was laughin' because I'd just thought the verra same thing, though I think et's only ten days now. Maybe I can make et ten days, but et's gonna be bloody difficult."

"Agreed." She rolled over and got out of the bed to use the bathroom. When she returned, he was sound asleep, so she climbed in next to him and listened to his heartbeat as she drifted off.

Chapter Fifty-Seven

RUN AWAY

Tuesday morning arrived, and neither of them wanted to get up. Erin rolled over and snuggled up against David, laying her arm across his chest. She wanted to feel him and smell him, engraving the memory into her mind.

Early morning sunlight was filtering through the shutters, allowing her to see the bits of dust in the air. The room was still dark enough that everything looked grey, except where the light hit it. There was one bar of sunlight, revealing a rectangle of green paint on the wall, and one of David's feet was bathed in a beam of light. "I don't want to go," she said as she ran her fingers over his chest hair.

"I dinnae want yeh to go." He kissed her hair, inhaling her feminine scent. "This has been—*you* have been brilliant, and I dinnae want tae be away from you. Do we have our next treatment date scheduled yet?"

"I don't know. We should do that as soon as possible. As far as I know, the only thing on my calendar is this coming weekend. My friends are having a girls' weekend."

"A girls' weekend, eh? What do girls do together on a girls' weekend?" he asked, amused.

"Girl things, like drink, talk dirty, play games, eat, and talk about boys. That's all you need to know."

"Will yeh talk about me?"

She smiled at him. *If he only knew!* "Every time," she said. Most of her friends were fans of his, so his name came up quite often at their weekend retreats.

"What do yeh mean?"

"Let's just say your name has been known to come up more than once at every girl's weekend, and now I have firsthand knowledge! Don't worry, I won't tell them about that, though."

"Ach, are yeh embarrassed, then?" he asked, only half-joking.

"What? I would expect you to be the embarrassed one! My friends would be the greenest green possible—they'd be the Ireland of jealous if they knew! I just don't want to have it—us become a 'wink-wink, nudge-nudge' kind of joke or get teased about it; it's too special."

"Aye, darling. I ken what yeh mean. And, for the record, I'll no' be embarrassed about you, ever. I'll call Tina to find out if there's one scheduled." He reached over and turned on his mobile. Touching the phone icon, he scrolled through his contact list, seeing familiar names Erin would probably find incredible. Kenneth Branagh, Gerard Butler, and Bradley Cooper, to name a few. Tina was a Cullen, so that's as far as he got. Someday he'd show her the crazy list of people he could call on a whim if he felt so inclined.

He touched the call icon and heard the familiar double-tap, *ring-ring, ring-ring*, but it went to voicemail. "Hello Tina, it's David. I need to know—" Just then, Erin moved her hand down his body, stopping to fondle his genitals. "Hmm—Ah, please send me my, uh, schedule for the next … two weeks. Thanks." He rang off and would've scolded Erin for what she'd done, but he didn't want her to stop. She smiled wickedly as she continued to touch him. "If that didn't feel so good, I'd—"

"You'd what? Hmm?" She rolled onto her hands and knees, moving down so that her face was just above where her hand had been. "What would you do, David? I'd like to know."

"Mmm," he groaned as she blew puffs of cool air on his rapidly growing cock. "Never mind. Nothing; I'd do nothing. Ohhh—" he moaned as she took him into her mouth, wishing he could last forever. He would've liked for her to continue for an hour, but he wouldn't last another twenty seconds with the way she was using her tongue. "Stop! Come here."

She slid up his chest, and he rolled her over, laying on top of her. It was her turn to moan as he put his arm under her leg and lifted it up, plunging himself deep inside of her. He could feel her body responding to him, getting ready to yield itself. "Run away with me," he said impulsively. She smiled, and he felt the tide of release coming from inside of her, which in turn, triggered him.

"You know I can't run away with you, David," she said lightly, not realizing he'd been serious.

"So, ye'll choose *him*—him, over *me?*" He still had her pinned to the bed, and she struggled to get him to move, but he stayed put. "I need yeh, Erin. Come away with me, please. I'll take care of you and love yeh better than he can."

"Let me up, David." She pushed him off her and rolled over, sitting up at the edge of the bed. "Please don't talk that way. Todd is a good man who also needs me, and I … need him. I do love you, but I have to choose my marriage." She walked to the bathroom. "I'm sorry," she said and closed the door.

How could he ask me to choose? It's not fair of him to do that so soon, she thought, as she paced the marble tiled floor, getting angrier and angrier.

Don't get mad; he doesn't have love waiting for him at home. Why should he want to go back there? Try to see his side. She was torn and wanted to cry.

Oh, come on, Erin! Running away with David Elliott would be a dream come true! Don't pretend you don't want to.

Even if she wanted to, she knew doing that would be the most horrible thing she could ever do to Todd.

No, I'm not going to let him say things like that anymore. He's going to have to understand and get used to not being able to influence me. Is that what he does? Is he manipulating me? Well, he's doing a good job at making me feel guilty, that's for sure. She heard him knock lightly on the door.

"Erin, I'm sorry. That was inexcusable. Please come out and forgive me?"

Her reflection stared back at her in the mirror. She looked tired, and her hair was a complete mess. What on earth did he see in her to make him need her so badly? "I'll be out in a few minutes," she said. *If he's unhappy in his marriage, he could have a million other women: why me? What should I do?*

Oh, Erin, you're such a fool.

She ran her fingers through her hair, making it behave a little better, and opened the door. He opened his mouth to say something, but she put up her finger to stop him. "David, I need to make something clear. I want to be with you. This has been the best five days I've ever had, but … I'm not going to tolerate you belittling my husband. I understand how you might feel about him, but he's been good to me." Her emotions got the better of her, and she felt the tears welling up in her eyes.

Dammit, Erin, could you have one conversation with this man without crying? she thought and took a deep breath. "I want to continue to meet with you as often as we can, but I'm not ready to destroy my marriage like that … and, well—"

Good night nurse, are you actually saying this to David Elliott?

"… that's how it is. I know you don't have love at home, but I do, and I'm not going to throw it away because … because sometimes the grass isn't greener on the other side of the pond. I'm sorry, but for now, my marriage comes first; I hope that's enough for you."

God, now you've done it! He's not going to want you anymore! You've ruined everything, you stupid—

"You're right, darling. Et's not right tae say those things about him. I'm sorry," he said and wrapped his arms around her in a full embrace.

363

She held him tightly, thankful the voice in her head was wrong that time.

Chapter Fifty-Eight

BREAKFAST BLUES

I'm going to take a shower," Erin said as she let David go. Her heart was now torn a bit further, wanting it all and knowing she couldn't have it. She understood why he said what he did, of course, but it was too much. She had to stop him, even if it meant he became more distant, and she knew it would most likely come to that. He'd advance, and she'd retreat until he gave up the fight. The eventuality of it all made her sad.

"A'right, I'll do the same," he said, seeing the sadness, or was it still anger, on her face. There was enough room for them both in the shower, and he would've suggested joining her, except he hoped she'd continue to cool off from his arrogant and presumptuous suggestion.

She made her way to her bedroom and saw the alarm clock sitting on the counter. Unplugging it, she carried it into the bathroom with her and set it on the wooden chair. After plugging it in again, she pressed play and heard the first notes of the music. She turned on the water, gathered her clothes and towels, and then took off her compass necklace. The warm water felt good on her tired body. *I'd never get the rest I need to recover if I weren't going home,* she thought. All the lovemaking would see to that. She smiled as she washed her hair, singing along with the music while shaving her legs and as she rinsed off.

Stepping onto the bathmat, she heard David in the kitchenette, singing, as well. He had a lovely voice, and she was determined to find a way to get him to sing more often. After she wrapped her hair in a towel and dried herself off, she stood at the mirror to pluck her eyebrows, which had been neglected for far too long.

David came to the door, smiling at the much-too-small towel wrapped around her. "I'm goin' tae get somethin' from the Garden House for breakfast. Would yeh care to join me?" he asked.

"No, it'll take me a while to get ready, you go ahead. I wouldn't mind a cup of coffee when you come back, though. Thanks, honey." The atmosphere changed in an instant. As soon as it had left her mouth, she wanted to catch it and bring it back. His face revealed that she'd wounded him.

"A'right," he said quietly and walked away.

That one damned word! He knew she called Todd honey; he'd told her that's what she'd called him when she was recovering from her episode. She heard the French doors open and close as he left the cottage.

You idiot! she thought, berating herself for being so thoughtless.

She knew she'd messed up, especially after getting mad and scolding him earlier. If she hadn't been naked, she'd have run after him and begged him to forgive her. She got dressed as quickly as she could and combed her hair without putting anything in it. Slipping her shoes on, she grabbed her room key and ran to the door, determined to at least meet him in the building where they served breakfast. As she stepped out the door, she felt the sun on her face; even that early in the morning, it was hot.

The gate latch caught as she hurried through the private courtyard, which annoyed her. When the gate finally opened, she rushed to the pool area and saw him at once, tall and lean, standing next to a beautiful woman in a microscopic bikini. Her heart jumped up into her throat, and she froze.

Shut up brain ... shut up!

She tried to talk her mind down from the edge of the cliff of terror before it had a chance jump. The woman actually took his hand in hers, pressing her ample, barely covered, breasts against his arm, and leaned in to whisper something into his ear, making him smile.

Oh, God! Erin don't—

But it was too late after that.

There were a lot of people out there, especially for a Tuesday. She realized they must have booked up solid because of the airport shooting. All she could think of was making a scene, but that would only make her look stupid. She didn't know what to do. The last thing she wanted to do was turn around and go back into the cottage. The only things she could come up with were childish and absurd, but the last time something like that had happened, she had been very young.

Think! What would someone—anyone else do in this situation.

She was terrible at that sort of thing; her heart was racing, and she wanted to throw up. Being at a complete loss, she took a deep breath and walked to the Garden House, ignoring David and the beauty queen. No longer having an appetite, she poured herself some coffee. The smell of sausage links and eggs in the chafing dishes made her feel even more sick to her stomach. Turning around, she saw that David hadn't even noticed her walk by. He was still standing next to the woman, and she was still leaning against his arm, obviously coming on to him.

Why in the fuck isn't he pushing her away? she thought.

Why would he, Erin? Look at her! She's curvy and fills out that bikini top quite well indeed.

She knew she looked frumpy, old, and tired. It didn't help that she hadn't done anything with her hair and guessed it was a big frizzy mess by then.

All I did was call him honey; why this? she thought, trying to reason it out in her mind.

Yeah, and you also told him you were choosing Todd over him, didn't you?

But he said he'd been wrong and asked me to forgive him!

Oh, Erin, he's exactly like all the rest of them. No matter what they say to you, it's always someone else. You should know that by now. There will always be someone better, or prettier, or less likely to choose the other guy.

Everything he'd said about why he was attracted to her and not liking skinny women left her. She watched for a moment longer, but when the woman stood on her tiptoes and kissed his cheek, she couldn't take it. Swallowing hard, she walked back into the cottage, grabbed her empty purse, then hurried down the path leading to the street, not knowing where she'd go. Her flight didn't leave until 3:55 that afternoon, and it was only 8 am, so she had plenty of time. A walk was what she needed to clear her head.

It was hot and muggy as she turned left onto Rue Dauphine; her clothes were already sticking to her skin. The scene was etched in her memory, replaying in a never-ending loop. That woman—pressed up against David, and him—allowing her to do it while smiling his beautiful smile at her.

Wow, Erin, you've fucked it all up this time! You had to go and stick up for Todd and humiliate David, didn't you?

That's when the tears started. It literally felt like her heart was breaking, her chest hurt so badly. Not wanting to have a complete breakdown right there, she tried to control herself, but the tears didn't get the message. Bawling like a baby, she continued down Dauphine, staying away from the city center. She didn't want people to see her; she just wanted to cry and get it all out.

What she should've been doing was resting and making sure everything was in order before she left, not wandering around in the heat. There wasn't a bench or chair in sight, either, so she walked, blinded by her tears until she saw a grocery store. Crossing Esplanade Street, she went in to use the toilet and get out of the heat. A police officer was standing at the counter, talking to the woman who worked there.

Erin came out from the bathroom and heard someone speaking with a lovely southern drawl. "You a'right, ma'am?" the officer asked. She didn't know he was talking to her, at first, not until he put his hand on her shoulder. "Ma'am? Are you a'right?"

"What?" She used some toilet paper, taken from the stall, to wipe her nose. "Yes, I'm fine," she lied. She was technically fine, only her heart was pounding, and she couldn't stop crying. "I only need to sit down for a few minutes." The image of David holding the woman's hand and allowing her to kiss him flashed into her mind again, making her break down into fresh sobs of grief.

"Come here," the officer said to her, motioning for the cashier to bring her stool over to him. She did what he asked, and Erin sat, thankful for the rest. "Now why you *boudein'*, darlin'?" he asked kindly, sounding as though he really cared. He took out a clean, white handkerchief from his back pants pocket and handed it to her. It smelled like Irish Spring soap.

"*Boudein*? I don't understand?"

"It mean upset; why you cryin' like dat?"

Erin shook her head, not wanting to tell him her troubles, sure he had more important things to do. "I'll be okay. I—" she started to say, but there were more tears.

Fucking control yourself already! God, you're such a baby! she scolded herself.

"*Mais*, now you just sit here and relax yo'self. You look exhausted, yeah," he said and then said something to the woman behind the checkout counter. He went over to a drink cooler, grabbed a bottle of water, and walked back over to

Erin. "Here you is, now take a drink, and you feel bettah." He twisted the cap off for her, and she gratefully accepted it.

"Thank you. I'm here for a medical treatment, and well, it's far too complicated to explain, but we had an argument, and then I saw him, my friend, with this beautiful woman, and I'm feeling ugly and—" she said haltingly. Her tears fell, forming a puddle on the brown tiled floor.

"Now, what make you think dat?" he said. "I see nothin' ugly about you, no suh."

Erin knew, with the heat and humidity, that her hair was a frizzy mess. Her face was splotchy, and her eyes and nose were red and leaking. He was only trying to make her feel better, and it did, a little. "Thank you, officer."

"Now you call me George, ya hear?"

Erin looked up at him and smiled. "Okay, George, I know I'm overreacting, but I didn't know what to do, so ... I took off. He's gonna be worried to death. Oh, crap!"

"What it is?" he said, genuinely concerned.

"I don't think I have the strength to walk back." She was fighting the urge to cry with all her might, but one tear and then two escaped her eyes. She knew the deluge was coming again, like the waves of a tsunami. As soon as she thought it was clear, another one would rise up, flooding everything once more.

"Now, don't you worry none. I'm gonna get you back. Where you stayin' at, darlin'?"

"We're at the Audubon Cottages," she said, and he nodded to acknowledge he knew the place.

"Now, you just let me know when you ready to leave," he said.

Erin felt soothed by his gentle Louisiana accent. "Okay, I'm ready then. Thank you so much."

He smiled down at her with bright blue Creole eyes and long black lashes. He had a dimple on his left cheek, and it was impossible for Erin not to smile back. She stood up and thanked the woman for letting her use the stool, then she and the towering police officer left the building.

His squad car was parked on the street, and he walked around to open the front passenger door for her. There was equipment everywhere, and she wondered how he could re-member where everything was. She waited while he moved the stand that his laptop swiveled on before she got in. It was in-tensely hot in the car, so she was glad when he turned the air-conditioning all the way up.

As he pulled away from the sidewalk, they heard the dis-patch officer on his radio. "Headquarters to all units: BOLO for missing/endangered female, last seen on Dauphine, on foot. Named Erin March; Caucasian; brown hair and eyes; five feet five inches tall; approximately 180 lbs.; near forty years old; has Fertilis Defect. If located, advise."

"I'm thinkin' that you, then?" George said and picked up his handset, replying: "Two-one-seven-four to headquarters: out with female matching description."

"Ten-four, 2174," came the reply.

"Thank you, George. I didn't mean to cause any trou-ble."

"Darlin' you ah no trouble at-all, ya hear? I'm glad for the good company."

Chapter Fifty-Nine

LOST AND FOUND

O		fficer George drove down Dauphine Street and parked in front of the cottages, lights flashing. He got out of the squad car to make sure the distressed woman reached her door safely. She did look exhausted, and he didn't want her to fall on her way in. A man came out of the green courtyard door, and George did a double take. *No suh! It cain't be!* he thought.

David caught Erin as she lost her strength. "Oh, darling! Where were yeh? I was beside maself with worry!" He looked up at the enormous Black police officer standing over him. The man looked like he wasn't pleased or trusting of him, and he wondered what Erin had told him. "Could you please help me with the door?" David asked.

Officer George lifted Erin up as though she were a small child and waited while David opened the doors for him. He carried her all the way inside and gently laid her on the sofa. "Is there anyone else in the house?" he asked them, and David shook his head.

"No, it's just us," he said, resuming his RP accent. George crouched down to speak with Erin. He picked up her purse, which had fallen to the floor, and handed it to David.

"Thank you so much, George; I don't know how to repay you for your kindness," she said and handed him the handkerchief, "Thanks for letting me use this too."

"Now you keep dat, I have more; you can repay me by assuring me you okay. Dat man don't hurt you, now, do he? 'Cause if he do, I'll brought him in, right now." He eyed David up suspiciously as he walked back from putting Erin's purse on the table.

"He doesn't hurt me, I assure you; I'll be fine now," she said. "You're a good man. Thank you for taking care of me and being my hero." She leaned forward and hugged him.

"It's my pleasure, Miss Erin. Now, do you need medical attention?"

"No, I'm alright, I've overdone things this weekend, and I'm really tired, that's all," she explained.

"A'right. Now I'm gonna talk to your friend here. If you need anything, you call us, ya hear?"

"I will." She laid on her side, sipping her water while the two men went outside to talk. *How am I going to explain this to David?* she thought. *He doesn't know I saw him, and I don't want to come out and accuse him of anything.* She was so hurt and confused, though she knew it was partly her fault.

And what about his excuse, whatever that might be? Should I believe it?

Does he need one? You refused to run away with him, why wouldn't he do it?

It was all so exhausting. *At least I know what to expect with Todd.*

David walked out to their private courtyard with the officer. "Thank you so much for bringing her back! I was—"

"Do you know what led up to her leaving, Mr. Elliott?" he said coldly. He knew who it was standing there, and he wasn't going to let him use his fame to excuse himself. Erin said she'd seen him with another woman, and he didn't much care for that sort of behavior.

"Ah, no, I honestly don't," David said. He was uneasy; the officer had recognized him and didn't seem at all impressed. "I'd come out to grab some breakfast ... unless she saw that woman standing with me. She was too close, but there were a lot of people around, and I didn't want to cause a scene by pushing her away."

"*Mais*, now I don't know what she seen, but she were real tore up 'bout it. Ya might wanna go mend things, and soon!" George said.

"Yes, sir, I intend to. Thank you again," he said sincerely. Officer George stepped out of the enclosed courtyard, and David took a deep breath, hoping he could figure out what had actually happened.

He walked back into the cottage and saw her lying on the couch, sound asleep. A water bottle and handkerchief were clutched tightly to her chest, and her knees were up in a fetal position. He could see the hankie was soaked, and her eyelids were puffy. *Is that what it was?*

He sat in the armchair next to the sofa waiting for her to wake up. *I reckon, seeing me with that disgustin' woman pressin' herself up against me and makin' a scene of tryin' to get my attention—It might've—but Susannah has never cared about that. Wake up, Erin, I want tae explain,* he thought, hoping to somehow wake her telepathically.

If that was what she was upset about, he wanted to explain so she'd understand what had actually happened. Finally, he couldn't stand it any longer and sat on the floor in front of her. "Erin, darling, why did you leave?" he asked tenderly.

She stirred and opened her eyes. "Really? Isn't it obvious? Why don't you ask the slut you were entertaining by the pool earlier?" she said, wishing she could keep her temper in check, but she was far beyond that at that point.

"I'm ... sorry you saw that, but the woman attached herself to me like a parasite. She didn't turn me on; in fact, she disgusted me."

"I'd say she was holding your attention pretty well, and you didn't look anything close to disgusted; I saw you. I went all the way into the building, and you were so interested in her that you didn't even notice me." The memory was still haunting her, and she sat up, not wanting to cry anymore but felt it welling back up, like it or not. "You seemed to be enjoying her company, smiling and laughing at what she was saying to you. She was ... and then she—and you didn't stop her."

Erin thought she was going to throw up, so she stood and stumbled to her bathroom. She lay her arm across the

377

marble toiletries shelf above the sink and laid her forehead on her arm. The cold stone felt good against her hot skin. Taking deep, cautious breaths, she willed the bile back down.

David followed her and sat on the wooden chair next to the tub. "But—"

"I don't understand. If she disgusted you, then why didn't you let go of her hand? Why lie about it? I saw the way you looked at her ... I saw it! Why do men always lie? You let her press her ... breasts against you, and then she ... kissed you! I ... can't do this ... again."

It was too much. She reached the toilet just in time, but all she'd put in her stomach were a few sips of coffee and the water Officer George had given her. She was bawling again, speaking incoherently. "I didn't know what ... and I couldn't ... but ... and why? And ... and I couldn't remember ... and my heart, it hurt so much. I'm sorry I called you honey, it ... it just came out, and I know I said I choose Todd, but—"

David was now on the tiled floor next to her, holding her hair and rubbing her back. "Ach, Erin, et's not yer fault. I'm not lying, darling; I didn't want tae make a scene by pushing her away. I could tell she'd make a huge ordeal of et, and et would be a bigger mess than just allowing her tae get her fill. As soon as she kissed me, I walked away, but I imagine you'd already left by then.

"I wasn't thinking about ... what ye'd think if you saw et. I've never had tae worry about that before. Sus—well, she never cared about that sort of thing. I wish you'd have come up tae me, then I could've escaped the twat," he said, trying to explain. "Et must've looked so bad. I'm truly sorry, darling. I wasn't angry about yeh calling me honey. I didn't know how tae respond, but I wasn't upset."

He remembered how he'd felt as he walked out of the cottage after she'd said it. Honestly, he was torn. Obviously, he didn't much like it, knowing that's what she called Todd, but on the other hand, it meant she was comfortable with him. *She thought I was upset about et, and then she saw me with that clatty whore!* he thought, miserable and angry about the whole thing. "Et was nothin' tae do with you sayin' you choose Todd, either. I understand that—yeh must believe me."

He was now sitting with his back against the wall. Erin's head was on his lap, and he was stroking her hair. "I have women of all kinds grabbing and touching me, constantly. They think they own a piece of me, and I can't escape et. I dinnae have any desire for them; they're obnoxious and make me sick.

"Truly, Erin, ma darling, *you* are all I could want, all I'll ever need. Please believe me. I've seen a thousand women in all forms of undress. Many of them have come on tae me or invited me tae be with them, but that's no' what I want. I'm not out tae get laid or have as many women as I can. I want love, Erin; real, honest love. I want a home and a family who love me and whom I love," he said, desperate for her to understand.

"The thing is," Erin said softly, her voice hoarse from crying and heaving. "I believe you now; I can see it in you. That's who you are, and I know it, but if I were to see something like that happen again, I wouldn't be able to remember.

Your words would leave me, and that horrible, evil thing would rise up again and kill all faith I have in your love. I can't control it; I tried today, I honestly did. David, you aren't mine; I have no say in what you can and can't or should and shouldn't do. I had no right to say anything, although I really wanted to."

"I know, darling, but I want tae give that to yeh. I dinnae want you tae be upset like that again, ever. I can tell yeh I'll not be allowin' that sort of thing tae happen again, damn the consequences," he said vehemently.

"But what would the consequences be for politely telling the slut you weren't interested in her attention? I don't see how that should affect you negatively."

"That's where the problem lies. Et should be my right tae say no, shouldn't et? The thing is, if I do, she may say that I was coming on tae her and that I misused her. Or she may post on social media that I was abrasive and rude tae her. People will believe anathing written down, so I try tae be strategic and figure out the best way to get the bird tae unhand me without a scene. Et can be a real tightrope act. Now, had yeh come up tae me, I would've had an excuse tae walk away with you, which is what I'd have preferred over her company, any day! I'm an actor, Erin, and sometimes I have tae act in ma real life. Sometimes I have tae pretend to be happy when I'm about tae cry or pleased when I'm angry."

Erin sat up, looking at him skeptically. "But—" she said.

"I ken, ye're gonna ask how ye'd know if I were actin' when I'm with you, right?" She nodded and lowered her head. "Erin, ma love, you are the only person I dinnae have tae act with. I have tae be posh with Susannah, a proper dad with ma children, and a good sport with Martin, as well as women who decide tae hang onto me. With you, I'm just David, and I haven't been able tae be him for a verra long time."

Erin thought she couldn't be more worn out, except right after an episode. "Thank you for saying that, and I realize you're pouring your heart out to me right now, but I can't listen anymore. I'm sorry, but I'm so tired, David. I need to sleep," she said, hardly able to keep her eyes open.

"Et's a'right, love."

"Could you please help me to bed?" She happened to glance at the clock. "*Le potage*! Is that the time?" She sighed at her second faux pas. "Sorry, but I told you, I can't help it."

"The soup! Honestly, whoever came up with that as an exclamation was either brilliant or mad; maybe both. Et's a'right, only don't quote *my* taglines to me. You've no idea how often I hear et!" he said and helped steady her as she stood to her feet.

"I make no promises. I use those and a few others every now and then! I don't know when one might come out, but I'll make an effort."

"That's all one can ask."

She took a step, a bit of adrenalin kicking her energy up a tiny bit. "We should be getting ready to go, shouldn't we?" she asked, feeling hurried suddenly.

"Shh. We've plenty of time," he assured her. "The car won't be here until half two, and et's only 10:15 now. Come, let's get yeh to bed." He helped her to her room, zipped up her suitcase, and set it on the floor at the footboard. "Erin, please say all's forgiven. I'll nev—"

"I don't want to think about it anymore. I have a lot on my mind, and I just can't do it now. I need a bit of time." He nodded and turned to walk out. "Hey!" she said, so he turned back toward her, "You didn't kiss me! And I was wondering if you looked at your phone today?"

He bent down and kissed her mouth, then he kissed her nose, cheeks, forehead, and finally, her eyelids, which made her smile. "Sleep well. I'm gonna have a look at what yeh did to ma mobile!"

"I hope you like it. Oh, no! I didn't think about Susannah. You can change it if—"

"What was et you said earlier, dinnae *fash*? Et'll be a'right." He stepped out of the room, unlocked his mobile with his fingerprint, and had to laugh. She'd changed his wallpaper to one of the close-up shots the waiter had taken the night before.

Suspecting that wasn't all she'd done, he opened his contacts and searched for her under March, but nothing came up. He tried Erin and found her smiling at him from one of the selfies she'd taken; it was lovely. She'd filled in all the information she possibly could; her birthday, address, phone number, favorite color, birthstone, astrological sign, and her maiden name, which was Wallace. *A good, Scottish name!* he thought. For their anniversary, she put in May 16, the day they'd met, and for relationship, she'd typed in 'lover.'

His photo gallery was next, where he viewed all the pictures she and the waiter had taken. Most of them were crap, either one of them had their eyes closed, or the shot was blurry, but there were three perfect ones. The time on his mobile read 10:25. *Plenty of time.* He wrote her a note saying he had to run an errand, and he'd be back in about an hour, just in case she woke to find him missing. Hoping it would be a good enough disguise, he grabbed his ball cap and sunglasses, then he took his room key and walked out the door.

Chapter Sixty

LACK OF CONFIDENCE

An hour and twenty minutes later, David returned, hot and sweaty, but he had what he'd gone out for. Opening his closet door, he picked up his holdall and rummaged around in it until he found his photo album. He slipped two of the wallet-sized photos he held in his hand into the slots with the family photos. The third one would go straight into his wallet when he got home. It was his favorite; he was blurry, but Erin was looking up at him with the most beautiful smile.

Once the album was returned to his holdall, he searched the room to see if there were any missed articles of clothing. He found a sock under the duvet, which was in a heap on the floor at the end of the bed, and then thought to look near the headboard, where he saw something shiny. It was a gold locket, which had slipped off the back of the nightstand.

On the front was a monogram with filigree etchings, which he assumed were Erin's initials, a small E, a large M, and a small G. The M would be for March, and the E for Erin; he wondered what the G stood for. He grabbed his mobile, found her profile again, and read her middle name, *Grace. Fitting.* On the locket's back there was a small T, a large M, and a small M. *Todd's initials. Humph.* He opened it and read *All my love, forever.*

He would've liked to put it back where he'd found it, but that wasn't the kind of man he was. Instead, he quietly slipped into Erin's room and placed the locket on the toiletries shelf in the bathroom where she wouldn't miss it. The small photographs he'd gone out to have printed were then tucked carefully inside her purse. She was still asleep, but it was getting late and time for lunch. At that thought, her stomach growled so loudly it startled him. He remembered she hadn't eaten anything all day, so he left her room and called the butler.

Erin woke up fifteen minutes later, her head pounding and her stomach yelling at her for not feeding it. She made her way to the bathroom and turned on the light, which made her head pound even harder. Remembering why her head hurt brought back all the morning's memories, which, in hindsight, seemed like a massive overreaction on her part.

Will you ever grow up?

Probably not.

Will you ever be able to adjust to seeing him the way you did today?

Probably not.

Are you willing to try? That is if he hasn't already decided that you're too messed up for him?

I don't know.

She splashed cold water on her face and brushed her teeth, noticing the locket Todd had given her on the shelf. *David must have found it and put it there.* She picked up her bottle of ibuprofen and poured three of them out onto her hand. The bottle of water from Officer George was on the sink, so she washed the pills down with it and then groaned when she saw her reflection in the mirror. She looked worse than she'd imagined, like something the cat wouldn't have bothered to drag in. Her hair was a mess, her eyes were puffy and sore, and her nose was now flaking bits of skin around her nostrils from having to wipe it so often. She wanted to hide; letting him see her natural 'morning face' was one thing, but it was so much worse than that.

The only thing to do with her hair was to wash it again and hope she had time to dry and straighten it that time. She started the shower, quickly took off her clothes, and got under the water. It felt so good, washing away the dried sweat and tears from earlier. Once her hair was washed, she stepped out and wrapped it in a towel, then she put new clothes on and headed out to the living room.

David was sitting on the couch with his book on his lap. "Oh, good; I heard the shower and wasn't sure how long ye'd be," he said cheerfully. "I ordered takeaway; I hope yeh dinnae mind. Et should be here any minute."

"No, I don't mind," she said quietly, feeling shy with him for the first time since they'd met five days earlier. She felt unsure and off-balance, but mostly, she was embarrassed at how she'd behaved and didn't know what to say.

"Did yeh sleep well, love?" He patted the cushion next to him, wanting her to sit there. She hesitated and looked at her feet. "Erin? Are you—are we a'right?"

"I think ... I don't know. Yes ... I mean, yes." She sat on the front edge of the sofa; her hands gripped the top seam of the cushion, and her head was still down.

"What's the matter, hen?" he asked, tenderly. There was a knock at the door, so he stood and answered it. A young man handed him two brown paper bags and thanked him for the tip before leaving. David closed the door, took the bags to the dining table, and left them there, returning to Erin. "What is et, love?" he asked, crouching in front of her and lifting her chin with his index finger.

If she'd had any tears left, they would've been there, her constant companion that week, but she was dried out. She tried to put her head back down, so he wouldn't see the state of her wrinkled and sagging face. "There's so much, but right now, I'm embarrassed at how I reacted today."

"Ach, ma darling. Yeh don't need tae be embarrassed; et must've been terrible for you, and I dinnae blame yeh one bit." He stood, holding out his hand for her to take, but she hesitated. "Are yeh sure we're a'right? Are yeh havin' second thoughts about yer ... feelings for ... me?"

She shook her head and took his hand. "We're okay, but I'm not sure about anything right now. I still want to love you; I'm just so messed up, you know?"

He pulled her into his arms and held her. "I understand," he said and then remembered what Dr. Nan had told him about the effects of oxygen deprivation. "We can work this out, but right now, let's have some lunch. I'll help yeh get yer things together afterward, a'right?"

She nodded and held him tightly around the ribcage, placing both hands flat on his back, feeling his warmth and hearing his heartbeat. He smelled so good; she didn't want to move from that spot and couldn't imagine her life without him. She just didn't think she'd be able to deal with what being with him would mean. "Please hold me for a while longer." Her stomach was aching with hunger, but she needed to be held more than food. After a few minutes, she looked up at him again, gave him a weak smile, and let him lead her by the hand to the table.

Chapter Sixty-One

REASONS & DIRTY SECRETS

I need to tell you why I freaked out so badly," Erin said after they were seated, and David started taking the food out of the bags.

"Et's a'right, darling. Yeh dinnae—" he began, but she shook her head and kept talking.

"I've struggled with my weight nearly all my life. When I was younger, I thought that if I ever hit two hundred pounds, I'd kill myself. I never would've done it, but I figured my life would be over, at least my love life, if it ever got that far out of control. Well, I hit two hundred pounds long ago."

"Et doesn't—"

"Please let me get this out. I want you to understand."

"A'right, go on then."

"I did lose weight, quite a lot, actually, before I met Todd. A country bar opened near me, and I learned how to dance. I was there all the time, but that's a story for another day. Once the bar closed I had to resort to other forms of exercise, like Zumba, biking, water aerobics, and Pilates, which I really liked, but after an episode, I'd have to stop, and it got harder and harder to pick it back up each time. Pound after pound I'd vow to start over, to try harder, but episode after episode, I became more and more tired; eventually, I gave up. I know you don't care about my size, but I do. It affects everything in my life."

"Et doesn't need to—" he began and then remembered what she'd said. "Sorry, continue."

"I think maybe I should start a bit earlier, so please bear with me. My first serious boyfriend was Joe Hickman. He was into fast cars, deer hunting, the Packers, and drinking. I was … fourteen, he was sixteen, and had a car. One night, a few months after we met, I let him have sex with me in his parent's basement on an old, rust-colored, velour couch. His parents weren't home, and … he said he loved me. It was my first time, so I was too young to realize that it didn't mean the same thing to him as it did to me. Anyway, a month later, of course, he dumped me for Kelly Snyder, who had red hair, a flatter stomach, and perkier breasts than I did."

"Ma Losh, Erin, yeh were only fourteen? That's brutal," he said, frowning and held her hand.

"I dated a few other guys, and with each one, it was the same thing, 'I only want you!' they'd tell me, or 'Come on, my parents aren't home, let's go to my house!' When I'd tell them I was afraid things would change afterward, they'd say, 'Of course things won't change; I love you.' I desperately wanted to believe them, but it always ended with unanswered phone calls, avoiding me in the hall, and telling me, 'I never said we were exclusive!' or, 'Quit calling me, don't you get the hint?' Oh, and how can I forget, 'I never liked you that much, I just needed to get laid.' That was my favorite. At least he was honest."

"Someone actually said that to yeh? That's just—" he began but saw the look on her face and stopped. "Sorry, but that's just horrible."

"I know it is—that's why I'm telling you about it. I even had one guy ask to marry me, but he found someone better than me too. Anyway, a few years later, I met Todd, but by then, I had major trust issues. I was always worried that he wasn't really alone when we weren't together. I would freak out if I saw him standing next to another girl, even if they weren't touching. I just knew that whoever the girl was, she'd be in some way better, prettier, thinner, or just not me. Todd would never have cheated on me, but there were days when I simply couldn't trust him.

"Now I know who Todd is and I've learned to trust him, for the most part, and most of the time, I can get over my anxieties. Though, to be fair, there were things I didn't know about him before we were married that I wish I'd known earlier, but I take each day one at a time. I have learned to deal with those things through a lot of heartache and forgiveness as they come up. The important thing is that he doesn't cheat, and he loves me."

What're the things she needs tae forgive him for? David thought but didn't ask.

"That's all; I just wanted you to know why I'm so messed up when it comes to other women."

"I'm glad yeh told me."

"I am too, but this is who I am, David. I don't think I can change, so please make sure you can handle it, before … I mean, if we—" She sighed and hung her head, waiting for him to tell her he'd changed his mind about loving her after the way she'd behaved.

"I love who yeh are, Erin, and you dinnae need tae change." He kissed the hand he was holding.

Erin nodded and took a deep, shaky breath. She tried to eat, but her heart was in her throat, and it was hard to swallow. They were silent for a while, and finally, the question that was plaguing her tumbled out. "Can I ask you a very personal question?" she asked and pushed her food away. She shook her head, not wanting to ask, though not able to stop herself.

"Sure, anathing," David said, smiling. She looked at him, unsure if she really wanted to know. "Erin, ma life is an open book, just say et. I promise I'll not get upset if that's what you're worried about."

"The thing I'm worried about is honesty, that's all. It's about something no one seems to be honest about, and it's important to me."

"I promise tae be honest." He thought she was about to ask him how many sexual partners he'd had, which were only two, including her, so he wasn't worried about honesty.

She still hesitated. *It's none of your business,* she thought.

"Erin," he said, interrupting her thoughts.

"Okay, do you enjoy … pornography?" she asked simply and then looked down at her lap.

"Well, that's not what I was expectin'," he said and thought about the wall of porn at the Registry. "The honest answer is, no, I've never fancied et. I need tae have an emotional connection when et comes to sex, not tae look at or watch strangers getting' it on. Why do yeh ask? Are you?" he asked, smiling wickedly, "Because I may be able tae get into somethin' with you as the subject."

"Ha! No thank you!" she said, laughing, but then her smile faded, and she continued looking at her jeans.

He frowned, knowing his reply wasn't good enough. He needed to take it seriously and elaborate. "The boys at school, but mostly Martin, had stacks of magazines. He was constantly at me, wanting me tae make use of them, and questioned my sexuality when I'd decline his 'generous offer,' which is rather odd, isn't et?"

"Makes no sense to me."

"Occasionally, I'd take one just tae get him to shut up, but they didn't do anathin' for me." He lifted her chin with his finger and looked into her eyes. "That's the truth, Erin."

She nodded and gave him a weak smile. "There's something I need for you to understand about … Todd." She hadn't planned on telling him, not wanting Todd to be villainized, but he needed to know.

"Go on," he said gently.

"He's … addicted to pornography." She closed her eyes and blew out a long breath. "I know some women don't care about it. They believe it's a natural thing, and bravo for them, but I'm not one of them. "I found the first stash near our first anniversary. He vowed to get rid of it and to never have anything to do with it again after I told him how it made me feel. I should've known." She felt stupid, both for having believed him and for not being able to handle it in the first place.

David frowned and turned to face her. He was starting to better grasp why she'd reacted the way she had. Having been discarded by too many lovers and then being made to feel like she had to compete with pornography on top of it would not be easy to take.

"It might have been different if he'd involved me. Maybe I would have been able to accept it if it wasn't hidden. I've even tried including it by asking him to watch videos or … to try new things. To be supportive, you know, but he's too embarrassed. So, every year, I find things hidden, and each time I confront him, he tells me he won't do it anymore. He will swear up and down that he doesn't have anything else, but I always find more," she said, sadly.

David kissed her hand again. "Needless to say, I have issues. I'm tired of being lied to every year, and I'm tired of feeling like I'm not sexy enough. I know I told you what an amazing husband he's been, and that's true. When it comes to my disease and companionability, he's great, but I'm finding it hard to live with the rest of it. I just can't compete, and I don't want to anymore."

It shocked her to realize just how much it was still traumatizing her. She thought she'd been dealing with the issue fairly well, but apparently, she had only repressed the whole thing, and it hit her pretty hard. "So, if … what I mean is, I wouldn't be able to … go into another relationship with someone who has the same inclinations," she said haltingly, not wanting to get ahead of herself but needing to make herself clear.

"Aye. That would be hard tae live with, and I reckon et wouldn't do much to improve yer self-image, especially seeing how other men have treated yeh. You don't need tae worry about that with me, darling," he said.

"The thing is … well, that woman today … she was a living, breathing, porn-star-worthy, nightmare. One of the pages of the magazines I've found under drawers, hidden behind the pegboard in his basement workshop, and between the lining of an old suitcase he'd had since he was a kid, come to life … touching you … and trying to … oh God!" She stood and began pacing. "What am I thinking! This will never work!" she whispered, wringing her hands, and shaking her head, knowing she'd never get used to seeing women with him like that.

"Please don't say that. Believe me, Erin, those women repulse me, though I can see how et would be hard on you. I don't know what to say tae help yeh understand. Et's the price I must pay for the profession I'm in. I wish I could somehow put yer mind at ease."

Erin frowned and looked at him suspiciously.

"What?" he asked.

"I'm curious, David, if those women disgust you, why would you choose to play a role with a sex scene in it? That seems to contradict what you just said."

He blew out a long, slow breath, "Aye, you're right, et does seem that way, but I took the job without readin' the script. Ach, Erin, et was foolish, but I was tryin' to escape. Et's a long story, and I'll explain et to yeh when we've more time. I promise yeh I didn't know that's what I'd be doin' until I'd already agreed. I give yeh ma word I didn't take et because of the sex scene."

"Okay. Thank you for listening to all my problems," she said, praying she could believe him.

"Thank you for trusting me."

Erin sat back in her chair feeling as though a heavy weight had been lifted off her. Sighing, she pulled her food towards her and smiled bravely at him.

Chapter Sixty-Two

TEN DAYS

"Mind if I ask who called you so late last night?" Erin asked as they ate, wanting to change the subject.

David's eyes grew bright at the memory. "That was ma agent, Becky. Apparently, she tried several times tae call, but I was too busy bein' swept off ma feet tae hear my mobile. I've been offered a once-in-a-lifetime role. I can't say what et is, no' even tae you; et's that big. She wanted me tae know as soon as possible, so she continued ringin' until I finally picked up."

"That's great!" she said, only half meaning it. She wanted him to get the part, presuming it was for James Bond, as Graham Norton had hinted at. It was a life-changing role, but it meant he'd be recognized more often and couldn't be seen with her. "When will you know for sure?"

"There's a meetin' set for Monday, but those things usually change. I'm no' gonna plan on et for at least three weeks from now."

She began zoning as she watched him talking. *"You are the only person I dinnae have to act with,"* he'd said to her. So, this was the 'real' David Elliott? She liked him a lot; he made her laugh and was easy to be with. He looked at her as though she were a priceless gem, even after everything that had happened that morning.

"... and yeh know 'Irn Bru' gets yeh through," he said, and she snapped out of her reverie. "You're in another world, hen. What could be more important than listenin' tae me blathering on?"

"Sorry, I was thinking about ... and watching you ... well, being yourself. Never mind, I was daydreaming, that's all, now what were you saying?"

"I'd rather hear about yer daydreams."

"It was nothing, really," she said, but he raised his eyebrows. "Fine, I was thinking about how much I like being with you ... I mean, how much I like ... you, the real you." She blushed and rolled her eyes, "See, it was nothing."

"I wouldn't call that nothin'; I'd say et was a real somethin'." He took her hand, which had been resting on the table, and kissed her fingertips. "I've had a brilliant time with you this week. I'm glad yeh still like me. Often, people have an idea of who I am or how I'm supposed tae be, based on what they've seen on the telly. When I can't live up to et, they dinnae like it."

"I like you more now than I did before. Everything about you is better in person." *Let's get married and have a dozen children*, was what she wanted one of them to say.

"Erin, ye're the most amazing and refreshing person I've met, and I can honestly say I've never been as comfortable as I am right now with anaone before. You dinnae have demands or expectations; no criticism of what I do, how I talk, or what I say. I've lived the last forty-five years not knowin' if I was sayin' the right thing tae the right person at the right time.

"With you, I dinnae even think about et. I ken ye'll just laugh if I say somethin' stupid, or more likely, you won't think et stupid a'tall. But ye're no' like a fangirl; ye're genuine and honest. You've no idea how that feels for me. Et's waking up, and having a good day, everaday," he said and gave her his best smile.

"No demands or expectations? No criticism of what you do? Are you kidding me? Where have you been for the last six hours? I'd say I'm quite demanding and have high expectations."

"No, love, you expect tae be treated with respect and tae be told the truth. Those are reasonable expectations, and yeh weren't criticizing what I … did this morning. You were worried, quite justifiably, about ma intentions and what yeh saw must've seemed like a betrayal; that's not the same thing."

"Well, you haven't known me for long. It's not fair to say that I don't have any unreasonable demands or expectations. I'm sure I could find a few if I tried."

"I can handle et," he said.

She couldn't help but smile. "Ten days, huh? It's gonna feel like ten years. How'd I live my life before you were in it? Well, I guess I did have a version of you, but how did you survive without me all this time?" she said and gave him a sassy grin.

He stood, took her hand, and pulled her up. "By the skin of ma teeth, and I nearly didn't make et," he said as he kissed her. He unwrapped the towel she had on her head and let it drop to the floor. The smell of her filled his senses. Her hair was still damp and slightly warm from the heat of her body, and he grabbed a handful of it. *I can't live without this woman!* he thought desperately.

I can't live without this man! she thought, though her heart was divided and confused. She kissed him back fervently, wanting somehow to be permanently connected to him forever. *How will I live my life without him next to me?* "I don't want to let you go, but it's getting late, and I have to do something with this mop," she said, pointing to her hair.

"I'm sure ye'll have time after I'm through with yeh," he said, pulling gently on his fist full of hair, making her lift her chin to reveal her soft, pale neck. The hickeys were so faint that with her tan, he could hardly see them. He took his other hand and placed it firmly under her ear, wrapping his fingers around to the nape of her neck.

She closed her eyes as he nuzzled her with his nose, taking her earlobe between his teeth and nibbling on it. Each of her nerves was coursing with energy, and every part of her tingled. Reaching down, she touched him, feeling his excitement. He was rock hard, and she wanted him urgently. She didn't know if she had the physical strength, but she'd do everything she could to get him to make love to her once more before they parted.

"Look what yeh do to me!" he said once she'd pulled his trousers down, revealing his erection. He undressed her and helped her sit on the edge of the dining table. He looked her in the eyes as he lifted her legs, wanting to see her reaction when he entered her.

She yielded to him, even though she was sore from all the lovemaking, and it hurt a little. It would be a while before she'd be able to have sex again, but she wasn't going to let it stop him. Gasping, she threw her head back as he thrust deeply into her, again and again.

She was so utterly spent as they both reached their orgasm, that she could hardly move. It took all her strength to stand and get dressed when all she wanted to do was go to sleep. *I can sleep later,* she thought and wished they had more time to hold each other, but they were now in a hurry. They only had forty-five minutes before the driver got there, and she still had to fix her hair.

Chapter Sixty-Three

MAYBE SOMEDAY

David and Erin searched the cottage, making sure not to leave anything behind. As they took the keys to the butler's office, a somber mood came over them. All they needed to do was leave the key in the cottage, but they wanted to speak to the butler before they left. Erin hugged him, thanking him for arranging their romantic dinner. David shook his hand, giving him a substantial tip. Then, they walked down the tree-lined path, stepping through the green wooden door for the last time.

Their driver was waiting, hat in hand, ready to take them to the airport. "Good afternoon," he said as he opened the door for them. The interior of the vehicle was exceptional. Soft leather seats and dark tinted windows embraced them, making them feel safe and anonymous.

What would it be like to travel this way all the time? Erin could only imagine. She would've said something about how foreign it was to her, but David didn't seem phased by it at all. *He's used to things like this,* she thought and said nothing. The driver put their luggage into the trunk and then got into the driver's seat.

Erin took one more look at the outside of the cottages; so much had happened there in such a short time. She'd met the man of her dreams, been mugged, had the most passionate and fulfilling sex she'd ever known, had her worst episode, been brought back by the police after running away, and had fallen completely and totally in love, to name a few things. She was feeling melancholy.

David watched her as he raised the privacy window. "Maybe we'll return someday," he said, trying to reassure her.

"Maybe," she said but doubted it would ever happen. She looked forward to future adventures but leaving that one was bittersweet. It meant their time together was at an end, and she was going home to Green Bay, where nothing exciting ever happened. It was also where she'd be expected to sleep with Todd again. "I'm going to miss this place." The car rolled past the now familiar houses and businesses they'd walked past nearly every day, and in only five minutes, they were on Highway 10, heading toward the airport. Erin closed her eyes and laid her head on David's shoulder, fighting the urge to cry.

"We'll come back, darling, we'll have tae plan on et. Besides, there will be many more weekends together, right? We can make each one an adventure," he said, trying to convince himself as well as her.

"Yes, of course, you're right." She looked up at him, and he kissed her. It was most likely the last of that kind of kiss she'd get from him until her next treatment, so she made it last. If she'd had any energy left whatsoever, she would've wanted to rip their clothes off and have sex, right there in the back of the luxury sedan.

Unfortunately, she didn't have an ounce of stamina left in her, and from what she could remember, it wasn't a long car ride, anyway. They sat quietly, each lost in their own thoughts. "You said you were going to take care of some things when you got back; can I ask what they are?" Erin asked, breaking the silence. She didn't want to be nosy or pry, but she was curious. He didn't say anything right away, so she thought he didn't want to tell her. She was about to ask about something else when he sighed.

"I'm plannin' tae find out how Susannah knew about us, and since I'm sure et involves Martin, I'll have a few choice words for him. I'm also relatively certain Susannah will ask for divorce, and I'm goin' tae let her have et. A divorce that is, not a beating," he said with a laugh, realizing how that might have sounded.

"Oh, David. I can see how that might be the way things should go, but I feel bad for your kids. Even if they know you don't get along, kids usually have a tough time with divorce." He nodded and put his head back against the headrest. "Why do you think Martin had something to do with her finding out about us?"

"Just a feeling. Martin thinks ma life is perfect. He sees my success, ma trophy wife, all the *things* I have, and he's jealous, I know he is."

"And you say he's your friend?" she asked, not understanding why he'd have someone like that around him.

"Aye, I've known him forever, and I'm no' gonna let fame come between ma old mates and me. I know he's toxic, but I … well, I feel sorry for him. He's got no life, except his schemes, which usually end up gettin' *me* into a right bloody mess.

"To put everything on the table, et's because of him I'm here," he said and explained how he'd gotten roped into signing up for the Registry. "I agreed to the television job in America, sight unseen, tae avoid … this and everything that went along with et. I was hoping I'd be too busy and too far away tae meet my match. I should've known better; I mean, what are the odds that the person I was aiming tae hide from lives in the place I wanted tae hide? Et was becoming a 'Sod's Law' situation, except et isn't, is it? Et's perfect, so maybe I should thank him." He looked at her and sighed.

"Anaway, he thinks I've always gotten what I want in life, but he's wrong. I reckon I've always gotten what he wants. He wants my lifestyle, and I'll be honest, I've enjoyed et for a long time, but et's becoming a burden. I ken et sounds ungrateful, but all fame does is make yeh worry as et slowly changes yeh. I'm turnin' into someone I dinnae want tae be. Susannah, on the other hand, loves et. She can't live without all of ets trappings, but I dinnae care anamore, I want somethin' else, something real."

Chapter Sixty-Four

DEPARTURES GATE

The driver parked in the drop-off area at the airport terminal and got out. Erin was about to open the door, but David whispered that she should wait until the driver did it for her. Once the door was opened, she stepped out into the afternoon heat and felt her forehead bead up with sweat instantly. She thought about what the weather must be like at home and was grateful for the warmth. They waited while the driver removed their bags from the trunk, then David thanked him.

After walking inside, they used the kiosks to check in because they weren't checking any luggage. David's flight was two and a half hours later than hers, but he was supposed to be early since his was an international flight. They walked side by side, occasionally brushing up against each other as they made their way to security and deliberately chose separate lines.

David's heart was heavy as he stood in the queue watching her while trying to keep his head down. It didn't take long for them to get through the line and meet up again. He wanted to put his arm around her, but all that was over until their next treatment weekend.

They found her departure gate and sat in the plastic seats to wait until it was time to board the plane. David wrote down his mobile number in case she needed to contact him, and so that she could add it to her new phone when she got it. They made small talk, avoiding the gaze of the people surrounding them until the dreaded time came when first class was called for boarding. They stood and hugged, holding on as long as they could, then she kissed his cheek.

"I love you," she whispered as quietly as she could before letting him go. "I'll see you in ten days. We can probably handle ten days, right?" She turned toward the gate and walked away from him.

"I hope so!" he said and waved goodbye.

Erin found her seat and placed her small suitcase in the overhead storage area. Pulling the compass pendant out from beneath her top, she held it, hoping she wouldn't cry again. She took Todd's necklace from her pocket and was about to drop it into her purse when she saw something she didn't recognize. In the side pocket she found three wallet-sized photos from the night before, the magical night. They were beautiful, and it was hard to keep her composure as she stared at them. The thought of her and David Elliott together was still unbelievable!

She had to find a way to deal with the emptiness she was feeling, so she decided to do everything she could to conjure up Todd, to bring her feelings of love back from the depths she'd buried them in. It was going to be difficult, but it was the only way she thought she'd be able to cope. Somehow, she had to find a way to love both men at the same time.

David's departure gate wasn't difficult to find, so he made his way to the VIP lounge. He was approached only once by a woman wanting a selfie. He tried to smile but knew it wasn't his best. When he arrived at the lounge, he found an out of the way seat in a corner. Taking out his book, he hoped no one else would request anything from him. It would be too difficult to have to deal with people just then.

He knew he was being petulant, but he wanted to sulk. Loneliness was something he hated, always had, though he'd gotten used to it with Susannah's aloof attitude toward him. It wasn't because of the recent fiasco, either. She'd been growing increasingly distant over the years. He loved it when his kids were home, as he could talk to and play with them. It didn't matter that he was forty-five; deep down, he still liked to play. The game didn't matter either, he loved laughing, and most games involved that.

He reckoned that was why he'd finally accepted Martin's poker game invitation. Knowing Susannah wouldn't want him to go, he had declined at first, but a night of poker with a group of blokes seemed a paradise compared to the silence and boredom of home, so he gave in and went. How was he to know Martin would use booze as a tactical maneuver in order to ambush him.

What should I say tae him when I get back? he wondered as the lounge waiter approached him and asked if he wanted anything to drink. A Guinness was tempting, but he thought better of it, asking for a coffee instead. *How can I be angry with Martin? After all, I met Erin because of his checkmate, didn't I?* he thought.

That's no' the point, though, is et? His plans may have backfired this time, but next time something serious might happen. He didn't want to find out what kind of mess that would cause. The waiter came back with his drink, and there he sat, pondering how he could never stand up to Martin. He was a bully and a nudge, begging and bothering until he went along with whatever scheme he'd cooked up. *I can't allow him tae do that tae me anamore.*

He opened his book and saw Erin's makeshift hairpin bookmark. It already seemed a long time since he'd laid next to her soft, warm, naked—*Okay, David, dinnae go there now. You'll have plenty of time once yeh get home tae dwell on her naked body; this is not the place.*

Leaving her bookmark where it was, he turned to the spot where he'd last stopped reading. He read and reread the first paragraph three times but couldn't concentrate. Finally, he gave up and wrapped the strap on his holdall around his leg, closed his eyes, and slept, dreaming about crème brûlée and a beautiful woman making blissful noises whilst eating it.

DISCLAIMER

Meet Your Match is a work of fiction. Any resemblance to actual events or main character persons, living or dead, is entirely coincidental and not intended by the author. Even if you have the same name, occupation, birth location, and/or city of current residence, it is a complete and amazing coincidence that the author was unaware of at the creation of any character in this book unless otherwise stated. Real celebrities used in this work of fiction are done with the utmost respect, and no defamation or insult is intended. Most importantly, the drug, Fertilis, the disease, the Fertilis Defect, and all treatment methods for the disease are a work of fiction and have come from the author's imagination. Any resemblance to real diseases or drugs is coincidental, and no offense is intended on its portrayal or treatment.

ACKNOWLEDGEMENT

There are so many people to thank that I'm afraid I'll leave someone out. Just know that if you helped me, even in the most minute way, I'm so very grateful!

First, I'd like to thank my amazing husband, Scott Boede, for putting up with my obsession and for reading my book(s) over and over, even though it's not his favorite genre. Also, for finally getting it through his head that he is NOT Todd! He encouraged and helped me while writing this book and believes in me. I love you!

I'd like to thank my daughter, Elizabeth Murphy, who has also read my book(s) ad nauseam and has given truthful feedback, even when I didn't want to hear it. Also, for being one of my best cheerleaders.

I want to thank my mom, Christy Aronis, who read to me and didn't use baby talk when I was little. She taught me how to speak well and sparked my imagination. She also told me that I could do anything and be anything I wanted to. She always believed in me, even when I didn't.

Thanks to my son, Christopher Schneider, just because. Also, for being a good sport about 'Brussels Sprouts" for all these years.

Thanks to Jamie Gould, who was correct when she suggested that my third or fourth chapter should be the first. Also, for giving excellent feedback! (I'm tellin' you, gurl, you need to do that for a living!)

Thanks to Laura Grotenhuis, my third-grade teacher, who taught me how to spell beautiful. Thank you for seeing something special in me way back then. Also, thanks for reading one of my early drafts and giving me excellent feedback. My teacher is B E A U T I F U L.

Thanks to Christy Oswald, for meeting with me every week almost since we met (until covid hit!) and giving great feedback!

Thanks to Kevin Manley for reading my girly book, saying you liked it, and for being my go-to expert on all things police and negotiation tactics, etc.

Thanks to Emily, for teaching me about null alleles and surfactants; your knowledge helped me to write the parts I had no clue how to write!

Thanks to Pragya Chaubey, I'm so glad we met at the Airbnb in Edinburgh and then became Facebook friends. Thank you for giving me amazing feedback, sending me really great articles, and helping with the medical stuff. You are a God send!

Thanks to Ashley and Mark Chmielewski for encouraging me and asking questions instead of laughing at my premise. Also, for trying really hard to read it, and I love you, even though you failed … haha

Thanks to Cindy Raasch, for being my best friend since kindergarten and for saying that I "Shouldn't change a thing," and "Send it to a publisher asap," even though it still needed tons of work! You're the best, next to a whopper and a whaler.

Thanks to Becky Knuth, for being #5 and for crying at all the right parts. Also, for being an excellent cheerleader.

ACKNOWLEDGEMENT

Thanks to the Fellowship of the Heart—you know who you are. You didn't laugh at me when I timidly told you (the first people other than Scott I ever told) the premise of my book.

Thanks to Karen Gebhardt, for your help and encouragement.

Thanks to Sue Graham, for loving my book(s) and begging for more—also for the use of her and Chris's spare room on more than one occasion! Also, to Chris Graham for inviting Elizabeth and me to visit what's become my favorite place in the world. It's because of you that I know anything about the United Kingdom. P.S. Thanks for forgiving me for being an idiot. xoxo

Thanks to John Hartley, who put up with all my "Does this sound British enough?" Or "I need a British word for..." sort of questions.

Thanks to Donica Mohr, who was the first person, outside of my family, whom I allowed to read the first draft of my baby and for loving it! (It's changed a LOT since I printed the whole thing out, a few chapters at a time for you.)

Thanks to Liz Kannangara, for being an amazing woman and for allowing Scott and me to visit her in the blue chalet (what an amazing treat), for letting us stay with her in her lovely home a few years later, and for helping me with one of her areas of expertise—Can't say what—(spoilers).

Thank you, Steven Brandt, for my headshots and the many laughs. You are an amazing man, and a really great photographer.

Thanks to Diana Gabaldon for being an inspiration for me to write a novel in the first place.

Finally, for everyone who put up with me asking, "Where are you now?" and "What did you think of it?" over and over, a great big thank you!